CURSE OF THE LAST DAUGHTER

CURSE OF THE LAST DAUGHTER

L.N. WANDREI

~ v

Contents

PLAYLIST

Something Blue- Voilà
Another Love- Tom Odell
Emergence- Sleep Token
How do I say Goodbye- Dean Lewis
Sad Beautiful Tragic (Taylor's Version)- Taylor Swift
Far Behind- Candlebox
Toxic-2WEI
Kingdom Come-The Civil Wars
Hey Driver (feat. The War and Treaty)-Zach Bryan, The War and Treaty
Truck Bed-HARDY
Keep The Wolves Away-Uncle Lucius
Full Moon- The Black Ghosts
Just Pretend- Bad Omens
Salvatore- Lana Del Ray
A Bar Song (Tipsy)- Shaboozey
Pink Skies- Zach Bryan
Love Me Harder- Steven Rodriguez
Carry You (feat. Fleurie)- Ruelle
I Remember Everything- Zach Bryan and Kacey Musgraves
Fall Into Me-Forest Blakk
If You Want Love-NF
Zombie-Yungblud
I'll Be Good- Jaymes Young
Ends of the Earth-Lord Huron
Almost (Sweet Music)-Hozier
Scared to Start-Michael Marcagi
Dirt on my boots- Jon Pardi

Save My Soul-Noah Rinker
can you see me in the dark?-Halestorm &I Prevail
touch me- Ex Habit
Like You Mean It- Steven Rodriguez
Wicked Games- Daisy Gray
It's Ok- Tom Rosenthal
Maine-Noah Kahan
Broken- Jonah Kagen
Dangerous-NEFFEX
wait in the truck-HARDY & Lainey Wilson
Wicked Ways- Nolan Tyler
Spin you around (1/24)-Morgan Wallen
Man or a Monster (feat. Zayde Wolf)-Sam Tinnesz, Zayde Wolf
Man of the Year-Lorde
Eine kleine Nachtmusik: Andante- Mozart
Me and the Devil- Soap & Skin
Requiem, OK. 626: Lacrimosa-Mozart
When You Say My Name-Chandler Leighton
Bloodletting (The Vampire Song)- Concrete Blonde
Forbidden Fruit-Tommee Profitt, Sam Tinnesz, brooke
Something In the Orange- Zach Bryan

Playlist can be found on Spotify

TRIGGER WARNINGS

Your mental health matters, and if any of the trigger warnings could be something that would be detrimental to your mental health, it's okay not to continue reading. Writing is a form of therapy for me, as is reading others with similar genres and tropes. While this list is as complete as it can be, there may be other scenes that may be triggering or disturbing to the reader.

Anxiety
Assault/Domestic Violence
Alcoholism
Depression
Explicit Sexual Scenes
Extreme Violence and Gore
Grief and Loss
Implied abuse of a child- not on page/Kidnapping
Implied Prescription Drug Abuse
PTSD
Trauma
Torture of a woman
Violent Death

This is a paranormal romance with dark notions, featuring an FMC who is healing through her grief and a MMC who grows and heals with his PTSD. They both experience many changes throughout the story, and how they handle them may not be what you would have chosen.

AUTHOR'S NOTE

Please note that while the places are fictional, they are based on real-life locations, and I have taken some liberties with the areas to embellish the story.

Also! Your girl loves to use grammar-appropriate diction in her writing, so with that, you will find the dreaded em dash — and eclipses ... throughout.

What this means is that ABSOLUTELY NO A.I. was used to help me write this book. It was just lil' ol' me and my MacBook Pro, a ton of Red Bulls, and an obscene amount of replays of my favorite songs.

Book 1 in The Blood Cursed Series took me well over a year to draft, edit, and compose this entire book myself. So, with that said...I hope you enjoy my debut novel!

For the sexy, sassy, and sometimes too-petty-for-her-own-good ladies. For the ones whose trauma can no longer define them. For the ones who use sarcasm and fake smiles to hide their pain. I see you, and you are not alone.

1

Faith

Oxburn, Maine

Do you know what the worst sound in the world is? I do...it's the sound of a gun being cocked, not the actual sound of the gun firing, but the undeniable sound of the hammer being pulled back. It's a sound that reverberates throughout your whole body, igniting a fear so deep it wallops panic straight to your psyche and ensures your worst nightmares are made real. I'm not sure if I've ever heard a worse sound.

A few hours ago...

Soft lace drifted up and tickled the tip of my nose, prompting my eyes to squeeze closed while my Dad gingerly lifted my veil, folding it behind my head. When I opened my eyes, his happiness pulsed from his steel blue eyes, accented by the wrinkles creasing the corners. My ribcage stretched against the silk of my dress, lungs searching for another gasp of oxygen, all the while my fingers flexed around the satin-wrapped stems of a white calla lily bouquet. Dad's hushed voice relaxed my nose from crinkling up and soothed the stinging burn of tears threatening to smudge all of Eliza's hard work on my makeup.

"You look beautiful, sweet pea," my Dad rasped, all choked up as he moved next to me before the mirror. My sweaty hands ran down the pale ivory of my gown, sunlight beaming through the stained glass, painting colorful splotches over the silk. Dancing back and forth on my feet, an ache in my belly burned and crept up my throat.

Pretending I wasn't about to cup and claw at my throat, my fingers ghosted over my grandmother's sapphire necklace, and a heavy sigh escaped my lips, that I hadn't realized I'd been holding. This day had been a long time coming, so why did I feel so off? Like a condensed bubble of dread was close to bursting.

I'm marrying the love of my life today. The happiest day of any girl's life... right? I thought, not for the first time in the past six months.

"You alright, sweet pea?" Dad's voice broke through the shadows, beginning to drag me under.

With a quick nod and a small smile, I cleared my throat, "mmhmm...yeah, Daddy, I'm alright, just nervous- I mean excited...probably the jitters, ya know?" My voice wavered alongside the growing pit in my stomach, that all-consuming feeling that something was wrong or was going to be.

It was normal to be nervous and second-guess your decision, moments before your wedding started, right? Doesn't every bride-to-be smother the urges of panic and chase them off as jitters? Surely everyone questioned their doubts one last time, only to talk themselves back into walking down the aisle. Yet, here I was contending with my doubts, like I was about to do something wrong, but couldn't put my finger on it.

Mom had said last night that if my wolf had sensed that my fiancé wasn't my fated mate, her energy may have been trying to seep through to me, but since my wolf was MIA, I chalked it up to nerves. I may not have been able to confirm Connor was my fated mate, but he was my soul mate, and I'd believed him when he'd said it in our senior year of high school. And I still believed it, deep within my soul, regardless of whether my wolf could confirm it or not.

If I could've had a conversation with my wolf about it all, this would've been solved years ago, and we could be raising pups by now, but my wolf refused to make herself known within my conscience.

While Dad tenderly draped my veil back over, the halo of delicate lace forced me to blink away my nervous thoughts. Through the sheer white, Dad's loving gaze lingered and soaked in his last moments with me before walking me down the aisle.

"If you're not sure, sweet pea, we can walk out that door right now, because there are nervous jitters and then there is doubt," Dad said, running a hand up my arms, cupping my shoulders.

"Yeah, this is what I've wanted for so long..." I trailed off, nerves threaded through me as I focused on the doors. The music had started, and the doors to the entrance of the temple swung open. Suppressing a flinch, I robotically looped my hand into Dad's arm, we shared a quaint smile, and then, gripping my bouquet tighter, I took the first step towards my future. My bright, beautiful future, filled with regret already.

We took one step, and my knees wobbled weakly, like Jell-O. What did Mom say to do when I'd get anxious? Find three things you can focus on, and breathe in to a four-count, slowly. My lungs expanded with the first inhale of four beats, and the sweet florals perfuming the late spring air held easily for the next four beats. Another inhale, and I took in the swaths of tulle and silk sweeping over the rows of pews with bundled calla lilies and baby blue satin ribbon. Exhaling, my lips parted in awe at the aisle dotted with flower petals, scattered perfectly. Connor would be pleased.

Three steps down the aisle, my breath hitched in my throat when I laid eyes on him, waiting for me at the altar. He was so handsome standing there in his three-piece tuxedo, blonde hair quaffed back, not a hair out of place. His chiseled jawline, smooth and free of the beard he usually kept, revealed the dimple in his chin.

When Connor's piercing green eyes locked on my amber brown ones, a trickle of ice ran down my spine. Reactively, I straightened, pulling my shoulders back. We marched down the flower peppered aisle, arriving at the steps of the altar way too soon, and I wasn't sure who was more reluctant to let go, me or Dad?

So when the shaman asked morosely, "Who gives this woman?" Dad glanced at me and gave my hand four short squeezes, one squeeze for each of us: Mom, Dad, Hollie, and me.

"*One last chance to wait, sweet pea,*" he mind-linked through our private family connection.

"*I'm ready, Daddy,*" I linked back to him, but I really couldn't say if I was or not. I didn't even know why I was questioning anything. Perhaps I *was* as crazy as I'd been told countless times before.

"We do, her mother and I." My muscles strained not to flinch as Dad's voice boomed in answer. His smile widened, and he lifted my veil, placing a kiss on my cheek. Cordially, he laid my hand into Connor's, and if looks could kill, then the one my Dad laid on my groom would've had him six feet under before I could've blinked.

A pang of pain ached in the back of my throat as I followed Dad when he took his seat next to my Mom. She dabbed the corners of her eyes with his favorite handkerchief but still managed a smile for me when our eyes met.

Scooping up her hand, Dad laced his fingers with hers and pressed a kiss to the back of her hand. A little surge of envy ran up my chest from the way my Mom and Dad's love leeched out from one another. They could melt the ice caps with the heat that poured out from them. The love they shared was an undying flame anyone would be envious of; I wanted that same flame. I hoped and prayed that Connor and I would share the same passion as theirs.

Eliza, my maid of honor and best friend, reached out from behind me and took my bouquet, smiling with tears lining her lashes. The shaman began talking, but all I could see was Connor; everything else was blurred and surreal. Holding his hands in mine was the only thing that registered; it was the only thing I could focus on.

Having been tuned into everything Connor, I found it odd that his palms were sweaty, and he seemed a little on edge...my lips immediately curved up, just enough to have my dimples show, but not too much. I scanned his eyes and breathed in, waiting for the burn of vodka to assault my nose. I sighed internally, relief whooshing over me at minty fresh breath and clear eyes.

Except, Connor kept swallowing and darting his weary eyes behind me, and then over to my parents. Did he break his promise? Or did he think I'd told my parents?

I met his gaze again, searched for any hint of displeasure, and relaxed a little when I found none. He was fine; there's no way he'd break his promise to me again. I chalked it up to wedding day jitters and kept smiling.

"Do you, Connor Morgan, take Faith Bennett to become your wedded wife and chosen mate, to have and to hold from this day forward?" My eyes darted from his lips to his eyes, ready to memorize the moment, and that's when I saw it —really saw what was happening.

The rapid shifting from me to the temple, full of our family and pack, and back to me, the tiny muscles around his eyes twitching, the slight clench of his jaw. He dropped my hands like a hot potato and wiped them down his pant legs. My heart fell out of my chest and cracked wide open on the wood floor.

"I do-n't," he blurted, and then my cracked open heart burst and bled all over the steps. He glanced over his shoulder and then back at me as if he had been searching for someone. His cousin stood behind him, mouth hanging wide open, eyebrows to the vaulted ceiling.

"I can't do this, Faith," he professed with not even an ounce of remorse, and stepped down from the altar. A stunned gasp rushed through the seated guests.

My Dad bolted from his seat, nearly knocking the pew over, his irises flickering between the bright blue of his eyes and the black of his wolf. He was seething and struggling not to shift, barely keeping his wolf under control.

My feet were rooted to the floor while the world tilted. If I'd moved, I would've fallen right over the edge, lost to space. It felt like being on one of those rides at the fair, you know the kind that have one too many twists and loops, making you regret that extra funnel cake. And all I could think about was why my heart breaking felt a little like relief and guilt rather than the soul-crushing experience it should've been.

Connor stormed down the steps of the altar, blowing past both of our fathers.

"Son, what is the meaning of this?" his father, Russell, chastised. Connor brushed him off as Russell reached out for him and strode down the aisle, not even glancing back, not once.

Russell's voice penetrated through the fog, calling after him again, rendering my vision with horrifying clarity at what had happened. A nauseating coil of shame slithered around my heart, twin fangs piercing the withering muscle, pulsing its venom deep.

Shouted whispers and murmurs flew around the temple, about me, about Connor; shock and sadness radiated from the crowd on my behalf.

A wrinkled, age-spotted hand clasped down on my shoulder, my eyes flared, and my pulse kicked up from the touch.

"Come, dear, let's get you out of here," Osmin, our shaman, vacillated, gesturing for me to follow, his aging features full of sorrow and pain. I swayed, but didn't, couldn't move, no matter how hard he squeezed.

My eyes weaved over the temple guests and landed on the doors at the end of the aisle. Osmin tried again, tugging harder on my hand. My feet refused to budge despite my legs being overcooked noodles anchored on jellied ankles. I couldn't tell you if I was breathing or not, but I remember the gasp that raked its talons along my throat as it blew past my lips.

"No..."

A sharp stabbing pain spread out from my chest, cracking it a little. That horrible burning pit I felt earlier boiled over, flooding my veins, and shadows crept into my vision again, blurring my sight. I couldn't think, couldn't speak.

Blinking through the haze, Mom appeared out of nowhere, grabbing my hand, giving me a burst of life, calming the bubbling sensation in my chest.

Twisting around, her hand encircled mine as she wrapped her arms around my shoulders, surrounding me in her unyielding love. Pulling back only a little, she wiped away the tears I hadn't known were falling.

"My darling sweet pea, everything will be okay, alright, just breathe with me," her voice shook while she mimicked my movements, encouraging me to keep breathing. Her hands, bitterly cold, smoothed up and down my arms. "Your Dad will handle everything; he will command everyone to go enjoy the reception, and to never speak of this day again."

My lips parted, and a tiny hiccup squeaked from my throat. That wasn't what I wanted at all. People would think what they wanted to; no matter what my parents did to help de-escalate the problem, they'd no doubt ask questions, ones I didn't want to answer.

"No, Mom, he doesn't need to do that, j-just..." I struggled for a breath; my voice sounded more like a frog's than my own. I was not myself; something was entirely off. "I-uh, have them enjoy the reception, I guess. I will—" I added and stopped mid-thought, wincing just as the exterior doors to the temple burst open.

The heavy wood doors slammed into the walls simultaneously as Mom said, "Faith, you don't need to do anything, not yet. I need to tell—" Her eyes were glued to mine, searching for something I couldn't decipher.

You see, the thing is, you never see heartbreak coming. The proper kind of heartbreak, the one that wrecks you, the kind that wraps grief around your soul and chains it deep below fossilized ground. At least I didn't, because in the moments before my soul shattered, it wasn't Connor's words that wrecked me; it was the cocking of a gun.

It happened in slow motion, a flash of a steel muzzle aimed down the aisle. The gun fired from the end of the temple. I watched that bullet fly straight for us, and before I could shove my Mom out of the way, she spun us both faster than should've been possible.

Her blood-red eyes flared wide; fangs lengthened and then retracted. She'd tried to shift, but it was too late. Suddenly, her hold on me lessened, and a warmth spread from her abdomen onto me. Gripping her body the best I could manage, my sight shot in the direction of the shooter, but they'd vanished before my eyes could ascertain who they were.

Colored glass exploded from my Dad's guttural roar, "Alaina!" The shattered glass flew from every direction, slicing into the skin of my bare back and arms. My arms jerked forward as Mom's body started to slip from my hands.

Determined not to let her fall, I took most of her weight, and we collapsed together to the floor. The skirt of my dress billowed, fanning out around me, and her limp body landed onto my folded legs, thumping with a wet smack. Her erratic pulse was weak and fading fast. My breathing hitched, a coppery tang of blood stung the inside of my nose and mouth, clogging my throat.

When my mind eventually caught up with time, Dad was shifting mid-leap, landing in a thunderous thud, his giant gray wolf howling in agony, and raced for the altar from the back of the temple—thick warmth soaked into the ivory of my gown. I clung to Mom tighter, shaking her and pressing a hand to her stomach.

"Mom! No! Momma, please!" I screamed, my throat raw and ragged; she wasn't moving. With shaky fingers, I brushed a fallen strand of chocolate hair away from half-shuttered eyes and swooped them to her neck, checking her pulse; it was still there, but weak.

"Someone help," I whimpered and choked when her bloodied hand traced the curve of my jaw.

Mom's eyes flashed between her honey brown to her wolf's blood red, "My darling, sweet pea, it'll be alright, you'll be—"

I wanted to scream that no, it was not indeed alright, but my voice disappeared. I craved to have the ability to shift and chase after the shooter, but I couldn't. My wolf refused to surface even then, when I needed her most. Strangely, though, I could sense her, wavering beneath a shroud of darkness, but closer than she'd ever been.

"*Bitch*," I tried to mind link her, and received no answer. Red-hot fury raged through my body.

Mom's eyes rolled up, joining mine, her lips curled up, blood-coated teeth peeked out from her faint smile; more crimson poured out of the corner of her mouth.

She raised her arm weakly again, cupping my cheek, her lilac scent seeped into my skin, "it'll b-be o-okay F-Faith, don't b-be... a-fraid...choose l-love..." she whispered, stuttering every word. Her hand slipped from my face, gravity slowed.

Mom's pulse faded to muffled knocking, blood-filled lungs gurgled on a cough, and the rattling of death drowned my ears. All was quiet the moment her heart beat. One. Last. Time.

The beat, similar to a thunderclap, jolted me. Her body released its hold on her soul, becoming an utterly limp pile of flesh and bones. The cool air of the ceiling fans above sent shivers like a tingling prickle biting at my skin.

Dad reached us, and my arms pulled her limp body close to my chest. A weak and pathetic wail tore from what remained of my soul, piercing the deathly quiet. It was the kind of pain that rips through your body without remorse. An overwhelming sadness that splits the heart wide open and pours out its despair.

My Mom was gone.

Shot.
Dead.

She's gone.

Gone.

2

Faith

No, she can't be gone, refusing to believe this, I shook Mom's shoulder.

Nothing. No. This was not happening. I prayed and prayed again.

"Momma...please, p-please Momma...please wake up...please, what did you need to tell me?" My voice cracked pathetically as I begged her and pleaded to the Goddess. My hand caressed her still-warm cheek over and over again while I rocked her in my arms.

Dad's wolf hung his head low, licking her other cheek, nuzzling her with his elongated nose. His onyx eyes lowered on her, then his wolf's nose tipped up, and he howled the call of mourning. An eerie howl, low and ragged, conveyed his grief, his wolf's grief.

From behind the tabernacle, blue denim flew over my head once Dad shifted back. I stared blankly as Dad took Mom from me, scooping her up like she was nothing but a feather. My hands lingered, hanging awkwardly in the air, before finally dropping to my lap.

With Mom tightly held to his chest, his anger seethed and pulsed beneath the surface of his skin so palpably I felt it vibrate into my own. The dark aura radiating from him kept everyone at a distance as he walked his mate towards the entrance of the temple. Not one member uttered a word; their heads hung low. Their Luna was gone.

Blood caked my hands, and my body shook like a scared mouse about to be eaten by a barn cat. My ivory dress, soaked in my Mom's blood, crumpled under my clenched fist. Her blood squished out from the crease of my palm and pinky as I tried and failed to stand. Every fiber of my body wanted to erupt into flames, and the heat of anger rushed over me like a tidal wave.

When I was finally steady on my feet, a scream tore from my throat as a cracking of bone snapped; the crack echoed like a stepped-on branch in a dead forest. Another scream rent the air as my legs bent and snapped backwards.

My body flung forward in a bend, curving my spine, and I heaved the contents of my stomach onto the steps, splattering vomit everywhere.

My dress shredded into a mass of silk, and the beads pinged across the floor as more fabric tore away from my skin. A tingle rushed up my spine; the bones ached as they lengthened. A fire singed under my skin, burning away my flesh, and fur sprouted in its place, like fresh new grass. I fell forward, landing hard, onto paws, shaking a furry head and a twitching tail.

"Faith, we must make haste," a familiar, soft voice echoed in my mind.

Wait! What? I shifted! Holy shit! I shifted!

I finally had my wolf. I shuddered with a release of relief and a mix of confusion and excitement, quickly followed by anger. But why now? Why today?

My head shook side to side, and with the eyes of my wolf, I caught the sable brown fur, dappled with bits of gray and white, along my body; the colors were a perfect mix of my parents'. A boulder of sadness weighed heavily on the realization that my mother never got to meet my wolf, and she never would.

"Faith! Snap out of it, we must go now, your Father needs you." The ethereal female voice shouted against my cerebrum. I'd wondered what her name was, but I dared not ask, too afraid she'd leave again and I'd be forced to shift back, left naked and alone. Rejected once more for not being good enough.

The shadows of my parents stretched down the aisle, and their silhouettes in the doorway grabbed my attention. Sensing my gaze on him, he glanced over his shoulder. Pain filled his darkened eyes, but his lips curled up briefly before the gravity of grief took over.

"Come, daughter, we must prepare your Mother's body for the Goddess, and your wolf must be recognized immediately." He linked to me, as stoically as he could've been. His soothing, calm voice baffled me, yet I heard the agony and sadness seeping in.

Not waiting another minute, my wolf flew down the altar steps in one leap, landing on the aisle with a graceful thud, rattling the pews. My wolf directed her glare straight at Connor's family, her contempt a solid slab of granite. His Mother and Father just stood there gawking.

Connor's Mother was the only one who never truly believed my wolf would surface; she thought I was defective and had no issue telling me at every opportunity. Right then, all I could muster for either of them was hatred. Anger raged inside, demanding retribution. I realized a minute later, that anger was my wolf's emotions merging with mine, and it was exhilarating.

Russell, my Dad's beta, had yet to move, yet to do what he had sworn to do: protect the Alpha, Luna, and my family, at all costs. He hadn't moved an inch during the whole fiasco after his son disappeared. I'd like to say it was shock that rooted him to the floor of the temple, but it was pure and simple cowardice.

The floor quaked with every step I took. I felt so powerful, yet so weak. At Dad's side, my head tipped up and over, a whimper escaped, and my head dipped to rub against his thigh.

We left the temple in silence.

I was wrong when I said the worst sound in the world was the hammer of a gun being cocked. No, it's the rattling breaths of your Mom drowning in her blood as her soul leaves her body.

THAT was the worst sound I've ever heard.

3

Faith

Present

If Mom were still here, she'd tell me to look for the silver lining, and the only good thing that came out of today was my wolf awakening. Who still seems mad at me, but I guess I'll deal with her later. And, no matter what my feelings are regarding Connor and my Mom, my Dad needs me. Hollie will need me. So, for now, I'll be there for my Dad and sister. I'm not sure how he's staying strong with the loss of his mate, Luna, and best friend.

The tires of the limo whir over the pavement as it crawls up to my family's mansion. Every single member of the pack lines the driveway with their heads bowed. Well, I guess everyone, but Connor.

Scanning the rows of the pack, I see his mother is also missing, no loss there. Russell, surprisingly, is here, and he should be. Beta or not, he's my Dad's best friend and the closest person he has to a brother. The burning rage I felt earlier flares anew under my skin, melting away any iciness left frosting my heart.

Leather creaks and scrunches as I lean forward in my seat to glare at him, hoping he can feel my wrath through the window.

"Faith, reign in your anger," Dad snarls, then sighs. "For now...I need you to collect your sister, then we will go inside," his voice barely a whisper holds every ounce of despair he is in. The visible pillars of his strength, wavering, break through my anger, soothing it back into the deepest depths of grief.

With all the commotion from Connor and then Mom, I had somehow managed to forget about the safety of my baby sister, Hollie—*way to win sister of the year award, Faith.*

The pressing weight of guilt hangs over me, crushing me. I'm a horrible sister, I know, but it's been a recurring theme since we were little. She's twelve years younger than I am, and at seventeen, she's still a tad naive and impulsive, but overall, she's a good kid.

I can't believe I forgot about her. She was one of my bridesmaids, standing right behind Eliza. How could I have been so self-absorbed that I didn't think of her and her safety?

"Yes, Dad, I understand, I'm sorry I—" my words choke on the crushing weight of pain pressing into me.

"Faith, you do not need to be sorry, my Delta found her right after that pitiful excuse of a wolf made his exit," Dad grumbles, nostrils flaring.

"Oh," I whisper, feeling incredibly stupid. I should've remembered that we have a protocol in case anything ever happened to leadership. Everyone was to head to the pack house. My Dad's top 4 Deltas were to secure any children belonging to the alpha and beta. The Gammas helped to ensure the rest of the pack's children. In the event of a death, the pack lines the driveway and awaits the alpha and any further orders.

Gaze swiveling to Dad, then down, landing on Mom, her stiffening body is held tight in his arms. He hasn't failed in keeping her close to him since lifting her away from me.

My fingers clench, flaking bits of dried blood onto a black suit jacket. Earlier, when we reached the limo, I shifted back before hopping inside naked. Our dutiful driver, Delco, immediately removed his jacket so I could cover up.

A glimpse in the window's reflection reveals the blood splattered all over my face, neck, and arms. Both of us are covered in her blood, a dreary painting of death. Scraping my nail over a splotch of the dried red iron, a cold shudder rakes through my body.

My Dad, Gerrant Bennett, cradles Mom closer, pressing another kiss to her ashen forehead. Each time he does so, a tear slips out, sliding down over his tanned cheek, vanishing into his thick, but groomed, black beard. His aura, usually a beautiful golden ray, now hazily hums a dull blue-gray; his voice has already begun to dwindle in its richness with each word spoken; I don't expect anything less. The ache in my chest tightens a little more with each pulse of his aura.

The limo comes to a halt in front of the pack mansion stairs, and Delco's eyes catch ours in the rearview mirror.

"Alpha Gerrant, when you are ready," he says solemnly, his eyes etched with the same agony we're all feeling.

Dad's and mine heartbeats sync with one another; each painful beat shattering another piece of our family. Hollie's heart beat joins ours from outside as she rushes down the wide stone steps, and I reach for Dad's hand and squeeze it.

A shadow passes over the window from Hollie, who stumbles over her ruined bridesmaid dress. A Delta snatches her arm, saving her from face-planting. Dad nods to Delco, and he exits, skirting around the front of the limo.

The door opens, and Dad dips his chin for me to exit first. Holding the lapels of Delco's jacket closed, I carefully step out to the side, waiting, and my sister's fingers lace with mine.

With Mom tucked carefully into his chest, Dad easily departs the limo. Her hand flops down over his arm as he adjusts her weight. Her arm dangling, blood trails down her wrist and drips onto the cobblestones, the splattering rattles my core. Together, Hollie and I collect her arm, replacing it over the top of her chest. For a moment, our hands linger, then Dad leans in, and the three of us bow, pressing our foreheads together. Our family's heartbeat is weakened, but our resolve will rebound. I just don't know when, or how.

Hollie takes one of my hands, and my other hand cups Dad's elbow, and the three of us walk into our family home. Russell, the Gammas, the Deltas, and Mom's Omegas solemnly follow behind. Dad gently lays Mom down on a carved mahogany table in the center of the long hallway. Several servants scurry about, and Nora touches each of our arms as she hands us each a bowl of water.

A black haired maid follows behind her, giving us strips of cloth. When she reaches me, her hands shake, and her eyes dart down and away from mine. Scrunching my nose, I accept the items, ignoring her odd behavior. From over my shoulder, I follow Nora's movements, catching her dragging the girl away by the elbow.

Sniffles echo off the white marble flooring, dragging my attention back to Hollie; my sister gives up wiping away her tears. Her once bright eyes are barely discernible through the red and puffy flesh around them. The same can be said of mine and Dad's. The three of us are rooted to the floor, staring at Mom's bloodied, lifeless body sprawled out on the table. Her hauntingly blank eyes stare up at the crystal chandelier above.

"Someone needs to close her eyes," I link to Dad and Hollie as I dip the cloth into my bowl of water, carefully wringing it out; the cool water numbs the tips of my fingers. Hollie's stagnant gaze focuses on my shaking hands, barely able to hold the cloth steady, and I wipe away the blood from Mom's arm. I hold out my other hand over Mom's body.

"Hollie?" She startles, realizing I'm talking to her, and grasps my hand. I squeeze, and tears fall down our swollen faces in never-ending streams. Both of us look at Dad. He gingerly strokes Mom's face, sweetly and softly, with the blood-stained cloth. Choking back a sob, he leans in and presses a kiss to her forehead and tenderly closes her eyelids.

* * *

At some point, Hollie shooed everyone from the hall, allowing me to photograph Mom's gunshot wound and body for evidence. I had nearly vomited when Dad and one of his trusted Deltas had rolled her to her side so Osmin could retrieve the bullet. The bullet was laced with wolfsbane, and the pungent scent made all of us recoil.

* * *

With Mom's body finally clean, she remains in the hallway, with two Gammas and three Deltas standing watch over her. The five of them stand stoically, but despair laces their features. There isn't a dry eye in sight. I do not wish to depart from her side, but I must.

Hesitantly, I climb the stairs to my rooms. My hand lingers on the handle of my door, and all I can think about is the whys.

Why Connor?

Why did he do this to me?

Why did Mom get shot?

Why did she stand in front of it?

Why did any of this happen?

Why didn't she shift?

Why did the Goddess take her from me? From us?

Why?

Why?

Why?

Whyyyyyy?

I shove through the door, into my rooms, collapsing to my knees, a loud smack cracks when they connect with the floor. Tears streak down my face, splashing onto my bare thighs.

* * *

Bolting awake and disoriented, the softness of a pillow behind me causes me to freeze. My eyelids are stuck together, with crust lining the lids. Balling my fists to rub at them and force them open, I bite back a curse from the grit grinding into the swollen skin. I don't know who moved me or when, but I'm in my bed, and still in Delco's jacket.

On my way to the bathroom, I shrug the jacket off and let it fall to the floor. Pausing at the counter, I tilt my head to the side and take in my appearance in the mirror. My wedding hair is in complete shambles, my makeup is destroyed, and my face is swollen from sobbing. Dried blood freckles all over my skin, and the trail of my tears has formed canyons through the red splatter caked to my cheeks. A visual representation of what my heart feels like.

Nine loud chimes ring out from the clock on my mantle. We will be taking Mom's body to her pyre in an hour, sending her ashes to the Goddess.

Mustering up every ounce of energy I have left today, I step into the shower, turning the knobs in a practiced habit, the slight squeak of the knobs flicks a wince in my cheeks, the sound too sharp for my oversensitive ears.

Not bothering to wait for the water to warm up, I step in under the cold water. The icicle streams slice over my numb body, slowly melting to warm with each second. Bloody water pools, circling the drain, swallowing the cloying copper remnants away. I lift my chin to the spray, letting the water assault my face. In a cloud of steam lifting around me, a stabbing pang erupts in my chest. I lost two people I love today.

Loved.

Mom has passed on to the Goddess, and Connor, well, only the Goddess knows where his pathetic ass has disappeared to.

Stepping out from the shower head, slick, cool tiles soak any remaining warmth away from my skin. With my back against the cold tiles, I crumble to the floor, bringing my knees to my chest. Shrouded in a fog of steam, I bury my head between my arms and knees, as an acute numbness settles in.

A short knock at the door jerks me from my ravenous grief. Rising to stand, my pruney fingers swivel the slippery handle off, and I step out. Wrapping a fluffy towel around my body, I open the bathroom door, finding Nora. Her grief-stricken eyes betray her normally stoic features.

"Come, I have laid out your dress," she laments in a raspy tone, her words choking on a silent sniffle. I look over the top of her head to the bed, spying the white muslin dress spread over the dove gray duvet.

I begin to walk past her, but her petite hand lands on my arm, stopping me. A measure of panic whips up, ready to react at the contact. She wraps her arms around my waist in a hug, her warmth seeps into me, dwindling the shock. I stand there awkwardly, unsure of what to do with my arms hanging in the air. She squeezes tighter, and my numb body begins to wrap them around her instinctively.

After a moment, she silently pulls away, bows her head in a nod, and disappears into the walk-in closet, returning with my undergarments and sandals.

Nora's reflection in the vanity mirror blurs with the threat of tears as I watch her work. Her dainty fingers pull a bobby pin from the line of them that she has clamped between her teeth. One falls, bouncing across the floor as she pins half of my long, chocolate hair up. I didn't argue earlier when she insisted that the rest cascade down my back.

Chimes ring again, marking forty-five minutes past the ninth hour. The pile of bobby pins pings against the stone top of my vanity, directing my gaze up to join Nora's.

"I am so sorry, Faith," Nora sniffles, her voice little more than a croak. She swipes the back of her hand under her nose once, bows once more, and leaves.

Subconsciously, I reach for my Grandmother's necklace coiled in the shell dish on my vanity when my fingers freeze mid-air, hovering over an empty dish. Frantically, I search in and around the vanity, opening each drawer and slamming it shut; it's not here.

My jugular pulses erratically through my skin as my hand slams into my chest. Trembling fingers inch up to the hollow of my neck, brows shooting to my forehead when bare skin meets the digits.

Flashes of touching the deep blue sapphire in the temple filter through my mind. Where could it be? I don't remember taking it off at any point, and jewelry is one of the few items that doesn't get destroyed during a shift. It couldn't have just disappeared. I'll need to ask Hollie and Dad if they removed it.

Spinning towards my vanity, my whiskey brown eyes focus on the mirror. An odd sensation pricks at the back of my mind and spreads down my back and arms. A gasp slips past my lips as my irises swirl and flicker to a shimmering copper, akin to a shiny new penny.

"*Hello, Faith. I am Sienna,*" my wolf links, appearing in my subconscious. I bite my bottom lip, stopping the trembling, but not cooling the irritation and resentment I have for her right now.

"*So you finally decided to appear? Today of all days?*" I complain.

"*Faith, you must know I've tried to connect and talk with you several times, but you've never listened, and then our connection grew so weak I couldn't,*" Sienna retorts in a huff. *Wait...what?*

Her concern ripples through me; she's restless, but also in pain, my loss is hers too. Choosing not to focus on the loss of my Mom, because I just can't, I have to know something else. "*Did you know about Connor?*" I challenge.

"Yes, I knew that he was not our mate, you should've known too with what he did—"

"Stop! Please stop, okay?" I plead, choking on a humiliating pain bubbling to the surface. Sensing my turbulent emotions, she relents and tucks her tail, hiding in the shadows once again.

Wave after wave of pain and unanswered questions collide, leaving me no choice but to allow Sienna to go. It's probably best for now, since I need to tend to and keep together what's left of my family.

* * *

With Mom cradled in Dad's arms, Hollie and I walk on either side of him up to the sacred meadow where Mom's funeral pyre will be. The trek up the hill from the mansion isn't long, but it feels like it takes an eternity with the entire pack following behind us.

Dad lays Mom delicately atop the beautifully decorated pyre, and a hush ripples out across the meadow. It's as if all of the Goddess's creatures hold their breath for the loss of our Luna; not even the song of the crickets can be heard.

Her body is rapidly becoming rigid in death, which highlights the pallor of her once radiant skin. Dad fidgets with her limbs, ensuring her body is nestled exquisitely within the ring of wildflower bouquets.

He cups her head in his hand, hovering over her body, and a single tear breaks free and slides down his cheek. With his other hand, he runs it up the length of her leg, tracing his shaking fingertips over her skin, cementing his last touch of her in his memory.

The dam keeping my grief at bay breaks loose, and a river of tears flows, exploding into sobs, shaking my body. They loved each other so deeply, passionately, and for such a long time. 33 years going on 34 in a month.

Through glossy eyes, I rub at a pain bursting in my chest when he clutches her hand, cupping her head with the other, and presses one long, final kiss to her lips. Dad's body shakes uncontrollably at the contact, his sobs bellow deep from within.

Trembling, he reluctantly releases her hand and head, falling to his knees alongside the neat vertical rows of pine and white cedar bundled branches. Not yet willing to let go, he reaches up to touch her arm. It's pure torture watching my Dad's soul rip in half. No one prepares you to lose a parent. No one prepares you to lose a mate.

I take Hollie's hand in mine, joining behind him. I give her a nudge on her elbow, encouraging her to say her goodbyes before me.

Waiting for my turn, I glance up at the moon and squint from the glistening light sparkling on my cheeks from its full, bright light. Unfiltered thoughts roll through my mind at the Moon Goddess's cruelty. How could she take my Mom from us? Frustrated, I swipe a hand under my eyes, bruising the sensitive skin.

As Hollie steps away, her whispers of farewell are lost in her sniffles. It's my turn. Air balloons in my lungs to the point of a sharp pain edging the sides of my ribs. With a step forward, grass grazes the sides of my feet, and the cool night air kisses my skin. I tell myself I can do this, I have to do this, but another ache swells, stalling my approach. Dad's bowed head and whimpering whispers draw me forward. If he can do this, so can I.

Tiny, wild violets, and white and orange lilies kiss along her skin, their perfume hardly masking the stench of death slowly seeping from her body. Inhaling through my mouth and thinking of anything other than the smell, I lean in.

"Goodbye, Momma...I love you," I whimper, barely recognizing my scratchy and weak voice. I brush my lips over the ice-cold skin of her cheek and rest my forehead against hers. The flicker of firelight in my peripheral ignites a rush of emotions that I'm not quite ready to deal with, but I must.

Stepping back, I spot Osmin carrying a flaming torch; the fiery tendrils waver and dance above his head of short white hair. His eyes, too, like everyone else's here, are rimmed in red, glossy and painfully swollen.

"Daddy, it's time," I choke, tasting the salty tears streaming down my lips. Gently, I tug on Dad's shoulder, and his body leans into mine before retreating with me.

The crackles and snaps of the fire lick the dry wood, then flare and engulf Mom's body in a whoosh. The bundles of dried herbs and flowers are a flimsy mask over the odor of her burning flesh.

The scent will forever be imprinted in my nostrils. One by one, every member of the Mystic Keepers pack drops into their shifts. They lope in a single-file line towards the burning pyre. They bow their furry heads briefly, then tip them back in a howl, singing a goodbye to the moon in honor of their Luna.

* * *

The first rays of light stream through the thick trees encircling the field in a golden glow. The last of the ashes and embers of Mom's pyre slowly fade and die.

Waiting on our knees in the grass, Dad, Hollie, and I remain, staring at the pile of ashes, praying to the Moon Goddess to send her winds to carry them away. The sky glows with deep violets, magentas, and oranges spreading up from the top of the forest, illuminating the dawn. Birds trill, warming up their bodies from the chill of night, their tiny breaths fogging the crisp morning air.

Hollie silently rises, but a sniffle escapes, and she bolts, disappearing down the hill. The rolling meadow steals the last of her cries when she reaches the bottom. Dad and I, refusing to leave, stay and stare blankly ahead at the thin layer of misty fog burning away from the dew-covered grass.

Time has stood still until now, and now, the quiet morning brims with life, one tick of my watch at a time. Staring at the charred remains of my Mom, a slight tug drags my eyes away.

A doe and her fawn gracefully walk past, grazing. The doe lifts her long neck, ears twitching in alert, fully aware of the predators kneeling before them. The doe blinks, piercing her dark, round eyes directly into my soul, and a tingle spreads warmly over the part of me reserved only for loved ones. The pair lowers their heads slowly in a bow and then prances back into the forest. I steal a glance at Dad, whose head is slightly bowed, with eyes that are unmoving from the ashes.

"She was sick, you know," Dad croaks, his voice a shock to the ocean of quiet around us. "It's why she kept insisting you wait for your mate... well, until recently." His eyes never leave what remains of his mate as he imparts that tidbit of news, as if it's a relief to relinquish his secrets.

Finally, a breeze swirls the ashes, and the wind picks up, blowing all around us.

Wrenching my neck like a wet towel, squeezing out the shock, my head snaps to him. I swallow hard, choking on my emotions, "What do you mean she was sick?"

The breeze gusts again, lifting the swirling and whirling ashes higher into the sky. At the sight, I release a breath I didn't know I'd been holding, as bittersweet relief floods my veins. Blinking back more tears, I scoot forward on my knees, facing my silent Dad.

"How long did she know?" I croak, blanching. I hold my breath and wait for the answer I need to hear. It feels important to know, perhaps it will be the band-aid I need to heal this gaping wound in my soul.

Mom had insisted adamantly that I wait for my mate and not marry Connor for years. Not once had she ever given up on it. Not once, during our nine years of engagement, not until recently. And I assumed she relented purely for the sake of my happiness. I was so selfish to think that...

Unmoving, Dad sighs out the weight of the world, his pain holding him rooted in place. "She only found out 5 months ago," he breathes, and runs a hand through his thick black hair, streaked with gray, and cups my cheek.

"Come, daughter, we must formally introduce your wolf to the pack," he commands.

We head back down the hill, and I glance back over my shoulder one last time before we reach the steep incline. Something plucks at my heart, halting my feet. I wait and freeze as a tinkling of bells rings.

"Do not be afraid to follow your heart, Faith..." a distorted whisper caresses the shell of my ear. My back twitches, and a shiver races down my spine at the ethereal voice. A tendril of wind curls up around my legs, swaying the skirt of my dress, and wraps itself around me.

"Listen to your heart..." the voice whispers again, taking the stream of air with it.

A single tear rolls down my cheek, and as I follow the current, it catches the last of Mom's ashes. They drift upward into the sky, twisting in an elegant dance on the wind, and disappear forever.

4

Faith

Standing in the kitchen, I stare hollowly at the heavily stocked shelves of the pantry. I can't decide what to choose. I know I should consume something, anything really, after shifting twice in twenty-four hours for the first time, albeit 11 years too late.

In a huff, I grab a bin of fruit leather Mom made earlier, chips, and cookies, and toss my goodies on the counter. Plopping down onto the stool, my fingers run up between my brows, erasing some of the tension lingering from earlier. A cyclone of distorted voices replay in my memory from when Dad had me shift in front of the pack and announced me as his heir.

"Finally, her wolf!" An older woman exclaimed, her hands cradling her cheeks, pure happiness radiating off her.

"I heard she was left at the altar," says another, her fake concern unmistakable, but it doesn't cut as deep as I thought it would.

"Took her long enough, clearly neither wanted her..." a close friend of Eliza's whispered barely loud enough for me to hear. One part of that still hurts, but there's nothing I can do to change the facts. I was left at the altar, and my wolf most assuredly took her time to show herself.

At least one person had some genuine care for what we were all going through, and that's what I'm choosing to cling to. "How horrible to lose both your beloved and mother in the same day," a warrior of my Dad's rasped.

Tucking each one of those away in a little glass box, I mentally shove it with the growing stack and tear open a bag of chips. The salty crunch and aroma of fried goodness drowns out everything else. Bite after bite, the rude comments replay.

"I heard she was left at the altar like the loser she is." Another chip. Crunch.

"No wonder her wolf took so long to appear; she clearly has something wrong with her." Another handful of chips.

Crunch. Crunch. Crunch. What do they know? Nothing. My fingers scrape along the bottom of the bag, empty.

"Dammit." Guess I was hungrier than I thought.

Crumpling the bag, I toss it to the side and glare at the remaining pile of snacks. A sharp stabbing pain pulses from behind my eyes, which isn't soothed with any amount of massaging. Their comments don't, shouldn't bother me; I've grown used to them over the decades, I'm merely hungry, that's all.

Regrettably, some of the pack members are right. Most wolves do shift sometime between their 13th and 18th birthdays for the first time. Unfortunately for me, that never happened until yesterday, and I'll be celebrating my 30th birthday in a month. I guess you could say I'm a late bloomer.

Peeling off the lid of a container, the tips of my fingers stick together from the long strip of dehydrated fruit I pick from within. Wrenching my jaw on the fruit leather, I chew and swallow roughly. An embarrassingly loud noise rumbles from my stomach, and I rip another piece of the tangy leather off. A groan escapes over the mouthful of the sweet and tart chewiness settling in my aching belly. Sated, at least for now, I shove away from the counter and wince at the stool legs scraping over the tile floors. I hesitate, glancing one more time at the snacks and sigh.

"Nope, I don't need to eat my feelings today." Giving up on food, I spin and head to my rooms.

I don't get too far before someone pounces on me from behind, wrapping their legs around my waist, and slinks down to the floor, their hands cupping my shoulders. A shiver racks down my spine and then dissipates in relief when my brain recognizes Eliza's lemony tart-filled scent.

"Faith! I cannot believe you finally have your wolf! And fucking Connor, Goddess, what an absolute asshole..." she rambles, talking so fast it's difficult to make out the rest of what she's saying.

"Eliza, I don't want to talk about Connor...or anything really," I mutter, shrugging her off my shoulders. Today is not the day to be so cheerful. She steps around me, arching an expertly shaped brow. Although her eyes are less puffy and bloodshot than mine today, she, of course, is glowing, radiant as ever. How is that fair? To retain such beauty after sobbing, meanwhile, I look like a ragged she-wolf returning from war. I guess she's not as depressed as I thought she would be. Whatever.

* * *

The leather chairs in Dad's study don't appear to be as comfortable as they should be, and I have yet to find a position in which I can sit for more than a few seconds. Grumbling to myself and standing, I tip-toe over to the window. Long black mourning panels hang from the eaves of the house and billow in the gentle breeze. Soon, the sapphire blue panels, embroidered with the symbol of our pack, will replace them, announcing our period of mourning is over.

A whole week has passed since Mom's murder, and each night I've managed maybe a couple of hours of sleep. Finding rest only after I've cried myself into oblivion, numbing the pain of Mom's death. For now, that pain far outweighs Connor's humiliation.

"When will you depart?" Dad asks in a low voice, startling me from my thoughts. I glance over my shoulder, skimming my inquisitive eyes over him. He doesn't bother to stray his attention from the paperwork cluttered over his desk when I don't answer right away. He hasn't slept more than an hour each night, and it's showing. Late at night, the pitter-patter of his wandering echoes in the halls of the mansion, drawing me from my own sleepless nights to spy on him from my door.

When he's not shuffling up and down the hallways, he sneaks into our rooms, checking on us. I pretend to be asleep when he covers me with a blanket and brushes a hand over my forehead. It should be Hollie and me checking in on him, but he's ignored all of my insistence to do anything that may help. He has gone so far and even refused to eat until Hollie or I force him to. My heart aches for him and the pain he's going through. I wish he would let us help him.

It's said that being rejected by a mate is excruciating and can take months to years to overcome. But, losing a mate in death, especially in such a traumatic way, well... I can't imagine that. Not many survive losing their mates in such a manner, and I worry my Dad's fate will soon follow. I see it in the way the vibrant life has left his once bright blue eyes and replaced them with a sorrowful, sunken soul that reflects in his now gray and dull aura.

"Tomorrow is when Con–," I hesitate, not wanting to mention Connor's name, knowing it will upset him. Dad narrows his eyes at my half-answer. He's livid over Connor effectively casting me aside that day, and by hurting and embarrassing me in front of most of the pack. So, when I approached him hours ago with the idea of taking my honeymoon by myself, I was worried about what his answer might be.

"It's the originally planned departure day for the Outer Banks," I correct myself. Going to his desk, I lean over, resting my chin on his shoulder, and wrap my arms around his chest. "But I don't have to go if you need me here."

He squeezes my wrist, breathing a heavy sigh. "No, Faith, you should go; it will be good for you. It will give you time to get to know your wolf, too." He pats my hand and releases it. "Go and heal, bring me back some seashells, yeah?"

At the mention of seashells, I find the shelves of them across the room. Hundreds of the creamy and multi-colored items from the aforementioned collection peek out from between rows of books in blown-glass jars. A few memories flutter to life from when I'd gifted him some of the more unique shells over the years, twitching a smirk across my lips. Planting a kiss on his cheek, my arms fall away, and I cross the wooden floors of his study, departing, but a thought halts my retreat.

"Daddy?" He looks up with a smile, removing his reading glasses, and raises his brows.

"I don't have to go, I can continue to help with the investigation if you want," my voice trailing off when his smile falls.

"No, I want you to go, sweet pea, you need to heal too–" he sips his coffee, and adds, "but I will forward any files that I need help with, okay? And I'll have Russell send you copies of his findings, too. Now go, pack, and try to enjoy the time away."

* * *

The third suitcase is nearly finished being packed when Eliza pops in, unannounced, into my rooms. Her loud complaints come through the sitting room walls where I'm gathering up a few more books and my camera gear.

"Honestly, Faith, I knew something was up when he made you wait practically a decade to get married," she yells, most likely lying on my bed. Her comment grates on my nerves, but I shove the irritation down. I don't have the energy to deal with it. She means well, she's my best friend after all, and a strong candidate to become my beta when I take over the pack, but sometimes she doesn't know when to quit.

"Fuck!" My elbow bangs into the bedroom door, tingling the funny bone. The motion knocks my arms full of the identifying shells, plants, and animals books, just enough that they start to slip free.

"Dammit!" Stumbling forward, I manage to juggle the mess and smack my other arm into the door in the process. "Fu-dammit-oh no, no, no!" I shout, watching in horror as the camera bag, full of specialized lenses, swings to and fro, from where it hangs in the crook of my now bruised elbow.

Eliza sits up on my bed, scrunching up her nose, glaring at my armful of books.

"Gee, thanks for the help, Liz," I mutter and ignore her, tossing the books into the tote bag next to the three suitcases. She scoffs, shrugging her shoulders, acting as if nothing could possibly bother her.

"Can you honestly tell me, Faith, that you're actually gonna read while on your vacation to the beach?" she sneers, pulling one of the books from the tote between pinched fingers like it's a dirty diaper.

I catch her disgruntled face from the corners of my eyes and roll them. "It's not a vacation, Liz, I'm going on my honeymoon alone and will probably work on an article," I say, annoyed, and snatch the book from her fingers, replacing it in the tote.

She huffs and shimmies off my bed, gives me a side hug, and air kisses. "Well, ta-ta."

The groan I'd been holding in releases more like a growl as the door to my room slams. "Ta-ta, to you too...good grief."

* * *

The last suitcase gets loaded into the trunk of my 1992 forest green Jeep Grand Cherokee with a thud. I slam the hatch and round to the driver's side. My father stands next to it, holding the door open; his appearance is horrible with hollowed cheeks and purple splotches under his eyes. I should stay, he needs me here, I know it, and I'm about to say that, but he manages a smile, stalling my words.

"I wish you'd take one of the newer vehicles, sweet pea. I don't know why you insist on driving this old thing," Dad mutters, with his hand on the hood.

My lips curl up into a half grin, shoulders shrugging, I rise on my tiptoes to kiss him on his cheek, his whiskers tickling my lips. His strong arms wrap me up in a bear hug. "I'm gonna miss you, sweet pea."

I breathe in the scent of him, fighting the urge to cry. The last hints of Mom's lilac mingling with his pine and ash are beginning to fade. My earlier thought returns, I should stay. I should be helping him run the pack, getting to know my wolf with his help, but I know I would only end up smothering him, and he wouldn't be any better for it. We both lost so much last week, and there is no quick fix for any of this.

"I'll be available on my cell the whole time, Dad. Remember, my location is automatically shared with you, and ask Hollie if you have any problems with it." He chuckles at my reminder and mumbles something under his breath about children these days. Last time I checked, I am a full-grown ass woman, but I won't poke at him now.

He steps back, his hands rubbing up my arms, a slight curl lifting his lips. "I'm sure I can figure it out. Please be safe, and check in when you can. I love you, Faith...my lil sweet pea," Dad's voice shakes, breaking off another shard of my already shattered heart. His gentle kiss brushes over my forehead, the warmth sinking below my skin. He steps away, allowing me to enter the car.

I slide onto the worn beige leather seat and close the door, its hinge squeaking. I really need to get that fixed soon. The only thing remotely new in my car is the stereo and navigation system. It was a gift from Dad after I got my first photography job out in Phoenix. He upgraded the out-of-date system to a touchscreen with navigation and cell phone connections shortly before I drove out to Arizona, instead of flying, and potentially risking all of my equipment. I appreciated the update, and while I should take one of my newer cars, driving this car is purely sentimental at this point.

My family could've easily bought me any car I wanted when I got my license, but they know the value of hard work and have encouraged both my sister and me to earn our first car the good old-fashioned way. I'd bought this one with my first two paychecks. I had wanted a jeep in my early teens. And when I spotted this forest green one with a for sale sign in the local garage shop's parking lot, I walked in and offered a couple of extra hundred for it. They put new tires on it and got it tuned up before I picked it up a few days later.

That was almost 10 years ago, and this old thing has taken me all over the US, and back and forth to college every day. A month ago, I had taken Mom with me on a shoot up to Canada. We laughed most of the drive north, munching on Cheetos, sour gummy candies, and drinking and spilling way too much coffee.

The memory draws my gaze down to the passenger side floor. The coffee stain in the carpet remains from when she laughed so hard her coffee sloshed in the cup, spilling everywhere. I didn't have the time to get it cleaned when we returned with all of the wedding plans. I don't have it in me to clean it now; it would feel like I was erasing a part of her.

The address having been pinned into the navigation to my Airbnb earlier, I select my playlist for the first part of the journey, and start up my old jeep, the aging engine rumbling to life, loud but purring. I wave a few times to both Hollie and Dad, both standing on the steps, holding onto one another in a side hug. I'd said goodbye to my sister earlier when she accosted me in the bathroom, full of tears and ramblings about Dad. She has never been great with goodbyes, even if they are temporary, but I know she will take good care of Dad while I'm gone. I have every confidence she'll call me the moment something is wrong.

Circling the driveway, tears sting the corners of my eyes when I glance in the rearview mirror at Dad and Hollie. Their forms shrink away the further I get down the long drive to the gates. Those blasted, unwanted tears slide down my cheeks, moments before I reach the guard shack at the perimeter of the pack lands. I nod to them, and they wave and open the gates. Both guards tip their heads in a small bow and continue their watch.

Stopping at the end of the long winding road into the pack lands, my eyes dart to the stain on the floor mat again. Mom's laughter echoes in my memory, another batch of warm, wet tears curl over my wobbling bottom lip before falling and absorbing into my pants.

5

Faith

There is something to be said about solo road trips, being able to listen to whatever you want, eat whatever you want, and decide to stop o n whenever you want, which is utterly freeing. Since I left later than I intended, the 18-hour drive from the pack lands in Maine to the Outer Banks in North Carolina has taken a little over two days. I could've flown, but I enjoy driving; the journey often is, for me, the best memory maker.

The worst part of my drive so far was through New Jersey. I got lost for a moment when I missed my exit off the turnpike, and ended up having to backtrack a little. It was pretty stupid. I don't know who de-signed the jersey turnpike, but they didn't think it all the way through. Too many roads converging into one, confusing signage, and horrible drivers, but it was still better than having to drive through D.C.

Mid-morning on the second day of driving, I'm somewhere along Highway 113. My hips shift in my seat as I stretch an arm over to the passenger seat, blindly rummaging through the snack pile, only to come up empty-handed.

"Ugh, great," I groan, and a pang of emptiness gurgles in my stomach. Glancing at the navigation screen, a line of gas stations and fast food places is coming up.

Awesome, I need to fuel up and get more snacks anyway.

I should probably consume a healthier meal and not just chips and sugar. Yet, those little wrapped goodies always do the trick and keep me awake.

The reminder of what Connor would say lingers, but I brush it aside with all the other unprocessed emotions for now. Besides, it wouldn't be a road trip without obscene piles of sugar and junk food, along with copious amounts of caffeine.

* * *

Brittany Spears' *Toxic* blares from the speakers as I roll into the Royal Farms station a little while later. The gentleman pumping gas in front of me raises his brow at the song and smiles, his wrinkles creasing at the sides. Embarrassingly, I roll my windows up and hop out, crossing the parking lot in an awkward sprint.

As soon as I grab the nozzle to pump gas, my nostrils flare, a pungent musk of a shifter wafts past on the breeze, and whoever it is is nearby. Sienna springs forward, attempting to gain control.

"Rogues are nearby, hurry up and be done, I don't think we should be lingering," she demands through our link.

I'm not nearly as confident of their scents as she is, but I know I need to trust Sienna even if I'm still a little pissy with her. Sienna's senses are ten times stronger than my own, and if it is a small pack of rogues, there is no way I can handle them alone. I just don't know if it would be the most brilliant move to give her control at the moment.

Casually browsing around and smiling at the others pumping gas, I struggle to resist the urge to lift my nose into the air, knowing that would make me look ridiculous. Sienna forces my head to swivel down in silent protest.

A few minutes later, the reverberation of passing cars and the occasional tweet of birds fill the now-empty lot. Only crumpled-up wrappers and an empty fountain cup roll over the pavement. It would seem I'm the only one left.

Right then, the hairs on the back of my neck rise, spiking goose flesh to pebble across my arms. Shaking the unease off, my muscles tense up again when I sense the shifter approaching, much closer than it was 5 minutes ago.

I wiggle the nozzle. It clanks against the metal as it slides out from my tank, and I replace it in the cradle. My fingers shake uncontrollably as I turn the gas cap, waiting for the click. Slamming the tiny door closed and scanning the area again, I sigh in relief at seeing the area clear of danger. But that niggling of something or someone is watching, won't quit. My hand doesn't quite reach the door handle when a creepy voice raises the hairs on the back of my neck again.

"Lookie, what we have here...a little she-wolf out...*all alone*," the voice sneers, he's so close his rank breath heats the skin of my neck. An eerie sensation creeps down my spine, and ramps up my pulse, it sputters out of control, and leaches fear into my blood.

He reeks of cheap, soured beer, dry pine needles, and campfire; the smell rolls my stomach upside down. My heart races, but I stand there frozen, watching his reflection in the glass of the jeep's door. His dark brown eyes flash gold and then back to brown. I cringe internally when he smiles a big, yellowed-toothed grin.

The creep leans in, sniffing me, his bulbous nose catches in my hair as he snakes it up my cheek. I choke on a yelp when he grabs my sides tightly, holding me captive. Ice slithers through my veins, gathering a dark, resounding calmness in the pit of my gut.

There are so many things that I should be doing right now, but all of them could end up on the internet or land me in jail or both. I wrestle with control over my anxiety and the icy calmness. The anxiety I can manage, it's the dangerous veil of darkness I'm afraid of. Inhaling, I refocus, allowing the calm to take over. Remaining as still as possible, I scan in between the vacant gas pumps; only the buzz of cicadas and birds' songs fills the air, not a soul in sight.

"Mmmm, you smell like heaven, little wolf, and a little scared," he murmurs into my ear, breathing deeply. "Mmmm, my favorite combination..." he smells me again, diving his nose into my hair—a sickening rope coils in my stomach at his touch.

"Oh! I know who you are, a bit far from home, aren't you, Lil Faith Bennett?" he adds, his voice low, rumbling excitedly, it sends shivers down my spine.

What? The– Fuck!

Sienna, who's chomping at the bit, pressures me to be released. *"Sienna, not now, I can handle this, just relax. Please?"* My attempts to calm her fail miserably, and she surges forward again.

"Oh, I'm sure you could handle it as if we were a little weakling omega. We're an alpha, and this punk rogue is being disrespectful and disgusting," she all but barks at me through our link. *"Let me out, I'll take care of him swiftly."*

I swallow roughly and muster my courage, ignoring Sienna, and anchor my control over her. The pain of near shifting rattles my bones. She knows we can't move where humans could see, but I don't understand why she is fighting me on this. The penalty alone should be enough to stop her.

Eyes creasing, my body whips around, and I glare at the rogue and swiftly bite my tongue. The left side of his face is horrifically scarred, odd for a wolf, almost like he was burned before his wolf appeared, or he was unable to shift. Or worse, it was a repeated injury from—nope, not going there. His earth brown eyes narrow, and he steps even closer, shoving me up against the door of my jeep. My back slams into the metal, vibrating my spine. Now I'm pissed off.

Releasing my masked aura just a little bit, a coppery light flashes on his shirt, right before I shove him hard in the chest. He stumbles backwards into the gas pump, smacking his back and head into the metal with a sickening crack.

The prick throws his hands up in the air, frowning, "You bitch!" He snaps, staggering forward, bracing himself on the back of my car, dirt-caked fingers reaching for me. Out of nowhere, another rogue appears.

"Dammit, Eric," the newcomer spits, yanking his friend up and shoving him back and away from me and my car.

"Man, fuck you, Dirk! I was just having a bit of fun," the first rogue, apparently Eric, whines in a voice too high-pitched to be normal.

Dirk steps towards me, bowing his head slightly, "I apologize, alpha, Eric...is an idiot. We scented you a few hours ago around the last rest stop, and he wouldn't let it go until he saw who was traipsing through our territory," he murmurs, but firmly giving me no reason not to believe him. I've never much cared for rogue wolves, but I also understand the plight of many. What I can't comprehend is how they know who I am just by my scent.

My gaze skirts over Dirk. He's tall and fit, but his clothes are ragged and threadbare. An overwhelming urge to give him some cash and tell him to get new clothes weighs heavily against my conscience, but knowing how Sienna will react, I stuff the idea back down.

"You'd be right..." she growls.

"Leave me alone, I'm just passing through," I admit, and realize a second too late how stupid that was. Tracing my hand backwards, I reach and fumble for my car door handle. Sweaty fingers slip off the metal and screech down the door.

Dirk bows his head again and backs away, hands raised in the air. "Apologies, Alpha Faith, you are welcome into our territory any time, just keep an eye out, not all members of our lil' rogue pack are as friendly as I am," he warns, and then in an instant, he's gone.

Frantically, I jump into my car, lock the doors, and get back on the highway, my heart hammering throughout my entire body. I dial Dad.

The call rings and rings and rings, ramping my pulse to a punishing pace.

Finally, he picks up before it goes to voicemail, "Yes, sweet pea? Are you alright?" he rushes, concern lacing his out-of-breath voice. He's probably picking up on my thunderous heart pounding through the phone; it's beating so hard.

"Yeah, Dad, I am alright, but–"

"But what," he blurts, interrupting. The garbled connection makes it hard to hear over the rumble of the tires on the old road.

Sighing, "One sec, Dad." I grab my headphones and place one into my ear, and I wait for it to connect before answering. "I just ran into a couple of rogues, Eric and Dirk? They knew who I was just by scenting me, they knew my name and could–"

"Identify you as an alpha, yes, well, once I declare you to the council," he finishes my sentence. "But sweet pea, I haven't sent in the notification yet; this worries me greatly," he reveals in a sigh. Wait what? He hasn't sent in my declaration of status change to the council yet.

"Why not, and why didn't I know of this ability?" A rummaging of papers in the background muffles his curse. He must be in his study. My eyes drift to my rearview mirror, and a dark blue sedan closes the gap between us, riding my tailgate.

Signaling, I change lanes to pass a trucker and get away from the tailgater. After gliding back into the right lane, I glance in the rearview again, only to see the same sedan riding my ass once more. The dark window tint covers the top quarter of the windshield, blocking my view of the occupants. My pulse picks up again, thrumming in my throat. It could be nothing, but I'm still on edge from earlier, and nothing has been as simple as it should be lately.

"I didn't plan on sending in the paperwork until you returned, since they will more than likely want to meet with you," he answers, startling me from the tailgater. Knowing better than to respond, my fingers bounce over the edge of the steering wheel while I wait for him to finish.

"I thought I went over all of the duties and responsibilities of what the council does with you, but I may have missed one," he says, a little annoyed, but in that perfect Dad tone. "All alphas are declared to them so they can either reconcile or dispute the ascension; you may have to stand before them."

"You did, but how can they determine who I am just from smelling me? Like, I know we can sense our ranks, but they knew my name, Dad." I can't hide the worry in my voice as it rises in pitch. "Maybe you told me, but it was one of those times I spaced off," I laugh, eager to deflect my anxiety, a sour taste coating my tongue. I didn't truly space off when he'd told me, I knew what the council expected of me, and all alphas. However, I would've remembered if he told me about a special ability.

"Faith, what's wrong? I can hear your pulse. Are you safe?" He pauses, and I can hear the thoughts he's bouncing around, not wanting to say, but inevitably will because he's, my Dad.

"I want you to do this trip more than anything, but with what just happened, I'm a bit nervous with you being alone." And there it is. He sounds wrecked with justified anxiety. I know what he's going to say next, and it's something I most assuredly don't want.

Not knowing what to say to him, my breaths slow with each long inhale, and I explain that I'm okay, and there's no need to worry. I convince him that the rogues haven't followed me, at least to my knowledge, and that I will call at my next stop. I can't bear lying to him, but the last thing I need is for him to be worried right now. All that would do is force him to send his guards down.

He grumbles about me telling him not to worry, "it's my job, sweet pea," he says, his beard scratching in the receiver. I can picture him reclining back in his chair, running a hand over his chin while he debates his next words.

"I would've preferred it if you'd taken Eliza or one of my guards," he mumbles. I argue that I am to be his next alpha, and that he needs to let me defend myself and to trust my judgment. We say our good-byes in a huff, and I hang up.

* * *

Delaware and Maryland have come and gone, and dusk falls over the skies of Virginia. The blue sedan ceased following me about an hour ago, somewhere in between Maryland and Virginia. The entire time that damn car followed me, my anxiety ramped up tenfold, so when it disappeared, it was like I'd been hit with a dose of Xanax.

The warm, salty air at the Chesapeake Bay Bridge-Tunnel assaults my skin and lungs as I inhale deeply while stepping out of my car. It's disgustingly muggy out, the air so thick, you can practically chew it. I dig my camera pack out from the back seat and lock up the jeep.

A crop of rocks lines the side of the road, separating the turn-off from the beach below. With a glance over my shoulder, ensuring no one can see me, I squat down and jump over the rocks to the sandy shore in one giant leap. There is no way I would've made that leap before without Sienna's powers running through me. I could get used to these new abilities with my wolf now.

Bending over to remove my white, slip-on Vans, a groan slips out from the burn in my hamstrings. I tuck my shoes into a side pocket of my old, beat-up canvas backpack and pull my camera out. I found the pack at an army surplus store ages ago, and now I never go anywhere without it. Lifting the padded neck strap up and over my head, a soothing familiarity releases all of my tension.

Warm, powdery sand clings to my feet, the texture reminding me somewhat of the sand found in the Grand Caymans. Casting a fixed stare over the water, I note several fishing boats and a couple of sailboats motoring throughout the water between sections of the large bridge. The Chesapeake Bay Bridge-Tunnel is 17.6 miles long. The expansive bridge dips into two tunnels within the bay, allowing larger ships to pass without having to construct a drawbridge.

The sun hovers above the horizon, waving its deep orange fingers to all those watching, that it soon will set, and give way to night and the moon; the golden hour, perfect for water shots.

Walking along the shore, the cool water laps at my toes as I zoom in on a snowy white crane stalking its dinner in a small cove near the base of the bridge. I focus my lens and press the shutter button several times, rapidly firing off frame after frame. The golden hour light glints and bounces off the water's reflection, illuminating the fringy white feathers of the crane. Its elongated neck curves, and its head tilts to one side while it continues to wade through the shallow water, hunting for its supper.

Fifteen minutes later, I'm about to give up on my mandatory search for a shell and find a place to put my shoes back on when my toe scrapes against something under the loose sand. Wincing from the sharp pain, I lift my foot, and blood trickles from the tip of my toe. Bending over, I reach out and flick the tip of the protruding object back and forth, tugging out a fully intact Atlantic drill oyster shell.

"Aha! So, you're the culprit who cut my toe," I exclaim to no one in particular. Turning the oval-shaped shell over in my hand, its purplish color fades from the top spire down over its raised whorls to beige. Brown spiraling vertical stripes along the ribbed sides lead to the smooth inside, and curves out to a flared lip with a deep purple painting the walls within.

"This is perfect for Dad's collection." I pocket the newly found gem and make my way back over to the base of the rocks, plopping down and dusting my sandy-covered feet off. The scrape on my toe has scabbed over and, surprisingly, doesn't hurt at all anymore. After slipping my shoes back on, I climb and heave myself up over the rock wall. I heave a sigh as a shroud of grief wraps its arms around my middle.

The spiraled shell would've been Mom's favorite, too.

Shoving the sadness away back into its little perfectly shaped glass box, I hop back into my jeep and head over the long bridge.

* * *

It's a little past 10 PM when my jeep ambles through the small Outer Banks town of Danset, North Carolina. Passing a tiny surf shop, gift shops, and a bar at the end of the road, my foot hovers over the brake pedal, and I stare out my window. The click, clock of my blinker drowns out most of the music pumping out from the open-air section of the bar, and as much as I want to stop and grab a beer, I desperately need sleep more.

A small crowd of people hanging around the open-air portion is laughing, appearing to be having a great time. They all seem to be care-free and happy, probably because they have everyday lives that aren't weighed down with despair and fretted with grief.

I roll my window down more and lean my head out, inhaling the sweet, salty air, keen to wake up enough to make it to my rental. The aromas of a sweet floral and what smells like BBQ layer over the sticky ocean air, making my stomach grumble.

The jeep's tires smoosh and crunch over sand as I pull into the driveway of the vacation rental. A small rectangular patch of expertly trimmed Bermuda grass grows alongside large oat grasses spaced evenly on both sides of the drive, their long, tall-stemmed, fluffy tufts drift and sway in the breeze.

Pale moonlight shines on the large, light-blue house, with white accents and shutters. The wide steps lead up to a huge wrap-around porch, and a seashell wreath hangs on the wall to the left of an ornate door with a beautifully etched window. The house sits on stilts on a raised portion of land, with wooden steps in the back that lead directly down to the beach. I won't have far to go to enjoy the salty water and sink my toes into the sand searching for my treasures tomorrow.

Turning the engine off, my head hits the headrest, and a heavy sigh releases the aches and stress from the trip so far. A few minutes tick by before I finally retrieve my keys from the ignition and pull up the code for the door in my phone and send off a quick text to Dad letting him know I made it.

After struggling with the door code for ten minutes, the stupid thing finally unlocked. I let myself in, and my mouth pops open in awe. The entryway light switches on automatically, instantly bombarding me with its comforting ambiance. The interior is beautiful and simply decorated in typical nautical whites, grays, and blues. The coastal-designed furniture with splashes of blue hydrangeas on the throw pillows is inviting without being overly garish.

Shuffling my exhausted body over the wood floors, I scan the kitchen, and instantly, I groan. Sitting on a granite countertop island is a bouquet of long-stemmed red roses, their sweet scent curling through the air-conditioned air. A note card with mine and Connor's names on it is propped up on a box of chocolates. Water drips down the sides of an ice bucket containing champagne. Two flutes with outlined white hearts sparkle from a nightlight under the microwave.

Not wanting to dwell on the welcome gifts tonight, I head back out to my jeep and retrieve my suitcases. Lugging the last one out of the back of the jeep, I freeze at a prickling sensation racing down my spine and lifting the fine hairs on the back of my neck. The eerie feeling that I'm being watched scuttles through my amygdala, warning me. Tapping into Sienna's senses, I inhale deeply while standing completely still. If someone is watching me, I don't want to alert them.

"I smell and sense nothing," Sienna links. I sniff again, and she's right, there's nothing now, not even the creepy energy. Perhaps, I'm merely exhausted and sensing things. Shrugging, I lug the last suitcase inside, grab my backpack, and head up the small flight of stairs to find the primary bedroom.

A warmth washes over me, and I inhale deeply. The whole house smells of salty air, sand, lilacs, and hydrangeas. My hand rubs absentmindedly at the sudden tightness in my chest, lilacs... *Mom.*

The wheels of the suitcase echo off the wood floors as I drag my body into the primary suite. Letting go of the handle, it topples over, clapping against the floor in a too-loud clang. The bedroom is beautiful, a large queen-sized bed draws the eye to the center of the room from against the wall. Across from the bed are a set of French doors that lead out to a small deck overhanging the wrap-around porch. Two comfy-looking chairs and a table on the deck invite one to curl up and soak in the sun.

After showering and changing into comfy clothes, I collapse onto the fluffy bed. Puffs of the softener burst into the air, comforting my senses as I slip under and bury myself beneath the comforter. I have no idea what time it is, nor do I care. Easily, my heavy lids slide closed, and my body surrenders to the sandman.

* * *

The smell of burning flesh, flowers, and herbs fills my nostrils from the flames licking the sides of the pyre. Mom's body lies there consumed in fire, but a rage builds inside me...scanning the line of wolves, I want to charge and rip him to shreds...

My eyes dart open to a dark room, and shaky fingers wipe away a thin film of sweat from my brow. I fling the covers off and sit up, orienting myself to where I am, and shake off the nightmare that has plagued my sleep for the last two weeks. It always comes to a halt right before or after Mom sits up and points at me, her scorched face contorting in a silent scream, with words I can't hear but know. A pounding headache throbs behind my eyes, and a tightness squeezes my chest, making it hard to breathe.

Knowing that I'll never get any sleep now, I stretch to try and ease the grip on my lungs and pluck at my top, which is currently stuck to me like glue. I glide across the room searching for the thermostat. It has to be a good 80 degrees in here, at least that's what it feels like.

Fumbling along the wall, I find the ceiling fan switch and flip it on, and lower the thermostat.

As the room starts to cool down a little, I wander over to the French doors that open to a large deck. The glass is still warm to the touch under the tips of my fingers pressing into it. My breath hitches when movement catches my attention from the corner of my eyes. That eerie energy from earlier creeps back in and rattles my senses.

Squinting, I can barely make out the shape of someone walking beside the waves crashing to shore. Nausea burns its way up my throat, I swallow sharply and step out of the moonlight filtering through the drapes, observing the weirdo out in the middle of the night.

My pulse thunders, ramping up the crushing anxiety. It overwhelms me as the person stops directly in front of the house, and they look up directly at me. Shit, can they see me? My mind runs rampant through irrational scenarios. After the last two weeks I've had, it's hard not to be in overdrive or let the paranoia take root.

My hand goes to my chest while I hold my breath and walk backwards towards the bed. My eyes never leave the doors. I take one slow step at a time, reversing myself up the mattress and under the covers. A sharp pain slices the back of my skull when my head smacks into the headboard.

6

❦

Faith

I rudely bolt awake to successive bells chiming. Groggily, I blink so slowly it takes me more than a minute to decipher where I'm at again and where the chimes are coming from. My legs jerk, kicking under the blanket, I sit up in bed and swing my sleep-heavy head to the right, glaring at the offending chimes. *Ugh,* it's my phone.

I detangle my limbs from the offending blanket and snatch my phone off the nightstand. Scrolling through the notifications that so rudely chimed their way into my slumber when my phone mode automatically switched to morning. I flop back into the plush pillows, relishing in the softness.

Several texts had come in throughout the night and this morning, as well as three new emails from Dad and Russell. A part of me really should open them and reply now, but at the rumbling of my stomach, I toss my phone to the side and get up.

The house is even more stunning in the daylight, the dark polished wood floors gleam from the sun peeping through the curtains, scattering its rays over the planks. Shades of blue and gray painted walls accent the bright yellows and splashes of lavender in the decor, spread perfectly throughout. Passing by the kitchen island, I groan again when I see the champagne and roses.

"Might as well get this over with," I mutter to no one but myself. I wasn't such a self-talker before, because Connor found it "unladylike."

The only thing he liked, and I quote, "not ladylike behavior," was my tattoos.

Picking up the notecard addressed to the two of us, I suck in a breath as a heaviness sinks into my stomach, and watery tears blur the scribbled words.

Congratulations, Mr. and Mrs. Connor Morgan.

Please enjoy the champagne and don't hesitate to reach out to us should you need anything at all. There are a lot of amenities here for your use, and in town, tons of things to see and do! Enjoy your honeymoon!

Sincerely,

The Mills

With a flash of irritation forking out like lightning under my skin, I crumple the note and toss it into the trash.

Wandering through the kitchen, smiling widely when I find the coffee pot and an espresso machine tucked into a corner under pristine white cabinets with seashell pulls. Effectively snooping through all of the cabinets, inspecting what's in each, a bubbling, giddy sensation rushes through me when I find the coffee beans and a grinder.

Hot, steaming mug of coffee in hand, I curl my bare legs up under a blanket on the porch swing, it sways softly from my jostling and lulls a sense of serenity over me. A soft breeze lifts the loose strands of my bun, the waving pieces tickling the sides of my neck. Taking a long sip of delicious life bean juice, I view the shoreline over the rim of my cup; the waves are a bit calmer than the night before. They're lazily crashing and lapping the shoreline, soaking the sand in their wake before retreating with the low tide. It's mesmerizing and cathartic listening to the ocean; it's one of my favorite things to do.

An antsy tingle ripples throughout me from Sienna's growing excitement to run alongside it, and she comes to the front of my mind. *"Wouldn't it be fun to run alongside them tonight?"* She mind links to me, with a level of excitement I've yet to experience from her.

"I don't know, Sienna, it's not common to see wolves this far south," I link back, and a wave of her disappointment washes over me. Besides, I wasn't planning on running her until I felt more comfortable shifting and doing so without pain. A tingle quivers and recoils as she senses my line of thinking.

"You know the only way that can happen is if you practice," she gripes and turns away from my consciousness before I can argue with her. Her sadness pulses with each breath.

"Hey, we will figure it out...I promise." She ignores me and disappears further away from our link, leaving an ache stabbing through my chest

Maybe I'll run late at night? I think I hope it will spark her to come back, but it doesn't. She ignores me completely, leaving me in a pit of awful despair for rejecting her idea.

The whirring of wave-muffled voices penetrates my ears, jolting me awake. Disoriented, I rub my fingers over my temples, easing the budding headache. I must have dozed off a while ago, based on the sun's position in the clear blue sky beating down on the porch, it must be nearing noon.

The swing sways awkwardly, while I try to right myself. The voices get clearer and louder as a couple walking by the waves with big smiles, and shouting, "Welcome to Danset!" I lift my surprisingly still full mug in response, and they continue on their way.

Well, I could get used to this way of life, no one outright bothering me, but still kind and welcoming without too much chitchat or typical judgment. Small talk always makes me want to crawl out of my skin. I never know what to say, and I end up staring like a sideshow clown at a creepy circus. You know the kind that you find in horror flicks? Yeah, that's me, always messing something up. Connor would always point it out, more annoyed with having to remind me to be normal than anything else. I never understood why he bothered staying with me so long if everything I did was a mistake or not good enough for him.

Clutching a hand to my stomach, I remind myself he's no longer my problem and shove those self-loathing thoughts away.

I get dressed in a pair of old, dark-wash cut-offs, a yellow bikini, and a lightweight button-down that I tie at my navel. As I knot the shirt, it soothes the anxious need building in my stomach for a tiny bit of modesty. Wiggling my white-painted toes, with little flower stickers I added when I came back inside earlier, I slip into my flip flops.

On my way out, I about-face when my vision snags on the bottle of champagne on the counter. Fingers curled around the neck, I debate finding a glass and then quickly decide it's not worth it.

"Fuck it, ain't no need, less dishes." I laugh to myself and rip the bottle from the bucket of melted ice, slinging water everywhere. A gasp rushes past my lips from the still-cold bottle, kissing the sliver of skin on my stomach.

* * *

Beige sand cakes my feet and up my ankles after several hours of walking the beach, collecting all manner of shells and pieces of sea glass. Carefully, I tuck the last little treasure into a tiny pouch to research later in my shell identification book. Running my tongue over my dry lips, I find the bottle of champagne nestled between the blanket and pillow that I tossed down the stairs on my way here.

With the tip of my tongue sticking out to the side of my mouth, I work to free the cork. POP! My shoulders flinch, and my spine curves in at the explosion of noise. The sound of the cork popping out also sends three little sea birds jumping into flight, only to land a second later. I barely have enough time to lean back, avoiding the erupting, bubbling liquid.

"Ah pissah!" I groan as the alcohol spills over the lip and directly into the cradle of my thighs. Latching my lips over the mouth of overflowing bubbles, I suck in air through my nose and take a not-so-graceful gulp.

Legs covered in sticky alcohol, I run down and jump into the waves to wash it away. The cool water splashes up my legs, relieving the stickiness and heat permeating my skin.

"Goddess, this is amazing!" I shout, throwing my arms out wide, I spin around in a circle, and stumble over the crashing waves, and then make my way back up the beach.

Plopping my salty ass back down onto the soft blanket, I spin the bottle of champagne in my hands. The label is entirely in French, and mine is too rusty to make anything out. I shrug and continue sipping. "Who cares anyway? It tastes delicious, and I don't have to share."

I'm swallowing another "unbecoming behavior of a lady" swig when a petite woman with skin like dark leather walks past, scoffing. Glaring quite rudely, she mumbles something under her breath about the audacity I have to be so disrespectful in public. All I can do is smirk at her because all of the fucks I have left to give are currently zero. Gulping another sip of the bubbly, I raise the bottle in the air and toast her as she trudges by.

Seems I was wrong about the no judgment part.

* * *

A few hours later, my naturally tan skin is hot and stinging with an emerging burn. The blinding sting shooting across my shoulder blades screams for me to get up and go inside. I should probably rehydrate, too, considering the bottle of champagne I polished off earlier had a decent alcohol content, and I don't remember drinking any water over the past few hours. Blessedly, Sienna has been quiet and also blocked our healing capabilities to allow me to stay tipsy.

Too-tight skin stretches painfully as my fingers dive below the lava, also known as the sun-scorched sand. I push up to my elbows, but the ground blurs and spins a little. Eyes widening, I force myself to my feet.

Gathering my stuff in both arms, I wobble my way back up the steep stairs and toss the bottle into the trash with a bit of flair and too much oomph. The bottle clangs against the metal, and it smashes to the bottom. A trickle of lucidity spreads in my veins, and I decide I've not been drunk nearly long enough today, and I need to figure out how far away that bar I saw yesterday is.

"Saaahh-weeet! Not too far!" I shout after successfully googling. I've really got to stop talking to myself, or people are going to start thinking I belong in a nuthouse.

Hips swaying, shaking my ass, I strut out of the house. A bout of vertigo causes me to immediately flare my arms out wide as I navigate down the stairs to the road.

* * *

McCormick's Bar is a lot worse for wear in the daylight than it was last night when I drove by. Standing before it now, I can't decide whether the dilapidated shit look it has going on is on purpose or not. Holding up a hand to shield my eyes from the blinding rays of the sun, because Goddess knows where I left my sunglasses last, I squint my eyes to slits, scrutinizing the establishment. As lame and granny-like as those chains for glasses are, I should probably get some since I'm constantly losing my sunglasses.

"Judgey much?" Sienna scoffs out of nowhere and curls back up, ready to ignore me some more.

Hey, I'm buzzing good, and remembering stuff isn't so easy at the moment. I'm trying to forget a certain someone who broke my heart, remember? Oh, and let's not forget the savage murder of my Mom on my almost wedding day...m'kay?

But I digress, back to the shit-hole of a bar I'm standing in front of. The wood shingle siding is weathered, and some boards are barely hanging on by a single nail. The covered patio area I saw last night is bright with mismatched chairs of all colors, and pub tables take up most of the space.

Despite what I'll call a 'rustic impression' it's rather charming with the random surfboards, fish nets, and anchors for decor. However, the collection of motorcycle parking signs hanging along the front, near the entrance, sticks out like a sore thumb. Not to mention the random skull artwork that I can see inside the windows and out on the side walls, is a bit of a contradiction to the nautical theme; it's making my eyes twitch. Either way, I don't care too much because I want another drink, and this place is the only bar within a 25-mile radius.

The uneven boardwalk that surrounds the outside of the bar creaks under my steps, as does the rickety door with a circle of glass in the top center, when I yank it open.

Momentarily blinded, I rapidly blink and cross the threshold into the darker space. Blinking some more, for what seems like too many seconds, my eyes finally adjust to the low light, and I quickly find the bartender.

Feeling a little like my old self for the first time in forever, I glance down at myself. Ensuring my button-down ends are still tied into a knot above my belly ring and the girls are perky, I pat my pockets for my cash and saunter up to the bar.

Leaning on the old wooden counter, my fingers trace over the scratches and initials carved into the grain... interesting. That annoying voice in my head rudely barges in.

Can patrons do whatever they want to the property? Seems tacky.

Shaking my head, I internally gawk at my bitchy thoughts. What the hell is my problem?

This behavior is not me at all. Could it be the champagne? Maybe. Or perhaps it's the bitterness that has wormed its way into my heart from constantly having to be presentable at all times, never a stitch out of place, and the anxiety of seeing others or places not perfectly put together is too much. It's leaking out into uncalled-for judgment. Or perhaps it was the relentless worrying that our apartment always appeared perfect for guests and was always up to date with the latest styles. Nothing but the best was good enough for Connor.

Goddess forbid, I forgot to hide away the evidence of his disapproval from my skin; it happened one time, and that was one too many. It could also be picking nothing, but the best places to dine or go out to. No, it's definitely the champagne.

Yeah, we'll go with that.

With a gentle reminder to myself that I don't have to be in pristine operation anymore, unless I want to be, and that I can be myself without the worry of punishment, I assess the bar again with fresh eyes. The tip of my finger rubs back and forth in the deep grooves of a pair of initials that are inside a crudely carved heart.

A sharp pang pierces a deep-rooted heartache, breaking it open at the thought of the people who must've been so in love they felt the need to mark it forever in the wood. I wonder what that is like. No. Nope. Not today, misery. Quickly, I stuff the thoughts back down and think of something else.

I guess it adds character, right?

Lucky for me, as I glance around, the bar is in its slow part of the day. Hardly any customers occupy the tables or bar, save a few guys who appear worse for wear, nursing their Natty Lites. A couple of college-aged boys hang around a table near the dart boards. They lift their beers towards me in a silent, but flirty hello. They aren't my type, but I can appreciate their cuteness, though.

I shouldn't even be looking, but a part of me wants to feed this budding desire of revenge against Connor. I want to experience the rush of exhilaration when someone goes out of their way to make you feel good, because they recognize you are more than worthy.

My toes tap to the beat of the low music playing from an old juke-box in the corner. The bartender, who has been wiping down the already clean counter, finally sees me and greets me with a huge grin. He winks at me in acknowledgment and works his way over.

For a solid ten seconds, I let my gaze slide over every inch of his features. Taut chest muscles stretch out a dark blue t-shirt with 'McCormicks' embroidered over the left breast pocket. His biceps flex and bulge with every sweep of the counter.

Shifting my view back up and landing on his sandy colored hair, a weird certainty that he's only a friend works its way over any ideas of fun. A wide, sweet, but inviting smile spreads across my face, and I wink back. Not my usual greeting, but hey, champagne does weird things to me, I'm going with the flow.

"Well, hello there. Welcome to McCormicks. What can I get you, ma'am?" The dusty blonde asks, a huge grin turning up chiseled lips. Being in the friend zone is a shame since he's quite handsome, and oh, those pretty baby blue eyes. Ugh.

"Well, hello-ooo to you too, what's'yr-name,"my salutation comes out in a surprising slur.

Oh, my Goddess!

My hand flies up, covering my mouth. I'm glad a hiccup didn't escape in that embarrassing bubble of words; that would have been more than humiliating.

"Name's Flik, ma'am, a'you alright?" The southern drawl of his voice comes out thick with his concern. That concern is also clearly written all over his handsome face as he swipes the white cotton towel over the counter again.

Focusing hard, I force myself to appear a bit more sober than I actually am. "Uh, yeah...I'd love a beer, Flik, or cider if you've got any," I say, and an embarrassing squeak of a hiccup slides out. Flik's brows lift in disbelief.

"I'm alright, I promise. I just stayed out in the sun too long, is all," I add, trying not to slur my words again and fail miserably; I'm sure I'm giving off the drunken idiot vibe to him right now. I'm also sure the heat blooming under my cheeks doesn't help either.

Leaning over the counter again, I reach into my front pocket, causing my cleavage to press together, drawing Flik's baby blues straight to them. With my boobs shelved on the counter, I get a good whiff of him: sea salt, allspice, and wolf. Nostrils flaring, I step back as if he'd stepped in shit. Of fucking course, I would find wolves at the only bar for 25 miles in the Outer Banks.

Flik gives me an incredulous look, "Here ya go, enjoy, ma'am," he says, sliding a cold bottle of cider over to me. "D'you want to open a tab?" He asks with a giant smirk that reminds me of that one movie cat, as my hand dips into my back pocket.

What is the name of that damn cat again?

"Sure, I walked here anyway," I answer when Flik's head tilts to the side and smirks. Fishing the money out and sliding a crisp $100 bill over to him, I smirk back, wink, and take my cider over to one of the high-top tables near the open-air patio.

I set my cider down, and the table wobbles off kilter.

Well, that's annoying.

I hop off the chair too fast, instantly regretting that entire bottle of champagne as the room spins. I grab the edge to steady myself and then snatch a sugar packet from the little holder on the table. Dropping to a crouch, I find the offending off-balanced foot of the table and slip the sugar packet under. The powder-coated pedestal of the table is cool under my grip. I give it a good shake and nod to myself at my genius when it doesn't wobble anymore.

Jeez, who knew champagne brought out the arrogance in me?

"*I could've told you that,*" Sienna mutters and drops her head to her folded paws. I'm sure if she could roll her eyes, she would.

Smothering a snicker at myself, I freeze, the hairs on the back of my neck rise, and a scalding shudder rakes down my spine. From the bottom of my peripheral vision, a pair of square-toed cowboy boots comes to a stop right beside my bent knees. My eyes scan over the dark brown leather, then up to a pair of dark wash jeans.

"Ma'am?" A deep voice that sounds like it was shredded over rough gravel cascades down to the floor where I'm still huddled, coating my skin with a heat I've never felt before.

"Huh?" Pain erupts when I smack the back of my head on the table from rising too quickly. "Ouch, shit, that fucking hurt," I swear, rubbing the sore spot, and straightening, the room spins a little.

If my cheeks weren't so dang red already, my embarrassment would be center stage. Regardless of the humiliation begging to rise, I grip the table, waiting for the dizziness to pass before spinning around to see the owner of said boots.

And of course, he's the most gorgeous man I've ever seen. Isn't that what all romance authors write about? Not only that, but he has the audacity to stand before me with the most intoxicating scent wafting off his tight, huge muscles.

Another ripple of tingling jars me, and a wave of uneasiness washes over me. Inhaling, my lungs freeze; something's off about his scent. It's vaguely familiar, yet at the same time, it's not. The rather pleasant odor almost overpowers my wolf senses. It's woodsy, like a spruce. Bits of driftwood with a hint of the sea, too, and dare I say wolf? It's not pungent or foul like most males can come off as.

Perhaps a shifter of a different type, no. Yes...wolf, dammit.

Why can't I tell? Is he masking his scent?

The thought ping-pongs off my buzzing brain, and I check my masking magic. I don't need another issue like before with the rogues.

Shaking my head, I clear my throat awkwardly. I'm about to throw my hand out and introduce myself but catch myself mid-air when his lips part in a sexy smirk.

Oh, my Goddess, what was I supposed to be doing? Fabulous, now I'm distracted...

"Is there something wrong with the table, ma'am?" *the* literal walking sex on a stick of a man says. Goddess, this man's voice is so deep and gravely, he could make a killing reading romance novels, destroying housewives' panties one syllable at a time. I'd let him read me a damn dictionary.

With how far I've got my neck craned back, he's at least two heads taller than me, which is perfect for snuggling under his chin. He's got a strong build, but not so much that he comes off like those meatheads you find in the gym. No, he's got the kind of muscles that come from hard work outside.

Eyes dropping back down to his dark wash jeans, my tongue skims along the back of my teeth, scouring and ogling my way back up. The dark wash denim clings to thick thighs. Why are thick thighs on guys so hot?

A well-loved black t-shirt stretches over his chest and biceps with ink running down to his fingers. Oh, my goddess, *swoon... I love his ink*. Well, what I can see of it. Hey, don't judge me, you'd be drooling too if you saw what I'm seeing. Although, to be fair, I am acting like a bitch in heat.

A combination of tribal shapes, arrows, and interconnecting line work is inked into deeply tanned skin. The black lines dip from his neck, down the entire length of his right arm. He has several on the left arm as well, but blank spaces remain begging to be filled with a full sleeve. He has some kind of large bird on his bicep, but most of it is hidden by the sleeve of his t-shirt.

"Ahem," the man grunts, folding his arms across his chest, which only accentuates his bulk.

7

Declan

Earlier today

Everyone has bad days, right? Today started pretty rough and has only gotten worse as the day wears on. It started when I woke up late because I forgot to plug in my phone, so my alarm didn't go off.

After rushing out of my house, I realized too late that I had forgotten to fuel up my Ford F-250 yesterday, forcing me to change and ride in on my bike. Which, in turn, forced me to call Flik in early to meet the delivery guy for the kegs and crates of beer being delivered today at McCormick's. And, because the Goddess herself has a wicked sense of humor, several of those beer crates arrived broken, and beer went everywhere the moment we moved them.

We'd spent way too much time mopping up the hoppy mess sticking to the sandy-covered floors before I dropped into my worn office chair in a huff. The beat-up old chair squeaked as I spun to stare at my bottle of whiskey and glass nestled next to a half-dead fiddle leaf plant.

Cracking open a sparkling water, I settled in with the never-ending paperwork cluttering my desk. My laptop crashed right when I was in the middle of completing payroll. That red-hot irritation that was closer than my cousin reared its ugly head again. It was barely noon, and I already needed a few fingers of Jameson.

To avoid getting drunk, I headed out to the floor and helped Flik with getting the glassware washed and put away, since Lexi forgot to finish all her tasks of closing last night...again. And seeing as life has a way of sticking it to ya, especially when you think you've stacked the shit cards high enough, that last straw strikes out, toppling your tower of shit.

As soon as the glasswasher finished, I yanked on the rack and it granted me with a cloud of steam straight to the face. I was still blinking away the sting when I tripped and fell on a goddess damned rubber floor mat and ended up dropping the entire rack of glasses, breaking nearly all of them.

After an hour of picking up broken glass, I'd had enough. Grabbing my keys and sunglasses, I snap my fingers at Flik.

"Hey, hold it down till I get back, I need to get the fuck out of here before something else breaks... or I break," I grumbled, breezing straight past him, not bothering to check if he was solid with me leaving or not.

Present

Straddling my Harley, I turn the key and kick start my old baby, rev the throttle and spin the tires, kicking up all sorts of rocks and peel away from my bar.

Warm wind whips at my face, lifting the ends of my hair away from my cheeks. A soothing sense of calm flushes my body at the rumble of the bike's engine. This is precisely what I needed after the morning from hell; my mood is already a thousand times better.

After a couple of hours of open throttle and taking corners at dangerous speeds, I turn around. When I'm rounding the last open stretch of road, I open the throttle one last time and haul ass back to the bar.

Purposely parking in the back, closer to my office door, solely so I can avoid a certain annoying female who likes to drop in unannounced, I cut the engine, leaving it in neutral, and roll right up to the door. Kicking the kickstand out, I hop off and revel in the tension leaving my body and head inside.

Nothing like a good stretch on the Harley to even you out.

It's hot as sin today, which means it's sure to be a busy afternoon and evening, and I won't admit it, but we need it, otherwise, writing paychecks this coming week will be out of my account. But, before I get nose deep in payroll and quarterly taxes again, I pop in on Flik, making sure he's good for a while, and he waves me off with his Cheshire Cat grin and a nod.

The door to my office closes with a forceful thud, reminding me that I've gotta fix that damn door soon. Making it to my desk, I reach over to close the blinds to the only window in here, and my fingers stall on the pull. Staring out between the slats, my dick twitches at the sight of a hot little number standing at the entrance of the bar, appraising it as if she's some kind of revered member of society.

She's in the shortest cut-offs I've seen, well, if I'm being honest, since yesterday, but she takes the cake for the who wore it better category. Although it could be the high-quality ink she's got wrapping around one luscious thigh, making me think that. The ink stretches to the top portion of her calf, drawing my eyes there.

A tied bow of sunshine yellow strings peek out from the collar of a button-down that's left open, but tied in a knot, revealing her toned, tanned belly. The panels of her button-down balloon out for a moment from the breeze kicking up, wafting an incredible scent through my open window.

Tapping into my wolf senses, I get a good whiff. Frowning, I inhale again. I could be wrong, but it's like her scent is muted. Maybe she's a human or a half breed shifter? Though it's faint, the distinct perfume of wild violets wafting in reminds me of the ones that grow back home.

Like the big bad wolf I've been accused of being, I huff in the biggest inhale I can, why? Because fuck if I know. What the hell is wrong with me? I can't get enough. Layers of white pine and fresh mountain air layer over the violets. The combination hovers and tickles the inside of my nose.

Goddess damned it!

My hand shifts involuntarily down to my jeans, adjusting my hard-on. I keep gawking at her. Acting like a pubescent pup, I give my dick a few good, hard strokes through my jeans. I can't help it; she's so damn cute standing there debating on whether or not to come into the bar. Her little button nose scrunches up as a loose strand of her chocolate brown hair, tossed up into a messy bun, blows over her pink-tinged face. Comically, she's squinting at the building and lifting a hand to shade her eyes. Her aviators are on top of her head.

Adorable.

Seeing that I've never seen her around town, I peg her as another tourist and not a newbie. I know everyone who lives here in Danset, my little slice of small-town heaven. If she were new to town, I would've known the minute she drove down Highway 12. There are never any secrets amongst the locals here. I would know, they spun the rumor mill hard when I moved in.

This girl, though, there's something familiar about her, but I can't quite put my finger on it. *Fuck, she smells amazing!* Thorin, my wolf, stirs for the first time today, urging me to shift. He wants to get closer to her, too. Which he's never done before, piquing my growing interest, but I don't hand over the reins. He grumbles and stays in the forefront of my mind.

My phone pings, distracting me for a moment, but I can't pull my eyes away from her. Don't want to, either. An irrational desire to throw my phone against the wall comes out of nowhere when it dings repeatedly, forcing me to retrieve it. The simmering rage is rapidly replaced with guilt when I see it's my cousin. A sharp pain grates my teeth together as I pull my eyes away to read and type out a quick reply.

Wyatt: Hey, man, we still on for the end of the week?
Me: Yeah, man, just let me know when to expect you.

The click of my phone ignites the emptiness that crowds my heart as I glance back up and find her gone. "Whatever, I've got shit to do anyways, ain't got time for that level of drama I'm sure she'd cause."

A whole whopping two minutes later, curiosity kills me, and I find myself perched on the corner end of the bar. I spin my sweating bottle of beer on the worn-down wood, watching her as she sashays her little sunburnt body over to lean against the counter, waiting for one of my bartenders. She reminds of a Barbie doll.

Her tiny flip-flop feet toe the air behind her as she kicks up and twirls one ankle at a time. I zero in on the perfect white polish she's sporting on her pretty, petite toes.

Are those flowers painted on top? What the fuck is wrong with me? I don't notice nail polish and shit like that!

Shifting silently on my stool, I make eye contact with Flik. When he sees me and nods, he follows my line of sight as it swivels drastically to the beach Barbie. He gets my drift and wipes his way down the bar. Lexi should be serving her, since she's supposed to be on staff during the day and Flik tonight, but who the hell knows where she is. If I had to guess? She's at the beach. That girl has so much salt in her veins it's a wonder she doesn't turn into a fish. Lexi can't seem to resist a good set rolling in, and since hiring her, she uses all of her "breaks" to catch a wave or ten.

Refocused on the beach Barbie, my brows crease into a frown. She seems a little intoxicated, but I trust Flik; if he thought she was too far gone, he wouldn't even entertain the idea of serving her.

Hiding in the far corner of the shadows, I toy with whether or not I'm being a perverted creep or not with my leering at her; regardless of the answer, it doesn't stop me from ogling her like one.

Her drunken, flirty talk and the batting of her eyelashes is adore-fucking-able, but she's gonna earn herself a good spanking if she keeps that up with my boy Flik, or anyone.

I keep creeping on her from the dark corner, ignoring all of the irrational possessive thoughts tumbling through my mind. I'm so hyper-focused on her perfectly apple-shaped ass sliding onto a pub stool that I barely register what she's doing when she suddenly gets up. One hand on the table, she wiggles it, rolls her eyes, and then nabs a couple of sugar packets, drops to a crouch, flexing those strong thighs, and shoves the paper-filled packet of sugar under a table leg.

"What the fuck?" My confusion is swallowed with concern when her perfectly honed body sways even more than before when she grips the pedestal. I curse under my breath. She's going to smack her head or fall over, and the last thing I need is a lawsuit. My mind made up to stop her before that worry finishes manifesting into something else, my stool scrapes back. I'm moving before I finish listing all the reasons I'm about to get involved.

Stopping in front of her table, I stuff my hands into my pockets to avoid doing something stupid like...oh, I don't know, pulling her into me and sniffing her neck like a rutting whelp.

A buzzing energy hums around her and tugs incessantly at me, like a magnet on my grandma's old fridge. Clearing my throat, I rasp, "Ma'am?"

I swear I can hear the tick-tock of the cuckoo clock in my office as I wait for her to come out from under the table.

"Huh?" Her bewildered honeyed voice is thick and laced with a come fuck me essence. Resisting the urge to offer a hand to help her, knowing it's only an excuse to have her skin on mine, I sigh and wait.

Momma always says, "Patience is a virtue I swear I taught you, but you've obviously forgotten it." Perhaps, in my next letter home, I'll detail this trial in virtues to make her proud.

The girl stumbles and hits her head when she shoots up, rubbing the injury. "Ouch, shit, that fucking hurt."

Well, I'll be Goddess damned, she curses like a sailor, but I don't miss the slurring or the bloodshot eyes before she faces away from me and grabs onto the edges of the table with a death grip.

She's wasted...great. Based on how pink her tanned skin is, the heat has probably only exacerbated her inebriation. No matter how delectable she may appear and smell, I can't have a ding on my liquor license, damn thing took forever to get in the first place; she's done.

I connect with her chestnut gaze as she finally pirouettes and rakes those orbs up my body from my boots to my head. My lips twitch into a smirk. She's ogling me like I'm a fresh piece of steak.

Go ahead, baby, eat it up.

Clearing my throat, my smirk deepens, her cheeks turn a deep cherry red, flushing the shells of her ears too. My nostrils flare with the scent of her embarrassment and anxiety, both overpowering a hint of her arousal.

The trio of scents rolls out from her, and there it is, the fourth scent I couldn't decipher earlier. It's barely a hint, layered in between swaths of violets and mountain air, but it's distinguishable. She's a full-blooded wolf, not half, and not another type of shifter. The too-light, distinct odor all wolves have has to be because she's masking it, or she's a lower-rank wolf like an omega. How can she even maintain that level of power, being as drunk as she is? That's something for later.

Questions tabled for now, I'm curious what she will do if I redirect her evident appreciation away from me? "Is there something wrong with the table, ma'am?" I ask in my most convincing Southern accent and stare down into her swirling chocolate irises.

While I still have bits of my Northern accent, I've been picking up more and more Southern lingo the longer I'm around Flik and Rhett. Those two, born and bred Outer Banks boys, have worn on me, but they are solid and reliable friends; we've become a family over the last few years. They would tease the hell out of me if they heard how I sounded just now. My eyes dart to Flik and let loose a breath when I see he's got his back turned. Glancing back to the hot lil' number, I hold back my grin as she keeps checking me out.

Every inch of my skin prickles to life under her scrutiny, leaving a palpable sensation of flames. I've been checked out before, and ogled by hundreds of women, but never have I felt so exposed while this one blatantly eye fucks me with swipe after swipe of those dark, lascivious eyes while her pouty lips form a little 'O'.

On her next pass over my ink, I wait to make my next move. She's two flicks from converging with my gaze again, when I clear my throat, "Ahem!" I meant for it to come out a little softer, but it flies out as a pained grunt.

Her lips clamp shut, and she swallows hard, which I follow intently and wait patiently again to hear the voice of an angel. As soon as she opens her mouth again, though, I realize my shit day hasn't quite had enough of fucking with me yet.

"Oh...um-sorry, no...I mean, yes, it was wobbly, but don't you worry, I fixed it," she replies sweet as sin, and finishes in perfect smart-ass smacking a hand to her hip.

Fuck! I'm too much of a sucker for smart-assed women. Good Goddess, I should walk away right now, just turn the fuck around and walk away. I don't need any more women's issues or drama. Of course, I ignore my own advice, rooting my feet in more; I'm a glutton for punishment.

"There's no need to fix the table, it was fine the way it was, and who served you?" I ask even though I know damn well who served her, but I want to triple-check to see how drunk she is before I toss her out on her apple-shaped ass.

Giving me her back, she takes a long pull of her cider, and from the slight tilt of her head, she eyes me again, smirking.

"It's not my problem, the tables in this place suck, I bet all of them need a sugar packet or two." She snorts. She is stunning, but that smart mouth...*Mmm*...makes me want to—Her bottle smacks into the table a little too hard, causing the cider to bubble up and over the lip, dripping down the table to the floor.

A fast-moving fire runs through my blood, quickly burning through all of my give a damns. I know that damn cider is going to instantly turn sticky in this heat in a matter of minutes and attract ants in hours. My lips curl as I let out a growl, and my last nerve frays and plucks free. That's about all I can handle today.

My wolf perks up and starts pacing, grumbling about my anger issues and OCD. Reining my temper back in so he quits, I visualize myself *peacefully showing her the door and*— nope!

Shut it down, Declan. Shut. It. Down.

My heels dig into the wood floors, leaving a dent as I stomp back over to Flik, slamming my palms on the counter. A loud growl rages from between my grinding teeth. He gives me a once-over nonchalantly and continues drying a rocks glass. Not even a quiver of a reaction graces his relaxed body as he waits for the rest of my temper to unleash.

Movement to my left draws my predatory senses out. I spot Lexi spying from the back hall, her hair wet and dripping all over the floor; her eyes widen when she realizes she's been caught. Again. Shaking my head, I ignore her. I'll deal with her bullshit later and mop the damn floors for the third time today. Why the hell did I come over here? Oh, right...*her.*

"Flik, what's her tab?" I demand tossing a thumb over my shoulder at the *her* in question. He purses his lips, knowing I know this already, but checks the slip like I don't and hands it over.

"She ordered just the one boss and started a tab with a crisp Benjamin."

"Give me her change, she's cut off," I grumble, letting out a ragged breath. I need to take a vacation.

Whizz...Whomp... the undeniable sound of darts flying through the air and landing on the board forces my body to spin around.

Whizz...whomp...Another dart lands in one of the many dart boards along the wall.

A little squeal pierces through the hot air, rendering me to nothing more than a twelve-year-old boy who'd just about come in his pants from a pretty girl's smile. I resist the itch to adjust my dick, that's so hard it hurts straining against the zipper. Focus on anything else.

A bead of sweat rolls down my neck, sliding between my shoulder blades, effectively distracting me from my hard-on. I need to get the AC back up and running more efficiently. The basket-weave blades of the ceiling fans aren't cutting it today, given the high humidity. All they're doing is spinning hot sticky air and whipping up my hot temper.

I suck my lower lip under my teeth, letting out another low growl while I track her every move. She's dancing with her hands in the air, one holds her cider, the other a dart. That body, curvy in all the right places, sways and spins like a trained dancer, captivating me under her spell again. My eyes find her upturned lips wearing a smile so carefree, but a little sadness tilts the corners down a fraction.

I know she senses me watching her when she drops her ass to the floor, rolling her hips seductively and slowly rises. Unbeknownst to me until I feel it, my head crooks to the side following the motion, *damn that ass*. My tongue traces my lips, hungrily, what I wouldn't give to take a bite out of it.

The knot in her shirt rides up when she lifts her cider over her head again, revealing glistening skin, a belly button ring, and a peek of ink on her ribcage.

Damn.

My eyes bore into her while my mind runs away with wicked yet disastrous thoughts of licking each line of her ink, tasting each inch of her.

This girl, no, woman, with that viper of a tongue, she's older than a college chick, has my cock in a vice and close to bursting the zipper of my jeans. Leaning my elbows back on the bar, enjoying the free show, I sense Thorin stirring again. He wants out; he wants to play with her, too.

Absolutely not, "No, Thorin," I link to him, shutting him down before he gets any more ideas.

"No?" he growls at me, the prick.

"If you don't back down, I'll refuse to give over control later for you to run as you please." The threat seems to work, and Thorin falls silent once again. It's odd, however, Thorin hardly ever demands control around most women. He prefers to be in misery, he says, whenever I'm entertaining a woman.

A masochist, he claims he wants to wait for the right one, our fated mate. Constantly griping at me for all the meaningless romps in the sack, he's become unbearable as of late. When Thorin does come to the front, he complains they smell all wrong and attempts to take control, and when he does, he becomes an epic asshole all to get the girl to leave.

Whatever, they sate my needs just fine, so he can piss off.

Thorin and I have had some significant disagreements over the years, but not too many that our bond is strained. However, after we got back from Afghanistan four years ago, we did. While he had thoroughly enjoyed the war and what we were doing, in the end, I hadn't. Being part of the Army Special Forces used to be a source of both our pride, that is, until that one night.

The night we lost Quinn and Tybalt, all of that changed; we changed. It was from then that I hadn't let him surface as much, only for the occasional run or when he forced a shift on me. He became too unpredictable, and I feared what would happen again.

Thorin surges at my thoughts and then settles begrudgingly, bitching back into his shadows. Shoving off from the bar, I approach the spitfire cautiously. Thank fuck for jeans, they hide my erection somewhat, otherwise I'd look like another horny male. Desperate to get it to go down, I rack my brain for something entirely undesirable to dwell on. The problem is, I need to think about anything other than what her skin would taste like, and I can't.

Having made my way over to her with a raging hard-on, I thrust my hand out to the sexiest lil' distraction ever, "miss," my voice barely rasps, it sounds all broken and in need of a good drink. I offer up her change. The brunette spins on her toes and topples over into me, my arms loop automatically around her, preventing her fall, and damn me, I groan in delight at the contact.

"Oops, my bad," she hiccups, her speech slurring even more as her little hands splay out over my chest, the tips of her fingers pressing in a little bit. A pinprick zaps my arousal to life again. "I opened a tab, no need for change."

I stare at her in a daze.

What did she say?

Damn me all to hell, her body feels amazing snuggled up against mine. I roll my eyes at myself.

Goddess help me, why did I come over here? Oh right.

"You did, but you're done for the day. I can't serve you anymore," I reply, hoping my tone doesn't come off as too much of an asshole, like I'm sure it sounds.

"Excuse me? So, you're what? Kicking me out? A paying customer, that's so rude," she fires back, as a copper ring races around the outer edge of her iris. Her hands shove into me, pushing me away. Respecting her desire for distance, my hands drop away from her, with an incredible emptiness remaining.

My eyes narrow as I lay the bills and coins on the table. A shiny new quarter rolls over the unlevel table, straight to the floor, and of course, she doesn't fail to miss that either. She hinges at the hips, granting me another spectacular view of her pert rear. She tilts her head, catching the gap under a leg of the table, and great...

"Oh well would you lookie there, another crap table," she croons, and promptly grabs another sugar packet and shoves it under the wobbly foot. "There," she says, all proud of herself, with her hands on the edge of the table, trying to shake it.

A low growl lets loose from Thorin. Now, he's getting irritated by her. *"Not irritated at her...irritated at you, Declan..."* he informs me, snarling like I did something wrong. *The fuck?*

"Perhaps if the owner spent more time encouraging the customers to drink more, and investing it in this shit hole, he'd have better tables." She takes a swig of her drink and slowly brings it down, smiling around the mouth of the bottle. Absolutely not. Before I can entirely stop myself, I grab her arm and yank her to me; her intoxicating scent assaults my nostrils when her body slams into mine.

"Ouch, what the fuck...you brute," she squeals, but does not attempt to move away, too drunk to fight back properly.

"Oh? I'm a brute now...you don't even know who I am, but you will get out of my bar and do it now, or I'll toss you out on your pert little ass," I counter, not caring that I'm being an asshole now. No pussy is worth the bullshit she's put me through in 45 minutes.

Her bottom lip quivers for a moment before she sinks her teeth into it and squints her whiskey brown eyes at me. Did they shift color? Tiny hands shove at my chest again, and she storms away. Her hips sway as her flip flops smack against the wood; my view locks on her juicy ass.

A clatter of metal stops her momentarily, and Goddess help me because she bends over... again, to pick up her dropped keys, and I get a peek of a cheek from the barely there shorts. My too-tight jeans rub painfully against my too-hard dick once more.

"No need, I didn't want to drown my sorrows in this dilapidated shit hole anyways," her voice breaks on a choke halfway through before she turns her face away, with the barest of a sniffle reaching my ears.

Well, shit, now I feel like a gigantic asshole, but at least I won't be subject to losing my liquor license. I follow her out and watch her walk and stumble across the road a couple of times, before disappearing around a corner. Thank the Goddess she didn't drive, or I would've taken those keys and driven her myself, and that would've invited even more chaos.

"Hey, boss," Flik calls, trying to get my attention. Not moving, I crane my neck half over my shoulder, one eye still on the road, "Yeah?" I utter.

"Uh, she left her change...do you want me to set it aside or?"

Sighing, I shrug and head back to my office, "Just set it aside, I'm sure she'll be back."

8

Faith

The sandy gravel crunches under the cheap flip flops I picked up from the dollar store on my way down here. My drunk ass stumbles back to my rental, mostly in one piece. I fell a couple of times, and not even from the alcohol, my ears are still beet red, and the churning nausea has yet to cease its assault on my stomach.

Finally reaching the wide steps, I slump my ass down on the second stone. Sweat oozes from every pore on my body; I have sweat in places ladies shouldn't admit to. The heat is so oppressive, I'm pretty positive my ass is going to leave butt cheek sweat marks when I get up. The weight of my head easily drops between my knees at the thought, and once I've broken that seal of negative self-talk, it flows. I let out all the embarrassment, betrayal, anger, and sadness in sobs that rack my whole body.

Raising shaky fingers to comb over my scalp, my nails press in deeper than needed. The strands tangle around the digits, and the briefest sting of pain starts and then stops as I relax my fingers. The desire, the need, I have to pull on the roots of my hair, or anything to cause pain, is overwhelming. I need it to drown out this agony with a different pain, one that I control.

My meltdown is one reason I don't drink when I'm depressed; well, it's one reason that Connor didn't allow me to drink. My molars grind and crack at the image of his face, my mind conjures. Shoving it away, my hands slide over my face and dangle off my bent knees. I'd been fine the whole drive down here, and a bottle of champagne and one cider later, and I'm not just skipping the line to crazy, I'm diving right onto the hot mess express. I guess that's what I get for holding in all my emotions and staying strong for everyone else.

An unexpected pulsing ache stabs into my heart, the pain radiating all over as my mind processes what happened with the hot bar owner.

I will never be enough for anyone, not for Connor, not for my wolf, not for my pack.

The sharpness of my jeep blurs when I let the crack inside my heart spread, my arms fall limply to my sides, my head tilts up, a strangled sob rips from my soul, the salt of my shame slides over my cheeks and tangs my lips before gracing the skin of my neck.

Unable to control the spiraling thoughts, I let go again of the last string holding all the broken pieces of me together. The string unravels from my fear of failure, to not being a perfect daughter, a perfect girlfriend, and a perfect fiancé. Each piece cuts into me deeper than they ever have before. The tears fall until my body can't produce any more.

The late afternoon rays of the setting sun glimmer behind my eyelids. They fly open to what has to be an ax that splits my skull in two. Shit. Groaning, I sit up and try to gain my bearings. Jell-O legs wobble like an '80s waterbed as I make it to the door, and curse again while the damn lock refuses to open after I enter the code. I need to remember to call the owners and ask if there is a key, because this not opening shit is for the birds.

On my way up to my room, I swipe the chocolates and stuff two in my mouth, savoring the melty goodness, and collapse into the pillowtop bed. Today, I've effectively wallowed in my self-pity and grief, and now all I want to do is indulge in a dreamless sleep, not that I need any more sleep.

* * *

A buzzing across the nightstand yanks my head out of the pillows, slowly comprehending that it's my phone about to vibrate itself off the table and land on the floor, my body flops and fails to reach it. I'm too late as it silences. In an effort to locate the offending device, I slipped off the mattress and slid down the side of the bed, landing on my knees. Goddess, I'm a mess.

Swiping the screen, I have five missed calls from Hollie and Dad. Great. I forgot to check in this morning. I dial Hollie; she'll understand better than Dad right now.

"Hello...Faith?" Hollie answers in her sing-song voice. Always so sweet that one, but she's really a Tasmanian devil in disguise; she fools everyone with her sugary sweetness, well, except me. She'll tear you apart after batting those doe eyes just long enough to misdirect your attention.

Pins and needles sting the creases in my nose, as I scrunch my sunburnt face, "Yeah...hey...sorry," I grimace, holding in a hiccup.

Ouch. What the hell was in that champagne?

"Goddess hell, are you drunk?" Hollie worries in the only way she can, with her condescending tone.

"Yup...please don't...don-nt, tell...Dad...o...ok." I hiccup, running my hand over my mouth, cupping it, praying the bile burning up my throat stays put. Her harsh judgment is evident through the resentful sigh she tries and fails to hide. A creaking of a chair squeaks the silence; she must be spinning in Dad's office chair.

"Faith, you know I won't, but you *do* need to call Dad or at least check your emails. Russell found something that he wants your opinion on," she rambles out so fast I barely catch it all. "And, you have an assignment request from Nat Geo." She adds as an afterthought.

I sit up, a rush of excitement swamps over me, or maybe that's my blood rushing to my head. I haven't been on an actual assignment in almost a year since I'd taken the time off to plan for the wedding.

"What?!" I whisper-shout and crawl over to my tote, leaning against the white-covered armchair, and retrieve my laptop. "Getting it now, I'll call you later, okay, Hol?" I attempt to sound less drunk, making my words slow and concise, but it doesn't sound like it, even after the adrenaline rush of having an assignment.

"Sure...okay, love you, Faith." She hangs up, not even waiting for me to say it back.

So rude.

Opening my email, I click on the most recent from Russell first. My top lip curls, and my brows pinch together. I know he's Dad's beta, but the mere thought of seeing Russell Morgan's name makes me want to puke and scream at the same time. I wonder if he knows how much of an asshole his son truly is.

Quickly scanning the email, my eyes widen, taking in the information:

Alpha Faith,

First and foremost, I hope you will accept my sincere apology for my dishonorable son's actions.

I had no idea he would act in such a cruel manner. You have and will always be considered a daughter to me.

Now, for the hard part, after pulling some of the camera feeds from the streets near the temple, I was able to get the techs to clean up the damaged footage from one. It appears that someone had tampered with the cameras after the shooting. The one that was right outside the temple was completely smashed.

The attached footage is passcode accessible only. It's your secure code.

We are still waiting for results from the pack lab on Luna's blood samples and the bullet.

-Russell Morgan

Beta of The Mystic Keepers Pack

A dreadful iciness crystallizes and freezes my blood. Shuddering, I reread the email a couple more times to make sure I understood what he said.

Crap, what the hell is my secure code...think Faith. Oh!

My alcohol and sun-weakened body scrambles across to my pack, after removing my camera and lenses carefully, I dump the remaining contents to the floor. Frantically, I search the pile for a small blue notebook where I keep all my passwords and important information. Receipts and cartridges of memory cards fly in the air over my head, and composition notebooks land in a heap next to my thighs. I should toss some of the crap in here.

Locating the blue notebook a minute later, I open the attachment containing the footage, and not wanting to mess it up, I grip my hand to keep my index finger ramrod straight, to pluck each key one at a time.

A long breath exhales from the depths of my lungs, and when I hit the enter button, a new screen pops open, and my eyes strain into focus. A hooded figure lingers outside the temple and then disappears, only to reappear near the windows close to the doors. What moves that fast?

I zoom in, trying to get a better view of the figure. The video footage is grainy, blurry, and distorted, making it difficult to identify anything. I fast forward and slam my hand on the keyboard, when I see the flash of red eyes and silver.

Blinking several times, then balling my hands into fists to rub at my eyes, I lean in and rewind it about 10 seconds. Reducing the playback speed and enhancing the picture, I hit play again. For a whole 2 seconds, the video is barely clear, but better than before. But it's all I need to recognize the distinct claret flash of blood-red eyes of him, the vampire whose silver nose piercing is one I'd like to yank out, tearing the flesh with it. Mother fucker!

Well, there goes my inebriation...

9

Declan

The clinking of glass and the clanking of coins fills the hum of silence in the main space of the bar. That cute lil' brunette's smirking face pops into my mind again, disrupting my concentration for the hundredth time tonight. The tip of my finger jabs onto the clipboard beneath the count paper, the lead of my pencil snaps, scratching a dark lead line up the paper. Gritting my teeth, I spin and arch my arm back, pitching the useless tool across the back of the bar.

"Hey- oh shit!" Flik screeches and ducks just as the pencil javelins over the top of his head. He rises, sloth-like, staring wide-eyed at the wall behind, where only the tip of the eraser is protruding. "Uh-I'm heading out...You good, boss?"

Chest heaving, I reach for the unopened bottle of Jameson and wrench the lid off. "Yeah, I'm fine," I grumble and tip the bottle back, and gulp a few swigs before wiping my mouth with the back of my hand. "I'll be leaving shortly too. You coming tomorrow?" I add optimistic, that I sound a bit less agitated from the whiskey warming my belly and numbing the frustration.

"Yeah, man, my sister is coming though, I'm sure you'll be excited to see her as much as I am," he answers dryly, laughing, and combing a hand through his hair. I roll my eyes; he knows damn well I won't be. His sister has been trying to get in my pants since the morning after I'd arrived in town. I would have too, she's hot, but she's got 'the I'm better than everyone else' attitude, and I can't stand that shit, especially from a wolf.

I wonder if lil' miss artificial sweetener is like that?

"Alright, man, I'll see you tomorrow," he waves a hand, hanging his half-apron on the hook by the door before slipping out of it.

Grabbing and stuffing the cash left from the drunk girl earlier into an envelope, I snag a pen and scribble: '*UN-sweet sugar packet chick*' on the front. That girl needs a packet or two tossed at her; maybe it'd sweeten her up a bit.

Gathering my toolbox, I shuffle over to the pub table that Miss Grumpy Pants had stuffed sugar packets under. I set the toolbox down, squat down, tilt the edge of the table, and grab the packets. Tossing them in with my tools, I grab a wrench and begin the tedious process of tightening and loosening each foot of the tables.

"I oughta charge her for this," I smirk and head to the following table.

As I finish closing, I lock up and head over to my bike. The engine rumbles to life, probably waking anyone within a mile radius. The booming exhaust causes a slight twinge to grate my teeth. A couple of years ago, I wouldn't have given a shit, but now, I like these people, who accept me and treat me as one of their own. Sour regret swims in my gut again for not fueling up my truck earlier.

Winding through town and then down my street, I pass several of the vacation rentals, spotting a green Jeep Grand Cherokee with Maine plates.

Ah, that explains the scent then...

I roll to a crawl, motoring past, inspecting each window, and catch a shadow crossing in one, right as I pass the driveway. My pulse kicks up, and every bone in my body urges me to stop. I hover my boots over the road, but at the last minute, I pull up and engage the clutch, speeding off.

Pulling into the driveway of my house, I reach into my pocket for my phone to open the garage with my app. After parking and wiping down my baby, the wooden stairs creak underfoot as I step inside the house. Thorin stirs, wanting to take over and shift, but I force him back, much to his irritation.

"Keep it up, jerk face, and I won't let you out for a month," I scold, my thoughts teasing over our bond. He snorts and goes back into the shadows.

Pouring a glass of sweet tea from a glass pitcher I nabbed from the fridge, my free hand shuffles through the pile of mail I've been ignoring for the past week. Piling the majority of it into a trash stack, I flip through until I find the letter that I've been avoiding since it arrived a few weeks ago.

Since my day can't possibly get any worse, I rip it open, and I'm immediately thrown back to northern Maine. Rich mountain and blueberry scents burst from tiny bubbles rising from the envelope. So do the visions of home, and the sorrow that always accompanies my scent memories.

I'd spoken too soon...it can get worse.

I down the rest of the sweet tea in one gulp and kick myself internally for drinking all of the bourbon and whiskey two nights ago, all to get an hour of dreamless sleep. It was that or taking the medication I hate. It's a shame, either liquor would've gone impeccably well with this version of a peach sweet tea—stupid mistake. Lesson learned, I guess.

The words of the letter blur and seize my heart, the anguished words forming claws and ripping it in two. Old wounds reopening fresh as the day I got them, leave a raging fire to burn through my flesh. The letter is from Quinn's Mom, my pack mate and Army buddy. His Father died a month ago and left me everything in his garage, since his son is already gone. She'd wanted me to come home for the funeral to be there with her as she buried her husband beside Quinn.

Coward that I am, I somehow knew what was within the small envelope when it arrived weeks ago. I had shoved it to the bottom of the pile, not wanting to read the damn letter.

I'm a shit friend, and even worse alpha. I don't want my pack, and I don't deserve a mate. Yet, my parents both want, no demand, that I come home and take over the pack, find my fated mate, get married, and give them the grandchildren they've been begging for.

"It's high time you settled down, son, find your mate or a chosen, marry and make a new generation," my Mom constantly says. She's been unrelentingly berating me with her outstanding Mom guilt for years now.

It's not that I don't want to find my mate, I did, I do, but I'm too screwed up in the head for anyone to be safe around me, truly. One of my former beta's daughters can attest to that fact if only my parents would listen to me.

Sophia and I had been dating before I left for war, and when I returned, we attempted to pick back up right where we left off, but one night, I had a horrible episode. I almost killed her.

We were in bed and enjoying one another thoroughly when a car backfired outside her house. Unexpectedly, my flip switched, and I was thrown back to Afghanistan, the night Quinn had died.

Sophia, too wrapped up in her ecstasy, didn't notice the shift in me, not until it was too late. My mind whirled in a loop of the last images of my best friend being blown to pieces and me flying into a partially shifted rage and tearing the heads off of all those who'd planted the car bomb.

Unaware of what I was doing, my hands firmly wrapped around her neck, piercing my claws into her soft flesh. In my zombie-like state, I threw her against the wall. I'd half shifted and was prepared to rip the throat out of the ghost enemy haunting me, that is, until a sharp gurgling scream finally wrenched free from her raw throat.

By the time I'd snapped out of it, her neck was sliced open to her collarbone, and her right shoulder was dislocated, bones shattered. If she were human and I had gone any deeper, she would've been dead.

Tears ran freely down my face as I bent and scooped her up. Terrified of me, she fought me every step to the pack's hospital. While I waited for the docs' update that she'd make it, I decided to leave the pack.

Shame-fueled, I went home and packed what I could. Ladened with guilt coursing through me like a stomach virus, I shifted and bolted. Eventually, my Father found me and dragged me back to the pack house.

Ever the perfect Luna, my Mom attempted to smooth things over with Sophia's parents, but it was of no use. They refused to accept my Army-gifted mental disorder and instead blamed my genetics, as like it was my parents' fault for my ptsd. I finally admitted it, that I was broken, because this wasn't the first time something like that had happened; it just wasn't as severe. My Mom had suggested I take some time for myself and step away from my duties to the pack and perhaps seek out a therapist. I disagreed and argued with her about it; there was no helping me. I was damaged, permanently.

My Father, however, had no qualms about reminding me of my duties. He informed me that I needed to suck up my issues and deal with my responsibilities. He tried to reason with me and explain away my flashbacks and reactive behaviors to loud noises, smells, and constant insomnia, as my dominance coming out. It was utter bullshit.

The only one who didn't give me any ounce of grief was my baby sister, Estella. She hugged me until she collapsed and told me it would be alright. After I tucked her into bed, I vowed I would never put her in danger, let alone anyone else I cared about.

So, in the middle of the night, I packed my shit up again and left without so much as a goodbye. I arrived here in Danset the next evening and haven't looked back. That was four years ago. Since then, I've ignored my Father's letters, texts, and most of his phone calls. He saw me as defective, an utterly useless alpha, and deep down, I always knew he was right. I've kept in contact with Mom and Estella, though, and they're happy for me, but I miss them something fierce.

Funnily enough, I ended up becoming friends with several lone wolves. They became my employees when I bought and took over the bar six months after moving here, and now they are my closest friends. So, in a sense, we are a little pack, but we don't truly live as one with all of the hierarchy and bullshit that comes with it, and that quite suits me. We are a family, and not one of them judges me for having bad days or zoning out when we are around too many people. They've all rallied behind me, and my episodes have been fewer and fewer.

Thorin growls again, yanking me from my thoughts. He wants out, to be loose, to run. The letter crumples under my palm as the suffocating dark clouds creep in uninvited. Giving in, I strip out of my clothes and stalk to the back deck. Letting Thorin loose always keeps the darkness away.

Shifting in a leap, the large body of my wolf soars over the stairs and down onto the beach, landing in the sand. The pads of his paws smoosh the mounds lingering with warmth from the summer sun. The sand splays out beneath his claws as our weight sinks in, he shakes out his fur and takes off.

As is his habit, Thorin ends up chasing the shoreline in a matter of seconds. Sloppy, wet sand squelches under his massive paws, his prints washing away under the retreating foam. More sand kicks up from under the rhythmic pounding of his stride, the grains sticking to his fur. Thankful he gets to deal with that itchiness, I settle into his run.

Before I can garner where Thorin is racing us to, he slides to an abrupt halt, jerking our vision up to the vacation rental that...that she's in. I know it's her because that delicious scent stream is practically swirling right before our eyes. She's intoxicating and very bad news for me.

Lil' miss sugar packet stands in the uppermost window, wrapped up in a blanket, her eyes locked on the moon above. A longing shines deep within her eyes. To be honest, I am surprised she isn't out here herself running.

Most of us wolves in the area will be tonight, with the moon almost full, the pull to run beneath it will be nearly unbearable. Tomorrow, every wolf in the vicinity will be twitching with the itch to run and satisfy the ancient call of the moon.

Thorin ducks into the dunes and eases to his belly to cool down. His long tongue hangs out to one side of his mouth, panting, while his head cocks to one side and then to the other in his curiosity. Ears pricking forward, twitching, he leaps to all fours. He must sense her wolf, his black nose high in the air, bushy tail swishing back and forth happily. If he could purr, I'm almost positive he would be right now. Mentally, my eyes roll as I prod him, picking at the thread of control, to take back over, but he refuses.

"You have had control for weeks, Declan. Take a seat," He grumbles. *"This is the first she-wolf in ages we've been around that actually smells good...no, she smells divine, and I want to enjoy it,"* Thorin whines through our connection. He can be such a big baby sometimes.

"I like her, you should talk to her tomorrow, maybe we can get lucky," he suggests, a sliver of possession and desire slides into his tone through our link.

"Stop acting like a possessive male, you prick. I'm not going to talk to her just so you can get your jollies off," I snipe back.

"*Says the assface who practically embarrassed himself in his pants earlier today...She's ours, dickhead. Get over it,*" he retorts.

"*Ours...what the?*" He can't mean what I think he means. I didn't sense anything earlier. I would've, right?

The slightest shuffle of sand snaps his head to the right side of the house, and he growls low, snarling his upper lip. He shares his sharpened vision with me again, and I see it, not an it, but a who. A skinny figure stalks around the woman's house. He keeps to the shadows, but it doesn't keep his undead stench from wreaking up the whole area for miles.

"*Fucking leech!*"

With one paw at a time, Thorin stealthily creeps closer. He crouches low along the sand and grasses. An angry grumble ripples the fur along his spine, spiking it straight up. When the stalker finally turns its disgusting head towards us, a pair of dark red eyes shine in the night.

"*This bloodsucker is creeping on our female...this is unacceptable, he must be dealt with.*" Thorin's statement reflects his soul's age...so stoic and chivalrous. Old wolf.

"*Besides, it's been a while since we've had leech for dinner,*" he adds, and I'm glad he's in control, because that thought would make me spew my lunch if I were in my human form and sent it across our bond. I ignore the 'our female' comment and tuck it away for later. She can't be our-nope, not going there.

Thorin prowls through the dunes, sticking to the tall grasses, staying hidden until precisely the right moment. Thank the Goddess we are downwind.

"*His acrid stench is burning my nostrils,*" Thorin growls seconds before he pounces.

In a flash, he lunges through the air for the vampire, but the bloodsucker speeds away before he lands. Thorin silently slides across the sandy walkway. The sand not halting our slide, he digs his claws into the pavers in time before we crash into the side of the house.

Thorin shakes his giant head.

Stupid vamp, doesn't he know we love the chase?

My thought dies on the wind as his hind legs launch forward, and off we go, hunting his favorite prey, leech.

* * *

Thorin chased that bloodsucker for 50 miles before it finally gave up in an alley in Stillpoint, a small town right off the jetty. Unhurriedly, the vamp walks towards us with his hands in the air. I wrench control back and shift, stalking to him, buck ass naked. Cracking my neck side to side, the loud snaps split an echo across the barren alley, muting my hurried footsteps towards the foul creation.

"What the fuck are you doing in wolf territory, blood sucker?" I demand and slam him into the brick wall by the throat. The vampire shrugs and smirks his thin, purple lips. I knew I should've stayed home today.

Tightening my grip, my fingers partially shift, and my claws slice into his putrid skin. "Answer the fucking question, before I remove your head from your neck," I growl, my teeth pressed together, lips thinning.

Narrowed blood-red eyes squint back at me, "That is really none of your concern, you mangy mutt," the vampire hisses. Thorin nudges me, reminding me that the worthless leech was hunting our little firecracker.

An unfamiliar rush of possessiveness fights its way forward, overpowering every other rational thought. I stretch my neck out and fight the burning of my canines lengthening.

My jaw tightens until the muscle throbs, and I snap, "What do you want with m-the girl?"

"Oh-hh, you almost slipped up there, but for the record, she is ours, get used to it," Thorin links to me and shoves his aura out to retake control. I ignore his bullshit; we can argue about it later.

"Fine flea bag! It won't matter if I tell you. That girl is of great importance to the clan, Benedict requires her; you won't have to worry your pathetic fur over her for long," he sneers. My eyes go wide. He chuckles at my reaction, the sound eerily smooth, rakes against my last nerve. I drop my hand and step back. Pure undulated fear warps my body. If Benedict is involved, that never ends well; he's a monster. Thorin tugs at me for control again.

The blood sucker senses Thorin snapping at the bit and purposefully creeps closer, forcing Thorin to burst forward. Swiftly, I release control to him, allowing his instinctual drive to kill his one true enemy, the vampires, to take over. Vampires rarely survive an encounter with wolves, especially alphas. This parasite must've known that he doesn't stand a chance, or he wants to die.

My wolf takes one graceful step forward and then pounces, shoving the blood bag to the ground. "She'll be his soon," the leech cackles and gurgles when Thorin rips his throat out. Dark, practically black blood sprays, coating the brick walls, and blends in with Thorin's midnight coat. Bones crunch under his maw as he completely severs the vamp's head from its neck. Thorin plays with the carcass for a while longer, ripping limbs from what's left of the leech.

* * *

Weak streams of the dawn's purple streak across the midnight sky, the last signal we need to get the hell out of here before we are seen. I say as much to Thorin, but he ignores me and drags the pungent, rotting corpse out of the alley, dropping it in a slap of flesh in the street.

Like a young pup playing with a new squeaky toy, he bounds back into the alley, retrieving the head. The mutilated skull dangles from what's left of his hair between Thorin's teeth. Any remaining blood splatters on his paws. He's so damn proud of himself prancing to the middle of the street, it wouldn't shock me if he decided to drag the head back to the lil' firecracker and leave it on her front porch as a mating gift.

"You know, that's not a half-bad idea...But I do not think our female would appreciate it," he growls and drops the leech's head on top of the body. Well damn, I didn't realize he picked up on that thought.

"No, that's a horrible idea, and she's not our mate anyway." I retort and roll my eyes at his grumble of disagreement.

Thumping down on his haunches in the shadows of the alley, tail swaying back and forth like a metronome, the sun crests over the horizon. The dome of light creeps up, winking good morning at the sleeping world, and then flashes. Bright bursts of oranges, pinks, and yellows fan out, tucking the moon into bed. The nasty odor of the vampire's body strengthens as its flesh smolders.

Shockingly, it bursts into a giant flame and disintegrates into nothing but a pile of ashes. So, he wasn't a Higher vampire then. Nothing but an underling. Only those who are Highers, vampires with gemstone dust injected into their blood frequently, can walk during the day; all others will burst into flames at the barest touch of UV light, instantly combusting into dust.

Thorin pads around the steaming pile of ash, nosing it, and snorts out the remains stuck in his nostrils. Without looking back, he takes off at an inhuman speed, returning to the banks.

* * *

Once we reach the outskirts of town, it's apparent that most everyone is still asleep, but not for long, which won't bode well for us. Thorin dashes along our normal zig-zag pattern home, but he freezes, nose high in the air. He keeps moving, but way too slowly for my taste. Sniffing with him, he clues me in; her scent lingers in the air, and now we are both distracted. Can't say I blame him. She does smell delicious.

"Why the hell is she so important to Benedict?" Thorin asks down the link. That was an incredibly random question, but valid.

"If I knew, do you think I would've been asking?" I answer with an edge to my tone, not one I typically use with him, but I'm so fucking over everything today, have been for the past twenty-four hours.

"We need to keep her close. Benedict being involved can't mean anything good." He says and closes our link. Rude.

Thorin follows the scent trail that leads us right up to the front door of my bar. A note tacked to the wood curls at the edges as the breeze whispers over the paper. Quickly scanning the area, he stalks around to the back, where I regain control, shift, and break into my establishment through the window in my office. This is a new low for me. Note to self, leave a hide-a-key.

The thought is abandoned when my foot falters and I tumble forward. I cup my balls and twist as I land on my ass behind my desk. Throwing my jeans on from the stash in the bottom of the file cabinet, I run a hand over my face, palm scratching over the stubble. I pause and think. I don't have the first clue how I could broach this subject with Sugar Packet Girl.

With my body still reeling from the chase and encounter, I shove all thoughts to the wayside for now. Flik and Wyatt will need to know we had a bloodsucker in our territory, if they don't already. I stalk to the front door and take a painful breath in and immediately regret it, when I get a nose full of her.

I rip the door open so hard I practically take the door off its rickety hinges, bits and pieces splinter off and fall to the floor. Tearing the note off the door, a chuckle bubbles up as I read the rushed scribble.

For the grumpish-saurus bar owner,

I wanted to apologize for my rude behavior yesterday. It's not in my nature to be so rude or blunt. Please accept my sincere apologies and keep the money from my tab, to perhaps fix your tables?

Sincerely,

Faith R. B.

P.S. That blueberry cider was delicious, definitely keep it in stock.

P.P.S Also, maybe next time don't be so brutish with customers, it's not a becoming look on a handsome guy.

She thinks I'm handsome, huh?

I'd gathered that much when she eye fucked me, but her admitting it, now that's a different story altogether. A whiff of her perfume wafts up from the note, a low moan rumbles from my throat as I bring the paper to my face and inhale deeply. What is that? Lilac? No, Lily of the Valley? Hmm... I know what that is, it's wildflowers, good Goddess, this woman. My cock twitches just thinking about smelling her, running my nose and mouth along her slender neck.

Fuck.

"*Told you.*" Thorin chuckles and curls up all smug, waiting for me to agree. Well, guess what, buddy, it's not happening.

* * *

A piece of rock that lodged between the curve of my toes and the ball of my foot earlier has irritated the flesh so much that no amount of rubbing the inside of my foot along my jeans is helping. Sweat coats my bare torso in a fine sheen and soaks into the waistband of my jeans. It's my fault, my dumbass keeps forgetting to stash a pair of shoes or boots and more shirts in my office; damn those natural consequences.

Luckily, it's summer, and the forgotten shirt and shoes are a welcome respite from the rapidly rising temperature.

Heaving breaths work in tandem with scuffing sneakers on pavement, and a low humming filters over the distance and snags my rapt attention. A hop, skip, and jump separates me from my drive, but something delays my barefoot pace. The humming and panting breaths get louder, and my eyes sweep to the top of the low hill near the end of the road. Immediately as my feet connect with the small rectangle of grass in my yard, I see her.

10

Isaac

Chanoît, Quebec, Canada
Palais de Sanc

An olive-skinned ghoul paces around my study, pieces of his rotting flesh dangling as he turns, facing me. He will need more vitae from me, the proof? One piece of the flimsy flesh tears like wet paper and falls away from his chest. The slimy bit sloshes to the floor in a splat. My nose wrinkles in disgust, my eyes bobbing up and down from it back to the ghoul, blatantly aware of my glare. He bends and retrieves it. Without hesitation, he gobbles it up and resumes his pacing.

Jamac obviously has bad news to impart to me, and whatever it is, it is undoubtedly going to enrage me; otherwise, he would've spilled it by now. My deadened heart beats a fraction of a second faster than its leisurely, languid pace. I roll my eyes and my pale, lanky fingers curl around the near-empty wineglass of a pretty, blue-eyed girl, who's currently crumpled over on the chaise by the window. The fading beat of her heart is music to my ears; one last tap of her veins should do it. Rising on tired legs, I make my way to her quickly fading life form.

From this high vantage point in the castle, the puffy white clouds can be seen rolling over the evergreen treetops. The mist that hangs down like a shroud from them distorts in the bubbled glass; you'd think by now my Father would update the panes in this decrepit stone relic to double panes. He'd preached something about leaving the 'raw authenticity' of his first home here in the new world alone. If you asked me, or the hundreds of other voices in my head, I'd say he is wholly abhorrent to change, even with the mundane things, but what do I know?

The cold seeping in through the imperfect construction sends a shiver over the human's skin, pebbling it beautifully. My pupils widen, blocking out the deep claret, they trace over the porcelain skin littered with my bites and slices from my claws.

"Any day now, Jamac," I croon, running my tongue over my bottom lip. My hand slips under the girl's limp wrist, and a twisted moan sounds from her bluing lips. Piercing the nail of my thumb into the weak flesh, reopening the vein, I raise my glass to it. The lukewarm crimson liquid sloshes against the glass with each fading pulse of her heart, lowering her arm below the chaise, my legs following in a crouch. Before the glass is full, a metallic taste floods my mouth, and my fangs lengthen, aching to pierce her silken skin.

My lips crash to her wrist, fangs ripping into her soft flesh, the girl moans again, relishing in the ecstasy of my venom. Her life's blood flows like a dying stream, coating my tongue in the sweetest honey. My eyes dart back to Jamac. He's a putrid statue, eyes locked on where my fangs are deep in her flesh.

Unbothered, I continue drinking from the girl's wrist. Pull after pull from the girl's vein brings her one step closer to the death she sought, my cheeks hollowing as her blood satiates my thirst. My ashy blonde brows rise in encouragement to Jamac, my lips tighten around the girl's wrist. Jamac visibly stiffens, and he heaves in a raspy breath.

"Niles is dead, we found the remains of his ashes in Stillpoint, NC...there was no sign of the alpha bitch anywhere, but Keir and Damon have been sent to finish the job," he grunts, but it's really more of a gruff, primordial rasping. A tinge of fear dripping with each syllable spoken sinks into my skin. "The beta has yet to return with the necklace to Benedict as promised as well," he finishes, dropping to his knees, head bowed low.

Ahh, there it is, what I really wanted to know.

"I'll accept my punishment."

Pop.

My lips release the girl's wrist, and it drops unceremoniously with a smack to the side of the wooden legs of the chaise. I draw my blood-coated lips in, running my tongue over them before rising. I set the full wineglass on the piles of papers atop my mahogany desk, spinning it so the crest of our house faces him.

"Bespoleznyy dog," I mutter in Russian, my roots still deeply ingrained in my being, much to Benedict's dismay.

After 1300 years, I've found that it's always best to do one's bidding oneself. I've yet to be proven wrong in this, and I doubt I'll ever be. "And do we know who killed an 845-year-old vampire so easily?"

Jamac lifts his sickly violet glower, those bulging eyes ringed in a purplish hue blink both sets of lids agonizingly slow, before he dips his wrinkly bald head again. "No," he groans.

The mirror above the large carved marble mantle reflects the darkening of my claret irises, the corded muscles in my neck twitch, and I twist towards Jamac, eyes narrowing.

"It's a pity..." I ponder, striding behind Jamac's spine. My arms tucked behind my back, my claws protrude and lengthen, curling into the meat of my palms. At the fresh bite of pain, the ends of my lips curl up mimicking that oh so famous green Christmas goons.

"Wha-" Jamac chokes, spluttering his last words, my hand shoots out, gripping around the decaying flesh of his neck, easily piercing through to his spine. A crunching of bone and shredding skin sounds as I rip the curved bones from his body as easily as one fillets a fish for supper. The vertebrae easily snap away from the ghouls' rib cage and neck; his bulbous head falls to the ground in a thunk. My fingers curl tightly around the frail ladder of bone, the end drags over the deep blue Persian rug, staining its ornate patterns in onyx blood as I meander over to the windows once more.

"It's a pity I'll have to replace yet another ghoul," I mutter, and my vision glazes over as the company of voices crowd my mind.

* * *

Transfixed once more with the fog burning away from trees below as the sun creeps higher with the dawn, I don't hear the door groan open over the rushing of blood in my ears. I just want some fucking peace and quiet.

"Fucking hells...again, Isaac?" Petra groans her distaste evident at her tsk-ing. I crane my head over my shoulder to watch her side step the mess of ghoul guts and gore seeping into the floor. The petite black haired beauty slides to my side, dark eyes grazing down over the spine still in my hand. "Your Father is going to drain you..." she reminds me for the hundredth, no, perhaps the thousandth time.

"If he hasn't yet, I don't see him doing it anytime soon; besides, he needs me..."

Petra snags the black blood-coated spine from beside me, pinching it between two lanky fingers, her nose wrinkles in disgust, and tosses it with what remains of Jamac. The wet slap of it landing with the rest of his rotting flesh is one more bar to my symphony, one I've been composing my entire life.

"Why are you here?"

My eyes cut to the side, taking in her profile. Resigning to deal with my antics later, she smirks, "You've been summoned."

* * *

The hallways of the Palais de Sanc, also known as the Palace of Blood, reek of old incense, copper, and stale, rotting flowers. The cold stone walls and black marble floors are offset with burgundy plush rugs lining the walkway. Flickering incandescent light bulbs provide inadequate light in the dank space, but Father insists those new types were too much, so the crappy lightbulbs stay. Hands deep in the pockets of my slacks, I stride to my Father's chambers at the end of the too-long and narrow passage.

Several heavy wooden doors close and click as I pass by. The inhabitants do not want any part of what's about to happen. My hand combs my platinum, pin-straight locks back, slicking them in place, save one errant strand that forever falls over my darker left brow.

I hate meeting with my Father. His expectations are ridiculous and outdated, like the arcane laws of our clan. One day, I'll have the pleasure of gouging out his throat, clawing out his heart, and squeezing his blood over my lips, giving me his power. All it'll take is *her*.

The tall wooden doors creak open on their own as I approach. Sighing, I enter, and they slam closed. Unflinching, I creep towards his desk. My Father, Benedict Valois, stands before the bay of windows staring at the same scene I have from my rooms. Except his includes the view of Beau Lake from this portion of his rooms, and on the other side, the river.

Benedict's long black hair lies in loose waves down the center of his midnight blue silk shirt, the ends curling slightly past his shoulders. My Father's athletic frame gives most everyone a false sense that he is frail, when he is far from it.

Benedict, or The Blood Prince as he is formally known, is every bit the psychopath his legends continue to write, and I would be lying if I said at one point in my long life that I didn't fear him. Now? Not nearly as much, but it's more of an annoyance than anything. With each decade, I become stronger, and the easier it is to brush away the tingle of fear, and I know without a doubt I will be superior to him soon, if not already.

"You're late, Isaac..." Benedict says, his svelte tone almost sings in that old-world lilt. I never learned exactly where he was born, but my best guess is somewhere in Eastern Europe, where the five princes and only princess are said to originate from.

Toeing the evergreen rug with the tip of my shoe for a moment while I gauge his mood, I wander over to one of the velvet chairs and collapse in a huff. "I am not late, I got your summons only minutes ago, and now I am here..."

My Father turns, folding the cuffs of his sleeves to the crooks of his elbows, revealing the ancient, arcane tattoos granting him far superior magical abilities from his supposed sister. His darkened pink lips curl into a snarl, one pearlescent fang reflecting in the low light peeks under the arch of his lip.

A sudden pressure grips deep inside my chest, restricting my air, choking dread paralyzes me in the chair. "I do not remember giving you permission to sit...son." The stark reminder grips my mind in its ever-growing claws of fear, and a bead of sweat rolls down my neck, soaking into the back of my shirt.

"I summoned you hours ago," he hisses, leaning on the back of his chair, his cruel eyes narrowing to slits as he glares at me. The pompous urge to roll my eyes is overwhelming, but I refrain, because I like my eyes in their sockets and frankly because I can't, not with his power's hold on me. The last time took forever to heal, and I still have a slight tic in my jaw from the bastard.

"I'm here now. What did you want?" I'm sure I'll pay for that sneer, but I don't give a fuck.

Benedict shoves off from the chair, re-buttoning several buttons on his silk shirt. I swear he never has his chest covered, ever.

"I'm told that you still cannot locate the female, or her necklace..." he replies dryly, almost unshockingly, like he already knows the details; he merely wants me to admit to the failure. Figures that my Father will only ever see me as the perpetual fuck up, unlike my brother, his only true son, Laurent. Too bad I'm all he has left now. I made sure of that. Poor, poor Laurent torn to shreds by an alpha wolf...it was a tragedy.

"No, like you'd instructed I tasked two to handle it. Niles was killed and that beta bastard has yet to return with the necklace, however Jamac sent out Damon and Keir to finish the job," I offer in hopes that this conversation is over, so I can take matters into my own hands like I should have from the start, but no dear old Dad wanted me to show him I can delegate and rule.

"Ah...I see," Benedict sneers, showing off a fang and lifts a bejeweled goblet of what I am sure is a sweet blend of mead and blood to his lips. His ghostly gray-blue eyes never waver from mine as he sips. I'm rooted in place; I have no other option other than to watch his Adam's apple bob up and down with each gulp.

He slams the goblet down on the massive desk and comes around to the front, leaning a hip on the edge. "Tell me, Isaac, what...am...I...to do with such incompetence? With my son, who can't be bothered to show his Father he can do as he's told?" Fuck all the demons in hell! If he rips into my mind again, I will be fucked.

As my Father's hands slide into his pockets, his glare sears against my skin, sending another bead of sweat to trickle down my spine. Gulping, I find his eyes, my glare hardening, and a snarl rips up my throat.

"I will take care of it myself...you will have the little trinkets before the next full moon," my voice a false bravado to what I'm truly feeling.

A dark brow quirks up, and he smirks whilst the sharp stabbing of claws digs deeper into my flesh, gripping my heart. My eyes widen to those of a frightened doe when they dart down to my slouched chest, taking in the crimson spreading across the white of my shirt front. When my petrified orbs collide with his again, he tilts his head, more animalistic than man, and then his hands withdraw from his pockets.

With one flick of his fingers, more claw marks rake across my chest and down my stomach.

Not able to hold in my scream, I bellow and fight against his hold on me. Benedict merely shrugs his shoulders and strides around his desk to stare out the windows once more, mumbling about three millennia waiting and waving me away like I'm the help and not his only son!

"Do not fail me again, or next time I'll actually have to wash my hands."

11

Faith

The ceiling fan needs a balance weight on one side; the blades are slightly off kilter, which has been throwing my daze off for most of the evening. Dropping an arm over my eyes, I groan, running through every possible scenario and theory why a vamp was at my wedding and mating ceremony. And why him? The longer I think of it, the more amped up I get.

The ticking of the bell and hammer alarm clock on the dresser clangs instead of ticking, rattling my brain.

Why is it so loud?

Shooting upright, I glare at the pale aqua device like it's going to obey me and stop. No such luck. I chuck a pillow at it, and it falls to the floor.

A loud pop snaps somewhere in my neck from the weight of my head bending shoulder to shoulder. The dryness in my eyes is the only indication I have of being exhausted. I haven't slept all evening. I lean back, enjoying the burning stretch before slinking to my luggage with a sigh. Sleep won't be found anytime soon, so might as well blow some steam off.

Changing into a pair of cherry red running shorts, a white sports bra, and a white tank, I lace up the oldest pair of sneakers I own. These ratty old things have seen better days; the hint of white and pink stripes barely stands out from the black. The soles have been repaired twice since I bought them; I used to run daily in college. I should buck up and buy a new pair, but these are my trusty companions.

Skip-hopping down the stairs, I pop my headphones in and stuff my phone into my mini fanny pack. Stopping in front of the entryway mirror, I throw my hair up into a ponytail and head out.

My feet hit the sandy gravel of the driveway, and the midnight blue of predawn greets me with the last remaining stars twinkling in the sky. After a quick stretch of my legs, I take off to the right in a jog down the road away from town.

* * *

The muffled sound of my sneakers pounding into the pavement matches the downbeat of Shaboozey's *A Bar Song*, currently blasting in my ears. The sun rose about an hour ago, along with the birds and the first rustlings of people headed off the banks. A burn in my calves shoots a cruel reminder that 5 miles after so long of not running was a few miles too soon.

Coming to a halt at the crest of the last hill, my hands grip my waist, and my head tips back as my panting breath regulates. The summer heat is already radiating up from the sandy pavement, and my body rapidly soaks it up. With a sigh, I kick up and trek down the hill, my pace slower when Pink Skies by Zach Bryan comes on my playlist for my cool down.

A tingling sensation zips over my skin as I near the bottom, and my eyes sweep the terrain, scanning. My tired gaze lands on the grump-ish-saurus man standing at the end of a driveway staring directly at me, in nothing but a pair of low-slung jeans. Why in all that's sacred does he have to look that good first thing in the morning?

I check my scent and lock my aura down, praying it holds. Keeping my pace, I plan to pass by with a nod and a wave, but Sienna has ulterior motives and takes control, freezing my feet. I skid to a stop at the edge of the driveway. I look like a baby gymnast, my arms flinging out to stop the inevitable forward motion of falling. If it's possible, my cheeks flame darker, and I regain my balance.

His eyes burn into mine and slide down my body, searing a trail of destroying fire in its wake before locking with mine again. Neither of us relents, not wanting to make the first move or say the first words. What the hell would I say to begin with? Um, hi, remember me, the rude ass customer from yesterday? I choke on my air when another thought slaps me straight in the face. Did he get my note? No, he couldn't have; he looks like he just rolled out of bed.

I pocket my headphones and draw my eyes up and down the length of him, stalling on his feet. For a man, he's got nice bare feet, even dirty, but all the same nice. Not sure why on earth I'm focused on them, but I can't seem to will my eyes up. It couldn't possibly be because the inked-up, rigid peaks of his sweaty muscles are on full display. He chuckles, forcing my eyes up anyway, drawn to the rough sound. It's comforting, like a shot of good whiskey.

"I got your note. Pleased to meet you, Faith...I'm Declan," he says in a voice so low and husky I almost miss him holding a hand out to me. Goddess damn me, he is hot as all hell, straight up sex on a stick, and that deep timbre is doing things to me. His mere presence makes my body ripple in tingles all over.

"*Would you like me to tell you why?*" Sienna asks, plopping down to enjoy the show.

"*No, thank you.*"

"Uh...wha? Oh, um-yes, well, I'm sorry. I don't normally behave that way," I stutter, quirking my lips to the side before glancing down and away instead of checking out the rippling veins and muscles of his forearms. Why are veiny arms and hands a thing? It should be criminal.

A shiver ripples over my body, reminding me that I'm standing in the middle of the road in my shortest shorts and a white sports bra, and I'm soaked in sweat. Great, I'm sure my nipples are showing through. Hot mess express train, anyone?

Self-consciously pulling my tank from the back straps of my sports bra, I pull it on, the fabric drags and clings to my dewy skin. A flush floods my cheeks when I catch him openly gawking at me. His jaw unhinges open and closed a couple of times, but he swallows and coughs into his fist.

"Um, do you want to come in for some water or sweet tea?" He probes, those mesmerizing eyes drifting to my cleavage, then up my neck, to land on my eyes waiting. I gulp down the Texas-sized frog lodged in my throat, and blink away the sweat stinging my eyes.

"*Do you plan on answering the swarthy male or not?*" Sienna grumbles.

"*This is your fault, you answer,*" I gripe back, annoyed with her games. The unbidden shift of the muscles around my lips curves them into a smirk.

"*Shit- I was kidding, Sienna,*" I whine, and wrestle for control from her.

"*Too late.*" She chafes and curls up, ignoring me with a huff.

White hot blood scorches my veins, it pulses into my ears, and my legs suddenly weak give out from under me. Stout warm arms wrap around my waist, one hand splays over my stomach, the other on my chest. Loose strands of my hair brush the ground with the tips, and a bead of sweat slides from my nose, splashing to the gravel. I'm going to kill Sienna, but maybe later, because this man smells delicious, I'll relent for a moment to wallow in it.

"I got you," he assures and helps me to stand again. Without much thought about why I feel safe, I let him lead me up to the stairs. He helps me to a black porch rocker and disappears inside. My head rests on the back of the rocker, and I let my eyelids slide down for a moment.

The creak of the wood under the rails of the rocker is disturbed by the squeal of the screen door hinges, snapping my eyes to him. Declan steps out with two large glasses of a dark liquid, ice swirling and tinkling against the tall glass. Handing one over, he jerks his chin to me to take the condensation-laden glass.

"Here, it's sweet tea, a southern staple around these parts. Figured you might need some sugar to sweeten your bite," his quip does not go unnoticed, but I'm too distracted as he leans against the post of the porch rail, looking freshly fucked, to think of a comeback.

"Or perhaps it'll boost your levels? I figured it might be low due to the amount you left under my tables rather than consuming it," he says sardonically, taking a sip, smirking at me. He lowers his glass and rakes those 'wreck me' eyes up and down my body again, my nose wrinkles at his jab, but my core squeezes at his perusal.

"The beverage isn't going to bite Faith, but I might. I promise you'll like it." My eyes narrow at his insistence and innuendo, and I take a whiff. The sugary tea seems to provide some comfort as it tickles my nose. Shaky hands lift the glass to my pursed lips. My tongue darts out to steal a taste before I gulp it. There's a burnt sugar, almost caramel taste that lingers on my tongue after I've taken a drink. The flavor intensifies after each sip. Tipping the glass back, I practically down the drink in one go.

"That was good, I've never had it. It's quite delicious, thank you," I say sweetly, praying the humiliation burning the tips of my ears isn't noticeable. I didn't plan on admitting to him that it was my first time trying it. I'm partial to the unsweetened iced teas from up north. Branching out and trying new comfort things is unsettling at the very least for me; I don't do well with change.

"You're welcome, sugar," he murmurs low and takes a sip. I didn't think my ears could burn even hotter, but the blood is surely spreading to my cheeks now.

"When my Mom would make iced tea, she used to add in random citrus like traditional lemon, but also sometimes limes, oranges, and even tangelos once," I add, sucking in my bottom lip. My head whips away from the rush of heat building in the curve of my ears again. Why the hell did I say that?

Declan scrunches his nose and shoves off the railing in a single long step. He's next to me and settling into the rocker beside mine.

"She used—" he stops himself, and he rakes a hand through his dark waves. Spying on him from the corner of my eye, I don't know what to think as he assesses, shakes his head, and redirects.

"Hmm, well if I'd known all it would take was a lil' sweet tea to cool the fiery vixen before me, I would've offered you a glass yesterday," he chuckles, it's a deep, throaty laugh, its soothing darkness shudders over me, and my clit throbs at the sound. The slinking of melting ice draws my view back to him. My breath catches, and I stare unabashedly as he lifts the nearly empty glass to his enticing, full lips.

Averting my stare before he lowers his glass, my fingers tap along the walls of the glass absentmindedly. My fingertips collect the condensation, and I roll and smoosh it between the pads. The ghost of Mom's laughter tinkles in like a small wind chime, sucking me into a wave of melancholy. Distantly, I hear Declan saying something to me, but all I can focus on is Mom's laughter.

"...It is quite good, and easy to make. If you'd like, I can give you the recipe, or better yet, I can show you how to make it," Declan offers and rocks back in his chair, tucking an errant strand of hair behind his ear.

"Huh? I'm sorry I drifted off there for a moment," I admit, my cheeks burning cherry red. At this rate, he's going to think there's something wrong with me. Perhaps it's for the best, though? I won't be here long, and anybody with a brain can see I'm starved for any sort of loving affection, and this is purely lust. It has to be.

"Haha-okay sure," he deadpans, laughing, there's that laugh again, like the sting of a smoked whiskey that bites and then finishes smooth down your throat, warming your belly.

Declan rises so swiftly from his rocker that it scares the crap out of me, and my shoulders flinch back. He notices, but says nothing. As his fingers brush along mine, he flicks his hooded eyes up, boring those hazel orbs into my soul, before taking the empty glass.

"I-uh- should get going. Thank you for the drink," I rush out and bolt up from the rocker, flying down the steps. I'm five paces away before he's behind me, fingertips grazing my elbow.

"Faith, wait—" his voice sounds strangled, but I shrug away and bolt down the drive.

I slip my headphones in, acting as if I can't hear him, and sprint the remainder to my rental. Declan makes it to the end of his driveway and then, like my Mom's gurgled last breaths, he gives up, which, all in all, is good, because I couldn't stay there a minute longer.

12

Faith

My skin tingles from the oppressive heat sinking back into my numbed flesh. After a solid thirty minutes of the best ice-cold shower that I've had in a long time, my body is still plagued with a grumpy bar owner-induced ravaging heat, but hey, the water pressure was terrific.

Tossing the fluffiest towel I've ever used to the end of the bed, I pull out and slip into my go-to outfit for assignments: a pair of army green khaki shorts, a cream tank top, my camel field vest, and boots. That pink battery bunny, what is its name again? I can't remember, anyway, it doesn't matter, that bunny ain't got nothing on me right now, my legs are pumped full of springs bouncing inside my veins. Excited to go out on assignment, I skip down the stairs and make a beeline for the kitchen.

Pouring another cup of coffee, I reach over and flip the last blueberry pancake on the griddle. I behold the towering stack of them and grumble. My eyes were undeniably larger than the pangs of hunger ravaging my stomach earlier. It's next to impossible that I'll be able to finish all of these for breakfast. Selecting half of them, I slide the rest into Ziplock bags and toss them into the pull-out freezer.

While twirling my spoon in my mug, I finish setting up my laptop on the island counter and promptly dig into the warm, fluffy deliciousness I slaved over earlier. I have no shame and shovel a forkful of syrup-drenched pancake in, closing my lips around the tangs narrowly escaping the dreaded dollop of sticky syrup dripping to my lap. I jut my chin over my plate to avoid the mess. Satisfied, I lick my fingers clean, and I go over the assignment request Hollie told me about last night.

Faith,

I heard about the wedding. I'm sorry to hear about your Mom. Your sister informed me when I called to send you my condolences that you were on your honeymoon alone. I did try your cell first before you get mad at her for divulging. I thought this would be a good distraction for you, and a great piece to add to the summer locations edition. I hear that the wild horses run the beaches down there all the time. We'd like you to capture them and help us tell their story. The boss man wants an in-depth article about the horses and how they affect the culture down there. You have a one-month deadline for the initial draft and photo submissions. Let me know if you've accepted, and send me a frame of your choosing by the end of the week.

-Charles

N.G.M.

Well, Hollie, you're still dead meat when I get home for disclosing where I'm at. I know she meant well, but Charles is a nosey ass. I adore him, I do, but sometimes I think he reads too much into our platonic relationship. Although he's made working with the magazine as a freelance photographer fantastic and easy, he always has a way of infiltrating every facet of my life.

Charles discovered me while I was a freshman in college, and I've worked as a freelance wildlife photographer ever since. I've never understood why I've been able to get as close as I do to prey wildlife while being a predator myself, primarily. I've always assumed it was, because Sienna hid away and they couldn't sense the predator within. Yet, the morning after Mom's funeral pyre, those deer didn't bolt; come to think of it, they didn't bolt with my Dad being there too. Either way, being a freelancer has worked out well with my busy schedule since I usually had events with Connor or pack business to tend to with Dad and Mom.

Mom.

Icy tendrils spread under my skin at her memory, and I suppress the stinging threatening to ruin my mascara. Goddess, I miss her so much. She would love it here, the ocean is—No. Was. It was her favorite place to visit for vacations. We used to visit Acadia's beaches in Maine during the summer and, in the evenings, explore down into Bar Harbor. We always ended the trip with a stop at the ice cream parlor to get Dad's favorite lobster-flavored ice cream. Not my favorite, but hey, to each their own.

The coastline in Maine is vastly different compared to here. Sure, there's sand and waves, but in Maine, there's rocky cliffs, and wicked cold water crashing up, frothing along the jagged edges, adding an element of danger. The forest dots along the beaches, too, and the way the morning fog moves in over the saltwater marshes behind the beach, oh, it's a sight that will never leave my memories.

A burn pricks along my nose, and I hold back my tears again; she wouldn't want me to be a blubbering mess. Mom would want me to live my life to the fullest.

Setting aside my grief, I poke at Sienna, who's currently throwing a tantrum in my cerebrum. She has remained pensive and mostly quiet since we encountered those wolves on the road here. She's only stirred awake when we are close to Declan, and now I'm worried she doesn't want to grow our bond or that I've made a mistake.

"You think I made a mistake leaving the note, don't you?" I ask her and sip my coffee, waiting for her reply. She hadn't said anything or pressed into our bond while I wrote out my drunken apology. She'd perked up when we approached the bar, but then curled back up with her back to me. Her walls were up, and I couldn't read what she was feeling or thinking. It left me reeling in all the negative self-talk swirling around me like a tornado. I can sense her nudging closer, but she's either ignoring me because she's pissed, or something else is bothering her.

"No, I think you did the right thing," she says softly. I spit my coffee out, spraying the counter with precious life juice. Not once has Sienna ever talked to me in a soft tone like that.

"Really? I figured you'd tell me it was a sign of weakness," I reply, expecting an explanation. She moves around and curls into a ball, lifts her head, ears twitching, and then lays her head back down. Okay, not going to get an answer then. It's fine, she doesn't have to—

"I don't think it was weak, Faith. It's a sign of humility; a good alpha has those qualities," she says matter-of-factly, but I can tell she's holding something back; her tone is off and not her usual snippy bitch tone, but I let it go for now.

* * *

My eyeballs hurt from scrolling and staring at my screen for hours. The research for the best locations to find the horses took a bit longer than expected, but I did learn some interesting bits of history surrounding them and how the people here are connected.

After meticulously cleaning and packing my lenses, I load the rest of my gear into the Jeep and head over to the grocery store for some snacks and aloe vera. The aloe, since I did not use sunscreen the day before. I'm a bit pink from my burn yesterday, but I'll be tan by evening. However, I don't want to walk around with my clothes rubbing all over the sensitive spots in the summer heat.

Sliding into the first available parking space, the door to my jeep creaks when I close and lock it. Walking up to the entrance of The Ringer Bros. Grocery store, I smirk, snagging the last carriage.

This place reminds me of Trader Joe's, but with less tree-hugger vibes. The dark wood floors offset the brightly colored fruit, and vegetable stands in the produce area, and an entire section is dedicated to only flowers, primarily wildflower bundles.

Selecting a bouquet, and then some berries and grapes, I turn down one of the many pantry item aisles, leisurely perusing, taking in all the unique items they carry. The clinking and occasional squeak of the carriage wheels blends seamlessly with the twangs of a steel guitar playing a sweet country song.

I'm so wrapped up in the ambience of the place that, as I round a corner to the right and check to my left, I startle when my arms jolt from impact with another carriage. I whip my head in the direction of the collision, pasting an apologetic smile on my face, ready to dish out pleasantries, when it falls, immediately frowning when I see *him*.

"Ahh, pissah," I yelp as my eyes land and roll up Declan. You know that feeling when you're utterly mortified, but also awed at the same time? Well, that is precisely what is happening with my face; it's all screwed up in conflicting emotions.

A grimace slides over my 'dealing with people' face. My bugged-out eyes drop into a tight squint, which embellishes the creases alongside my eyes, aging me a few years in the process. The blush of my cheeks adds to the ridiculousness.

"You've got to be freaking kidding me," I groan, instantly irritated more in my head than the rest of my body. His beautiful hazel eyes appear a little grayer today when they lock with my espresso ones. We take each other in, subconsciously drawing our wolves to the surface. Sienna is perky and, dare I say, fascinated with Declan and his wolf.

We both inhale at the same time. *Oh no, no, no...* my eyes bulge, ready to pop out of their sockets. I forgot to mask before I came in here. He's going to figure it out, and then all the damn questions will start, which will inevitably lead to other questions that I don't want to answer. Ugh, why didn't I remember to mask? But he also smells so—

"Shit," I blurt and start to back away from him, death gripping the carriage handle. "I'm sorry... again," I call out and attempt to make my escape. I yank on the handle of the carriage, retreating, but it isn't budging.

My vision blurs as I blink up to Declan. He smirks and holds the edge of the carriage in challenge. The slightest twinkle sparkles from his right eye, and something tells me I'm about to be in big trouble. He sways his hips out to the side, curving around the basket, heading straight towards me.

Oh fuck, oh fuck, oh fu- he's figured it out! Shiiiiitt!

I struggle to resist the urge to raise my nose in the air, but Sienna rushes forward, ears perking up, and encourages me to do precisely that.

Goddess damned wolf!

Declan reaches out and snags my bicep, dragging me to his chest. I collide with his puffed-up, hard-working, muscular chest, which I kind of want to bury my nose in. I'm sucked in, and for the first time in a long time, I feel...safe. He can't possibly be...no-nope.

Transfixed by our closeness, I revel in his heat, forgetting absolutely everything I was supposed to be doing. He shamelessly dips his nose into my hair, mussing it, and inhales deeply, popping goosebumps along the back of my neck. A low growl rumbles in his chest, and every muscle in my body freezes, lava reactively pools in between my thighs. In an attempt to quell this desire, I press them together, and it only makes it worse. He inhales again, his eyes darken, and mine grow round as a barn owl's.

Shit!

He trails the tip of his nose down over my cheek. He's so close, our lips are a breath apart. Is he going to kiss me? My heart thuds hard and takes off in a sprint. If I were a betting woman, I'd say the damn muscle could win the Triple Crown.

He pulls away, and my stomach sinks to my feet. "Hmmm...so you're an alpha?" he moans, almost questionably, with the way he cocks his head to the side. His wolf is in charge at the moment, and it's kind of cute. Declan leans in again, running his nose alongside my cheek.

"Oh-fuck," I whisper, and moan. I attempt to move away again, and Declan squeezes harder around my upper arm. I'm wrestling to hide my wince, but he doesn't miss a thing with the way he's staring at me, and loosens his grip, but doesn't let go. If anyone walks by, they'll probably think we are a couple of sexed-up psychos smelling each other up in the boxed goods section of the grocery store. Mortification slithers its cold tendrils down my spine and squeezes my stomach in a vice.

"It's nice to see you again, Declan. Sorry about running into you," I squeak. I freaking squeaked like a schoolgirl!

What am I, fourteen?

Getting a whiff of my heady arousal, every inch of my skin flushes. If I can smell it, I have no doubt he can smell it. That confirmation comes when his hazel eyes flash gold and then back to hazel gray, and he licks his lips.

Declan rakes his gaze torturously up and down my body and openly adjusts his cock in his jeans. At my mortified expression, he grins, flashing those almost perfectly straight, white teeth. One incisor next to his canine on the right turns a fraction inward, giving him a hint of an impish grin. Not so perfect, but perfect.

No! Bad Faith. We don't find the walking wet dream attractive.

I yank on the carriage again, and he snatches the side of the basket, effectively stopping my retreat. What the hell? How are one person's fingers that strong? My mind immediately dives into the gutter and swims in all the ways he could use those strong fingers. Tipping my head back to get a real good look at him, my breath hitches at the intense longing I catch ping ponging across his face.

Declan roams his eyes over every inch of me again, the silent studying is unnerving...kind of. The burn in my belly swells and swirls the longer he's in my bubble. My heart pounds uncontrollably in conjunction with my labored breathing. I'm hyperventilating. I should probably sit down before I pass out.

Yanking on the handle so hard that the bar bites into my stomach, I tug again. I refuse to show mercy. The metal finally jerks free from his vice-like grip. His fingers glide down my arm and over my wrist, lingering on my fingers as I back away. Little electric shocks bite at my skin in the wake of his fingers, and a bubbling burn boils in my stomach.

My eyes are glued to his when I walk backwards and duck into the next aisle. Mind in a cloud, my hands randomly toss boxes of Goddess knows what into my carriage and then make a beeline to the checkouts. I can come back later and get the rest of the stuff I want for the house.

Throwing my flowers, fruit, and junk food up on the conveyor belt in the most crazed fashion, I dance on the balls of my feet. Up and down, side to side, up and down. The lady across at the next cashier glares over her shoulder at me like I'm doing drugs. Resisting the urge to bob my foot so I don't look like a strung-out junkie, I try to wait for the young kid to ring up my items. My heart is lodged deeper in my throat.

Declan's scent billows stronger, like an Alaskan-sized cloud of it trails him; he pops out from an aisle close by. He peeks over his shoulder, points and winks at me, and walks through the store like he owns it. *Wait, does he own this, too? It would be just my luck, wouldn't it?*

"That'll be $33.79, ma'am," the young kid says, bringing me back to the moment. Straight up highway robbery for the few items I'm getting, but I'm at a loss for words. I stare past him; he appears so lost and sweet at the same time. A reflective sign above flashes a bit of light in my face, snapping me out of wherever the hell I went.

"Oh, right, here ya go," I hand over my cash and wait for my change. I flick my gaze back to Declan, but he's not there.

13

Declan

She's an alpha female.

I had her pegged as an omega with her weak scent yesterday, even this morning when she sat on my porch. She has been masking it, but why? Goddess, did she smell heavenly! If I thought her scent, even masked, was delicious, her actual scent is divine.

"Told you," Thorin mutters against my cerebral.

A potent field of wildflowers, specifically wild violets, mountain air, and white pine, all things home. If I didn't know she was a Mainer from her plates and the little accent she let slip a moment ago, her body's perfume would have identified her right down to a pinpoint on a map. White pines grow heavily along the border of my old pack and the Mystic Keepers pack. I don't recall the alpha's daughters' names, but if I had to guess, and I'd put money on this, I'd say she's one of his daughters.

Rounding the corner of the spice aisle, I hang back and get a side view of her profile. She's rather jumpy for an alpha wolf. Thorin comes rushing front and center, panting and sitting like a pup waiting for his goodies. His tail swishing back and forth, he licks his lips.

"Mine," he growls through our link.

"No, no way in hell! She's not ours either, just a fine as hell she-wolf who smells like the goddess herself blessed her," I snap back. He doesn't even flinch, simply cocks his head to the side and then back to the other side. He watches her check out and run from the store. Fuck, if I don't get him under control, he'll chase after her and pin her down. Goddess knows he loves the chase.

When I grabbed her arm earlier, she pretended like I didn't see her wince from the contact. It took a concerted amount of effort not to react to that when I leaned in to inhale her heavenly ambrosia closely, my cock jerked, but my mind focused on the wince, which wasn't intentional; it was reactionary from fear.

Yet, her arousal blossomed as I'd mussed up her hair and then again when I rubbed the tip of my nose down her cheek, her skin like the softest silk, sending sparks along mine. She would've melted into a puddle if I let her go, hell, I bet her panties were soaked like my boxer briefs were currently from my pre-cum that leaked every time my dick twitched at her breathy words; wince forgotten.

She's like a damn drug that I can't wait to get my next fix of, and that thought has me stepping back and taking breath. I can't let another addiction take root; it's bad enough that there are days I can't function without my meds, I don't want to know what would happen if I couldn't function without her.

So, to give myself some distance and release, perhaps I could take Gwen up on her thousands of offers, or call Nia; it's been a while, but do I really want that drama? Not really, no, neither option comes free of any strings or headaches. Groaning, I head down the aisle to grab what I need to make the sweet tea and BBQ for tonight.

The full moon gathering is later, where every wolf in the area gathers to shift late into the night, when human eyes, who don't know of us, will be fast asleep and not on the beach. Maybe she'll be drawn out later; the call to the moon usually brings nearby wolves together.

Isaiah, the cashier, eyes me with a questionable smirk as he rings up my food. The awkward silence creates the game of who speaks first, but I have no patience left today. That little vixen stirred me up and then dashed away, fueling the need to chase...to hunt.

"Spit it out, Isaiah," I snarl, curling my lip. This kid, whom I've known for the last four years, is a good kid, but really needs to get out of this town and spread his wings.

"Uh-is-sh- she yours?" He squeaks out and hesitates to continue scanning the food while he waits for my answer. My eyes widen at his response; it's not what I was expecting at all.

"Excuse me?"

"Everyone is talking about the new pretty girl in town, and some-one thought she was yours or something, but after watching that in-teraction, I'd say she doesn't know it yet," he says quickly and shies away from me to bag up my groceries. That took less time than I thought, the whole town already? My bet is on Flik's big mouth.

Well, shit, I wasn't aware we had an audience. I comb my fingers through my hair. Heat rises to my cheeks, coloring them a deep ma-genta, "uh, we..." What the hell was I supposed to say to that?

"No, she's not. She-ahh...had a really great perfume and we had an argument yesterday at the bar so..."

Isaiah stares at me, narrowing his eyes in disbelief, and then hands me my receipt and nods to the two bags of groceries. "We heard," he mutters, not believing a single word out of my mouth. Fucking small towns.

Shaking off the uneasiness that's currently creeping throughout my body, I duck out from the store and cross the parking lot with cement in my shoes. A prickle like an electric shock races up my forearm, and I jerk my head up, spotting Faith's jeep still in the parking lot.

Willing my legs to carry me to my truck faster and not to her jeep, I fight the yearning instinct every step of the way. Finally loaded up and blasting the A/C, I watch her leave, and a slight tug pulls on me from my chest. Without much thought, my hand slides up and rubs circles on my sternum.

My truck slows to a crawl, almost all on its own, when I creep by the place she's staying at. The top of her head bobs over the dunes as she hops down to the beach with a backpack. Pressing the brake pedal a little more, I hone in on her dainty fingers pulling that luscious hair up into a ponytail and popping some headphones in her ears. Those perfectly curved, cute ears.

"*Maybe we should follow her and see what she's up to... maybe rub our scent all over her,*" Thorin says to me, and I roll my eyes.

"*You are a dirty wolf, you know that,*" I mutter back and release the brakes, the sand whipped over the pavement squishes under the tires, but my eyes swivel one more time her way.

* * *

A new, shiny, navy Chevy Silverado is parked in my spot when I pull into the driveway, forcing me to park a bit into the sand. If I didn't love my cousin, I'd probably throttle his ass; he knows I'm particular about where I park. Shoving the shifter into park, I spot him leaning against the railing of the porch, looking all smug and shit; he knows what he did.

I hop out and jog up to him, ready to smack him upside the head, but I opt for clasping both arms around him, we embrace, and I pull back to take him in. It's been too long since I've seen him; he's not only my cousin, but my best friend.

"Wyatt! I thought you weren't coming until this weekend?" I wonder and send a quick prayer that it's not bad news for the earlier arrival.

Wyatt smirks and lets out a chuckle, "It's all good, Cuz, just thought I'd surprise ya, and come down a couple days sooner to share the best news of my life in person," he replies with happiness gushing out from his aura. It's been about four or five years since I last saw him in person. Sure, we'd been in contact over the years, but I haven't seen him in ages, and this is the best surprise.

A feminine giggle pierces the breeze. I spin and see a gorgeous blonde walking around my wrap-around porch. She's stunning, in a sunflower sundress and flip flops. Brows rising to my hairline, I turn to Wyatt, with a question sketched across my face. He smirks and claps me on the shoulders, steering me closer, but then abruptly stops, eyeing the distance between our feet.

Uh, ok...

"Declan, I present my mate, Julianna," Wyatt beams and lifts his arm. She tucks into his side, and he wraps her up in his arms, placing a gentle kiss on her cheek. "Julianna, this is my cousin, Declan," he finishes the introductions, beaming once more. I don't think I've ever seen so many of Wyatt's teeth before, but a mate, what are the odds?

Swallowing hard, I smile and reach out a hand in greeting. Tentatively, Julianna seeks out Wyatt's permission, and he nods. Julianna takes my hand in hers and squeezes lightly, giving it a slight shake.

"It's so nice to meet you finally, Wyatt talks about you all the time," she says so quietly I barely hear her.

"Likewise, why don't we get out of the heat and head inside?" I motion up the stairs.

"I take it you're staying in town, or do you still want to stay here?" I ask, not sure of the situation now that he's not alone as initially planned.

"Haha, here if that's alright? I'd rather be away from any unmated males; being newly mated is intense, man, but you're the only male I trust around my girl," he says sincerely.

His words wrap around my heart and squeeze. Wyatt knows what happened with Sophia, and despite that, he trusts me around his new mate. For him to offer such a deep level of trust in me, the honor of it, has my chest aching.

Lost in my memories, the clearing of Wyatt's throat tugs me back. Swallowing hard, my mouth opens and then closes twice before I can find my voice.

"Sorry...yeah, man, it's cool, there's plenty of room, pick any upstairs, there's one other primary suite up there opposite side of mine, if you want, that's the next best room," I offer and head into the kitchen. The two of them rub noses and head upstairs; that is disturbingly cute.

My phone pings when I enter the kitchen to unpack the groceries, and I glance at it, an internal groan almost slipping out; it's Nia. Nope! Diving my hands into the brown paper bags, I set to prepping the sweet tea and the pork for the BBQ.

Ping! Ping! Ping!

Ping!

Oh, my Goddess, she's relentless today. Rolling my eyes, I count, 1...2...3... and there it is, Flik's annoyingly drunken high-pitched mockery of her voice pelts out from my phone.

"Ring-ring. Rinnnggg-ring."

That honestly was the highlight of my month when we stayed at the bar for inventory and to scrape the undersides of the tables of gum and other unmentionables. Somehow, we'd gotten on the topic of women and how it was going with Nia. To my surprise, I learned how much Flik despises her and her red flag behavior. And when he'd mimicked her nasally, high-pitched voice almost perfectly after 6 or 7 beers, I had to record it, and now it's her ringtone.

The ringing continues, and sighing, I answer despite not wanting to. "Hey Nia, what's up?"

"Finally, oh hey Dec," she coughs and not so smoothly adjusts her tone. "How are you? Are you going tonight?" She croons like the primed ring seeker she is; that girl is the definition of thirsty.

I'm sure she's trying to stir up my lust for her, and while it would've worked before, I cringe. Goddess knows why, even when I'm in dire need of a romp in the sack to get a particular sugar packet off my mind, but Nia's doing absolutely nothing for me. What the hell did I see in her again? I debate telling her no for a moment and realize it's pointless; she'll be there regardless.

"I am, but my cousin arrived in town earlier, so I'll be preoccupied. Listen, I gotta go," I hang up before she can say anything else, and then silence her alerts on my phone.

* * *

The sizzling of meat on the smoker hypnotizes me as I check the pork's temp, my gaze flitting from the meat to the waves crashing and back. The ends of my hair lift on the sweet, salty breeze, the ends tickling my cheeks. I close my eyes and breathe in deep. The last twenty-four hours have been a whirlwind of emotions and changes, but I'm proud of myself, with no episodes.

Ticking them off in my head again: A new female wolf, an alpha to boot, strolls into town, I should say rolled in like a thunderstorm because she's upended my brain into a deep-fried corn husk. A vampire stalked into my territory, and my cousin showed up early, and...and with a mate. Any one of those would've usually had my brain in a tailspin.

Lost deep within the tangles of my thoughts, shadows in my peripheral startle me, and my stomach drops like a rollercoaster.

"Hey," Wyatt murmurs, approaching slowly, and joins me. It's been a long time since someone has gotten the jump on me without me sensing them first. Maybe I am going to have an episode?

"So, mated, huh?" Shifting around him, I hand him a beer from the porch cooler and sit back down in one of the Adirondack chairs. Wyatt smiles widely, the corners of his mouth reach his reddened ears, his dark blue eyes shine brighter, and he leans back against the railing, sipping his beer.

"Yeah, it's the best feeling in the world, but if I'm being honest, it wasn't something I'd expected at all," he admits and takes another swig of his beer.

"Well, congrats, man, I'm happy for you. "A twinge of something twists in my stomach before I raise my beer to him.

There aren't many people that I can enjoy the quiet with, but with Wyatt, we tend to do it more often than not. Wispy, soft clouds float over the noonday sun, giving our skin a moment of reprieve from its oppressive heat.

* * *

My eyes drift open and closed several times as the hours tick by, the waves crashing and the gulls calling practically lull me to sleep. Faith's pretty face pops into my mind, tensing all of my muscles awake. Wyatt tilts his head towards me briefly before snapping it right back to Julianna walking along the shore.

Slapping a hand to my thigh, "Well, I should recheck the temp on the meat," my voice is awkward at best, and I know Wyatt can tell, but he's not acknowledging it for now. The pork has reached the temperature I need it at, and I nod at him. Then, I head inside to grab the butcher paper to wrap it, and let it continue smoking.

Inside the kitchen, a strangeness rolls over me like a tsunami. Gripping the sides of my head, my eyes squeeze closed and fly open. I try to shake the weirdness away, but it knocks into me again, like a door-to-door salesperson who won't take no for an answer. I rip open the cabinet door and grab the butcher paper. My eyes land on the orange bottle of round white pills, the roll of paper still in my hand.

"No!" I grumble and slam the door, blocking the temptation to drown it all out. Supplies gathered; I head back to the patio.

Opening the side door, my arms tingle with numbness for a second, and I almost drop everything. Wyatt jumps up and rushes to me as I curl in on myself, when out of nowhere, an excruciating pain tears into my chest, burying it with a suffocating sorrow.

"Dec?" A hand slams into my chest, circling with slight pressure until the pain subsides. "Declan? You, okay?"

Blinking rapidly, my gaze jerks to Wyatt and then down to his hand on my chest and back up. He drops his hand, his brows pinch with the worry stitching across his face.

"Yeah, just a wicked pain in my chest, second time today."

"I noticed...you sure you're good?" He asks again. I know he hopes I will elaborate, but I can't.

"I'm good, probably a bout of indigestion or something."

"Indigestion? You're an idiot..." Thorin mumbles.

"Uh huh, sounds like it..." Wyatt deadpans. He grabs the paper from me and helps me wrap up the pork butt, and then we both head inside so I can make the sweet tea.

Wyatt's been watching me like a hawk for the past 15 minutes. Asking about the bar, my new friends, and any ladies I've been chasing, using it as his excuse not to leave my side. I tell him but still don't mention Faith. Something about her makes me want to keep her a secret for a little bit longer. Besides, I have questions of my own.

After I've got the tea steeping in the pre-sweetened boiled water, my lips quirk to the side, and I lean on the counter. "Can I ask you something?"

Wyatt drops his attention from his phone and morphs his love-stricken face into a cool, collected one waiting for me to ask my question. My heart thuds hard, pounding up my throat. I shove off from the counter and run my sweaty palms down my jeans.

"So, what's it like? The bond?" My voice squeaks at the end like I'm a teenager all over again, and suddenly the floor is fascinating.

Wyatt slams his hand down on the counter, "What?!" he stares at me, rapidly blinking.

"I said—"

"I heard what you said, but give me a minute to process what my cousin, who swore he never wanted a mate, questions me about mate bonds," he chuckles and smiles widely. A bit over the top of a reaction if you ask me, but I know he's doing it on purpose; he likely can sense something is going on and will pick and prod at me until I blow up and let it all out. That's an investigative reporter for you.

"I never said I didn't want one. I said I didn't deserve one, besides, even if I was blessed with one, it wouldn't be good for her to have to deal with my shit," I admit sourly and then catch the concern he's trying to hide pass over his face.

"I only wanted to know what it's like, you look so damn happy, I-I'm curious, is all," I drawl and stir the tea again.

He takes a swig of his beer, squints, and heaves a sigh. "Well, cuz I am...happy that is, over the moon. But how the bond feels is different for everyone, from what I've been told, but the main thing is the strength and depth of the pull towards one another. There's this unyielding desire for one another, and—" he swallows slowly and takes a swig of his beer.

"Uh...and being addicted to their scent." My brows tug upwards briefly, but enough that he notices.

My face must've screamed everything he needed to know, because before I could even deny it, he stood up and rounded the counter. Placing his hands on my shoulders, he stares deeply into my eyes and bursts out laughing.

"Oh shit...who is she?" He asks in genuine interest. Well, that isn't what I was expecting.

"I never can hide anything from you, can I?" I groan and roll my neck to the side.

"Nope...now spill or I'll go get Julianna and she can deduce it out of you," he chides, slowly turning away from me.

My eyes see my brain as they roll, "No, she just got back to nap, let her sleep, it'll be a long night anyways, and I'm not telling you and I don't want it anyways."

"Liar...liar...pants of fire." Thorin teases and shoves an image of Faith outside the bar, smiling.

Wyatt drops his hands to his side, the bright smile he had moments ago fades, and the corners of his lips droop down. His eyes soften, and sadness washes over him, pushing out towards me, worry wafts from him to my nostrils; dammit.

"You're planning on rejecting her before giving it a chance? Before it even forms? Do you have any idea how painful that is?" his questions are laced with concern for not only me, but her, too, and he doesn't even know her. I knew I shouldn't have bothered to ask; now he's going to hound me about this forever.

"I don't care, Wyatt, you know why I shouldn't have a mate, I'm too dangerous, I could hurt her..." I point out, shrugging, none to eager to remind him of my failed relationship with Sophia. I never have to worry with Nia when I'm with her, because she never stays long enough to see when my head goes into the darkness.

"Yet, here I am with a recent mating bond, and I am trusting you to be around her, am I not?" he argues back. "Haven't you had any relationships since?" A shake of my head answers his question.

14

Faith

Tingles pebble along the tight skin of the back of my sun-kissed neck, remembering too late that I forgot that one spot for sunscreen, again. I could shift later and heal, but I'm not sure Sienna will be willing.

She's still in a mood with me for running from Declan this morning and at the grocery store. Her anger is irrational, at least it is to me. She can't be mad at me, I don't even know him, and she wants me to what, mount him? No, no fucking way. She's starting to act like a bitch in heat.

Hot sand sinks below my boots as I trudge along, following the hoof prints, tracking the warm, sweet, musty scent of the wild horses. Their earlier neighing and whinnying have gotten closer, not too much farther.

The stalks of the dune grasses sway back and forth in a haunting melody. The mini prints of the sandpipers and willets rapidly disappear, the loose sand filling in behind, covering them. Spotting a small grouping of sandpipers, I squat down and sight them in my lens.

Warmth clusters around my heart. I love the way the tiny birds skitter and scatter along the shoreline, pecking at the sand for their food. It's adorable to watch. Snapping a few photos of them, avoiding the crashing tide, and smiling while reviewing the playback screen. A thought of Mom loving this glides its cold fingers over my scalp.

"Faith..." A distorted whisper of her voice shatters the box I had stuffed my grief into. "Do not be afraid...listen to your heart..."A band of barbed wire twists tightly around my heart, refusing to loosen no matter my internal pleas.

Why now? Why Mom?

Another twist, the barbs cutting deeper, gasping, my knees fall forward, crashing into the sand.

Relenting, I close my eyes and let the emotions crash over me, and tears rush down my cheeks like the spring melt in the mountain streams. Head tilting back, a guttural moan of sadness forces its way out of my throat. Chin dipping to my chest, I will myself to calm, inhaling through my nose and out my mouth.

Determined to pack this hurt away, a steel box appears, and I stuff it all in there and slam it closed before kicking it across to the shadows of my mind.

Calmer, I allow happier thoughts of her to drift again. She would've loved it here, she'd point out every single bird, naming all of their genuses. And then she'd give them proper names because 'they need proper names befitting their personalities and not just their species.' I get my love of bird watching from her. However, I'm not sure if it's a wolf thing or if it was merely a mom thing. As the breeze dances over me, I smile through the trickle of pain trying to seep back in.

"Well, I can't let this tradition die," I whisper to myself and pick out one little female sandpiper. The little sea bird ruffles its feathers and settles its tiny head within the fluff.

"Hello little one, I hear by declare, you will be known as Sadie the Sandpiper," I say, my voice cracking. Pushing off the sand, I swipe away the salt tracks and continue on my hunt for the ponies.

* * *

An hour later, sweating profusely and ducked down behind several dunes, my arms tremble as I hold my camera up to my face. Hot sand sprays up on a stream of wind, wafting the pungent, sweet musty smell from the small herd of wild horses only yards from my hiding spot. An image of Declan standing at the end of his driveway comes to mind. I wonder what he's up to.

A mare and her foal play and frolic along the waves, and several others munch on the nearby tufts of oat grass while a magnificent stallion keeps watch not too far from where I'm tucked in between the towering grasses. Every time I breathe, his ears flit forward and twitch, but the stallion makes no move towards me. Instead, he trots off again, closer to the mare and foal, corralling them back, closer to my spot. He's done this several times now, almost like he's showing them off to me.

The three move to stand closer to one another. All three sets of their ears prick forward, their eyes focus in on my direction, like they know I'm here and they aren't afraid. The tip of my index finger presses down, releasing the shutter. A quick peek at the preview screen shows a too-posed-to-be-real moment.

Intent on getting the right shot, I lift my camera again when the stallion steps next to the mare and runs his nose along her forehead and neck, messing up her mane.

Click, click.

Suddenly, the stallion freezes in alert and then stomps the ground angrily, alerting the herd. He frantically whinnies, and they take off, stampeding down the beach where I can't follow. Zooming in, my shutter button fires off continuous frames, capturing the sand spraying up under their hooves.

Aching legs and arms scream in protest as I pop up, scanning the area for the perceived threat. Tiny heat waves roll up from the sand, a gull calls above, and then disappears. Giving up, I slink back down on my blanket and click through the frames. Surprised, I didn't take as many as I usually do. So, I pick out my favorites: Sadie the sandpiper and the one with the stallion, his mare, and foal. Before my mind forgets the details of the moment, I jot down a few notes and repack my bag.

* * *

The sun hangs a bit low for the late afternoon, but I trudge on, fueled by the repetitive crash of the waves and occasional bird call. My mind wanders to Declan again and how he devoured my neck earlier. I can't quit thinking of him at all today.

The only thing ruining this moment is the grains of sand that have wedged their way under my watchband. Slipping a finger under it, I glance at the time, my shoulders slump, it's later than I thought. By the time I can get remotely closer to my part of the beach, it'll be well into the night.

"Oh well," I shrug and drop my pack, digging out my water bottle, and gulping it as I trek back to my rental, snapping pictures of anything and everything. I'm living in the moment and enjoying the sights, sounds, and smells.

Stunning carnelians and violets streak across the unending sky and reflect over the water from the horizon. A few scattered clouds stretch their cotton-like fingers over the colors, barely fitting in the frame of my lens when I capture the scene.

* * *

A burnt acrid odor wafts in my direction, its smoky tendrils curling around my tangled hair. A gust of wind blasts by, lifting the hem of my shirt. Another gust brings a myriad of scents my way. The majority of them are a smoky, smothered-down version of humans and shifters. Inhaling deeply, I pick up on BBQ and other foods; must be a party or something; maybe Declan is there. A loud grumble twists my stomach in hunger. I probably should've packed more snacks today.

My boots stomp into the sand, flinging more up and into my socks each time I quicken my pace to get to my rental sooner. The full moon is rising, and the new sensations of the pull to shift are getting harder to ignore, but thankfully, Sienna remains quiet.

It's not long before a soft orange glow lights up the dark. In the distance, a gigantic bonfire blazes, illuminating a crowd of fifteen or so shifters drinking and laughing. No matter how much I'd rather continue on home and have peace and quiet, their hoots and hollers draw my feet to a stop. I'm generally not a jealous person, but that filter of green plucks at me while I admire their carefree spirits.

Without much thought, I stalk closer to pass them. I raise my camera and snap a couple of shots. Focusing on the viewing screen, an excited shriek draws my attention up and away. A blonde woman in a sunflower dress runs towards me, waving like a crazed fan. Shit! I forgot about the few random crazies who obsessively follow me around on assignments.

The all-too-familiar pings of panic race in my veins, my head swings around, desperate to find some kind of escape. The wind kicks up again, and with it, scents of home and apples swirl around me, instantly calming me. Squinting at the woman sprinting towards me, her features start to come into focus, and a wisp of apple blossoms wafts to my nose. My heart sinks right out of my body.

It's Julianna, my cousin.

Why is she here? Last I heard, she was newly mated and still prepping to move to her new pack. I didn't speak to anyone save Eliza, Hollie, and Dad after my disaster of a wedding and Mom's funeral. I wonder if she's fully moved in with her mate, Wyatt, yet. He's a sweet male, intelligent too.

Years ago, we attended the same college for a bit, becoming pretty good friends. If he wasn't hounding me to go solo with my photography, he was frequently found at my Dad's resort eyeing a particular employee...Jules. She's worked there as our masseuse and resident coffee connoisseur for years.

Holding my camera out to the side, I spread my arms wide when she jumps up and wraps her arms around me. Legs faltering for a moment, we squeeze each other tight and find our balance. Apples, oak moss, and pine filter up my nose and squeeze at my heart. She's always smelled like home in the fall. I've only been gone a few days, but I miss it.

"Faith! Oh, my Goddess, I can't believe you are here," she shouts, her alto voice full of excitement. Her small arms hold me in a vice grip.

I giggle and kiss her cheek, and she kisses mine. I pull back to get a good look at her. She's practically glowing with happiness. My smile fades instantly at the reminder of why, and the icky chartreuse ghosts its cold fingers against my chest. It slices in more at the thought of my aunt, her Mom, who is still alive and well. It pings around in my brain. Two things I do not have anymore.

"Oh, hun," she coos, tugging me back into her chest. "It's going to be okay, I promise," she whispers, brushing the hair away from my face. An overwhelming swell of peace eases at her simple words. It's all I've wanted to hear for the past two weeks: that everything is going to be okay. Angrily smashing my knuckles under my eyes, I swipe away each tear that falls. Jules takes my hand in hers, tugging me along with her, and we walk towards the beach party.

"So uh, what are you doing down here?" I ask, hoping it has nothing to do with me. We used to be close when we were younger, but when I started going off on assignments while waiting for my wedding, we grew a little bit apart. Her smile shrinks for a second and then beams again at the squeeze of my hand in hers.

"Well, we came here to visit Wyatt's family, and then we are headed to Florida for an extended mating period to solidify our bond." Her words send a rush of relief flooding through me, *thank goddess.*

"Wyatt has family down here?" I ask. As far as I knew, Wyatt's entire family was on the other side of our borders. Maybe a distant relative? Someone retired, living out in a lone wolf lifestyle?

As we draw closer to the bonfire, an ear-piercing laugh steals my vision towards the sound, and I immediately find the source sitting on... Declan. The busty red-haired female perched on his knee laughs that horribly fake sound again, and is she licking his face? Oh. My. Goddess. She is!

Frustration percolates just below the surface of my self-control, and a pain snakes in my jaw from clenching my teeth. It's like watching a train wreck, but instead of rescuing survivors, you want to ensure they're dead by stabbing them through. She paws at his chest and licks his cheek again. I can't pull my eyes away, can't hide the disgust painting my face, or shake this burning sensation rising in my chest.

Glimpsing my cousin, I'm not at all shocked at the daggers Jules is slicing the bimbos' way.

"Seems there's one in every pack, huh," she whispers, leaning into my shoulder. Her sneer shifts suddenly, morphing into a bright, beaming smile, and in this moment, is almost as misplaced as my uncalled-for, irrational emotions at seeing Declan with that bimbo; these emotions certainly aren't jealousy, even if, for a second, they felt like it.

Tracking the direction of her sudden giddiness, Wyatt bounds up to us, answering her smile with one of his own.

"Faith! Ho-ly shit! I didn't know you were here, Jules said she thought she scented you earlier," he yells, ensuring I hear him over the partygoers and music playing.

Jules smiles, but it falls when she faces me, "I did, and you know I've been texting you for days. Even called a couple times, but you never answered," she accuses. I should have some kind of guilt, but I don't. I haven't felt much in the past couple of weeks. I'm not even mad she's mad at me.

"Uh, yeah, well, this was to be my honeymoon, remember?" I mutter low, trying like hell to hide the heaviness suffocating me.

"Right..." Wyatt drawls, squeezing my shoulder, and drops it quickly. "Listen, I'm sorry you had to go through that. Connor is a fuck-twat and doesn't deserve you. If you asked me, he never did," he replies, malice twisting his signature happy-go-lucky tone into a dark grunt.

His sudden sniffle brings my chin up, meeting his glossy eyes. "I pray your Mom rests peacefully with the Goddess," he adds, swiping a lone tear away. Mom loved Wyatt like the son she never had, and he was always sweet to her, always helping her around the resort and home.

Wyatt leans in, wrapping his arms around me. I steal a glance over his shoulder and roll my eyes as Declan stomps his angry self our way, glaring at me. Great.

15

Declan

The bonfire is hopping, and everyone is here. I spent about an hour introducing everyone to Wyatt and Julianna, saving Nia for dead last to avoid her. With Faith's scent lingering on my clothes, I desperately wanted to enjoy it before her sour, pungent perfume overpowered it. But, Nia, being Nia, she sought me out immediately, came over, took one whiff, and decided to lay her claim like she had one. I should remove her, but I don't have the energy to deal with her drama tonight.

Flik and his sister, Gwen, arrived shortly after, and she was positively distraught at seeing Nia sprawled out all over me. She's been casting me glares all night, and Nia's been taking every opportunity to dig her claws into me and incite Gwen's ire to a permanent glower.

Wyatt's tall frame shadows over me. He hands me a beer and nods at Nia, who promptly scatters off. "Fucking finally," I grumble and take the offered beer, chugging half of it.

"For wanting to be a sigma, Dec, you sure have a pack," Wyatt muses, side-eyeing me while plopping down beside me and smirking.

"Whatever, it's not the same," I retort. I never wanted to be the alpha of my pack back home; it's my birthright, sure, but it isn't something I need. As an alpha with no pack, pretty much a lone wolf, I'm considered a sigma. It's no fault of mine that the betas and others clustered around me when we formed strong bonds of friendship. I don't operate as their leader; they simply flock to me for advice and kinship. It's not the same.

Leaning forward, I face Wyatt a little more, "So you still planning on traipsing around town tomorrow?" Julianna had been buzzing earlier about scenting her cousin and wanted to know if they could go exploring the next day to see if she was here. The chances that her cousin is Faith are good, but I doubt it.

"Yeah, man, you're more than welcome to join us, you could be like our tour guide," he laughs, smacking my shoulder.

* * *

Four beers later, Julianna excitedly bolts upright and takes off down the beach, waving frantically at a passerby. Staring after her determinedly, Wyatt stands up, ever the watchful mate, as the two embrace down the coast. He sits back down a moment later, and I assume it must be her cousin she insisted she'd scented earlier.

That damn tug yanks in me again, I ignore it, and stifle a growl when Nia slides into my lap again. Another tug, and I purposely shove it away, and allow Nia to nuzzle herself into me. I could get laid tonight, and that would settle the compounding desire I have for Faith, because that's all it is.

At the thought of her, I get a powerful punch of her wildflower scent, strong even over the smoke billowing up into the night sky. My dick instantly hardens at the thought of her. I shift uncomfortably.

Nia moans in my ear, "Oh, well hellooo baby," she mewls, sounding more like a dying cat. Mouthwatering, I swallow sharply, and the bile rises in irritation at Nia.

Faith's striking features gleam in the firelight when she steps up to the fray, with Julianna in hand. Her smile drops the instant Nia licks the side of my face.

Tug, tug.

Well, now I can add Faith's irritated scowl to the list of nasty glares I've gotten tonight, while she slices her sharp glower over me.

Tug, tug, tug.

I'm so enraptured with *her*; I barely note Wyatt jumping to his feet. When he takes off in an unbalanced run, my eyes follow, making sure he doesn't fall on his face. A whoosh of air leaves my lungs as he bee-lines for Faith, calling her out by name, like he knows her. *What the—*

Tug, tug, tug...TUG!!!

Nia laughs, so loud and fake, at something someone else says, and then nuzzles into my neck again. I choke on the acid creeping up my throat, guiltily, my view flashes to Faith's. Those copper glowing eyes turn down, sweeping thick lashes over her cheek, a single tear falls, and her lashes flare open. That little, tiny ball of salty liquid sucker punches me straight in the gut.

I watch Wyatt scoop her up into his arms, hugging her, and a burning sensation flares like a wildfire all over. When her eyes join mine again, I'm up and stomping towards her; Nia tips over, landing on her ass in the dense sand with an oomph.

"Dec-lan," she whines, but she's immediately forgotten, my gaze locked on Faith. My feet sink into the sand to get to my cousin, so I can rip his damn hands off what is mine.

Wait, mine?

My breaths come faster and faster, but it feels like I'm being robbed of air. I approach the trio, a muscle along my jaw feathers, and my brow pinches again at the thought of her as mine. That feeling is overpowered with each second Wyatt has his hands on her.

Faith slips out of Wyatt's arms right as I stomp up to the group. She's wearing that 'don't fuck with me smile' and sunburnt again.

Does this woman ever wear sunscreen?

"Dec, have you met Faith yet?" Wyatt asks, breaking my scowl.

"We have unfortunately met Wyatt," Faith replies a bit too dryly.

The fuck does she mean, 'unfortunately?' Sure, we didn't get off to a great start, but I have intentions of fixing that; I'm not a jerk by nature. That is, until her scent drove me insane. It singed the inside of my nose, fried my brain, and hasn't left me normal in a little over 24 hours.

"How the hell do you know Wyatt?" I blurt out, but it's more of a snap. Narrowing my eyes further at her, my teeth grind almost cracking while I wait. In response, her lips twist up in a sneer directed right at me. Well, crap, that is not how I wanted to come off to her again.

What the hell is wrong with me?

Wyatt's eyes bob between us, then he randomly smirks. His face alights with amusement; he's speaking with Julianna through their mate bond. He chuckles and slaps his hand on my shoulder, dragging me towards him. I collide into his side, our ribcages thudding together.

"Well, *cousin*, if you must know, Faith Bennett here is Julianna's cousin, and my former college buddy...*my best friend*," he answers a little more sternly than necessary. Message received, Wyatt. I had been an ass again.

"Wait, what? This is Bennett, *the* Bennett?" I'm stunned, because for years I thought he had been talking about a dude, his friend Bennett from college. Wyatt had never called his friend anything other than Bennett, nor had he indicated gender at all. I guess I just assumed. Assumed wrong, it appears.

Wyatt laughs and gives me an incredulous grin; my cheeks flame a tad cherry. My gaze shifts to Faith, who shies away and turns to Julianna, whispering something behind a cupped hand to her cousin's ear. A beat of awkward silence follows as they both drill their judging stares into me.

Faith and I lock our glares into a battle of wills, and all sound drowns out behind the whooshing in my ears. The longer we stare, the harder my dick gets. The harder my dick gets, the more I want to wrap her up in my arms and take her away somewhere to bury myself under her skin. Julianna's voice penetrates through the waves of humming white noise, but I can't drag my eyes away from Faith.

"Oh, Faith, you must stay...please? We are going for a run soon; I would love to finally meet—" Julianna starts but stops when Faith whips her head and glares at her.

Meet? Meet who?

Julianna looks to Wyatt, and he shakes his head. I feel like I'm a third wheel and in the dark on the 4-1-1 of this shared connection between the three of them. Unscrewing my attitude and face, I soften my eyes from burning into Faith, anxious for her to sense what I need answers to. Tingles spread up my hands and arms when she bites her lower lip and shifts our steamy gazes, matching.

Tug...Tug.

Unbidden, my hand goes to my chest, rubbing at the ache building in intensity from the last time I was around Faith. Wyatt's eyes cut to my hand, narrow, and then cut back to Faith before his brows raise.

"I actually need to upload these photos and work on my article, and I don't want to intrude, but thanks for the invite," she trails off and sweeps an apologetic grimace to Wyatt, and then to Julianna. Her eyes turn glossy, and mine lock on her trembling bottom lip.

Little liar.

Suddenly, Faith shakes her head, spins, and takes off with a silenced whimper floating behind her. Julianna runs after her, shooting a hand over her shoulder, jerking her to a stop not too far from our circle of driftwood.

"Dude, you need to work on your facial reactions better, and your scent." Wyatt fans a hand in front of his face, nose wrinkling. "You smell like a jealous-horny male," he chuckles and turns to keep an eye on his mate. An easy smile smoothes his features as he stares longingly at Julianna.

"Whatever-Wyatt," I grunt, dismissing his very wrong assessment of the situation. I'm not jealous, I don't get jealous. "Why didn't you tell me that Bennett is a girl?"

He curls his lip and pinches his brow in confusion, "Huh? I never once referred to her as he, so that is on you, dude," he says mockingly. He nods in the women's direction, "I'm shocked she came on her honeymoon alone," he says, shoving his hands in his pockets. That gives me pause.

She's married? Something drops inside me and burns a hole through my body. I didn't see a ring on her finger; maybe she's one of those new-age women who doesn't wear one, or if her ink is any indication, she hasn't gotten the ring tattoo yet.

"She's married?" I ask, my voice dropping along with my heart. I have to know, I don't know why I do, just that I do.

"You know why you do, don't lie to yourself or me," Thorin growls and spins to lie back down.

"What? No..." Wyatt blurts, pauses, and turns to me and then back to the women now sitting in the sand watching the waves as the moon rises higher in the night sky. The silver moonlight glints for a moment over Faith and then disappears behind a passing cloud. Wyatt runs a hand through his hair and clears his throat.

"You know, she lost both her fiancé and mother in the same hour...barely over a week ago, and now she's here and working? Leave it to Faith to live up to her name," he says in a dispirited tone, as if he's been grieving too.

"What?! How?" I yelp, but the crushing sadness that is leaking from my chest doesn't come across in my tone at all.

Kicking the toe of my boot at a shell in the sand, I wait for an explanation, and a miserable blanket settles over my heart.

Wyatt shakes his head and walks over to a driftwood log and straddles it so he can keep watch over Julianna and talk with me. I join him after grabbing us each a beer. Handing one to him, I lean in, raising my brows, waiting for an answer.

"I'm surprised you didn't hear about it; it's been all over pack news throughout the country." Wyatt straightens and places his hands in front of him, his face slackens to a serious one, and he clears his throat roughly.

"Ms. Faith Rina Bennett was deserted at the altar by Mr. Connor P. Morgan today, the pair were reportedly to tie the knot after many years of planning and waiting. While the blow comes as a shock, the devastation did not end at the altar."

"Mrs. Alaina Bennett, Luna of the Mystic Keepers pack, was shot in cold blood. Unfortunately, she did not survive her injuries, and according to eyewitnesses, she passed in Ms. Bennett's arms on the steps of the altar. The pack remains in mourning while the culprit is found. In other Mystic Keeper news, Ms. Faith Rina Bennett has finally been named heir apparent; she will take over as alpha when her Father retires later this year," he says in his reporter voice, relaying it as he probably did over pack news.

He gulps a long pull of his beer, swallowing it so hard his Adam's apple bobs. I swear I hear that too.

"I was there Dec, I've never seen such heartache in my life, both Julianna and I scrambled for safety while we watched Faith clutch her Mother's dying body to her chest. That douche, Connor, had strung her along for almost a decade."

"Jules says, her Aunt never wanted Faith to marry someone who wasn't her mate, but you know how Moms can be," he sighs and drags his hand down over his stubbled chin.

"Her wolf, though, holy shit! It was her first shift that day, too, so much in one day. But her wolf, she's absolutely stunning and force to be reckoned with, no wonder her Father waited to name her the next alpha, he wanted everyone to see it for themselves," he adds, sounding almost proud.

"Fucking hell...shit," I reply, I'd been a complete dick to her since yesterday, she was probably drowning her sorrows, and I kicked her out of the bar. I mean, technically, I had a right to, because she was beyond intoxicated. She'd mumbled something about grieving or something on her way out, though, and I'd chucked it up to drunk mumbling.

At my face drawing into what can only be described as 'well fuck' Wyatt says, "Ohh, you fucked up, didn't you?" He smirks and shoves me off the log. I land hard, head thunking into the sand, when a thought slams into me, something he said is ping ponging around. He used her full name. It rings a bell in my head, for what, though? I rack my brain and then it hits me, I burst up, sand flying everywhere.

"Wait, she's Rina Bennett, as in the famous wildlife photographer Rina Bennett?" Wyatt gawks at me like I've grown another head, or I'm a complete idiot, not sure, could be both at this point. Leaning forward in earnest, he chuckles and sighs.

"Yes, the very same, a freelancer for National Geographic, she uses her middle name for all of her articles. I'm honestly shocked she hasn't sprouted out on her own yet; she's an amazing photojournalist."

Yes. She. Is.

He knows that I'm a little obsessed with Rina Bennett's photography, buying out several of her larger prints at galleries. What Wyatt doesn't know is that I have collected every single Nat Geo magazine edition with her photographs on the cover, stored away. So long as he stays out of my closet, my secret is safe.

Somehow, she captures the essence of the people's and animals' souls that she photographs. Her writing, along with it, ensnarls the reader to be right there with her as she journeys across the globe, forever capturing pivotal moments.

After my last episode, when I ended up in a hospital, I found myself staring at a worn-out copy of Nat Geo while waiting for the doc to come in. My fingers flipped through the article she'd written and photographed, falling into the deepest state of calm I've had since coming home from the war.

For the past three years, I've hunted down every copy I can find of her work, dating back to her first one. Reading over and over and admiring her work is what brought me out of, and has kept, my shadowed self. I've also purchased any photographs that were exhibited in art shows. Except I can't tell her that I am practically a fan boy now, not after how I treated her, and then practically assaulted her in the store with my nose.

Hanging my head between my bent knees, for a few seconds before glancing back up, I wish, not for the first time, that I could turn back time. My heart thuds erratically when Julianna stands up and holds out her hand to Faith, the firelight bounces off her glistening cheeks, and the pain that rises from my chest cracks open my rib cage. I'm not just sensing it, I'm experiencing her grief, and that is something I can't deny anymore.

"I'm going to walk Faith home. We will be back for the run, though. I want to make sure she's okay, and after what you told me about the vamps lurking around earlier, I don't want her walking home alone," Wyatt informs me while he pats off the sand covering his legs.

My head whips in his direction, and I jump up.

"No, I'll do it, I need to talk to her anyway, I need to apologize," I say and leave him standing there, mouth agape. "Don't wait up for me, I'll see you later."

Faith's form starts to disappear as she walks down the beach. Bolting into a jog to catch up with her. I zip by Julianna, who gives me such a look like I'm the biggest jerk she's ever met. Great.

16

Faith

J ulianna catches up with me moments after I start to head back to the rental. "Wait up, Faith..." she shouts over the crashing of the waves. Running up to me, she's panting hard and out of breath. I check her over to make sure she's okay.

"Are you alright, Jules?" I ask, and my hand reaches out to her arm. I lean over and find her eyes while she catches her breath.

"Yeah, I'm okay, just tired a lot lately, probably all the traveling," she says sweetly. I still can't believe she's here or that she's mated to one of my good friends, who's, unbeknownst to me, a cousin to Declan of all people. Why did he have to be related to someone I know?

"I'm sorry, I didn't know Declan was Wyatt's cousin until this afternoon. Are you two not friends?" Her sweet and shy demeanor counters her fierceness on most days, unless she gets upset enough that she'll fight you tooth and nail to prove her point or defend someone she cares for. She's going to be an excellent Mom when they decide to become parents.

"It's okay, I'm not upset with either of you, and no, we aren't friends. We got off on the wrong foot. I thought we might be able to be friends, but now, I don't know...it's awkward," I explain, glimpsing the moonlight's reflection bouncing and dancing off the water.

"You know what he is...stop denying it," Sienna links with annoyance thickening the space between our bond.

The ding-ding of a text alert peels through the night air, and both Jules and I jump from the sudden sound. "Sorry, one second, I should check, make sure it's not Dad or Hollie, they've been...well, you know." I tap the screen awake and open the text from Selene back home, a mutual friend of Eliza and me.

Her message knocks the breath from my lungs when several images and a video download one at a time.

Selene: Just thought you should know who to trust...

What in the hell? My eyes double in size, and the burning pain of tearing flesh ripples from my heart and stomach; I pull the screen up closer. There, in all seven photos and video, is Eliza, my best damn friend, all over Connor. One photo shows Connor with his tongue down her throat, another with Eliza on her knees blowing Connor at the pool cabana at our apartment complex. Another depicts the two of them holding each other in the woods right outside the mansion.

Finger frozen above the play button on the video, I swallow hot tears and tap the screen. The camera angle was as if it were taken from outside a window looking in.

"I can't believe you ditched her at the altar. I thought you'd do it sooner, like you promised...did you actually intend on keeping us both?"

Eliza says in her post sex voice, lifting her chin to Connor from his chest as he strokes her hair. "It was complicated, babe," he rasps. When the hell was this taken?

The gasp I hear isn't from me, but from Jules, leaning into my shoulder. "Oh, my goddess, that bitch!" she snaps, her hatred seething. Jules has never liked Eliza, like ever, now I know why. Jules always said she didn't trust her, said she seemed like a 'two-faced, fake ass bitch.' Eliza was always a thorn between Jules and me, and I guess I was blind to her two-facedness since we'd been friends forever.

My whole equilibrium wobbles side to side, shifting the horizon to and fro; I'm going to be sick. Not able to stay upright, I collapse, my ass hitting the semi-hard sand. The stinging in my nose and eyes wreaks havoc on my nerves, I swallow sharply and swipe at my face angrily, while my whole body trembles. Another blow, one I can't take.

Heat surges beneath my skin in a hot flash, sniffling through clogged nostrils, I gulp in air through my mouth, trying to calm myself. Failing, another snotty sniffle chokes me further, and I'm close to losing it. Jules wraps her arms around me, holding me close, letting me fall apart in her arms.

From over her shoulder, both Wyatt and Declan stare at us from their driftwood log near the bonfire. Declan's unblinking gaze soars straight past my walls and pins me in place, breaking in, demanding an explanation exactly like earlier.

Jules rubs circles over my back, and I angle into her for a hug, hiding my face from him. She murmurs that everything will be okay someday, maybe not now, but someday, and that I should get some rest. She adds that she'll come around tomorrow. I nod, and we both get up.

"Wyatt says he'll walk us to your place, so you don't walk alone, but we are going to come back for the run. I wish you would stay, but I understand why you don't," she leans in and brushes tears I didn't know fell away, kissing my cheek.

A fluttering brushes along that sense reserved for prey animals. Spying over Jules' shoulder, Declan heads our way, and that's my cue. I'm up and walking away before common sense freezes me to wait for Wyatt. He's still far enough away that I can get some distance in.

Or so I thought. Declan's huge body thunders over the sand effortlessly, and he's behind me before I can get much further than a few yards.

"Faith, wait," he calls out.

Stopping, I glance back at an angle towards him, frown, and continue walking. I don't have the bandwidth to deal with him. Sienna, however, ignores that memo because she rises and takes control of my body, rooting my feet in the sand.

"You'll thank me later," she says, teasing me, as my entire body comes to a standstill. She preens and sits up straighter, enjoying that she can control my senses and body now.

"You know what, fuck you...just fuck you, okay," I snap, and shiver as a breeze of wind curls up around me, and caresses my body in a swirl of winter.

"Do not be afraid...listen to your heart..." that damn ghostly voice whispers in my ear, kissing my skin, leaving an imprint of a snowflake in its wake. Declan's arms encircle me from the side, warming my frozen heart and skin. I can't think, I can't breathe. With each inhale, his scent overpowers me, his emotions clash against my own; he's worried.

"Mate," Sienna whispers through our link, vocalizing what I denied earlier. I want to deny it now, too, but I can't.

His chest curves around me, and he leans in, placing a gentle kiss on my temple. My hand holding the straps of my backpack falters, and my bag falls beside my feet. I crumble, my whole body shudders in a weird pain at his gentleness, and a blunt jolt slams into my knees as they fall to the ground. Declan follows suit, joining me on the sand. He wraps me into his chest, and while holding me tight, I wholly and utterly fall apart.

My throat is raw, and I've painted Declan's arm in my snot and ugly tears. He's held me the entire time, not once letting go, or uttering a word. His warmth sank into me, and his heartbeat, once it slowed from running after me, quickly lulled me into a peaceful calm, ending my explosion of tears. No one has ever been able to calm me so quickly.

Being in his arms is the equivalent of a warm blanket in the dead of winter. I can't remember the last time I felt so completely safe with a man, other than my Dad.

Blinking the last of my tears away, coming to my senses, I lean back from his chest. "I'm sorry, I'm a mess...I d-don't know what came over me. Thank you, you can go back to your party," I splutter in a croak and rise to my feet, dusting the sand off my legs.

Declan remains on his knees, his shorts stretching over his thick, muscled thighs. His leg tattoos are on full display as he rises beside me. He crooks an arm out, offering me his elbow.

"I'll walk you home, Faith, it's dangerous out at night, and I promised Wyatt, I'd see you home," he reasons, his brows slightly pinched, jaw set the skin over it taut.

"No, you don't need to do that, thank you, though it was a kind offer," I say with a shake of my head. My entire body is on edge and bristling at being told what to do.

"I wasn't offering, and I didn't ask," he states, his lips stretching into a tight line, and reaches for my hand, wrapping it around his arm. Peeking over my shoulder at the bonfire, a lovely emerald snake of jealousy works its way up my neck when I spot the bimbo from earlier.

"Won't your girlfriend get pissed that you're walking home with another female?"

"Girlfriend? " he tsks, shaking his head, face scrunched up in disgust. "She's not my girlfriend."

"Right, well, I am a wolf shifter, so I'll be fine, but thanks," I argue, tugging my hand from his arm.

He shakes his head and retakes my hand, tucking it into the crook of his arm, and pulls me in close to his side. I guess I don't have much choice, he's walking me home. I stumble over the uneven sand, and he stops, glaring at me like I did it on purpose. I huff at him, yanking my hand free and striding off.

Declan, not one to quit so easily or get the memo that I want to be left alone, follows behind like a lost puppy. He follows a foot behind like that for a few miles until I'm mere yards from the base of the stairs of my rental. I turn, starting to tell him, "Hey, so thanks, but-oomph," and smack directly into his chest. How the hell did he get right behind me without me hearing him?

"Fucking hell, do you always do that?"

"Do what?" His devilish smile tells me he probably does.

"Sneak up on people, causing them to hurt themselves?" I dead-pan. His warm, large hands wrap around my arms, sliding up and down, searing my skin in their scorching path.

"Faith, I-I'm sorry about yesterday, and today at the grocery store, I acted like a complete asshole," he says so low, it's like a whisper against my skin. His index finger lifts my chin to his face, and his thumb traces under my bottom lip, pulling it down and releasing it.

Goddess damn it, those gorgeous hazel eyes suck the fight right out of me as they bob back and forth searching for something. They soften, and he leans in closer. Not wanting whatever it is he thinks is going to happen to happen, I shift out of his hold.

"Wyatt told you, didn't he?" I sigh, resigning myself to the pity that is coming. He steps back, crossing his arms, and then, seemingly uncomfortable, he stuffs his hands in his pockets.

"He did, but that's not the main reason I'm apologizing. I shouldn't have behaved like a dominant, irate male with you," he attempts in explanation, yet the lingering hints of pity and grief lace his words, filling me with a hint of doubt.

I roll my eyes and turn back towards the stairs. "You're an alpha, Declan, I wouldn't expect anything less," I say, annoyed, and mosey to the stairs. Wincing when a sharp tug yanks at my chest, I gasp and clutch my shirt, bending forward from the pain. My head pounds, my eyelids squeeze tight from the ache behind them. The excruciating pain tugs again wickedly, as if a taut rope is between us, holding my heart in place.

Declan is by my side in an instant, helping me up. "Hold on to me," he instructs, and he slings one of my arms over his shoulder, becoming my human crutch. After three steps, he gives up and scoops up my legs and carries me bridal style up the steep wooden steps to the porch like he's carrying a sack of feathers.

The pounding in my head lessens, and the pain in my chest ceases, luring my ear to press into his chest. My body is so relaxed that my fingers strain to keep a hold of my backpack straps.

He reaches my front door in no time and keys in the code. I stare at him, my lips parting as the code is accepted. "I used to live here when I first arrived, good thing they haven't changed the code, huh?" he replies.

Stepping into the foyer, he flips the lights on and kicks a leg backwards, slamming the door. Only once we finally reach the kitchen does he set me down, his gaze sweeping the room. The roses are still on the counter, along with the ice bucket that held my champagne from the day before, and the random groceries I haven't put away. A bead of embarrassment forms in my throat at the mess before I can will it away, and it grows almost choking me.

To hide the burning sure to be flooding my cheeks, I curve my shoulder away, slip my backpack onto a chair pushed in under the island, and make my way over to the fridge. Grabbing a water bottle, I tip my head back, glancing out from the door.

"Um, would you like a water?" It's the least I can do since he walked me home and carried me up all those stairs. When he doesn't answer, I step back and peer over my shoulder.

His eyes are glued and glaring at the roses as if they did something unforgivable. His entire body is rigid, and his breathing is nothing more than short pants. What the hell is his problem?

"What?!" he barks, his glower not moving from the roses, a ripple of his aura releases, slamming his pissed off energy into me. Involuntarily, I flinch, swiftly turning away, I snatch us each a bottle, slam the door closed, and march over to him.

Irritated with his hot and cold games, I shove the bottle hard into his chest, the plastic crackling, and his hands automatically grip the top of the bottle. Without even bothering to acknowledge him, I stomp towards my room. He can be an alpha asshat anywhere else, but here.

"Lock the fucking door on your way out, Declan!" I shout. I'm so overwhelmed with emotions that I can't deal with anybody else's. Supposed mate or not, he can go back to his 'not girlfriend' and leave me the hell alone.

"Why are you being such a bitch to our mate?" Sienna growls, stopping me in my tracks.

"Really? Fucking really?" My blood is pumping hard; it thuds in my head while my entire body is engulfed in pain again as the bedroom door slams.

17

⟨⟨⟨⟩⟩⟩

Declan

Lock the fucking door on your way out, Declan!" she snaps at me, jolting me out of wherever my head went. Moments later, a door upstairs

slams. That's one way to say you're not wanted somewhere. I've never been dismissed like this before. Ever. There's a sharp tug pulling at my chest again, and my hand goes to rub it, easing the pain only minutely.

Dammit! It wasn't my intention to hurt her or anger her further. I've messed up again. The blood-red roses on the counter were a stark reminder that she's engaged, or rather had been, and a tepid anger had built near boiling at the thought of another man touching her. That she allowed it angered me unjustly.

"The male will lose both his hands for touching what's ours." Thorin linked, only encouraging the rage. My mind is stuck in an internal battle at the baffling emotions raging through me, when I have no rhyme or reason to logically have them, at least ones I'm willing to admit to.

Cocking my head to the side, I listen to her footsteps pad back and forth above me, and the creaking and whooshing of the shower turning on. The urge to take the stairs two at a time and demand she listen to me is overwhelming. I crack my neck from side to side, relieving some of the pressure. Thorin fights me for control, but I don't allow him; he'll go straight up there and be all dominant alpha up her face. She'd fight back, challenging him. I know she would, if not her, then her wolf. It's in her alpha blood to do it.

With the force of a hurricane, I take one step at a time towards the front door. Closing it softly and locking it, despite the compelling argument Thorin is spouting at me to return to her. As the whirring of the dead bolt slides in and clicks, I round the porch and head down the stairs.

A light flares to life at the bottom, it glows and stretches in the sand. I reach for it, bending down and finding a cellphone. The screen illuminates when my thumb touches it, and I see Faith's bright, beautiful smile next to an older carbon copy version of her.

Deciding this is the worst possible idea ever, but I'm not going to stop, I tap the screen and see that it's locked. From my time in the special forces and having to crack into phones and keypads, I angle the device, it darkens into sleep mode, and I see the prints predominantly in two places. The zero and the two, based on the location. The other fingerprints are too sporadic, indicating her typing.

Well, there's only a handful of possibilities, so I tap the screen to wake and attempt to unlock it.

0220. Nope.

0022. Nope.

0202. Also, nope.

A warning pops up that I only have a few more tries before the phone locks completely. *Shit.*

2002. *Bingo!* I'm in, and without thinking twice about the intrusion, I open her messages. The most recent from Selene was around the time we were still at the bonfire. Tapping it open, my jaw working silently, the muscles pull my ears back, my anger prickles over my scalp. The images I see have to be of Connor.

Closing that thread, I open the next one, from Russell Morgan.

Beta Morgan: Faith, no news on Luna's murder, but the photos you took of her body have helped with the lab results. It has been confirmed that gemstone powder was used. Please call me at your earliest convenience.

Goddess, she took her Mother's autopsy photos?

* * *

Only when I'm about halfway back to the bonfire do I stop snooping through Faith's cellphone for a moment to realize that I have gone through half of her messages. I have no regrets.

I open her email too, which shouldn't be happening either, but a compulsory need is driving me. My vision goes black when the email refreshes and downloads new messages. Scowling, I focus on several unread emails from Connor. Clicking each one open, my desire to shove his legs down his throat and rip them out of his asshole grows.

In each one, he begs her to take him back, that he'd made a mistake. Nope, not happening fucker. With zero remorse, I delete those permanently and block his email. She may kill me when she learns I not only kept her cellphone, but broke into it, snooped, and deleted stuff, but for reasons I'm still not willing to admit, I want to, no need to protect her from this scumbag.

Thumbing through her photos like a stalker, I'm mesmerized by her beauty. Every selfie of her and whoever has to be a sibling brings a smile and a twinge to my gut. She models a certain happiness in every photo, the kind of happiness I've yet to see on her face. I search through highly organized albums, tapping on the unnamed folder, and my heart falls out of my body as hundreds of photos appear.

It's her wedding album, or what should've been. Inside are loads of photos of what must have been the days leading up to it. Rehearsals in a temple, dinners with both families, etc. Selfies and others well posed with her and Connor. A blonde, fake ass, good for nothing, asshole by the looks of it. Swipe after swipe, I keep going, unable to stop, pictures of her in her wedding dress at what must've been her fitting, others of her with her Dad.

My rapid scrolling stops along with my feet at the photo of her with her Mom on the day of her wedding; she's positively radiant in her white gown. In this photo, her Mom stands behind her, fixing the veil, tears beaming in both their eyes while they stare into an ornate floor mirror.

I keep on scrolling, unable to stop myself, and I should have. The next several are video clips. However, the willpower to stop has left my body, and I press play.

The plucking notes of a harp play as her Father walks her down the aisle. The video rotates 180 degrees to Connor, who looks like he swallowed a puffer fish, and then back to her. Faith's smile spreads over her face, alighting it like a diamond catching in the sun, but I see a moment of shadow darkening her radiance.

Her Father hands her over to Connor, and the video stops. In a panic, I rapidly swipe to the following video. Her maid of honor reaches for her bouquet; it's the same girl from the texts Faith received from that Selene girl earlier tonight. The memory of her gut-wrenching pain she'd felt at seeing that betrayal wrecks me all over again in a way I wasn't expecting.

Swallowing down the sharp knives, I keep watching. Faith hands her flowers to the maid of honor, and Connor takes her hands in his. The room grows quiet as the shaman begins their service.

"Do you, Connor Morgan, take Faith Bennett to become your wedded wife, chosen mate, to have and to hold from this day forward?" Any fool watching can tell that something is off, and it takes Faith a minute to figure it out seconds before it happens.

"I... don't," he'd muttered. The prick glances behind him, and then back to her as if he had been searching for someone. "I can't do this, Faith, I can't marry you." He said completely robotic and without emotion whatsoever. An acute pain consumes me, for her, for the pain she's endured, but I don't stop watching. It's like some twisted form of empathy that keeps my eyes glued to the screen.

Connor stepped down from the altar, and a stunned gasp rushed through the seated guests. It's her micro reaction of relief, which I don't even think she was aware of, that glares at me, like a lighthouse in the darkness of a storm.

The video doesn't stop when Connor storms off, but it's when the commotion escalates, and the video remains focused on Faith. She's frozen, her alpha aura starting to bloom out from her, a golden hue fading into a deep violet. Tears race down her cheeks. The shaman tries to comfort her and remove her from the altar. Her Mom is there, and I swallow hard, knowing what's coming next. The person holding her phone hits the ground as the shot rings out, I blink in time with it. The video is jumbled and sideways, but still relatively focused on Faith.

The horror that shadows her features while she clings to her Mother isn't nearly as heart-wrenching as hearing her plead to her Mother to stay with her. I blink away the tears and watch in stunned silence when her Mother cups her cheek.

Something cracks inside me, as the agony cracks in her. I pinch and spread my fingers on the screen, zooming in on Faith. Her earth brown eyes darken to a dark espresso, and her pain, visible, radiates out in a rainbow of a broken aura. The person holding her phone gasps, and her Father tenderly scoops up his Luna and departs.

What happens next has Thorin stirring and leaping forward in my conscience, snapping his maw. He knows it's coming, we both do. We both are sensing it. A painful expression pinches her face as every bone in her body breaks. Her body slumps forward, and she shifts into her wolf.

By the Goddess, she has a beautiful wolf, the same as her human self. Her wolf's pelt, a sable of russet brown, is dappled throughout with bits of gray and white. Her gold and silver aura spins out around her, swirling with starlight and flecks of white and blue. I've never seen an aura like that before in my life.

The video cuts out then. I squint back down the beach to where her rental is, miles away now, and then back towards the fire. Clicking the phone to sleep, I pocket it and stride back to the logs around the fire.

"Hey, you okay? Did Faith get back okay?" Julianna asks as she sits down beside me. In my stupor, I nod yes and continue to stare off into the flames. "Everyone is ready to go when you are," she adds. I stare past her, unblinking.

Wyatt's hand clamps onto my shoulder, my muscles tense and re-lease, he knows me better than anyone else here, and where my mind has gone. He sighs and then holds his hand out for Julianna.

"Come, love, he's not going to run tonight, but I promise we will be here long enough for you to meet Thorin. Right now, Dec needs to walk his sorry ass home and go to fucking bed," he says pointedly, mostly to me by his intonation.

"Yes, Dad," I reply dryly, still zoned in on the flames.

A hiss and whoosh follow a plume of smoke and steam. Fluttering my lids at the bite from the smoke, I find Flik and Rhett dousing the fire with buckets of seawater, and everyone else stripping down, while others shift into their wolves. Thorin doesn't bother to nudge me into shifting. He merely sits there, tail swishing back and forth at the front of my consciousness, the rest of my body fading into numbness.

* * *

The early morning light streaks across the midnight sky when my feet finally reach the wooden steps to my house. I'd sat outside on the driftwood log all night, ruminating over what I'd watched and what I'd gleaned from snooping through her phone some more. We have so much in common, and yet we are so far from being even remotely friends.

I end up in my kitchen staring at the fresh brew in the coffee pot. Someone's awake, because I sure as hell didn't set the auto start on it. I never think that far ahead. Wyatt's smoky oak and amber scent perfumes the kitchen, growing heavier in the space, wrinkling my nose at his intrusion, I turn to see him glaring at me.

"You just get in," he says, his glare morphing to concern. I nod and pour myself a cup of coffee. Settling in at the table in the corner, I stare out at the beach, watching the gulls swooping and diving into the waves.

"We are headed over to Faith's for the day, you wanna come with?" My eyes swing in his direction, scanning over him, dressed in jeans and a dark blue V-neck.

"No, I should head over and get to work at the bar. I planned to take a ride later, but I think I'll stay in for the day, maybe take a nap."

Wyatt leans back before he shoves away from the table, quirking a brow at me, and then sighs. "Alright then, see you at dinner, Cuz." He leaves, allowing me to wallow in my well-deserved stupor.

18

Faith

Remember how I said the worst heartaches are the ones you don't see coming. Well, I lied. The ones that hurt the most are the ones you do see coming, but deny, and they're usually guided with a bit of false happiness from the start too.

Declan's my mate. My mate...yeah. That small, wishful part of me knew the moment we met, but I'd like to say I was in denial, or shock at the irony. It had nothing to do with the ghostly voice urging me to listen to my stupid heart.

Sienna scolded me for hours after kicking him out, not letting me sleep. I denied it over and over again until the incessant burning tug wouldn't allow me to.

He's my mate, and somehow, I know he'll reject me too, just like Connor did. I can't explain it, but my sixth or perhaps seventh sense tingles in the back of my mind, prodding me to prepare myself.

Shortly after I woke up this morning, following another icy shower, I started packing. I had no plans to stick around and be hurt. The doorbell rings when I'm halfway down the stairs, suitcase in tow.

A zing of anxiety flutters over my chest and plummets down into my stomach. No way he'd be here this early in the morning, or maybe?

No. Sneaking a glance at my watch, it's early, but figuring it's probably Jules, the zing dissipates.

Meandering over to the door, I paste a smile on my face and pull it open to not only Jules, but Wyatt too. I know how I look right now, no less than a hot mess with express tickets to hell, but I don't care, and based on the acceptance written on their faces, they know it too.

Pity and sympathy paint their expressions for a few seconds too long, serving only to irritate me. The pair embraces me and, in doing so, envelops their warm love around me, dissipating my irritation.

Leaving the short hallway, we make our way to the kitchen. Wyatt slows and skims over my suitcases and my disheveled appearance again. "You going somewhere, Faith?"

I glare at him over my shoulder, forcing my lips to quirk into a small smile. "Yeah, home." His brows pinch, wrinkling his forehead, and he shakes his head.

"Wait, what? How come? Didn't you just get here?" Jules asks a mile a minute, concern dripping from her sing-song voice. My heart hurts from a preconceived pain, but I can't explain this, especially to them.

Attempting my best customer service smile, I clear my throat. "Yeah, well, I finished up my assignment yesterday, and Dad needs me to assist with some pack business...besides, coming on my honeymoon alone hasn't exactly gone the way I thought it would..." I trail off, partially lying.

To avoid seeing their worry, I turn away to the living room. The bright blues and grays mixed with pops of yellow from the throw pillows, and watercolor paintings of hydrangeas bring an instant sort of happiness, but now it's as if I got gypped; I didn't even get a chance to enjoy this space yet.

Wyatt narrows his eyes at me, not believing a word out of my mouth. He has always been one to deduce the truth without asking too many questions. I blame the investigative reporter in him.

Bring it on, Wyatt, I'm in a mood.

"Oh," my cousin says, a little sad, "I hoped to spend a couple of days with you before we left, but okay, when do you leave?" Jules replies, a twinge of her fallen spirit impales me with guilt. I hate that I've made her upset, and if I spend a day with her, maybe our relationship will grow and blossom back to what it once was.

"Uh-m, well, I was getting ready to head out soon, but I guess I can wait one more day. What would you like to do?"

A sharp clap echoes in the foyer. Jules jumps up and twirls to Wyatt, planting a kiss on his lips before spinning back to me, dragging me to the kitchen. She opens each cabinet without asking me.

Finding the coffee and espresso beans, she finagles the espresso machine out and grinds the beans while she hums a tune only, she knows. Wyatt saunters up to me, and we both take a seat at the counter, watching Jules.

"She's really in her element, isn't she?" I supply in hopes he won't ask any more questions now that I've relented to staying one more day. He'd been on his phone a moment ago, I'm sure texting Declan. I don't think he bothered to hide what he was doing based on the reaction on his face.

Wyatt isn't a fool; he's always been excellent at reading people and their emotional states, seeing what others don't or won't admit to. Lucky for him, he gets both sides unfiltered. He nudges my shoulder with his, forcing me to receive his gaze.

"Yeah, she is, but what's got you running from yours?" Well, damn it, there goes all my hopes of not having this conversation; they leaped right out the window, committing hope-icide. I honestly can't answer that question without enduring more of them. Not sure if I even want to.

He fiddles with his phone again, waiting for my answer. I scan between him and Jules a few times, wishing I had what they had, but I know deep down I won't. Sometime during my nine years with Connor, I lost myself to the constant internal battle and let a part of myself die to keep him happy, to keep the peace. How had I let myself fall that deeply into a sleep-like state, that I was blind to everything?

And now, I'm one more failure closer to the edge of what's holding me together. There's too much on my plate, with my Mom's murder, the vampires being involved, and taking over the majority of the pack business as soon as I return home.

From being here, and taking on what could be my last assignment to Declan? I'm not ready to admit any of that. What does he expect me to say? Oh, hey, you know how you mated my cousin, well, I'm mated to yours...and I'm pretty sure Declan would rather drink battery acid than be tied to me for the rest of his long life if his actions around me give any indication. Too hot and then too cold, and frankly? I'm too emotional right now not to react poorly. See? I can admit some things to myself anyway...kind of.

However, I'm almost positive that Declan's kindness last night was from pity, not because he cared. My attraction to him? Well, as supernaturals, we can be sexually primed up beasts; it's in our nature. The Goddess links her children to have the best chance at producing a strong and long bloodline, and it makes sense, I guess. I can't help but think, *what am I, for him?* I'm new meat, that's what, fresh juicy steak so to speak, someone different than his day to day, like that bimbo.

I'm sure she tastes like gristle.

Even if we accepted the bond, he would have to leave here and travel north with me to be introduced to my Father and ask for his blessing, and then I'd travel with him to wherever his pack is for his parents' blessing. Then, barring no interference from the council, both of our packs would need to sort out any issues that may need settling and then join the two packs through our bond. A successful joining of packs hasn't occurred in centuries, and those mates ultimately had to live separately, creating a new set of problems. I don't want that.

Jules slides a steaming mug of what appears to be a latte towards me. Cradling it, the heat circulates through the ceramic into my palm. Lifting it slowly to my lips, I blow on it so as not to scald my tongue.

A loud pounding knock on the front door induces a whole-body flinch. I swallow a gulp of the piping hot liquid, burning my tongue and the roof of my mouth. "Shit, that is hot."

Both Jules and Wyatt give me an incredulous look before Wyatt scoots his stool back and answers the door. Low murmuring is indiscernible this far away, but the sweet sea salt, amber, and driftwood with hints of home float into the kitchen, my nostrils flare, and my heart thuds harder in my chest. Why does he have to be here? And why does the man have to smell so damn good, almost akin to an illicit drug? A person could get addicted to it. No, no bad Faith!

Wyatt walks in with Declan by his side. I glare at Wyatt, "You ratted me out to him, didn't you?" I ask defeatedly, and he shrugs with a smirk. My placating smile falls: he is so dead. My lips roll in and out, thinning the longer I glare at Wyatt and then at Declan.

Jules' humming stops, and I take in Wyatt's cousin, who's sporting quite the ragamuffin outfit today. Jeans slung low over his hips, and his wrinkled black V-neck clings to his sculpted body, barely flattening out the creases. Bits of his tattoos crawl up from his exposed chest, wrapping around his neck. His dark locks are in disarray as if he's been raking his fingers through them and pulling them straight up, letting them fall where they may.

"He did...we need to talk, Faith, it's important," Declan says, his voice rolls over that dirt road of sexy gravel and skims over my skin like a fine coating of sweat. Get a girl a fan first, sheesh.

Fine then, if I am going to be rejected, he can say it in front of our family. "Go ahead then, I have nothing to hide from either of them. I'm ready, say whatever it is you came to say," I retort, building a fortress around my heart, malice dripping from each word. My eyes close of their own accord, not wanting to see the relief on his face when he says the words I don't want to hear but know I will.

Declan clears his throat, coughing. "I-um huh?" he asks, confused. I open my eyes in time to watch his face contort into bewilderment.

"What do you mean, huh? You really must be dense. Let me help you out. If you are going to reject me, do it now and then leave. I promise I will accept if I can speak through the pain, if not, I'll do it the moment I am able," I ramble out in frustration.

Jules and Wyatt both gasp and find one another to hold on to. They know of the pain that will come because the reverse is said to be twice as painful as the pure joy when a pair accepts their bond.

If he doesn't do it, I don't know if I'll be able to; I don't think Sienna would let me either, but I'll respect his wishes if that's what he desires.

"You're right, I won't let you do something so monumentally stupid and asinine...why don't you think he deserves you?" Sienna says sharply, raging her displeasure through our link.

"Because he doesn't deserve my brokenness, okay?" I reply and block her for now.

My gaze zeroes in on him, his eyes flash gold, and then back to hazel. His face scrunches up, and a tear slips down his face. Why is he not saying it?

"Faith, why would you think—" he begins and takes a step towards me. I move, a polar opposite magnet from him, and flee to the screen door of the porch. I white knuckle the handle and yank it open, bursting through it. My body swan dives forward, and I grip the center of my shirt, panting to steal some breath.

Why won't he do it and get it over with? I know he can sense I'm not good enough for him, which would eventually cause him nothing but dissatisfaction and disappointment. I did it with Connor, so why not with him? I'd racked up a black star tally with the Goddess since she'd seen fit to allow my wolf to remain hidden and silent for years until I was completely a shattered shell. That's what I'm telling myself.

My chest heaves in air, my throat closes, the world around me spins in an off-kilter carnival ride. I make it to the porch swing, praying I can manage to climb into it before I keel over. One wobbly step is as far as I make it before a hot hand runs up my spine.

"Here...let me help you," Declan's baritone vibrates my bones.

"No, I've got it," I snap, and try to shrug away. He either needs to say the words of rejection and then leave or just leave. We can do this later. Maybe it will work over email?

A growl leaves Declan's lips, and then I'm being lifted and cradled into his warm chest. He deposits me onto the swing and moves a throw pillow to sit beside me. Surprise crosses my features that our combined weight doesn't crash the swing to the porch.

"Why do you think I'd reject you?" He cuts right to the chase, but his voice is soft, a placating tactic used to calm a jumpy person.

My head turns down and away, and a traitorous tear streaks over my flame-red cheek. Scraping it, I swipe the tear away a little more roughly than I intended. His palm rests on my bent leg, his heat seeping into my skin, luring me into his trap.

"Faith."

Refusing to focus on him and fall for the farce before the hurt, I scan the beach over my shoulder and watch the seagulls scamper across the sand, avoiding the rushing tide.

I know the feeling, lil' ones.

"Faith, damn it, look at me," he demands, sounding more annoyed than he did before. Fiddling with the hem of my shirt, I summon my voice to work without cracking.

"There's no reason for me to look at you, Declan. Say what you need to and then go, I can take it, I'm a grown ass woman," I croak out, entirely unconvincingly, and now I'm pissed that I sound so weak. I pulled on a loose thread, unraveling a length of stitching, and found the weak spot.

Declan sighs and tugs at my arm, forcing me to face him. I glare, lips thinning into a straight line. Our eyes connect and lock, strengthening the bond; the pull is unbearable to resist. It's a warm hug on a cold day, an icy lake in the hottest summer, and a promise of more. My heart is racing, sweat beads across my brow, I lick my lips, and swallow harshly.

His eyes widen at the movement, his weight shifting, and he leans away. He shoots up from the swing, causing it to sway angrily back and forth. Declan walks away backwards, shaking his head, "The mate bon-no...fuck...I don't—" he mumbles, his eyes locking with mine once more.

His nostrils flare, breathing in my scent again, but all I hear is the "I don't" that he was starting to say. *I don't want this; I don't want you.*

The all too familiar pang hits me square in the chest and sinks into my stomach. He's no different than Connor, and I am not shockingly wanted again. This is why I just wanted him to reject me outright, so I wouldn't have to hear the reasons or wait for him to figure out that I'm worthless.

Those hazel orbs bob back and forth over me, and what I already knew would happen takes root within him. The moment he figures out what I'm asking for, he turns away. His arms are holding his weight as he leans on the white wood railing that wraps around the porch.

"Yeah...I know. So, say your rejection and be done with it," I rasp, and gulp down the rapidly producing saliva pooling in the recesses of my mouth.

My vision bores into his back while I wait with bated breath for the words of rejection to slip from his strikingly sexy, chiseled lips. Instead of the rejection I thought was coming, he reaches into his back pocket and retrieves a phone, his arm stretches behind him holding it out to me.

"You dropped this. I found it after you kicked me out last night, didn't think you wanted to see me then, so I waited until morning," he mutters, his tone sounding despondent.

On unsure legs, I shove off the swing and retrieve it without touching his skin. The more we touch, the worse the rejection is going to be when he finally grows the balls to do it. I scan through my messages and catch him moving towards the stairs to the beach. My heart races. Where is he going?

"Wait, aren't you going to say it?" Declan peers over his shoulder, his hazel eyes glassy, the outside corners turned down and shakes his head.

"No, I have nothing to say," he supplies and then races down the steps, landing on the sand in record time. My gaping eyes follow him as he sprints across the hot sand, small waves of it fling up into the air after each foot pounds into it.

19

Declan

What the actual fuck just happened?

She wants me to reject her. I've tried to deny any acknowledgment of the bond trying to form between us, but I'm only lying to myself the more I deny it. That is, until she begged me to reject her, and I felt a crushing agony from her not wanting me. Like she knows I'm not good enough for her and wants to prove it by making me reject her.

Fuck that.

No, she's probably right. I purposely ignored all the signs of the bond earlier, pushing her away by being an asshole, because I knew I'd end up destroying her. Right now, the bond is weak as we dance around one another, avoiding and fighting it even as it forces us closer. And being as weak as it is, it would be easy to reject her; she wants it, but why? I know why I don't want a mate, and it's more of a need born out of protection from me, than me not having the desire to want one. But fuck.

It chapped my ass when she demanded I reject her. I was so flabbergasted I couldn't even get my thoughts into words and jumbled everything up, and by the confused hurt on her face, she mistook it as something else entirely.

And what did I do instead of attempting to fix it? I reigned in my anger at her wanting to cast me off and ran.

"Stop berating yourself like a coward right now and go back to our mate, accept the bond, her wolf wants us...I know it." Thorin growls, agitated, that I'm still racing down the beach back to my house. The bond pulls on me harder the farther I get away from her.

Thorin is irate and keeps attempting to take control of my body, and I continue to refuse. The desire to shove him back down and keep him from emerging is tempting with each demand he is making for me to return to Faith.

As I slow to a walk, an incessant bell dings repeatedly from my cell. I fish the obnoxious device out of my pocket and see several missed texts and calls from Wyatt. Before I can reply, he calls again. Rolling my eyes in frustration, I answer.

"What?!" I grit out, the cords in my neck tightening and pulsing.

"What do you mean, what? Get your ass back here, you either need to accept the bond or reject her before she leaves," Wyatt rushes, his breathing harsh, his voice angry and demanding. "She's leaving Dec, loading up her luggage as we speak. Jules is trying to stop her, trying to encourage her to stay...please come back," he says, the panic and worry edging over his stern tone.

"She wants me to reject her," I mutter, I can't get the words out without—

"I know, but you really shouldn't, and yeah, I know why you don't want one, but she *does*, well, did. She waited a decade for her mate, all while hoping it was Connor, only to have her heart ripped out of her chest. Until her wolf surfaced and she came here, finds her mate, which is you, by the way. It doesn't make sense as to why she would want a rejection now," he replies, worry threading through his tone.

A sensation of my heart dropping into my stomach shudders through my body, and I can't decipher if it's my emotions or hers. My feet are moving on their own accord, taking the stairs to my house two at a time.

"A decade, why?"

Wyatt sighs so loud, it's practically a yell in my ears. "Tell him he needs to come get his fucking truck. I want to leave," Faith's lyrical voice floats over the line, and my body freezes. She really intends to leave before settling this. I should leave my truck there. I didn't even remember I'd driven over when I made my hasty escape.

"No, I'll get it when I am damn well and ready." I bark, pressing my tongue to the back of my teeth.

"Ugh, Dec..." Wyatt pauses. "He says he'll come back later and get it...will you come inside so we can talk, please?" He responds to Faith. He's fumbling with something, probably her luggage. The wheels roll over the porch, thunking over the warped boards of the steps. The creak and slamming of a door over the line causes me to flinch.

"Okay, sorry, I'm inside now, what was I saying?" he pauses, and I swear I can hear his brain working its cogs. "Oh, right, she's waited a decade, because her parents didn't want her to marry Connor unless he was her mate. Her Dad explained to me once that they wanted Faith to be bonded with a true mate bond rather than a chosen mate. It's why their mate- no farce of a wedding...was stalled for so long, well, one reason anyways."

Okay, that makes some sense, but it still doesn't explain why we never picked up on each other; our packs are neighbors for Pete's sake. I'm about to say this when he sucks in a long breath.

"If you think about it, it makes sense why you two never found each other sooner though, you were gone for so long in the Army and you then moved down here, and she was without her wolf when you were near one another before that," he finishes, almost on a high from figuring it out. "I guess that also explains your obsession with—" he starts, but I don't even want to try to connect those dots.

"What? Wyatt, you're gonna have to fill me in later..." I fade off with so many questions that need answers, and my anxiety about the future pushes me into a black, spiraling abyss.

Dammit all to hell, a decade? All those years growing up, going to functions at each other's packs, we could've recognized one another sooner if only her wolf hadn't hidden away. I can't even recall if I'd met her when we were younger. I knew of the Mystic Keeper's alphas' daughters, but more as a formality, the responsibility of being a leader in my pack. But then I'd joined the Army and came back broken and then ran.

"Wyatt, I need time to think... tell her I'll be by later," I reply and end the call. Pacing over my porch, my ass lands on the padded patio chair in a huff.

A mate.

I have a mate.

I have a fucking mate who doesn't want me.

"I've been telling you this since I scented her, you never listen..." Thorin says not so nicely again through our link. I'm two seconds from shutting it down for the foreseeable future if he doesn't quit.

A mate, something I wanted, but knew would create nothing but heartache if I couldn't get my shit together and mend the broken pieces of my soul back together.

It could be worse; she could be an ugly, bitchy, annoyance who rejected me first, but she's not.

Wow, where did those thoughts come from?

Faith is anything but. Her natural beauty is an affinity most wish for and try to achieve with fancy cosmetics; it shines from within. I gathered as much over the night while dwelling on every article I could recall she'd written. She exudes passion through her caring nature, at least I think she does, based on her descriptions and the photos she takes, which reveal what she's seeking from life, because she showcases it in every single one. I'd know, I have them all.

A bubble of doubt surfaces. Does she not want a bond after what Connor did to her? Is she as unsure as I am?

Tug, tug, tug, tug...

My thoughts race through my brain at warp speed, flickering images of what I'd watched from her phone. Connor's rejection of their vows to her. And then it slams into me. I'd uttered almost the exact phrase, and then did the same damn thing he did, ran off. Fuck!

More thoughts crash together: her best friend's betrayal, her Mom being murdered. Then, as that vampire's last words to Thorin flash into my mind, an alarming question resurfaces, and everything else goes quiet.

Why on earth does Benedict want her?

Benedict is an epic and apathetic asshole, but a smart one with loads of patience. Known to be a born vampire, supposedly a primordial of his species, a genuine threat to the werewolf and other shifter communities. He alone can decimate an entire pack, so why would one wolf be the object of his desires?

My gut's telling me that they'll continue to hunt her down until she either is trapped and caught or she surrenders to him.

"Protect our mate Declan, if nothing else, keep her safe," Thorin grumbles through our bond again.

Anxiety-heavy lids slide over my dry eyes. I toss an arm over for good measure to block out the sunlight. The white noise of the ocean drowns out all other sounds. I'm too overwhelmed to think.

20

Faith

An unexpected sense of relief settles in my stomach as Declan's image gets smaller and smaller the further away he runs. When his form entirely disappears, I turn and stride back inside to find both Wyatt and Jules curled up on the sofa speaking in hushed voices.

Intending to make a light breakfast and then load my luggage, I make it about five feet before Jules sighs and wraps her arms around my waist from behind.

"I can't believe you found your mate...don't worry, he will be back," she murmurs. She's always been a hopeless romantic. I pat her clasped hands over my belly, and she releases me.

I fix my sight on her, shaking my head, "I don't want him too unless it's to break our bond," I say, my voice a crackling monotone. Jules's round eyes flare wide, and a hand shoots up to cover her gasp. I snag a toaster pastry from the freezer and pop it in the toaster oven.

Grabbing my keys, I drag one suitcase out and prop it near my jeep, returning for the other two quickly. Opening the back of the cargo area, I reach for one suitcase when Wyatt approaches.

"Faith, come on now, hang tight and wait. Please come back inside," he says, pausing to wait for my response. I don't offer any. He strolls over languidly and rests a hand atop a handle of one of the suitcases. Silently challenging each other in a stare off, this isn't the first time we've stared one another down and probably won't be the last. Today, though, I won't be the first to break.

"Talk to me, Faith. Why in all hells do you want to break a bond that you haven't even given a chance?" I turn away at his question and swipe an errant tear away, with no plans on answering because frankly, I don't know myself. I glance back at him to see him angled away from me, phone in hand. Wyatt's fingers fly over the screen, probably texting Declan. While he most likely rants to him, he frequently flicks his attention between me and his phone.

Shaking my head at him, he glares and lifts it to his ear. I grab a suitcase, lugging it to the back of my jeep. The sad tone of his voice as he calls Declan tingles across my skin, and an unease builds in my gut.

After loading in two suitcases, I crawl out of the back of my jeep and spot Declan's truck blocking the entire driveway with its massive size. I yell to Wyatt, knowing he's still on the phone with Declan, that his cousin needs to "come get his fucking truck."

Thankfully, Wyatt obliges me and relays the message. However, he yanks the suitcase he's had a hold of for the past ten minutes and rushes inside like he's a small child stealing candy. I glare after him.

* * *

The hours have ticked by, and still Declan has made no effort to retrieve his truck. Wyatt and Jules managed to sneak my luggage back inside when I curled up on the sofa and passed out. Jules mostly unpacked everything into the primary bedroom, too. She'd cleaned up the kitchen while Wyatt went to check on Declan, grab some clothes for them to stay over, and then head to Ringer Bros for ingredients for the dinner that he plans on cooking for us.

Much to Jules' delight and my misery, I'd resigned to staying at least until they depart for the rest of their travels. Despite my earlier declarations, I hadn't completed my assignment, and now I'm sitting on the porch with my laptop, alternating between editing the article and tweaking a photo here and there.

A cup of coffee in hand and my earbuds blaring my playlist in my ears, I am in my element. I have a steady flow going on, completely zoned in. Pulling out one earbud, my head rolls side to side to loosen the tension in my neck, and a slight crack pops the mostly silent area of the porch.

"A—" a low voice says, and I jump practically out of my skin. Declan appears, hands raised in the air. "Sorry, didn't mean to startle you. I was going to say a chiropractor would probably be able to release that for you...unless it's tension, then perhaps a masseuse," his voice rakes across my skin, leaving a path of goosebumps and the hairs on my neck standing up on end. His presence is akin to a lightning storm, with static pricking everything in sight.

My eyes sweep up from my laptop, taking in the beast of a man standing before me, and before I can stop the garbage from spilling, my mouth opens, and I ask, "You offering?"

Declan grins, all refreshed in a solid black button-up, with the sleeves rolled to his biceps. I don't understand why men do that, just wear a short-sleeve one, not that I'm complaining about how drop-dead sexy he looks right now, though.

What is wrong with me?

He's here to reject our bond, so we both can get on with our lives. I don't need to be drooling over him, but here my eyes go wandering over him again.

Those dark wash jeans fit snuggly around his oh so thickly muscled thighs, and if I had to guess, his ass too, damn my eyes can't break away. Spruce and amber with a hint of salted driftwood scent, it snakes its way to my nose.

Declan's eyes widen a fraction when he catches me inhaling. I need to ignore him, not fantasizing about anything he could do with those arms and thighs...those hands. I return my attention to the draft of my article, anxious that my cheeks and ears aren't as red as they seem.

"Faith, while I'd love nothing more than to make your cheeks flush more by offering to relieve your tension, we need to talk," Declan supplies, leaning against the railing. Almost in the same positions we were hours ago, the deja vu hits hard, and with it, the ache in my chest at why he's here returns.

"Speak then, I can't promise I'll listen," I snap. I shouldn't be acting like such a bitch, he's not yelling at me or saying anything cruel, at least not yet. Declan shifts, then before I know it, he's joined me on the swing, not so subtly snooping at my work.

"I, Declan Reed McCormick..." I hear him speaking the words I knew he would say, but then my vision blurs and a buzzing fills my ears. Subconsciously, I rub at my chest, preparing for the pain to come.

When I am sure he's stopped speaking, even though I hadn't heard anything past his name. I automatically reply, full well knowing the pain that is about to come.

"I, Faith Rina Bennett, accept-" I rasp, not able to fully finish accepting his rejection. Except the pain I'm waiting for doesn't peel through my skin. Instead, a warm, tingling sensation fills my chest, and then my mind is bombarded with conflicting emotions, and Sienna is howling with joy.

My head snaps to the right, discovering his stunned expression. "Wait...what happened?" My horrified reaction has to be amusing to him, because he stares at me, bewildered.

"What do you mean...I accepted our bond, and then you accepted it as well."

Oh no. No! No, no, no...this can't be happening.

When he decides later to abolish this bond, the rejection pain is going to be ten times worse. And he will discard me, I'm broken and discarded goods, why on earth would he want me? I have a weak bond with my wolf, and I have no real idea what I am doing with my life. Even Connor said I was a disgrace of a fiancé, and I'd almost married him...the hell is wrong with me? What if Declan doesn't want to go back with me to meet my pack? My Dad will approve of him, I'm sure;

this is all he and Mom ever wanted for me. But what if Declan doesn't? Why did he accept it?

A creaking noise behind me snags my attention, and then quick footsteps fade away, damn Wyatt and Jules eavesdropping. Knowing my cousin, it was probably her idea too; she was always hiding in corners listening in to everything when we were kids. They're most likely over the moon with this news.

Setting my laptop aside, I rise from the swing away from him. Leaning over the railing, the dizzying emotions crash over me, and I squeeze my eyes closed. I inhale long and steady. My pulse is raging in my veins, hammering inside my skull. Sorting out the noise of my mind, I listen to the waves crashing to shore, the small sandpipers chirping, the gulls overhead calling, the oat grasses dancing in the light breeze.

The thudding of my heart manages to even out once again, and my breaths ease back to normal, and I peel my lids open. Declan's heat seeps in behind me as he draws closer. That taut rope slackens, coiling into a pile with each step he takes towards me.

Without moving my head, I see his hand reaching out from my peripheral vision. I shrug away, shifting my body closer to the post. Heat floods my body, head to toe, so warm a prickling of sweat in every pore pebbles.

"Faith, look at me," he commands, using his aura on me.

Oh no, he did not!

He has some audacity. I'm his mate, not just another pack member. What he's doing is unfair; no matter my alpha status, he can force me to comply with his command.

So nice.

It's bullshit.

Instinctually, my head tilts, baring my neck to him, but I refuse to budge. I summon all of my strength to fight against his command. He ignores my defiance and gathers me in his arms, spinning me to face him. Pinching my chin, he forces my glare up. If I weren't so pissed and confused, I'd melt right now. I close my eyes once again in rebellion.

"Faith, please don't make me use it again. I want us to be equals," he murmurs, his tone a balm against my bubbling anger.

"Bullshit, if you did, then you shouldn't have used that on me in the first place," I say through clenched teeth. The steady rhythm of his breath tickles my skin, his grip loosens the slightest bit, but he doesn't move away. The muscles in his chest tense, and he leans in more.

"Please," he pleads, and this time he sounds sincere.

Deliberately slow, I open my eyes, glaring. "Thank you," he offers for my compliance.

"Why didn't you reject me? You should've rejected me," I rasp, my voice hoarse and breathy. We're so close our lips are millimeters from touching. Declan's beguiling hazel irises bob and narrow on me.

"Why? Because there is no reason to impart that sort of pain on anyone, but honestly? I don't know, okay, I didn't wa—" What? He doesn't know why?

He's too close, way too close, it's making my chest tight. I need space from him; the proximity is feeding the bond, and if he is to break it later when he comes to his senses, it will only be worse.

Warm fingers trace up my side, gripping my waist before they yank me against his hard body. "Will you come with me for a little bit?" His voice, low and sensual against the shell of my ear, shudders through me. The stubble on his chin tickles the column of my neck as he rubs it up and into my hair.

His grip loosens when my body flinches, "Sorry," he whispers, and slowly, almost hesitantly, his hands withdraw from my waist. The loss of his heat is immediate, a fissure of spider webbing cracks across a frozen lake, threatens to break and drown me in the well of sorrow buried deep in my soul. I turn, staring at him, old dreams and desires fight against what I've lived with knowing.

Those golden hazel eyes turn down at the sides, he backs away from me, and heads back down the steep stairs to the shore. I track his movements, my eyes never leaving his form. He stops at the bottom and glances back, grief and sadness casting a shadow over his handsome face. For reasons I don't want to dissect, my feet move before he finishes turning back.

Faster than I've ever moved, I fly down the stairs, jumping the last six, landing in a spray of sand. Declan stops but doesn't turn around; his breathing is frozen while I approach him.

"So where are we going?" Hazel eyes slice into my soul before he smiles at my question and then extends a hand. Heart thudding in my chest, I blink and then watch in a haze as my fingers curl around his. We leave footprints in the sand, silently holding onto one another.

Neither of us has uttered a word this whole time. When we walk up to and inside his garage, his fingers unlace from mine, and he pulls away, the loss messing with my head. He steps up the one stair, and opening the door, he calls over his shoulder, "gotta grab a few things."

Left alone, the gnawing thoughts stretch their spindly claws ready to strike. Shaking them away, my eyes go wide, taking everything in. It's surprisingly spotless, with glossy concrete floors, immaculate work benches with tools laid out, each in its own space.

The Harley Davidson, though, now that's something else. It's an older model, black, with black flames ghosting over the gas tank and trim. It's low to the ground and has stunning chrome throughout. My features reflect in its polished metals, and my fingers trace down the handlebars to the tank. I'm so wrapped up in the details of this beautiful machine, I barely notice the faint smell of woods and amber mixing with the motor oil and hints of gasoline.

"She's a 1979 FXS low rider, with a Shovel head motor. I have others back home, but this one was my first and my favorite baby," Declan offers before I even lift my eyes to his. He holds out one of two helmets and a leather jacket towards me, already wearing his. He puts down the other helmet and holds up the shoulders of the smaller jacket up to me.

The black leather is simple in its cut, stainless steel zippers, and leather tabs, but its smaller, feminine cut unleashes a bitter desire within to slash it to pieces. My face must show it because Declan offers up an explanation before it festers.

"It used to be my sister's," his voice dips, and he swallows, hefting the jacket up again. I slide my arms inside, bringing them together to zip up, but Declan's hands curve around my waist, doing it for me. "Be right back," his breath whispers against the shell of my ear, and heat blossoms in my belly.

He disappears into the house again and returns with a pair of dock martins and socks. "Here," he shoves them at me. "Don't want you to burn your shoes."

Snatching a look down at my sneakers, I shrug and say nothing, shucking them off. Bending to slip on the thicker socks and boots, he's before me in a flash, kneeling, and then rolls the socks up and laces the boots tight. I roll my eyes and hold onto his shoulders while he finishes tying the last one.

Gripping the helmet, he studies me, a shift in his aura captivates my entire attention. "Hold on to my waist, watch the mufflers, and lean with me into the turns...ok?" He instructs and pulls the helmet down over my head, buckling it himself, again not letting me do it. If he'd asked, he would have known I've been on the back of a motorcycle before.

He straddles the heavy bike and swings his head towards me. He taps his head, and then I hear him inside the helmet. "If you need to talk to me, ok?" Declan's smile grows. I nod, and he turns the key and kick-starts the antique machine.

Its loud engine thunders to life, he toes it into gear, and he backs it out of the garage. I walk out and follow him as he turns the bike around in the driveway. Hopping on, I slide my fingers around his waistband, my core a breath away from his back.

"Ready?" he asks, surprisingly clear through the helmet microphone over the roar of the engine. I don't bother answering and hike my other leg up on the foot peg and tap his stomach. Declan takes it slow at first as we ride down our street and past my house. Jules and Wyatt are on the front porch and wave to us when we drive by. He opens the throttle, and we speed off. We pass his bar, the grocery store, and the few other small shops before we are out on the open road.

The winding road we end up on a little while later is so far my favorite part of the ride. Trees dot the roadway on one side, and open farmland on the other. I lean in closer, wrapping my arms around his waist when we round a corner, and he stiffens before muscle memory takes hold of him and he relaxes, and we lean together.

* * *

The wind whips into the space around my neck and cuffs of the leather jacket, occasionally prickling my skin in goosebumps. The exhaust rattles beefy and loud, vibrations massage every muscle in my butt cheeks, hips, and back. But the heat of his hand over mine is all I can focus on. I'm still focused on it as we pull into Elizabeth City and roll to a stop in front of a brewery.

My hands are still clasped tightly around him, and he kills the engine and props the kickstand out. He runs a hand over my thigh, stuttering my brain. "Faith? We're here," he says, removing my hands.

"Oh, sorry." Only a little mortified, I've been clutching him so tightly that I slide off the back of the bike and unbuckle my helmet. One of Declan's brows arches at me. My hair is a total mess when I lift the helmet, but that doesn't seem to bother him because he inhales and then takes a step towards me like he's on a mission.

I've tugged my hair out of its haphazard ponytail and run my fingers through it before he's on me. His body presses up against mine, his hands skimming a feverish path up my leather-coated arms. The lightest touch of his finger on my cheek flares a potent need, as he draws it up to tuck one side of my long, layered ends behind my ear. His hungry gaze dips from mine to my lips, his pupils widen, and I suck in a ragged breath, waiting.

Expecting him to lean in and press those chiseled lips against mine, he derails the built-up desire when he takes my helmet and then my hand, dragging me into the brewery. I stare at the back of his head in confusion, a heavy, dull pain sinks to the bottom of my stomach, and I know he doesn't want me. He draws me in but then pulls away in every interaction. I'm so stupid, misreading his cues, it's not going to happen again, I tell myself, trying to shut down that gullible part of me.

Once inside, Declan hauls me along to a table outside on the brewery deck that overlooks this stretch of the Elizabeth River. It's peaceful out here, we're alone save for another couple in the opposite corner and the flock of ducks wading along the edges. The wood and steel pub table and chairs are modern and sleek, and warmed by the sun's rays all day.

Declan makes quick work of the umbrella after handing me over to my seat and then plants a kiss on the top of my head, stunning me, and disappears into the brewery. Thoroughly addled from his hot and cold advances, I don't know what to think. Am I reading him wrong?

Leaning on my fisted palm to admire the riverfront and not entangle comparison thoughts of Declan and Connor, I take in the seamless hustle and bustle in the small city that blends in with the calmness and quiet of the river. Contagious warmth crawls up my spine, curling its heat around me when Declan slides a drink in front of me.

"I got you a cider, I thought you'd like a blueberry one," he offers and sits down, not quite across from me, but more off to the side. My stare tracks his movements as he brings the frosted glass up to his lips, downing a gulp.

Raking my gaze down his throat, it bobs, and before I can pay attention to the craving that motion brings out in me, I flick them back up. A small bit of beer foam clings to his lips, and I shouldn't be staring at those either, but I can't help myself, especially when his tongue darts out to swipe the remnants away. My cheeks heat to an uncomfortable temperature when my eyes move up again and lock with his. Those sultry soul sucking hazel orbs are deliciously thinned, his pupils widening, staring at me. Maybe I did read him wrong?

"Thank you," I reply, taking a sip of my cider, pleasantly surprised with how tasty it is. "Wow, this is good."

Declan smiles, revealing a hint of those not-so-perfectly straight white teeth. The action sends a jolt of electricity down my spine. "Yeah? Good, because I'm ordering it for the bar."

"Oh? That'll be great." The awkwardness grows again. He dragged me along to sample drinks for his bar...wow. I have no idea what to say at all. He accepted me, but he is also keeping me at arm's length for what?

21

Declan

What crawled up my ass to show up at Faith's house, accept our bond, and then drag her out for a ride? Good question, I'd like to know too.

The situation with me not rejecting her was going to go one of two ways: either backfire on me, or she'd reluctantly give her acceptance. I can't tell if she's pissed at me for not rejecting her or if she's pissed at herself for accepting my acceptance. None of which is abundantly clear while we sit staring at one another, drinking, and fighting with ourselves to find words to communicate. I had felt a rush of her emotions on her porch, but she's been a blank slate since, save for the few glimpses that have slipped through our connection.

Her slim fingers trace the edge of the table, lips quirking into a sideways grin as she gently rocks the table. Inwardly, I groan, already knowing what she's going to say.

"You should maybe order some of these tables too," she shoots out in a smooth, smart-ass tone. She can't hide the tiny giggle either that bubbles from her plump, kissable lips as she teases me.

With a shake of my head, I raise my glass to her, "touché mon amour," I slip out and then swig a gulp down, averting my gaze to the river. If she picks up the term of endearment, she doesn't let on, but it does quiet her to an open mouth gawk her brows pinching together.

"You're right, though, I do need new tables, but it's been a slow season, and revenue goes to employees first during slow times versus back into the bar," I offer in reasoning why my wobbly ass tables haven't been fixed or replaced since the place was purchased. Faith's eyes soften and then brim with an emotion I don't want or need.

"Oh, I'm sorry, I didn't mean to-I'm not usually a spiteful person, I-I wasn't myself." She stumbles over her words, not sure of what she wants to say. I've got to get her to stop apologizing for shit that's not her fault.

My eyes hang and freeze on her lips, hugging the rim of her glass, and she gulps down the last of the cider. Her lush lashes sweep down and brush against her sun-kissed cheeks before fluttering up, gifting me with the radiance of those whiskey chocolate eyes.

We sit in a comfortable silence for a while longer before I find myself sliding a hand over to cover and interlacing my fingers with hers, for no other reason than I can't keep from touching her. She doesn't pull away, but the muscles in her fingers tense, and she glares down at our intertwined hands. There's a heaviness sinking my tongue deeper down my throat, choking the words I've been wanting to say to her since accepting our bond, and I squeeze her fingers, swallowing down the fear of her reaction.

"I know that my acceptance isn't what you wanted, but I hope you understand this isn't easy for me either," I start, investigating her eyes searching for any hint of emotion, her glare falls to a wide-eyed, pale expression. She swallows like she wants to say something, but remains silent, and I sense her shutting me out again as her fingers slip from mine.

"You have to understand, Faith, I never wanted-no, deserved to have a mate. I have my reasons and I'm not ready to get into it, but I want you to know that I'm willing to try if you are," I rush over my words, fingers playing with the paper coaster that's swollen from condensation, the puffed edges inviting them to be plucked and pulled.

Quacking from the few ducks swimming by the edge of the dock seems so much louder with her silence. The coaster is all but destroyed on one side by the time I lift my eyes to Faith's empty stare.

"Can we go back?" She says, squeaking on whatever she's trying to hold in. Her question leaves my chest caving in, and my ears turning red. I nod and stand to help her from the chair. I watch her as we walk back into the brewery.

The manager waves at me. "Nice to see ya, Dec, it'll be there in a few days." With a jerk of my chin and a wave, he dips his in response, and we continue out towards the front. This place always stirs a desire in me to better my ramshackle bar into something a little nicer, but then I get back there and remember why I bought it in the first place; it's cozy and perfect in its imperfection.

Helping her slide her helmet back on, I note her flushed cheeks and brush my finger over her nose and the small inch of cheek exposed under the helmet. She's gotten a lot of sun over the past couple of days, so I should drop off a better sunscreen for her.

A couple of hours later, we are almost to the turn that will lead us back to the inlet, and Faith's entire body shudders against my back.

"You, okay?" I ask, realizing I never even asked her if she's ridden a motorcycle before, but based on her ability to take turns and hold on without a death grip, I'd say she has. The thought makes me cringe, and a slight burn ignites in my gut over who she may have ridden with. Sure, as fuck wasn't Connor because he gives off the sports car vibe.

"Yeah, I'm good," she whispers back, and then flabbergasts the shit out of me when her hands leave my sides and her body inches away. In the mirror, I spot her hands splayed out to her sides as we hit the last stretch of the straightaway. Her laugh shoots ripples of joy from my heart. She soars her arms for a few more minutes before languidly wrapping them back around my waist. Maybe, I think, just maybe this might be okay.

* * *

The exhaust of my bike rumbles loudly as we roll up to the bar's full parking lot. Standing next to the bike, I help her out of the helmet and smooth her chocolate hair down her back.

"Thanks for today," her voice sings over the ends of my nerves, making them jump and dance to every word like a lyric of my favorite song.

"You're welcome. Come on, the night's only getting started," I say, scooping her hand into mine and turning towards the back side of the bar. "My office is in the back, we can drop our stuff in there," I explain at her questioning look.

Sliding my key into the lock and shoving the door open, my hand slams against the wall searching for the switch. Finding it, I flip on the light and groan as the light bulb buzzes and flickers before it finally burns to life.

22

Faith

The inside of Declan's office is, well, I'm not sure, disorganized? Chaotic? And yet not at all, at the same time. Dark wood paneling accented with one pale blue painted wall is covered in photographs of motorcycles, cars, and various scenes of the beach, some that are vaguely familiar, like the beaches in Maine.

Declan comes behind me, grabs my shoulders, spinning me to unbuckle my helmet, his eyes never leaving mine as he pulls it up and off, then smooths a hand over my hair. He places our helmets down and shuffles around a chair to stand near me while I take in his space.

A filing cabinet fills one corner, while in another corner, a short bookcase sits covered with numerous bottles of liquor and several glasses neatly stacked. His desk is average and is well-loved; the oak wood is stained to match the dark woods of the other furniture in the room. Two wooden armchairs face the desk, angled towards each other, and on the desk, a laptop and several perfectly aligned stacks of paper and ledgers are piled up. A dark ring stains the wood, probably from his drink, and next to it, three sleek pens are lined up next to one another in a neat, tidy row, the clips all facing the same direction.

The wooden blinds filter any light coming in, feeding the several hanging plants he has in each corner, dangling in varying heights. It's quaint and reminds me of my own office, only a smidge darker in tones.

"So, this is my office...buuu-t you already knew that," Declan says with a hint of pink kissing his stubble-covered cheeks as he runs a hand through his hair.

"Yep, I can see that," I laugh and spin into him, colliding with his chest. Heat floods from my head to my toes, and the room moves a little off kilter. Blinking rapidly to clear my vision, his handsome face comes into focus. His brows curve slightly, and his lips loosen at the sides while his pupils dilate and contract.

"Are you okay?" His voice drops low as he asks and steadies my body. In a daze and at a loss for words, I'm only able to nod. His hazel eyes crinkle in the corners as he draws one side of his lips back. Declan's fingers skim down the side of my arm and link with mine. He pulls me closer, his head tilting towards me, eyes darting to my mouth when my tongue sweeps over my lower lip.

Right as I think he's going to dip in and kiss me, his hand is on my chest and unzipping the leather jacket. Warm hands slip under the leather and glide over my shoulders, guiding the sleeves down, my arms retracting from them automatically.

His warm fingers slide down my arms and link with mine again. Facing me, he smirks and guides me to another door. What. The. Fuck! Is this some new kind of torturous edging? Or am I really that dense? A long exhale empties my lungs. I don't have any energy left to fight anything today, and I decide it's best to simply go with the flow for the night.

"Come on, let's grab a drink and then I'll take you home, okay?" His voice flames my already scorching skin, pinching the base of my ear and neck as his lips leave the shell of my ear.

Locking my gaze on his tall frame, I follow as he leads me into the bustling bar and over to a table opposite where I sat before, closer to the dart board.

"Be right back," he informs and kisses my forehead before strutting behind the bar. His kiss melts me a little. Cocking my head to the side, I devour the muscles in his back and glutes as they flex and stretch with each movement. The Goddess knew what she was doing when she brought his parents together.

The bar is busy, but not as packed as I thought it would be. People are milling about, and a musician is setting up in a corner close to the patio. The twangs and notes of instruments being tuned cut through the chattering of customers.

Leaning on the table, I immediately notice it's not wobbly, a smirk curls my lips, and I shake it just to be a brat when hot breath blows across my neck. Internally shuddering, I catch Declan in my peripheral vision, standing behind and leaning into me.

"Afraid I'm all out of sugar packets, sweetheart," he murmurs against the side of my head. I glare at him over my shoulder.

"Why's that? Forgot to order them?" I tease with a giggle.

"Nope, someone sweeter than sugar used them all to fix some tables." I clamp my legs together at his lowered voice, I swear he dropped it an octave. "That'd be you sugar," he groans in my ear, giving me tingles all over.

He slides a cider over in front of me and takes the seat beside me, motioning with a jerk of his rounded, but strong chin, and tips his bottle to his lips. Declan glides a hand over my thigh, my legs jerk in reaction, and he frowns.

"Sorry," I mutter, and then, spying the darts on a shelf next to our table, I grab them. "Um—you wanna to play?" I ask, distracting him so he won't linger too long on my reaction.

His frown eases, and he nods, "Sure, sweetheart."

The two of us walk up to the throwing line, and he lets me throw the one to see who goes first. Lining up my right toe with the edge of the line, I throw the first dart with a snap of my wrist, landing in the single bull ring.

"Close," he smirks and then lines his right toe up with the line and throws his dart landing in the double bullseye...of fucking course he's great at this. He has this air about him, you know, the one that says 'I'm naturally good at everything I do.'

"Guess you're going first then," I sigh and retrieve both of our darts and hand his over to him. I stand off to the side, observing Declan's form, and my hips sway as the band starts playing a cover of Michael Marcagi's, *Scared to Start*.

I roll my eyes at the universe and grab my cider, sipping when I want to guzzle. Declan's bicep curls and stretches the sleeves of his shirt, entirely drawn in to him, my lips curve behind the mouth of the bottle.

"Enjoying the view, sweetheart?" He drawls and smirks, throwing his last dart. It lands with a thunk right into the double-ring scoring of 20. My eyes drift to the other two darts, and my nose wrinkles; two are in the double bull, 120 points towards lowering his 301 starting score.

"Ugh," I groan, folding my arms across my chest. He breezes past me, grinning like a fool, and retrieves his darts, and gestures for me to take the line.

He grabs his beer and winks, taking a sip. I slide my boot up to the line. Eyeing the board, I draw back and close my eyes, inhaling and then crack one open and release. The dart flies and hits the single bull's ring, I barely resist the urge to whoop and spin. Grinning, I grab my cider from our table, and Declan grabs my waist. I freeze and then force myself to relax when he guides me between his spread legs.

"Nice shot, baby," he whispers in my ear. Involuntarily, my back quivers, and then, bracing my hands on his shoulders, I shove away and return to throw my last two darts. This draw to him is wickedly strong and too much at the same time.

The band's playing *Dirt on My Boots* by Jon Pardi now, and couples have broken off from the bar and surrounding tables to dance and sweat the day's worries away. I stare at them so long that I overlook Declan sneaking up behind me until his heat radiates into my back.

"Godde-" I stutter and swing around into him, my hands slamming into his chest, his rock, hard chest. He gives me a wicked grin, cupping the backs of my arms, then slides his fingers down to my wrists before dropping them. Utterly distracted, I spin around and line my shot up, aiming for the triple points ring in the 20 segment. Declan's breath scalds the shell of my ear. He presses his hard length into my backside, my cheeks flame, and my teeth grind.

"You're not playing fair, Declan," I grit out between my teeth, grinding. My blood is heated to a boil and pulsing to my nipples and throbbing between my thighs.

"No, I suppose I'm not." His swagger has no boundaries, and he proves it when he runs his hot fingers up the sides of my waist and languidly back down. My arm bends and I release, the dart soars through the air and lands exactly in the triple ring of the 20 segment.

Super proud of myself, I sip my cider and then crane my head back to him, aim from my peripheral, and throw my last dart blindly. The thunk of the dart is a relief that I didn't hit a person, as is Declan's face. His mouth pops open at the same time as his eyes widen.

"What?" I quip sardonically and then slowly turn to see where my dart landed, right smack in the double bullseye.

"-166 left to my -181...I'm not sure if I should be irritated that you're better or if I should be proud as fuck," he says, licking his lips, and scanning my body up and down, while he waits for me to retrieve my darts.

We take our turns back and forth, and then Declan busts his score on his next turn, and I'm 5 points from bringing it to 0. Technically, I've won, but I'm no quitter. I'm about to throw my last dart when Declan sweeps me up into his arms. I release the dart and giggle as he moves us to a space to dance.

"I love this song," he murmurs alongside my cheek, his lips grazing the skin. He glides one hand down to the small of my back and the other clasps my hand. He leads us into a slow swaying dance to *Save My Soul* by Noah Rinker. This cover band is excellent.

"Why?" I ask, darting my eyes up to his golden hazels, burrowing down into me. He brings my waist closer, our hips touching, and rests his forehead against mine.

"Why what?" He rasps, while running his thumb over the edge of my palm, and in that moment, it's only the two of us. The music fades to a whisper, the crowds blur and mute as our eyes collide and meld. The strumming of the guitar and the wheezing whistle of a harmonica sways along with the lyrics. The serenading words are reminiscent of our lives.

We only get one shot to lose, that we aren't perfect and we've been in love before and trust broken, but we need each other.

The music winds down to an end, but we've long since stopped moving. He brushes a strand of hair behind my ear, the tips of his fingers dusting over my skin. He leans in, skimming his lips over mine. A burst of tingles erupts in my body, spreading to every part and hitches my breath. I'm stunned, yet I know I'm safe when he combs his fingers up my neck and onto the back of my scalp, fisting my hair.

He tugs my head back, and his mouth is on mine. He groans as his tongue traces my lips, begging me to open. I do, and our tongues collide and curl around one another. He kisses me, deeply, passionately.

My core tightens, and a fire ignites low in my belly. I wrap my arms around his neck, and his other hand scoops down to my lower back, pressing me closer to him. He grinds his erection between our bodies, and instinctively, I lift my leg to curl around his hips. He grabs my thigh and keeps it there as he deepens the kiss.

The room spins, and I can't breathe, but that is okay, because he can breathe for me. Before I'm ready to let go, he gently lowers my leg and breaks our kiss and peppers more over my lips and cheeks.

"Wow," I murmur under my breath. He grins but says nothing. I'm too stupefied by that toe-curling kiss to speak more.

"Ready to head home?" He startles me with his question, but I nod, and he leads me back to his office. We both slip into our jackets and pull on the helmets. I get on the bike behind him, my body flushing hard with heat as I lean in and wrap my arms around his waist. I've never been this overheated before, like my entire body is about to be engulfed in flames. He cups my hand with his and then starts up the bike.

We pull up to my rental and head in, passing Wyatt and Jules curled up on the couch watching a movie. Wyatt smiles so wide, his happiness seeps into my bones. Jules wiggles her fingers at us in a wave and then snuggles back down with Wyatt.

Declan snuggles us in on the porch swing and then shifts, angling his body to face mine. His warmth cools a little, and he sighs.

"We should talk," he says while brushing his thumb over my cheek, leaving behind a singed path of skin. He swoops up to my neck and abruptly drops his hand. A pang of nerves slides in under my skin, my stomach sinks and dread starts to cloud my thoughts.

"Faith, I don't know how to say this, so I'm just going to be blunt," he says cautiously. His timbre dropping with each word, his eyes hardening. My heart does a little flip-flop, and my tongue sticks to the roof of my mouth. He looks away for a brief second, meeting my eyes once again.

"The other night, you had a vampire outside the house here. I followed it, well, Thorin, my wolf did, and he killed him...the vamp was seeking you out," he rushes out, his grip on my arms tightens.

In slow motion, my lips part, a gasp releases to the wind, and my legs tremble. It's my stomach's turn to flip-flop upside down; so, I was being followed, but I thought it was those rogues, not vampires.

I have no words, nothing, but a creeping heat that is rapidly taking over my body. He instinctively wraps his arms around me, my body a limp noodle in his embrace. Declan does not falter; instead, he bends and lifts me from under my knees and walks us back inside.

My arms curl around his neck, and I rest my cheek on his collarbone. Jules and Wyatt sigh contentedly in the background. Declan bypasses them and heads directly up the stairs.

The stairs creak and groan with his heavy steps. He turns, pushing the door open and backs into my room, setting me down on the bed. I should be questioning why he knows which room is mine, but I guess it wouldn't be too hard to guess. He settles on his knees on the floor before me.

"Faith." My eyelids blink sluggishly, savoring each beat as they match my slowing heart. Why am I so hot?

23

Declan

With a tentative hand, I reach and brush a chocolatey-caramel swirled strand behind Faith's ear, my fingers tracing along each piercing and curling down to her lobe. I can't seem to keep my hands away from her; the need to touch and caress is almost fucking unbearable, but the concern that something is wrong is substantially worse.

Like a moth to a flame, my knuckles brush along her cheek and jawline, falling down her neck; she's burning up. "Faith, please look at me," I try again, longing to reach through the thick fog that she's shielded herself in earlier, and pierce through the wall of her emotions.

A sharp inhale startles me when she finally dips her head down, lifting her honeyed eyes to mine. An ache in the back of my throat takes hold as her emotions flood back to me in a raging river. Chills race across my skin. Her emotions and thoughts are all over the place. I search her rapidly moving eyes, a stark contrast to her lids that are still blinking at a snail's pace. Dread and sadness pour over me, and I sense her deflating from the inside out. I force myself to take a breath and not bombard her too much, but I have to know.

"What has you weighed down, lil one? Please talk to me, I want to help." Faith's head moves side to side, the movement so quick and subtle I would've missed it had I not been staring at her so intently.

We sit there in crushing silence while she still refuses to answer me, I'm begging her on my damn knees for Goddess' sake, and she's a mute statue. What is it going to take to get her to answer me?

She can hate me later, but I need answers, and this is the only way I will be able to protect her, because if Benedict is involved, nothing good will come of her silence. Releasing the hold I have on my aura, I grip her chin in my fingers, forcing her to meet my eyes.

"Faith, tell me what you know about the vampires, about Benedict, everything so I can protect you, right now," I command, almost growling, but reining it in at the end. I hate using my alpha aura on anyone, and I've used it twice now with her, my mate, and she was...she was devastated earlier. I'm such an asshole.

The guilt crushes me like an elephant is sitting on my chest. How could I do that to my mate? My mate...I still have no idea why I accepted the bond. I told myself I'd accept our bond to protect her from Benedict and his horde, but in truth? I don't know, not really, but maybe, I think she can hold my broken pieces together, and I can hold hers.

Zeroing back in on her, I hold in my cringe as her body fights the command. Those heavenly eyes narrowing to slits, her upper lip curls up in a snarl, peeking a flash of white canines, warning me to back off. Yeah...that's not happening. I let the fullness of my aura radiate out again.

Finally, my aura pushes into her, and she resigns, baring her neck with a growl, eyes cutting to mine, her pupils growing. A flash of metallic irises glows into a swirling of copper, silver, and gold.

Good goddess, she's so beautiful.

Crouched before her, I release her chin and cup her cheek. Pure instinct drives her as she leans into my touch. I jerk my chin towards her, encouraging her to speak, so I don't have to use my alpha command again.

"Please...please, sweetheart." Her eyes flash before she blinks the metallic away, and then her cognac irises darken to rich chestnut. The pink tip of her tongue darts out over her lips, wetting them, her bottom lip curling in under her canine, and finally, her voice cracks through the stillness of the room.

"Fine. But I don't know what I'll tell you that you don't already know. La Luxure de le mort clan lives not far from my pack lands, and extends into Canada. Benedict is the leader, and his asshole son, Isaac, is his second, and he—," she answers almost robotically, like a history lesson, but I don't stop her. Faith's whole body contorts, shaking off whatever it is she's reliving. She recites the rest of what she knows and ends her monotone history lesson with a sigh.

A strand of salvia clings and stretches between her pouty lips as she opens and closes them. She runs a hand under her nose, silencing a sniffle. Faith studies my face, her eyes roaming over each plane and ridge, a single tear races down, curving over her cheek to her chin.

She lifts a hand, skimming feather-light touches over my brow, cheekbone, and down to my chin. A trifle longer than the other touches, she rubs a too-warm thumb over the stubble peppering my jaw.

Perhaps I'll grow it out again.

Her chest rises and falls deliciously and aggravatingly slow. Her fingers trail down my neck, her thumb stroking my Adam's apple before resting in the hollow of my throat. Sweet whispers of her skin trail heat in its wake when her hand reaches the apex of my neck and shoulder. She thrums three fingers over the spot, where her mark will go if...no...when we complete our mating.

With both of us being alphas, we will both mark each other as is custom, the magic swirling in our blood that controls our shift, given to us by the Goddess herself. Our bodies will absorb our teeth marks and morph into a blend of our family's symbols. I can't help but wonder what mine will be? Will it be my family's or nothing since I have no pack here, not really, anyway?

A deafening crash from downstairs snaps both of us out of the bond's hold. Faith retracts her hand faster than an asp viper. A painful shudder trembles down from my head to my legs, lingering around my chest, and sharp stabbing sensations wrap around my heart.

Yeah, there is no way in hell I'm breaking the bond now, not with that slight pain simply from her removing her touch. I may not have wanted a mate, but if the pain I felt is anything compared to what she must've felt the night before and earlier, I can't imagine inflicting the rejection pain on her.

Rising, I join her on the bed, our thighs touching, soothing the ache in my chest. "Why do you think they are after you, Faith?" I ask, my intonation soft.

Angling her shoulders towards me, she flutters those chestnut eyes up over my face and tucks her chin to her chest. Another single tear runs down her cheek, hovering on her chin before one more slides down and forces it to splash onto her exposed chest.

"I think...no. I know a vampire was responsible for my Mother's death. I've watched the recording over a hundred times, and each time I see the flash of *his* red eyes," she croaks, sniffling. A gurgling noise rumbles from her throat as she clears it, mustering her courage.

Tentatively, my hand rises, running up her spine, rubbing small circles over it, up to her shoulders, and in between the blades. The bed jostles, and she jumps up, striding over to the door. Grasping the knob, her hand slips off it, and she spins around. The muscles in her neck contract and relax. She swallows and sucks in her bottom lip.

"Are you coming?" Her sweet voice is a welcome surprise in my mind as she uses our bond to link with me for the first time. My brows lift in astonishment. For a female who, for all intents and purposes, didn't want this bond, just strengthened it threefold.

Sifting through to find that thread within my mind to hers, I smirk before replying, *"Yes, sweetheart."*

She yanks the door open, "Don't call me that," she snaps at me, and I follow her down the creaky stairs, already solid in my decision to keep calling her that, forever.

She slips out to the porch. Side eyeing our family members as we pass, I catch Wyatt busy at the stove, sautéing something delectable, and Julianna seems content while pinching the ends of the pie crust in a fluted pattern next to a collection of pans stacked haphazardly on the counter.

Ahh...that explains the crash earlier.

The hinges squeak when I walk out to join Faith. She gathers her laptop and walks around to the other corner of the wrap-around porch, flopping down on the patio sofa. Placing the laptop on the rattan and glass tea table, her fingers fly over the keys.

Those alluring chestnut, almost chocolate now, irises lift to mine. I've never met anyone whose eye colors change as much as hers do. It's enticing, like a shiny lure. I'm hooked and let her reel me in. Her soft, round eyes wrinkle at the sides from the frustration written over her face.

"My Father's, well, I guess mine too for now...anyways, the beta sent this over to me the other night. I had to slow it down and enhance both the audio and the resolution. It's from a nearby traffic camera, I believe."

Joining her on the sofa, I drag the laptop closer to me and press play, slowing down the recording even more, frame by frame, until I can see a familiar face. His nose ring is a dead giveaway.

24

Faith

Declan's sharp intake of breath confirms what I had suspected, but his declaration solidifies my answer. "Mother fucking Isaac."

Like a turbulent storm, my mind reels from thoughts and anxieties rising to the surface. Experiencing Declan's emotions melding with mine and knowing I can trust him with this is entirely foreign to me. Trusting others hasn't been easy for years, especially not after Connor had- well, that doesn't matter now, does it? I'd stayed, made my choice, and got no less than what I deserved.

It's been a long time since I've been able to trust so easily right away, at least not with anyone I hardly knew. If I were being entirely truthful with myself, it's like I've known Declan my whole life already, and that thought alone is disconcerting to say the least. Yet, the warmth and sincerity of his concern ultimately drives my decision to divulge.

He is an alpha, and if anyone can help me, it would be him, at least with this. His instincts and aura are powerful, more so than my own, and Sienna agrees that I need additional strength to weather this storm since she hasn't objected to me deciding to do this. I think she's running high off the giddiness she was yipping through our bond when he'd kissed me earlier.

"Why do they want you, Faith?" he asks again, tilting his head to the side, and then righting it, I lift my own. My heart beats faster with each passing second. He stares into my eyes, inches from the precipice to the door of my soul. Each thud of my heart reverberates in my rib cage as Declan barges through that door and tenderly clutches my soul, keeping it captive. I blink, closing the connection, and think back to what my Mom had told me years ago.

A strong, brine-filled gust of wind blows around us, loosening my hair further and ruffling my button-down shirt. Knitting my hands into the flaps, I close my eyes and let my head fall back. Another gust of wind races past us. Sea mist and lily of the valley perfumes the wind, stinging the inside of my nose, and tears burst to the surface and spill over my swollen eyes.

Mom...

My hands drop from my shirt ends, and I stand summoned by my Mom's spirit. Facing the warm wind, I let it whip around me, bristling along my skin, and the essence of her magic sinks beneath it with each gust.

"Tell him, sweet pea, it's okay." The whispers of her voice echo in the colliding wisps of air. Before I can protest, Declan is behind me, encircling my waist in his strong arms, resting his chin on my shoulder. I sink into his embrace and let him hold me up.

"I'll protect her with everything I have, all of me, with any means necessary...I promise," he whispers so softly, raising the hairs on the back of my neck.

Somehow, he knew, felt her presence. The spirit-laden wind kicks up again, a blast of her strength, and courage soaks into my skin. She came, reminding me that I'm not alone. If he weren't holding me, I'd crumble to the decking and crack open like a broken vase.

The silver glow from the moon reflects off the ocean as it rises, and the waves roll in the evening high tide. The wind dies down within moments, and a calm settles the sea into a glimmering layer of gloss. He presses a kiss to the side of my neck and shifts to face me. He gathers me in his arms and presses another kiss to each of my cheeks, whispering.

"I promise Faith, I will keep you safe." I believe him; the truth of his sincerity keeps me anchored enough to spill my own.

"*I cannot say this aloud, for it has remained a secret for many years. I do not share this frivolously, but at the behest of my Mom.*"

"Go on," he encourages and holds out a hand for me to sit. Returning to the sofa, I sink into the cushions, curling my legs up underneath me with an arm propped over the back. I fixate on the serene sparkling water, conjuring what I need to remember and how I can explain this.

"*My mother is-was,*" I start and then heave a breath in and try again. "*Many believed her to be a rogue omega my Father found in the woods, whom he mated, but that's not even remotely close to the truth. She descended from a line of gifted shifters, alphas specifically. She hid her gifts to protect herself from the vampires, and also the other alphas who could use her as a weapon.*"

To his credit, Declan doesn't react as I expected. His hand runs down over his chin and neck, eyes sweeping back and forth over me. A heavy fog clouds the path to his mind, keeping his mood and emotions unreadable to me at the moment. Biting my lower lip, I hesitate, do I keep going? Or will he think I'm crazy? Heart in my throat, I lean into that earlier fluttering of trust and continue.

"*My Mom is a descendant of the Goddess herself, and the vampires believe that she could cure them. She was a skilled healer, but also a fierce warrior...and I-I carry part of her gifts,*" I add, I've never admitted that to anyone, not even to Dad. Mom knew when I was 4 years old, she saw them wisp out from my fingertips during bath time. She started teaching me to mask my powers and alpha aura before I got out of the tub. The gifts have only shown themselves a couple of times in my life, despite Sienna's hiding, but they've been silent for so long that I've essentially forgotten about them.

If I had the forethought to record Declan's reaction, it would've been priceless. A blank stare combines with a dumbfounded contortion smoothing over his face, after he scrunches it open. His mouth hangs agape, and I lift my hand to his chin, closing it.

"You have to promise never to speak of this to anyone," I command, a hint of my alpha aura slips out to make my point. It's only fair, since he used his aura on me. A flicker of confidence flares to life within and encourages me to straighten my shoulders and hold my head high.

He arches a brow at me, bobbing one eye up and down my body at the tiniest use of my alpha command on him. The longer he stares at me, the more my newfound courage falters, and an impulsive desire to flee grows. I cast my sight up, and instantly my shoulders curve in, because he's not staring, he's scowling. Every muscle and tendon in my body flexes and freezes in alert. Immediately, my eyes dart to the storm door and then to the stairs. If I have to escape, the safest place might be inside with Wyatt and Jules to block him.

Out of nowhere, a rush of boiling blood races through me. Declan's scowl twitches, and then his aura whooshes out, reminding me of my place. I cower and lower my head, but keep my gaze fixed on him. Pulse racing, I start to inch backwards, and then in a flash, he freaking smirks at me, closes my laptop, and leans in.

What is happening?

Shrinking back into the cushions, my chin drops to my chest. I want to crumble and disappear into a hole, never to come out again. I knew I shouldn't have attempted to use my alpha command on him or told him anything. Why did I trust him? I never should've believed my gut feeling, it's been wrong so many times before.

A tug of war ensues within me; on one side, I acknowledge Declan's superior strength as an alpha, and on the other, the wilting of my courage reminds me of my insignificance and weakness. A cruel declaration that I'll never be good enough for anyone. All men, save for my Dad, want to do is exert their power over me.

My arms curl around my knees as they unfold from underneath me, bending up. Tucking my head into the cradle of my arms, bitter hurt spills from my heart, engulfing my whole being. I miss my old self, and I wish I could get her back.

Retreating further within myself, I ignore his pleas to let him comfort me and his rapid apology for dampening my spirits. Ha, my spirits? No, Declan, you didn't dampen them; you thoroughly washed them away.

The back door swings open, and I lift my head a fraction to find Wyatt standing in the doorway, wiping his hands on a towel.

"Dinner is ready, you two—oh, Faith, honey, are you okay?" He asks, stepping towards me. His tender voice is sickly sweet and tinged with genuine concern. Declan snaps his head in his cousin's direction, his nose wrinkling and lip curling. A low growl rumbles from his chest, and Wyatt backs away, hands in the air.

"Right, new bond. Sorry, I meant no disrespect, Dec... but can't you sense her pain?"

Face red and wet from tears, I shrug away from Declan's hand reaching for me. I inchworm my way back on the couch, smashing my back into the upholstered arm, and bury my head once more.

"Of course I can," he croaks, like he's crushed with pain himself. He glances at me from the corner of his eye, and then, inhaling, he squares his shoulders. "We're only working out some kinks...alpha to alpha," Declan explains. His voice is similar to the velvet notes of a cello.

While I can comprehend his notion, he has no clue that I've always felt inferior to other alphas my entire life. For so long without Sienna,

I grew to accept my fate of being reduced to an omega and my powers weakened. Perhaps it was my acceptance that dwindled my inherited magic, or maybe I was found unworthy, because I masked my true nature and aura.

My aura has matched a powerful alpha's only twice, and one of those was when I shifted. The other time was when I was eleven years old, and a visiting alpha's son hurt Julianna. I'd gotten so mad when the bully's father came to make her apologize for something he did, my aura crackled out. It streaked like lightning and toppled a tree, landing inches from their feet.

My Dad was ecstatic that I had finally shown my alpha blood, but that joy didn't last long, because my aura practically disappeared after that. He never knew I'd had them since I was a toddler. Mom made me swear to keep it a secret, even from him.

I'd assumed my aura fading was his reasoning for not naming me as his heir until my wolf appeared a couple of weeks ago. Truthfully, I believed he was going to name Hollie by my 30th if my wolf hadn't appeared. I kind of wish he had done it sooner, to spare me the humiliation of being less than everyone else, all to keep a secret.

The other reason my aura dimmed so efficiently...well, I've buried that so far down I can't bear to think about it, and Declan can never find out about it, or anyone else. The weight of that crushes my soul daily.

Another squeak from the storm door hinges pops my head up as Wyatt retreats inside the house, leaving me with his broody cousin. Broody, but oh so handsome. Oh, what in the Goddess is going on with me? One minute, he's driving me crazy, reminding me of my worthlessness, the next, I want to straddle him.

Declan grazes his hand up my calf, and I jerk my leg back, curling deeper into the cushions. Then, like a shot of hot sauce, a scalding heat fans my skin. Wave after wave brings intense sensations of needles poking every single pore in my body, stinging, from the sweat pushing through. I glance up and squint. Declan's body sways and rocks like he's aboard a boat in uncertain currents.

Hooded lids drag over my sand-scraped eyes, and my head lolls to one side. Everything is muddled and too heavy. Another rush of flames surges through my body, leaving my breasts aching. My nipples bud, and a fierce warmth pools and floods between my thighs. Forgotten are the notions of unworthiness as the unwelcome signs of my heat devour every coherent thought. Fuck.

25

Declan

Faith's scent abruptly changes, flaring my nostrils, and her body flushes a deep scarlet, sweat beads across her forehead and brow in a sickly sheen. My throat constricts, and it's hard to swallow at the realization that she's most definitely not okay, something is wrong, and I should've done something sooner.

Is she sick?

I shuffle towards her, and folding, I scoop her up, tucking her into my chest. Her too-hot body is limp and pliant in my arms. Even though this is hardly the time, it's pretty amazing that for the second time I get to hold her, all the chaos of my mind settles and locks in place. If something wasn't wrong, I could drown in the feelings rising within.

Moaning, she nuzzles her face into my neck, and I get a whiff of arousal. "Fuck!" She's not sick, she's going into heat. I've never aided any females through their heats before. However, I know what happens, but I've always been too afraid to lose control to aid any girlfriend.

What the fuck, am I going to do?

For a second, my knees buckle, and everything shifts around me, until Faith whimpers.

Get your shit together. She needs you.

Toeing the edge of the storm door open, I burst inside, seeking out Julianna. Faith stretches up, nipping the underside of my ear. Wrapping her arms around my neck, she pulls herself closer to suck at the skin, tasting me as I walk towards the open design kitchen and dining area. The slickness of her tongue against my flesh tightens my skin. "Mm, you taste like the smoothest whiskey," she moans, pricking hot desire straight to my dick and distracting the hell out of me.

When Julianna spots us, she stops mid-placement of a fork and knife, dropping them, the metal clattering on the plates. She rushes to us, immediately touching Faith's cheeks and forehead.

"She's burning up," she says worriedly. Lifting her pert nose in the air, she sniffs, and her doe eyes widen. "Oh shit, she's in heat...oh um—you need to get her upstairs, into a cool bath, lock all the doors and windows." She spins, glancing at Wyatt, and then back to me, scrunching her face up.

"We will send your food up and leave it outside the door. Keep her cool, Declan, and be prepared to sate her needs," she orders, urgently moving around to my back, shoving me towards the stairs. "Go, the first heat after a bond is accepted is almost ten times stronger," she adds and shoves my shoulder harder.

My gaze lands on Wyatt, who's a frozen statue near the kitchen island, concern written all over his stark white face. Cold sweat runs down my temples. He catches it with a flick of his eyes and blanches. He gulps the water he's holding to his lips and slams the glass down on the cutting board. He knows why I'm truly swallowing every ounce of panic sketching across my face. I can't hurt her. I downright can't. I won't come back from it if I do.

"I got you, bud. You need to trust yourself," he murmurs, his eyes cutting behind me to Julianna. "And seeing as you two are still relatively unfamiliar with each other, and I doubt she has any form of protection here, I'd stick to uh, non-intercourse activities Dec," he instructs, swallowing several times, a little embarrassed, undoubtedly from experience, but I also hear his unspoken message. Sticking to things I can quickly extricate myself from the moment I sense myself slipping, I can go to him. However, it doesn't make this situation any less awkward, and I find myself blankly staring from him to Julianna.

"You have to keep her fever under control or—" Julianna states, trailing off, staring at Faith. Her worry snatches me out of my stunned stupor. Looking down at the beauty tucked into my chest, I brush my nose over Faith's. "She's never had a true—" she adds, but doesn't finish, when Faith whimpers again, this time in pain.

Not wasting another minute, I nod and glide to the stairs. Faith's growing arousal floats to my nose, burning a path straight through me. Lust thick and hedonistic coats the back of my throat. A quick shake of my head returns my senses momentarily, allowing me to rush up to her bedroom. My stomach turns with worry settling in. If the fever from her heat rises too quickly and takes over, she can suffer drastic repercussions within her body.

Kicking her door open, I race to her bed and peel her arms from around my neck. Her tiny mewls of protest ping pong inside my chest. "I know, sweetheart, but I must draw you a bath first."

She finally relents, allowing me to unhook her arms from my neck so I can lay her gently on the bed. Making a quick turn about the room, I lock every window, the balcony doors, and the bedroom door. My cock painfully presses against the rough denim of my jeans with every stride, and I don't think it can get any harder. Every single sensation is heightened and strung out.

I lean over the large tub, turning the knob to cold. A hiss escapes from the pipes before it finally begins to fill with cool water. The groundwater here is warmer than home, and it's tepid at best, but unless I want to shout down to Wyatt to get ice, this will have to do. I love and trust my cousin, but there is no way in hell that I will allow him in here at all. Not right now. Not with the bond pulling and yanking on me to protect and claim her.

Returning to the bedroom, I skid to a stop when I find Faith sprawled out on the bed with her hands roaming up over her stomach. Torturously, she inches her shirt up over her tanned, taut skin. Closing my eyes, hands balling into fists, I rein in my desire and lust and stride towards her.

"Faith, I need you to come with me," I rasp, getting a mouthful of her piquant arousal. Her tantalizing stare lasers in on me, a sinful smile stretches her luscious lips as she leans up, propping on her elbows. She drags a lengthened canine over her bottom lip, piercing it. A pebble of blood beads and slides down her chin.

Fuck me, why is that so hot?

Bewitched, I tilt my head to the side, watching it trail down her throat, staining her white tank top inches above her breasts. It spreads, followed by more blood that rolls down. Her brow arches, and she sucks in that lip and releases it, another bead of blood races down her chin. Desire thick and syrupy scalds inside my veins. I don't know what about this is a turn on, but it's fucking sexy as hell.

A growl rolls up my throat, and all sense and reason leave me. I am at the edge of the bed in three steps, gripping her neck. With firm, but tender fingers cradling it, I lean down and hover over her. My breath is ragged as I press my lips to her chin, darting my tongue out to taste her blood.

"Godsdamned...the sweetest honey." I groan and keep feasting. I glide my tongue over every trace of it on her chin and down her throat. A heady moan slips from her lips as her head falls back, revealing more of her slender neck.

Reluctantly, I pull away and tug her up from the bed by her wrists, walking backwards and leading her into the bathroom; I'm going to need a cold shower soon myself.

Maneuvering her in front of me, I turn our bodies away from the mirrors and peel her button-up shirt off her shoulders. A shudder shivers across her body when the material falls from her arms. My hands fist several times before I can tamp down the lust building deep in my groin and the tingles spreading up and over my lower back. This punch of desire is utterly foreign to me, but I have to admit it's not unwelcome.

Sliding my hands up her sides, I lift her arms above her head, "Keep them up, sweetheart," I murmur, brushing my lips over the shell of her ear. She presses into me, rubbing her ass along my heavy, aching cock. Eyes closed, I tug on the hem of her tank and slide it up, my fingers skimming over the velvet skin of her rib cage, the tips brushing along the outside curve of her bare breasts.

"Fuck." I barely recognize my voice as it grates over a swell of desire. Her skin flushes again, and another coating of sweat instantly glistens on her body. Tossing the tank top with her other shirt, I make quick work of her bottoms, only to stop short when I find more bare skin beneath.

Goddess help me, not a stitch of underwear on, I might die tonight.

The contact of my skin on her hips sends her into a frenzy. She turns abruptly, cupping my neck and bringing my lips to hers in a crushing kiss. Her tongue demands entrance while she presses her body against mine, seeking friction. Obliging her, because frankly, I don't think I have much control left, I return her kiss, this tasting of her, renders my mind stupid.

"I need you, Declan," she whispers between our lips, crashing into one another, shattering my resolve. I grip the back of her neck, angling her exactly how I want, and slide my other hand up and fist her hair, holding her still. She tastes like blueberries and honey. Breaking away, I internally berate myself for what I'm about to say, but I have to get her temperature down.

"Fuck...I know, baby, but we can't...not like you need, or I want, but—" I confess. Ignoring me, she pulls away and goes straight to for my shirt.

She's struggling with the buttons and, giving up, she rips it completely open. She meets my gaze as buttons fly and ping off the tile floor. Devious.

Good hells, this woman.

Faith's chocolate-chestnut eyes flicker to that molten metallic, glowing heavily with copper and hints of gold and silver. They roam up and down my chest, landing on my tattoos, and then a saucy smirk forms when she lifts her hands and runs her fingers over the barbells piercing through my nipples.

A ripple of blazing tingles spread over my skin from every one of her delicate touches. My pulse races, funneling all of my blood to my cock. I don't know how much longer I will be able to bury the two-ton want I have to bury myself deep inside of her.

"Keep ogling at me like that...and I can't promise I'll be able to restrain myself..." I mutter huskily.

The tub is nearly full to the brim, distracting me enough, so I reach behind her and shut off the flow. Lightly tapping her shoulders, I guide her back to the tub. Lifting her naked body up, holding her tightly against mine, I take a moment and soak in the titillating sensations from holding her before reluctantly placing her in the cool bath. Water splashes over the side, soaking my jeans.

My girl giggles and slips her head beneath the water, her breath bubbling up. She emerges with a small spray of water, tugging a hair tie at the back of her head, trying and failing to remove it from holding her messy bun.

Kneeling next to the oversized porcelain tub, I motion for her to come closer. My hand slips into my front pocket, covertly adjusting my lust-hungry dick, and then retrieves my pocketknife.

Flipping the blade open, I catch her flinching; I'll dig into why that is later. I stretch the hair tie, letting my blade slice through it. Gently tugging the elastic from her knotted hair, a warm sense of contentment at her sigh ripples in the air.

Once more, she slips beneath the water, emerging quicker and smoothing her hair back, flitting her whiskey eyes over me. Goddess help me, she's exquisite, her eyes still glowing that metallic copper gleam. Wet skin sparkling, tendrils of her caramel ends curl around her shoulders and neck. Her full breasts bob into one another in the water, capturing every ounce of my attention.

Seeing my unrelenting stare, she drags her knees up, hiding the delicious globes from my sight. With a groan, I slam my hands down on the side of the tub and shove myself up. I'm three steps away from the counter when her arm shoots out, slippery hand gripping my wrist and tugging.

"Join me, p-please..." she pleads, voice petite and nothing more than a breathy rasp, but oh so sexy.

Stepping towards the counter anyway, I turn from her, sucking in several pulls of air, filling my lungs to the brink each time. As her mate, while she's in heat, my body too will react and send me into a rut-like state. The purpose is entirely driven by the need to procreate, and man, it's driving me clean over the edge right now. The thought of bending her over the counter and being balls deep inside her bombards my mind and heats every cell in my body.

Fighting the building lust that is coiling within me, scalding my insides along the way, I debate obliging her. Enchanting whiskey eyes connect with mine in the mirror, challenging my resolve. I can do this.

Reminding myself not to sink into her, I strip out of my clothes and step in behind her. I gather her in my arms; she fits like a puzzle piece. My cock jolts when I yank her closer in between my legs. She wiggles her hips, and a tantalizing friction forces a moan from me. I instinctively press harder into her backside and band my arms around her middle.

"Stop before I lose all sense and bend you over this tub and fuck you raw until you can't walk for a week," I growl, and she laughs. Her devious little giggle is malicious and tantalizing.

Sliding my dick up between the globes of her ass, it cradles itself. I guide her to lie back, and she settles easily against my chest. Her nearness calms the caged Thorin, begging to be released.

Her lithe fingers lace with mine and ghost over her quivering, hot flesh, heating the blood coursing through my veins to a boiling point. Breathy little moans rush from her lips, and she cups her breasts with our entwined hands. My heart gallops to a thunderstorm and then stalls when she slides the other of our entwined hands down the front of her stomach. My fingers brush against something hard and metal. Glancing over her shoulder through the clear water, a glint of silver protrudes from her belly button.

Well fuck me.

I vaguely recall seeing the tiny piercing that first day in the bar, but I had forgotten. How? I don't know. It's been impossible to stop looking at her since that first afternoon. Unable to drag my eyes away from her flesh, I skirt over the black ink of her tribal and Celtic tattoos on the left side of her torso. They're distorted a little under the water, but still alluring enough that I drag our hands up over them.

Furthering my study of her body, my other hand lazily caresses her budding nipple, tugging it to a peak. Grazing her skin from her ribs to her leg, my fingers skate over the wolf tattoo on her left hip and thigh. She throws her head back into my shoulder to look at me. Agonizingly slow, she lifts a hand to cup my cheek and run her fingers over my lips. I capture them and lightly suck on the ends before dipping my head to her shoulder and nipping the skin. She gasps and moans, undulating her hips, cascading my hand from her thigh.

A need so compelling to touch and explore her skin overwhelms my senses, and I can't think straight. I have to keep a clear mind; I can't hurt her. Refocusing myself, I go back to her tattoos.

A large piece stretches from the top of her hip to the top of her knee. It's a blend of half a woman's and a wolf's face. Runes and other symbols related to her pack are inked into the flowers and white spruce branches framing the blended faces. Delicate strings and chains are draped and hanging from various spots around the wreath of plants. The ink is dainty and feminine, yet powerful. It had to have taken hours to complete; an irrational burning of jealousy creeps up my throat at whoever touched her skin for that long.

Swallowing sharply, I shift behind her, bending my lips to her neck and place a kiss on the base of it. Inhaling as my nose brushes up the side, little black spots flicker behind my lids. Placing open mouth kisses up the curve, I drag my teeth up and nibble on her lobe and then back down. Potent arousal blooms in my stomach and sinks, flooding my legs.

A quick shake of my head clears it. I have to stay clear-minded; it's a necessity. My eyes land on the largest tattoo on the other side of her body, the black and gray ink swirls from her upper pelvis to right under her knee on her calf.

The ink seems to be a compilation of every creature she's ever photographed, centered around a haunting skull in the center of the outside of her thigh. Deer, horses, butterflies, foxes, rabbits, leopards, a variety of birds, and wildflowers. Even a snake wraps around the base of her calf, but it's the large black wolf face that draws me in. I swear it could be Thorin.

Tracing over one of the skulls, I realize the haunting bone is not the only one. Noting the several smaller skulls scattered throughout the ink, but it's the faded streaks of white scars peeking out from under them that raise several alarm bells. I rake my eyes over the side of her profile, taking in her peaceful and beautiful visage, and wondering, *what is she hiding?*

My gaze flits back down, and the tattoo is filled with swirls and more of those dainty chains. It stretches the whole expanse of her flesh, save for the blank space remaining from the top of her leg and the middle of her calf. Her back is bare from ink, as well as her arms and neck.

A carnal need to mark her skin pulses from the roots of my canines, spreading throughout my body.

"Claim her," Thorin growls.

"Go the fuck away, Thorin, I can't, not right now." He snorts and walks back into the recesses of our connection, grumpy and snarling.

Staring down at her cleavage, I lift our hands back to the other breast, squeezing. Faith breathes out a provocative moan, arching her back. Deep-rooted satisfaction rumbles from my throat as she sighs contentedly from my touch.

Her body flushes red again, thighs squeezing together seeking friction for release. Sucking in a breath, needing to clear this haze fogging my mind, I unlace my fingers from hers. And following an ancient instinct to please and satisfy, I skim my palm down her front, cupping her between her thighs. My dick twitches at the contact. I need more, but I have to behave myself for her.

She hisses when my thumb rubs against her swollen clit. Her hips buck when my finger strokes down and up her slit, and circles her swelling clit again.

This girl is going to wreck me.

"More, Declan, I need more," she pleads in between breathy moans. The sound of my name coming from her lips, bawdy and erotic, is almost more than I can bear. I capture the skin of her neck between my lips, sucking, while I trace a finger from the base of her pussy up, and my thumb continues rubbing circles over her clit. Her center pulses, trying to suck my finger in.

I reverse direction and slide back down, delving inside. Her heat wraps around the digit. Her gasp floods my body with a wildness I've never felt before, and it takes a herculean effort to stay level-headed. The heat of her pussy clenches and engulfs my finger. I add another and curl it up as I stroke her.

The haughty and sultry moans of my name leaving her lips again, tease the very sanity of my willpower not to lift her hips and seat her on my aching cock. My fingers stroke and thrust into her, her arousal pooling around them, mixing with the water. My head tips back as I plunge in and out of her in a sloppy, sloshing rhythm.

Her panting breaths and quaking legs leave my body heavy with a want so powerful it's taking everything in me to focus on her pleasure...she's close. Her pussy flutters around my fingers, and I swiftly add a third. With my other hand, I increase the pressure on her nipple, pinching and tugging before releasing it. Then I glide it down her body, lightly pressing over her womb, and continue my ministrations.

Licking up the side of her neck, she cranes her head back, stealing a kiss. Our hips buck together, both seeking more friction, causing the water to slosh over the side.

Do not come...do not come...do not come... I tell myself over and over. My mouth covers her cry, I pinch and flick her clit, then slowly rub it to ease the pain.

I curl my fingers over the spongy spot inside of her pussy again, her thighs clamp together, squishing my hand. She flushes pink to a deep red from her cheeks to her chest.

"Oh...I'm going to," she breathes, pressing her head into my shoulder. Arms wrapping up around my head, raking her fingers through my hair, pulling on the ends. The sting of pain races down my spine in an inferno.

"I know, baby," I rasp. "Come for me. Drench my fingers, I want your mess all over them," I murmur in her ear. She arches her back, tensing every muscle in her body, her pussy pulses, and she shatters around my fingers, coating them in her climax.

"Oh—fuck," she lets out on a scream, her body tenses and grows limp in my arms. I continue thrusting my fingers into her, riding out each wave of her pulsating orgasm.

She tries to rub her thighs together. "Nuh-uh," I command, keeping her thighs wedged apart with my fingers still buried inside her, torturing her clit with the pad of my thumb.

"Declan...not...fair." She moans. Her petite feet slide over and against each other. A muffled pop sounds, and the plug releases. The water whirlpools over the small opening and gurgles; the water quickly drains from around us. I wiggle my fingers inside her pussy, eliciting another delicious and heady moan from those inviting lips.

She squirms, attempting to flee my hold, "nuh-uh...they stay where they are until I say so." Her little nose wrinkles, pinching her brows in confusion at me over her shoulder. She shakes her head as her hands find the sides of the tub. I follow up with my fingers still tucked inside her. Only when she's about to step out of the tub do I withdraw them.

26

Faith

Twisting my torso, my naughty expression rakes over Declan's glistening, wet body. My thighs clamp together as he ever so calmly brings his fingers, drenched in my climax, to his lips, sucking every last drop of me from them. If that isn't the hottest thing ever, I don't know what is.

I want to devour him.

His hooded lids fall, and nostrils flare. My core flutters when a delicious and deep growl rumbles from his chest. "Fuck..."

He steps out of the tub, reaching for a towel, and I stand there naked and dripping water, ogling him like a two-bit hooker impatient for a quick fix. My teeth sink into my lower lip until the metallic tang of iron coats my tongue. He could command me to bend over the counter and spread my legs right now, and I would do so with no complaints.

This draw to Declan is so heavy and dominant, I can't help myself. With every stroke of his fingers over my clit and thrusting inside me moments ago, he undid another knot I hadn't realized was tied. The reminder throbs between my thighs, begging my body for more.

Blissfully, Sienna is quiet and tucked away in my subconscious. The last thing I need is her two cents on what I should be doing. A few of my friends have shared what it was like suffering through their heats before they were mated, but none of them told me how unbearable it would be once a bond was formed.

Sure, I've been so ramped up in lust that I've wanted to fuck an entire football team before, but never have I experienced the burning of my body from the inside like this. Never has the drive to claim and be claimed been so strong. It never once felt like this with Connor; when I was with him, it felt like a glacier in comparison to Declan's river of lava.

Another wave of my heat comes on, and it burns through my body like a firestorm. I toss any and all rational thoughts out the window as he steps up behind me. I want, no, I need his skin on mine, his tongue tasting me, his cock, swollen and stiff inside me, and not torturing me by brushing against my back. I know the risks of sex during a heat, and frankly, at the moment, I don't care. I need to sate this raging inferno and now.

Spinning to face him, I drag my body up, looping an arm around his neck and walk my fingers up over his pecs. My nipples graze over the coarse hairs on his chest, puckering them to sharp points. He cups my cheek, tracing his thumb over my bloodied lip. Snagging his fingers in mine, I guide his index finger to my lips. Those hazel eyes hold mine when my tongue wraps around the digit. I suck, pulling it slowly out and then back in, twirling my tongue around it, tasting my lingering climax mixed with his skin.

"Fuck...sweetheart that's—" Declan grunts in more of a deep rumble from his chest than actual words. I release his finger and turn, stalking from the bathroom. The water sluicing down my body leaves a tantalizing trail for him to follow. I glance over my shoulder, biting my lower lip.

"What are you waiting for?" I whisper, with a coy smile playing over my lips. I'm fully aware of this inner sex vixen, I didn't know I had before, coming out to play. Declan full body shudders, dropping the towel, and then immediately chases after my sashaying body out of the bathroom. I take off, giggling.

With each quickened step into my bedroom, my thighs rub together, a delicious friction against my swollen center—the remnants of my climax and renewed arousal snake down my thighs in rivulets.

Declan's hands seize my waist before I reach the foot of the bed, and I shriek in delight. The callouses of his hands graze along my damp skin, gripping deep into my hips, and he yanks me into his hard body. His pulsing curved length presses into my ass and lower back. I lean into him, rolling my head to the side, exposing my neck for him. The things I want this man to do to me right now are unholy and downright filthy.

He obliges me and places a kiss on the exposed flesh, moving to my shoulder next, sucking the skin between his teeth, then flattens his tongue and runs it up the column of my neck with a delicious pressure swirling along the cords. My eyes roll into the back of my head, my lips parting on a moan.

He slides his large, warm hands up, cupping my breasts, tweaking my peaked nipples, rolling them between his fingers. Lacing my fingers with his, I tug his hands down and step towards the bed. Curling down, I crawl up on the mattress, ass up in the air, inviting and teasing Declan. Can't get much more wolfish than that, can it?

His weight shifts the mattress and then covers me from behind. I collapse under his weight, the muscles of his chest and stomach hug my curves in the most salacious way, and it feels so right. He paints my neck with his tongue and then peppers kisses down my spine, forcing my hips to dip forward and my ass up into his dick.

"Please..." I plead breathlessly, I'm not above begging to get what I want right now, and that is him thrusting into and filling my wet cunt.

Stifling a giggle, from his answering groan, I wiggle around to face him. As soon as I have turned over, Declan pins my wrists above my head and dips his lips to mine. His kiss is anything but passionate; it's all carnal and pure destruction.

He rolls his hips into mine, sliding his cock between the slit of my pussy. Twin guttural groans erupt from both of us, muffling the slippery noises from between our sexes. My hips lift, connecting with his, dipping and grinding into me, the head of his cock presses against my opening before sliding up to brush over my clit again.

Frustration bubbles at the missed connection but is quickly replaced when the stubble of his beard scrapes along my chin and lips, leaving the skin there raw. I moan into his mouth when he grinds harder and retracts before his cock can slip into my drenched pussy. A sinking ache shrinks in my heart. Doesn't he want me?

He breaks our kiss, whispering, "We can't, sweetheart...I want to, Goddess knows I want to, but we can't...not yet." You know that feeling that you get when you work so hard to get that gold star and then are told you have to wait for your prize? Yeah, this is similar...no, not really, it's worse. I may be pouting like an insolent child if we are basing it on his reaction.

He smirks, leaning back on his heels between my legs, running his strong hands up them. They're all veiny and shit, and so are his forearms too.

Goddess help me.

My eyes follow, trailing up over thickly muscled thighs, then to his hard cock jutting up to his navel.

Continuing up to a sprinkling of hair that traverses up his chest, spreading out over his taut pecs. The silver barbells piercing through his nipples twitch as he flexes under my heated gaze.

He's so damn sexy.

My wandering eyes skim over every inch of black ink swirling across his skin, and the urge to clench my thighs triples. The tribals are a collection of differing repeating patterns, shapes, swirls, lines, and dots. Rune symbols climb up his torso and up over one side of his chest, a small wolf running with an owl in flight sprawls from his chest and shoulder, and up the side of his neck. All of it adds to the natural sexiness he already exudes.

"Like what you see, sweetheart?" Declan's voice draws me out of my stupor of drowning in all things him. Who said I needed air? I'm perfectly content with drowning.

I smirk and dart my tongue out over my bottom lip, drawing his eyes there before they trail down my breasts and linger on the tattoo on my side, to my belly ring, and down. They hover at the apex of my thighs, to the triangle patch of dark curls above my bare pussy. The need to torture him a little bit urges me to draw my knees up, spread my thighs wide, and slip my hands down the inside of my thighs.

His nostrils flare, drinking in my scent, and then, without warning, he dips down, gripping my thighs hard, his fingers digging into the flesh at my hips as he drags my dripping pussy to his mouth; I'm sure to have bruises tomorrow, and for the first time, I don't care, I want them.

The first swipe of his tongue arches my back, and my head drops back into the pillow in a sultry moan. He chuckles, the sound reverberating against my slick center, tensing all the muscles, making my clit throb. He clamps his lips over my nub, sucking and then thrusts a finger into my drenched pussy, filling me, but not full like I need. The sensations and slick sounds are almost too much, but not enough. I need more of him.

My hands find the ends of his hair, raking my fingers through, I dig into his scalp and hold him as he indulges. Lap after lap of his blazing tongue, he brings me closer to exploding.

A seductive heat pools low, building with every thrust of his finger in between my slit. He adds another finger and curls them inside and suckles on my clit.

"Ohhh...gods—" The curve of his smile brushes against me when I buck my hips with each flick of his tongue.

"The gods aren't making you come, sweetheart... I am...your mate," he groans against my lips and then flattens his tongue in one long, hard lick up to my throbbing nub. His hands cup the underside of my knees as he lays them over his shoulders and clamps his arms over my thighs.

My hands slam down on either side of me, clenching the bedding in a crush grip. His tongue slides exquisitely in and out of me, but then he stops, peering up from between my thighs, his chin covered in my juices. Biting back the ripple of disappointment, I catch his smirk; he's waiting for something.

Without breaking his focus on me, he darts his tongue out again, tasting my clit. Flick after flick, teasing me to the brink of explosion.

"Dec-lan," I moan. He sucks it in again and lifts his head in awe.

"Say it again," he groans so low it scrapes against the primal lust caking my insides, igniting little fires all over my skin. I do, and he dives right back to my pussy with a renewed vigor, eating me without abandon, driving me higher up the mattress.

The muscles in my stomach to my toes flex, tightening, and a rush of heat builds from my head to my core. The walls of my pussy pulse and clench as he alternates fucking my hole with his tongue and fingers.

My clit is so sensitive and raw from his mouth and beard, it won't take much more for me to detonate. The stubble on his face scrapes the sides of my thighs and over my pussy in a delicious burn.

"Come for me, sweetheart," he commands, my pussy quivers from his voice dripping with desire. Surprising the hell out of me, he takes my clit in between his teeth with a tiny nibble and tug, and I'm sent over the edge. I scream his name out, climaxing and shuddering from the release. He drinks from me until I'm a puddle of liquified mush and then gathers me into his arms, as exhaustion takes over.

* * *

Throughout the night, Declan brings me to release three more times with either his mouth, fingers, or both, but never how or with what I wanted, and needed. No matter how many times I begged and pleaded for him to fuck me, he refused. The sting of rejection only settled for a moment before he destroyed all thoughts of it with his mouth.

I must've dozed off again at some point, because when the mattress dips and bounces, my eyes crack open following him. He walks that perfectly muscled ass into the bathroom, and I stare at his retreating form unabashedly, landing on more of his tattoos. I never really had a chance to admire them that morning he'd offered me sweet tea. He was shirtless, and now I'm kicking myself for it; he's utterly beautiful.

The phases of the moon are tattooed along the length of his spine, and a spiritual tribal version of the tree of life that wraps from the center of his back to his side, with names scrawled along the bottom that I can't quite make out. In addition to those, a large howling wolf with a flock of ravens in flight over it on the other side. The pieces, while separate, seem to mesh well and tell a story that I'll have to ask him about later.

Not looking back, he disappears into the bathroom, closing the door behind him. A rush of hot pain flushes my body, curling my spine in on itself, anchoring a solid weight of agony, forcibly pushing my mind into darkness.

27

Declan

Her breaths finally evened out after that last round of pleasure. I silently give reverent thanks to the Goddess for giving me the strength to endure all of that without taking her. I would fall to my knees in my gratitude if I could feel them. I thoroughly enjoyed bringing that beautiful woman to ecstasy, but fuck, if my balls don't find release soon, they will burst. I want nothing more than to sink into her slick heat and complete our bond, marking her as mine forever, but I want her to want it, want me, and not from a heat-driven lust.

I slip from the bed soon after I sense she's asleep and head to the bathroom for a long, preferably a cold shower, but—

Little minx.

My lips curl up, and I stifle a chuckle.

Her eyes are burning into my backside as I cross the bedroom on noodle-like legs into the bathroom and close the door. I have half a mind to text Wyatt and send him to my house to grab my box of condoms.

Locating my cell a minute later, I open my text thread with Wyatt. My jaw unhinges at the amount of missed calls from my father and texts from Wyatt.

Wyatt: I hope she's alright...Jules is panicking down here.

Wyatt: Okay, never mind, we can hear she's alright.
Wyatt: Well done, cuz, I now never want to hear your name again...
Wyatt: Food and essentials are outside her door.
Wyatt: Don't forget to come up for air. LOL.
Wyatt: Your father just called, looking for you.
11 Missed calls: Father.

My head falls back against the wall, the last of my lust fading at the mention of my Father. Deciding to shower off and then call him, I turn the knobs of the shower on and let the bathroom fill with steam. It should be a cold one, but at the thought of my Father, the need to cleanse his ick off me is greater.

The hot water sluices over the ridges of my body, relaxing my aching muscles I hadn't realized were tense. One hand leans against the tiles, the other sloshes the water over my hair, and then runs down my chest. An image of Faith running her hand down my chest earlier, and then another of her gripping my hair while I devoured her flares to life.

My hand slides lower, grasping my hardening dick at the memory of Faith spreading her legs wide for me, revealing her slick, pink pussy. I groan, shuttering my lids, rolling my lips in under my teeth, the tangy-sweet yet slightly salty taste of her still lingers on my tongue.

Gripping my length in my hand, I fist it up over the mushroom tip and slide back down to the base. Flashes of Faith arching her back, running her hands over my shoulders, darting those sultry glances at me run through my mind over and over. Her moans and whimpers fuel the hot blood rushing over me in waves.

The way she submitted to my demands and, in turn, demanded more of me was divine. Fuck I need her. Each stroke grows faster and harder, as I recall the taste of her arousal on my tongue again, sweet and tangy like sweet tea.

The base of my shaft and balls tighten, and tingling spreads over my lower back. Pressure building as my climax rises in my shaft. I groan and with one last pump of my fist, rope after rope of my spend slings over my hand, to the tile wall and floor. I'm so lightheaded, I have to lean my head against my propped arm on the tile. My panting breaths slowly return to normal as my climax washes away. I've never come that hard in my life.

With hands stretched out above me, I lean in under the shower head, letting the water pound into my skull. Thoughts of earlier on the porch before Faith slipped into her heat run rampant in my mind again. The puzzle pieces of every flinch and the scars she's hiding pick at a nagging suspicion that's rapidly growing. Someone's hurt her, and that fuels a rage I haven't felt in a long time. It also reignites the fear of that night with Sophia, only solidifying my resolve to keep myself in check. No amount of forgiveness would ever come close to meaningfulness if I hurt her.

I keep telling myself that I accepted this bond because she needs protection, and that if she genuinely didn't want to accept a bond that she craved for a decade, then she would've. Yet, when I repeat my reasoning to myself again, I don't believe it. There's something about her that I can't quite let go of. I need her, but I don't know how to keep her. Rejection would be easier, I think.

Frankly, if I'm being honest with myself, I don't think I'm strong enough to withstand a rejection if and when she eventually smartens up, either. It's as painful for males, but it doesn't leave lasting effects on our bodies like it can for females. I know I'd kill any male if that ever happens to my sister, so I wouldn't put it past Faith's Father to do the same to me if our bond is broken by either of us. It would be no less than I deserve.

I'm not afraid of dying, but I would never put someone through that pain purposely. Whatever it was earlier, urged me, pushed me to make her mine, and now she is. Well, mostly until I claim and mark her. I pray that I won't hurt her. I know I won't survive another Sophia moment. The ghost of that evening is inked into my psyche forever.

Stepping out of the shower, I wrap up in one of the towels and swipe my belongings off the floor. Cracking open the door, I pad back into the bedroom as steam escapes behind me, and the slight cool air from the ceiling fan brushes against my skin.

Silently, I slink across the floor and dump my clothes on the chair with hers and unlock the bedroom door to find a tray full of finger foods, sandwiches, and water bottles, and two glasses of sweet tea. Alongside the tray is an unopened box of condoms with a sticky note attached.

You can thank me later :)
-Wyatt

Barely holding in a chuckle at the poorly drawn winky face, I snag the tray and toss the box on top and ease the door closed, sliding the lock back in place. Spinning, tray in hand, I freeze when a pair of dark chocolate eyes lock with mine.

"Hungry?"

Faith licks her lips, and her eyes flicker to copper and back. "Mhmm," she gives a little nod, smirking. She sits up, and the sheet slips down over her puckered nipples.

Oh yeah, she's hungry, and something tells me it's not for food. The hand gripping my towel drops, and all hells, she licks her fucking lips like I've presented her with a Christmas feast. Never before have I wanted to be roasted meat in my life, but right now, she can carve me up and serve me; I'll gladly provide the gravy.

I set the tray down on the nightstand and face her. Faith crawls to me and slides her hands up my damp stomach. My hand cups her neck, bringing her closer, dragging her up the length of my body.

Skin to skin, a surge of lust ignites in me, and my fingers grip tighter around her neck. I lift her and crush my lips to hers in a bruising kiss. Her arms wrap around my neck, pulling me down to her. We collapse as one to the bed, her legs wrap around my hips, grinding my hard cock over her wet slit.

Our hands are wild, slipping over each other's skin. My lips claim her neck, nipping and licking. My hands cup her full tits, pinching and pulling at her nipples. An erotic moan shatters any restraint I have to take her gently. I pull away, despite her protest, to grab a condom.

"Please, Declan, don't tell me no again, I won't survive another rejection," she whines, the tips of her fingers holding onto my neck. Hand freezing mid-air, her protest paralyzes me.

She felt rejected?

Fuck, I knew I should've asked Wyatt before I locked the door earlier.

"I–Faith," I try to explain, but figure words are useless. I reach behind me, fumbling for the box. Sneaking a glance over my arm, I snag it and bring the box to her face with a grin.

"Oh," she blushes.

"Oh," I reply in turn, and she turns her head to the side. That won't do at all. I set the box beside us and pinch her chin to make her face me.

"Don't hide from me, sweetheart...ever," I command, not as an alpha to his mate, but a lover to a lover. Faith nods, taking my hand, and brings my finger to her mouth. Her hot tongue slides under it, then her mouth closes over it, sucking. A flash of gold from my eyes glimmers over her cheeks. She smiles with my finger in her mouth and then releases it, guiding it down between our bodies.

Catching my rapid breaths proves futile when she slips my finger inside her weeping cunt. I don't bother holding in the groan that comes out. With her hand guiding mine, sliding in and out of her, I lean back on my knees, enjoying the view of our fingers disappearing inside her. My cock jerks, it's so hard it's painful.

With one hand, I fumble to open the box of condoms and snag one. Bringing the wrapper to my teeth, I tear it open. When her fingers take the condom from the package, I spit the wrapper off to the side, and with both of our hands, we roll it on.

Sliding our joined hands from her cunt I take hers into my mouth and slide mine in hers. Her moans are so sweet and sensual, I can't wait any longer.

Taking my throbbing cock and rubbing the head against her slickness, teasing her, she whines. "Please...Dec...please," and that is my undoing, I slam into her, almost blacking out in the process.

Oh, Goddess help me, I'm seeing fucking stars. She tightens her legs, wrapping around my back, and her hips buck up with my next thrust.

"Fuck...so...good..." I have no idea what I'm muttering to her; all sense and ability to think have left. All I know is that I'm a goner.

She is so tight, hot, and wet. And when she clamps that enchanting pussy around my cock, I almost lose my load. Focus on anything other than that right now, I tell myself on repeat, like going to the dent—

Fuck.

She rakes her fingernails down through my hair and to my neck. I shudder and growl out a groan, "Fuck me, that feels good baby." I grip one of her inked thighs upwards, angling her body to get deeper, thrusting so hard her tits bounce.

"Goddess...sweetheart, your body was fucking made for me," I groan at the sensations of her body against mine, my cock pumping in and out of her, reinforcing our bond, solidifying it. The all-encompassing, heady passion drowns me with each thrust of our hips, our skin clapping together. All of her provocative want and emotions slam into me, melding with mine, heightening the sensations.

"Who are you praying to Declan? Because it's me you're pounding into." She breathes, tilting her chin up. It takes everything in me not to chuckle at her taunt. I dive in and suck her bottom lip between my teeth.

"You sweetheart, you're my goddess."

Her nails rake across my back, slicing, leaving little scratches in my skin. The sensation ripples a tide of tingles down my spine. Sweat beads and pebbles over our skin, creating a slippery friction.

The slapping of flesh against flesh creates a sultry symphony, one I can't wait to repeat. My hips piston into hers in a steady rhythm, our racy moans and the undeniable scent of sex fill the air. In a snarl, my canines lengthen as we both climb to our climax, and as much as I want to, need to, sink my teeth into her neck, I won't, not yet, not while she's in her heat. I want her fully present in her mind, not clouded with primal lust fueled carnage.

"Declan...don't stop...I'm close..." I grip both of her legs, hooking them over my shoulders, and rock into her to the hilt. Her slick warmth clamps around my cock, her body flexes rigid, and a rush of heat floods around my cock as she screams my name. I follow her, pumping hard and shuddering, yelling hers as she milks my cock dry.

28

Declan

The counter chair creaks as I shift in the seat, a shaky thumb hovers over the call button to my Father. It's the last thing I want to do this morning, but I've put it off long enough. He's called at least a dozen more times since last night. I haven't bothered listening to the voicemails, knowing he will repeat whatever is in them.

I've got time to handle this while Faith's upstairs sleeping; she looked so peaceful that I couldn't bear to wake her this morning, no matter how much I wanted to slide into her from behind. I did, however, leave some ibuprofen and a fresh glass of water for her on the nightstand.

A squeaking floorboard above draws my eyes up to the ceiling. The aroma of oak and amber with a hint of smoke assaults my nose next, and I stifle a groan. Wyatt saunters into the kitchen, scuffing his slippers along the wooden floor. He's fixing the waistband of his wrinkled flannel pajama bottoms, and his honey blonde hair is a complete mess.

It seems I wasn't the only one with a late night. "Morning," he greets, his voice a bit hoarse and groggy from sleep

"Morning, did *you* sleep okay?" I tease. Wyatt quirks a brow at me, I'm sure wanting to know the same, but I refuse to answer his unasked question. We may joke like we're still kids, but the kiss and tell stories aren't my thing anymore.

"Sure, we had to put in earplugs...y'all are far from decent roomies," he teases back, and heads to the coffee pot. "But on a bro level...well done, Cuz." He adds, chuckling. I roll my eyes, not going there this morning, and trace my finger over the edge of my cell and then look up again.

"I—uh made a fresh pot earlier and ground up some espresso beans if anyone wanted one of those instead," I offer, and glance down at my phone again. Whether or not Wyatt notices, he doesn't say anything about it.

My fingers tremble as I pick up my phone for the fifth time. An unexpected churning in my stomach distracts me from the number on the screen, and I cover the screen with my palm. Wyatt brings the coffee pot over to refill my mug and stops mid-pour, pulling it back as he realizes my mug is untouched.

He sighs and closes his eyes for a moment before setting the pot down and snagging my mug. He furrows his brows, then swiftly softens the corners of his mouth and eyes, dumping the cold contents of my mug into the sink.

"You know, when you make it hot, it's usually best to drink it hot..." he mutters and refills my mug with fresh hot brew. "There, black like your soul," he chortles, sliding the mug my way. The bitter citrusy and chocolate aroma wafts on the steam rising to my face. I give a curt nod and focus on the screen of my phone again.

An unwelcome series of thoughts pester the edges of my mind. Why has he called so many times? Has something happened to my sister Estella? When my other sister, Estella's twin Elena, was killed by vampires he'd called incessantly when I was on leave, having only returned stateside. I had over 30 voicemails from him then. At the moment, I have 25 missed calls and half as many voicemails. Cold dread pours over my head to my toes.

I know I shouldn't be speculating over what it could be about and call, but I linger and sit in denial. Setting the device down, I cradle the steaming mug of black coffee between both palms. My foot bounces rapidly in its restlessness. My gaze darts up to Wyatt, who leans on the other side of the white and gray granite island. He's shooting me a knowing look; one he's given me countless times over our lives.

"So...are yo—" he starts, and I shoot him a glare.

"Don't fucking start, Wyatt...I don't need your psychological bull-shit right now." I reply tersely and instantly wish I hadn't said anything; he doesn't deserve my mood swings. Heaven knows he puts up with a lot more than that from me.

Wyatt flinches and backs away from the counter to lean against the opposite side next to the coffee pot. He stares at his mug of coffee and nonchalantly drinks some before setting it down. I don't deserve his patience, but I'm grateful for it.

A bloom of wildflowers, and mountain air envelopes me in an embrace of comfort when Faith descends the stairs. The khaki shorts she's wearing hug her hips and sculpt her shapely bum. The forest green tank top she has on shifts with each movement, snagging my eyes directly to her breasts swaying with the loose fabric, *and* no bra again...that's downright cruel.

Those stunning chocolate and caramel tresses are tied up in a pony-tail, showing off the slender curve of her neck. I graze over her curves, and a wistful smile plays at my lips. Last night was the first night that I've slept throughout the night without nightmares or waking up in a cold sweat in years. A night without the clawing, burning need to drown myself under the cloying clouds of my meds is a welcome gift.

There's a part of me that knows I should've told her about my PTSD last night before I went and accepted the bond, but that nag-ging sensation of fear pulled at the recesses of my mind, and I couldn't.

Unbidden images of Sophia's bloody neck flash before my eyes, causing my hands to jerk. I knock over my mug at Faith's voice. What did she say?

"Oh shit... Wyatt toss me a towel," she demands, rushing to my side. Snagging the towel mid-air, she promptly wipes up the still-hot coffee spilling all over the counter.

A small drip of it lands on my thigh as she chases it towards the lip of the counter. Her worried gaze drops to my jeans and then back up. "Are you okay?" she asks, softly. She straightens, but her eyes never leave mine.

"What? Erm-Oh yeah, I'm fine." I didn't even notice the sting from the hot coffee splashing onto my thigh. I lock eyes with her, diving deep into those chestnut rings, rimmed in amber and copper flecks. Those soul-devouring irises are ever changing and strikingly radiant; it's so damn difficult to look away. I'd rather claw my eyes out than blink. The side of my face heats at her lips pressing into the skin. I'm swimming in a puddle of joy, floating out of my body.

"Earth to Declan!" She coos, snapping her fingers. Her hand waving in my face, I blink rapidly and study her features. In a huff, she spins away from me, breaking our eye contact, and deposits my mug in the sink.

Faith stands at the counter, thrumming her fingers to the side of the metal sink, staring at me. I can't tell if she's pissed, annoyed, or thinking.

"*Oh, I'm not pissed, should I be?*" She arches a brow and waits, but my tongue is lodged in my throat. "*No, Declan, I'm not mad, but I am worried though...what's wrong?*" She links through our bond, stunning me with the intrusion.

With a slight shake of my head, I hope she'll take that answer for now. I'm not quite ready to speak, let alone string a solid connection to our link. "*Okay, Declan...I'm here if you need me.*"

Grabbing my phone again, I glare at the screen and hover my thumb over the call button. My leg starts bouncing again, faster this time, and my hands begin to tremble once more. The screen lights up with my Father's face. Hot irritation sparks to life at his impatience, and the thought of his nitpicking for me not calling right away sets in.

I let it ring several times before both Wyatt and Faith's stares bore into me so much that it sends a pang of guilt through my chest. I swallow sharply, clearing my throat, and answer.

"Hey Dad, I was literally getting ready to call you..." I trail off as his voice cuts into mine.

"Dec-lan? Thank fucking Goddess. I've been trying to get a hold of you for the past day...it's—" his raspy voice dies off, the hoarse tone merging from worried to miserable in less than five seconds.

"What is it? What's happened? Just tell me!" I yell, panting, my eyebrows shooting together. I tug on the collar of my shirt, wrenching it around my neck. There's not enough air. Why is there not enough air?

Bolting up from the chair, I start pacing the throw rug in the living room. "It's...your Mom...she—was—killed, vamps," my Dad replies gloomily, sniffling, and choking, a sob tears through his throat. The phone slips from my grip and crashes to the floor.

Icy claws grip my throat, slicing panic through the tendons and muscles. My vision blurs with tears, and slowly my head shakes back and forth, faster and broader as the news of what he told me sets in. Wyatt is by my side in an instant, both hands cupping my shoulders, shaking me, but all I can do is search for Faith.

From the kitchen, her stare widens, freezing on me when our eyes meet. It takes me a second too long to realize she's already tuned into everything I'm reeling in. Shit.

A strangled sound, like a dying hyena, erupts from my throat, and I collapse to my knees. How fucking fitting, those soulless blood suckers have killed both of our Mothers, and within weeks of each other. What are the odds? The Moon Goddess sure has a hilarious sense of humor.

"Don't fall into the darkness, Declan, you're not alone," Thorin wails through our link, but it's muted and fuzzy, and I can barely register what he's trying to communicate.

"Dec, what is it? What's happened?" Wyatt questions, firing off in rapid succession, he squeezes my shoulders and shakes me again.

"Faith, can you tell?" He asks her, and she doesn't respond, just stands there like me, frozen.

"Declan!" My Dad shouts through the phone, Wyatt grabs it, and rises. He paces across the living room, burning a hole in the rug.

"Uncle Emron, it's Wyatt. What's happened? Declan can't physically speak—" Wyatt freezes, stumbling and catching himself on the arm of the couch to keep himself upright. "What?" He squeaks painfully, holding a hand to his chest. "Alright, I understand...okay, yeah... we will be there."

He's in my space again, cupping my shoulders, his fingers digging into my collarbone. The thrumming of blood in my ears drowns out whatever it is he's saying to Faith. They sound like they're underwater. My eyes don't leave her, while I try to grab for our link. She recoils, and a surge of sharp pain slices through my entire body as her emotions roll through our bond.

Wyatt's face comes into focus at a snail's pace, like tuning in an old TV. Finally gulping down a heaping of air, my lips part and then clamp down again. Wyatt turns unexpectedly, stomping into the kitchen. He drags Faith to me, her feet skidding over the floor.

"You need to snap him out of it before he has an epis—" he stops and then clears his throat. "We gotta go as soon as possible, his Father is sending a plane in an hour, and it'll be here in three," he says, and then gently pushes her into me. If my body weren't a frozen mess, I'd rip his damn hands off for handling my mate that way.

A cluster of asters, daisies, and white violets perfumes the space between Faith and me. Our bodies are so close, I can see the tiniest beads of sweat forming above the arches of her eyebrows. Her chestnut eyes, now a lighter shade closer to honey, brim with unshed tears.

Look at me. Please. See me, I think.

Bring me out of my head, I can't do this, I scream internally, hoping she can hear my silent torment and ease my torture.

Warm hands cup the sides of my face, her thumbs rub back and forth over the softening stubble of my beard. Her honey eyes bob over my pensive face, and a breath shudders from me in relief. My lids flutter close, squeezing out the first tears that race down my cheeks. Faith's warm lips collide with mine, and my eyes flash open. She doesn't demand or pry. She briefly connects our lips and then leans back, still cupping my face, eyes searching into the depths of mine.

"Hey...I see you," she whispers and pecks my cheeks. A weight lifts from my chest, replaced with a tender warmth that wraps around me. "Wyatt told me, I-I am so-so sorry, Declan...what do you need from me?" Her voice is barely a whisper as she consoles me, offering her sympathy.

When she wraps her arms around my neck and pulls me into her shoulder, I allow my body to follow and sink into hers. Sobs rack my body like a ghost, clogging my ability to hear anything else but her heartbeat.

* * *

I don't know how long we stayed like that, but the next thing I know, Faith is putting my truck into drive. I deduce that she's either dragged me or at least gotten me to move my feet at some point to get me in the passenger seat. A suffocating darkness creeps in, carving a hollowness along its path; it would be so easy to slip into it and never come back out.

"It's a couple more houses, Faith...oh, that one," Wyatt guides from the back seat, pointing.

"I know," she says dryly, in a voice full of guilt, but she makes no other offering for explanation to him. When she pulls into my driveway, Wyatt leans back, patting my shoulder, and tugs Julianna into his side.

Wyatt, Julianna, and Faith quit the truck while I sit there blinking like a zombie. Wyatt is at my door before I can finish unbuckling and, pulling my arm, dragging me up the stairs.

Absentmindedly, I hand over my keys; my hands are shaking too much to function. I flick my gaze up to the non-moving porch fans. I must've forgotten to leave the switch on. The sticky air hanging under the overhang clings to my skin, but the irritation that generally accompanies it is nowhere to be felt.

Wyatt deposits me on the couch, and Julianna hustles through my house. The slamming of doors and slightly shouted commands filter to my ears, but I'm curling into the soft comfort of nothingness. Faith hovers in the living room, eyes boring into the back of my skull. I sense her brushing against our bond, but I shut her out and sink further into the numbing fog.

Hello, nothingness, it's quite lovely to see you again.

It's nice here in the blank state; you notice things you didn't before, like how my air filters need to be cleaned.

Did you know that if you don't change your air filters monthly, the amount of dust that settles daily is almost double? The picture frames on the fireplace mantle are covered in a layer of dust, and I know I dusted a couple of days ago.

Without too much thought, I shuffle to the kitchen, find my cleaning rags, and slide back over the wood floors in my socks, shocking myself on the arm of the couch from the static created.

Where are my shoes?

Wiping the green cloth over the silver frame of the picture of my parents, the dust instantly clings to the microfibers. Once it's sparkling and free of the pesky debris, I set it back on the mantle.

I wipe each frame, remembering when they were taken. One of my sisters, when Elena was still alive, hugging one another at the lake, slices a pang down my chest. Another one of Estella, a year ago, rips that cut wide open. But, the one of my Mom, stalls my hand, holding me in a paralyzing grip. I wipe the surface, over and over and over again, maybe if I—no. I gently return it to its place in the center, juxtaposed to Estella's.

29

Faith

Declan is drowning in his grief, and I don't blame him one iota. I wish I could say I don't understand what he's going through, but unfortunately, that has been my life for almost the past two weeks. Wyatt didn't need to tell me something awful had happened earlier, because a tidal wave of unfiltered, raw pain smashed into me the moment Declan dropped his phone.

All morning, I lay in bed debating on getting up after he snuck from the bedroom, his anxiety had been streaming into me like the winter runoff from a mountain brook in the spring. I didn't know what was wrong and tried like hell not to think it had something to do with me, that perhaps he regretted his decisions from last night.

In the past, Wyatt had talked about his dear cousin and how much he worried for him, but never truly explained why, and I never pushed. I most certainly didn't know it was Declan he was speaking about. I didn't even know Declan then, and it wasn't my place to be concerned, but there was a sliver of it wedged into my heart. I have my suspicions, but for now I'll leave it until I can't. I'm far from perfect myself, so I guess if we are going to try, then I need to be accepting of whatever it is.

A dull ache pulses in my chest while I watch him clean off the picture frames. He's trembling as he sets his mother's photo back on the mantle. Needing the distraction from all of the too unfriendly emotions starting to wrap their spindly dark fingers around me, I glance around the space.

His house is similar in design to the rental I'm staying in, but darker woods occupy the space, leather, and random bursts of colorful throw pillows complement the decor. If I didn't know he lived alone, I'd assume his spouse decorated. The walls are littered with all manner of paintings, tying everything together.

My senses are assaulted with Declan's spruce and amber scent with drips of sea salt and driftwood as it wafts around me in a savory comfort. Dozens of photos dot the walls, but I'm too far to see the smaller ones.

Julianna calls for me from the top of the stairs. I stutter to a stop when one photo in particular snags my attention along the wall to the stairs, but before I can get a second look, she calls again.

"Coming..." I shout back and glance at Declan one more time before I climb the stairs. I wish I could soak up the grief he's swamped in, if only for a moment.

The deep forest green paint in the stairwell is a stark contrast to the bright cream in the hallway. Light overflows and brightens the stairwell; it reminds me of when the sun streaks through the trees in the woods surrounding my pack lands.

Julianna's head pops out from a set of doors at the end of the hallway, "Here!" She waves at me to join her.

My mouth drops with an audible pop as I enter Declan's room. A rich Prussian blue accents one wall, sucking all the light from the windows into it. Thick dark wood beams overhead accent the vaulted creamy white ceiling. Photographs framed in white and black woods, and differing metals hang haphazardly above a dark wood and leather headboard.

My fingers trace over a large, darkly stained cedar trunk with leather straps and oil-burnished fittings that rests at the foot of the bed. The fluffy, creamy comforter draws my eye sharply to the mattress; a slightly lighter navy blue knitted blanket is tossed at an angle over the comforter. But that isn't what has my full attention, it's the photos in the frames, my hand covers a gasp, and my heart takes off like a thundering of hooves.

Every single one of them is one that I've taken over the years. Ones that were exclusively in art shows, or ones that I won awards from and were offered up at auction to benefit different charities. One of a stag with a wolf in the background is one of the largest prints I have ever sold, and it's centered over the bed. The fog rolling through a meadow with Maine's deep woods in the backdrop. The wolf is crouching low, but you can see his gold eyes and dark black fur glistening from the early morning light that bounces off it.

I remember that day vividly. My heart was in my throat the entire time I was squatting behind a tree, zoomed in with my telescopic lens about 300 yards away. Too far to sense if it was a shifter or a wild wolf. I'd snapped the photo and ducked out as quickly as I could.

That photo only had one print made, and he of all people has it?

The room dips to one side, and then to the other. My hands brace on the footboard, my lungs grasp at what little air I can suck in past my lips. How does he have it? I was told that one sold to someone in Maine. Why does he have all of them?

Julianna's lovely face appears in my line of vision, and she's tugging me into the closet. "Here, help me grab clothes for him...stars know he isn't capable right now," she mutters and pulls hangers off the top rack in his walk-in closet. I'm not sure I am either, but okay.

Shaking my head, I stride past her and squat down to grab boots and two different pairs of shoes. In the far corner of the narrow walk-in, several protective plastic bags are hanging. Curiosity piqued; my fingers run over the tops of hangers as I walk to the end, and spread the clothes back. Army fatigues, dress, and formal dress uniforms are zipped up inside the protective bags. My fingers press into the dress uniform, gliding over the ribbons, medals, and insignia pins I don't recognize. He has so many.

Seeing the army uniforms now explains so much of his personality, his commanding and dominating presence, and not solely his alpha aura demanding respect.

My eyes drift down, spying several bank boxes in an impeccable line along the floor and pressed up tightly against the wall. Each one is labeled with a period of years. One box is labeled award-winning. I start to squat down and peek inside when Jules pops back in.

"Hey, can you grab him that black jacket above you, and one of the green and black ties hanging on the tie rack, please?" Jules's voice cracks through my cat like curiosity, jolting me back to reality. A rush of almost getting caught red-handed flushes my cheeks and ears.

Grabbing what she asked for, I carry the haul of clothing out to the bedroom and begin neatly rolling and folding his clothes into a suitcase on the bed. Covertly checking to make sure I'm alone, I snatch and bring Declan's hoodie up to my nose, breathing him in. A homelike warmth cloaks my skin, and for a moment, a tranquility eases my anxious heart. The door creaks, and I quickly shove the hoodie down, roughly folding it.

Wyatt comes in with a garment bag, his eyes rimmed in red and swollen. He lays the bag out flat next to me, jerking his chin at the suit next to me. Gathering the suit jacket, my hands start to shake as a memory of helping my Dad out of his suit jacket at my Mom's funeral flashes behind my eyes.

Wyatt's welcoming hands lift mine and squeeze, stopping the shaking. "Are you okay, Faith?" He swallows and holds my gaze, and swipes away a stray tear that slides down my cheek. "I can't imagine that this is easy...I'm sure it's reopening the wounds of your Mother," he whispers.

Blinking slowly, my lips roll in on themselves as a wave of pain washes over me, causing my chin to tremble. I can't explain what it is

I'm feeling right now. My heart hurts for my Mom, but the weight of Declan's grief pulls me down and crushes me with Earth's gravity.

"Yeah, it's hard, but this isn't about me right now," I reply shakily and place the finely cut black suit jacket inside, followed by the starched white button-down and black slacks. Folding the ties in a loose loop over my hands, I lay them over the shoulder of the jacket and run my hand under my eyes, finding Wyatt standing before me. His shoulders slumped, his head barely holding itself up.

"He's going to need you, Faith," Wyatt says, wrapping me back up into a hug that I'm sure he needs more than I do. He lost his Aunt today. I rub my cheek over his shoulder and step back.

"I know, I just—" I choke on my words and give him an imploring look. "I haven't even processed...my Mom's. I don't want to get in the way-" I admit and turn away. Wyatt remains silent, but I know he understands without needing further explanation.

After a few minutes, I suck up my sadness and finish helping Wyatt and Jules. The zipper closing around the garment bag reverberates through the silence, and as a unit, we pack up the rest of Declan's clothing and needs to travel.

I stand in the hallway, staring back into Declan's room at the wall behind his bed as Julianna and Wyatt take the suitcase downstairs. I'm still standing there when they head back up the stairs and down to where they must be staying at the opposite end of the hallway. I hadn't even thanked them for staying with me last night, even if Declan wasn't there, I know they would have for me. It's comforting to know I still have honest friends in my life.

Suitcase wheels roll along the wood floor and carpet runner. Wyatt nods at me and swings it off its wheels effortlessly and stomps down the stairs. Jules who's following right behind him, stops, staring at me as I meander down the hall and find more of my photographs along the walls. The garment bag hook is digging into my shoulder and as I adjust it, I give her a tiny twist of my lips and we head down together.

There is a stillness in the living room when I step off the last step and set the garment bag over the back of the leather couch. Crooking my head to the side, I search for Declan, but he's no longer in the living room.

"*Where are you?*" I call out over our link, praying he responds.

"*Come around the corner...*" he answers, his grief compounding minute by minute, hits me in a wave. I don't know if I'm strong enough to withstand his grief on top of my own.

A few steps past the couch, I round into the spacious and spectacular kitchen. Declan stands stoically in front of a set of windows overlooking the wrap-around porch. Hands stuffed in his jeans pockets, he stiffens at my approach making me hesitate and linger a moment longer.

My clammy hands slide against my fingers as I fist them and fidget, unsure what to do with them. I hold them behind my back and take measured steps towards him.

I reach inside my mind and close the doors to my mental shield, blocking the emotions rushing towards me from him. I don't want to close our connection, but there is no other way for me to keep standing otherwise.

Warily, my hand stretches out to his elbow, our skin brushes against each other, exquisite tingles radiate down my fingers to my wrist and flow down my arm and wrap around my heart.

My fingers flex and cup his elbow and spread up to his bicep. Declan's muscles flex and twitch under my touch. When he turns, anchoring his gaze with mine, I gasp a mini sigh. Those light hazel eyes are a dull hazel gray, bloodshot shot and swollen.

In choreographed movements, we come together, my eyes never leaving his, I cup the side of his face, and he holds the opposite side of mine. My other hand lingers over his arm, sliding up his shoulder to his neck. He scoops the curve of my spine, bringing me closer to him. My breath hitches at the contact.

We haven't spoken about last night, or exactly what we plan to do about it all or our bond. Plenty of females don't recall their heats, what they said or did during them, but I do, and it was delicious. The pleasure I'd experienced even before we finally had sex was immensely mind-blowing. When our bodies did come together last night over and over again, I wanted to peel his skin up and bury myself underneath only to get closer to him. I shouldn't feel this way after such an extremely short amount of time. I barely know him, but I know him, my soul knows his. Damn, mate bond.

"Will you come with me?" He croaks, his timbre raspy and broken. Those once dazzling orbs sweep over the crown of my head and down to my eyes.

My tongue darts out, wetting my lips, swallowing, and I open and close my mouth several times before I can respond. Do I want to go? Of course! I want to be there and comfort him, but I'm also terrified. I don't think I'm strong enough to stifle my grief without giving off the appearance that I'm making it about me. I'm not that kind of person and bringing me with him at a time when he needs to be there for his family...well, it's not the right timing. Right? In all honesty, I am terrified, but I'm also so conflicted that I don't realize my mouth has opened and I've started talking.

"I want to more than anythin-"

"But you won't," he interjects, his hurt slicing into me, leaving me raw and vulnerable. The twinge of pain that grips the base of my throat closes off any air I sucked in.

"That's not fair, Declan. I want to, but I'm barely scraping by as it is with my grief...But I will be here waiting for you...please try to understand." I manage the half ass explanation laden with anguish that's hard to bury, but how can I explain that something is holding me back? And that it has nothing to do with him.

"Oh, I see, so you can use me for when you need me, but when I need you—You know what, just forget it." He snaps, his tone biting to the quick. The color drains from my face. I stumble back a step and try to understand what's happening.

"That is not fair—" I retort, but he stops me, grabbing my arm, pulling me back to him.

"You're right, none of this is fair," he whispers, hurt laces with confusion at his words, and I stand there frozen. "I'd thought out of anyone here, you would understand, not just because you're my mate, but because you know this pain, but I guess I was wrong."

Ouch. This has to be his grief talking right now. I know I said some awful shit when my Mom's murder had just happened. What I said is a mystery to me, but Hollie told me at one point I was being a spiteful bitch. Shock does wonders for us, doesn't it?

Before I can tell him, I'll meet him there, his hands drop, and he angles away from me. He winces, and then turns back, placing a brief kiss on the top of my forehead. Wyatt appears in the doorway, sun shining behind him.

"Time to go Dec," he reminds, and then turns away. I fight back the urge to grab his hand and bring it to my chest, to tell him I'm sorry, that I'm going to go, and that I'll meet him there. I can easily call my Dad and ask him for our jet, I know he'd have no problem with me using it for this.

That internal tug begs me to keep him close, to soothe his heartache, but my feet drag across the wooden planks of the floor and step out onto the porch. Declan soon follows and locks up his house. He glares down at me. Nothing leaves my mouth. What could I say anyway?

"We can drop you off on our way," he says gruffly, offering his hand. A slight shake of my head is all I can muster for a response, and I step down the steps one jolting step at a time. He thinks I don't want to be there for him, and he's right in one way, but his heart is hurting to much to hear me. I've messed up and I don't know how to fix it.

"I'll walk," I finally mutter when my feet hit the pathway to the drive.

"Faith—" Peering at him over my shoulder, my lips thin, and I turn away and swipe a rogue tear from existence. I'm regretting my decision already and he probably thinks I'm a selfish bitch. What's the point of changing his mind?

"No, it's alright, Declan, go. I'm sorry about your Mom. I'll see you soon." The 'If you still want to.' goes unspoken.

The overwhelming amount of saliva welling over my tongue practically chokes me while I trek back to my house. I pick up my pace to get some distance away. Truck doors slam in the distance as I pass the second house from his. I'm a horrible mate, I knew this before when I was with Connor, I shouldn't have believed it could change with my fated.

From the corner of my eye, I watch Declan's Ford F-250 creep by and spy him in the back seat, facing forward, not even acknowledging my presence.

Why would he?

The sting that quickly pricks at my eyes hurts more than I thought it would. I glance away and decide to walk on the beach instead.

Slipping between two houses, I jump down and remove my shoes. The sand is warming this early in the morning, but I run down to the waves and walk in the salty water, cooling the humiliating heat working its way through my body.

The waves lap at my ankles as they race ashore and retreat, swallowing up my footprints, leaving bits of foam. Tiny bits and pieces of shells litter the damp sand, freshly brought ashore by the tide. With my shoes pinched in one hand, I bend over and snag one perfectly intact scallop shell.

Turning the wet, cream colored shell over in my palm, I continue and focus on my breaths with each step. It does nothing to soothe the building ache inside. I have half a thought of diving beneath those deep, aqua-blue waves, washing away everything that's pounding at my skin.

I should've gone with him...

The climb up the steep stairs to my rental seems to take a lot longer than when I've climbed them before. Circling the wrap-around porch, I punch in the code to the door, and, shocker, the damn thing worked on the first try this time.

Walking into the hallway, I zero in on my reflection in the mirror above a small table in the foyer. The end of my nose is red and raw, my eyes puffy, and red lines the edges of my lids. My palms grind into the sockets of my eyes, stamping out the grief lingering there.

A couple of blinks and I paste on a smile. I can do this today, I will be fine, I will do what I need to do today. I have several emails to go over from Russell. Then, I will call my Dad to discuss coming home early and about Declan. What I should be doing, is packing my bags and calling my Dad for the jet and figuring out where Declan's pack is. I freeze and decide that's exactly what I'm going to do.

Walking to the kitchen for my cell, I yank the ponytail holder from my hair and comb my fingers through the ends, detangling it. My fingers snag on a knot, right when a sharp rapping at the door cracks throughout the hallway. I jump and fling my hands to the console table behind me.

"Declan," I whisper, hope blooming in my chest. Another sharp knock raps against the wooden door before I can head towards it.

"Coming," I call out and take the four steps to the door, pulling it open. My heart lurches and falls completely out of my chest.

"Faith-"

30

Declan

My ears pop when the plane reaches its flight altitude, and my mind drifts to Faith's form walking down the road, peering at me from the corner of her eyes. The pain laced in them and her lips falling gutted me, remembering it now, claws what remains of my insides out. The stabbing pain she'd inflicted when she'd said she wouldn't come with me buried itself in my already deep grave of grief, but when I searched her copper orbs, I saw it. The heart-splitting sadness she couldn't swim above, and while it still hurt to understand, I did.

I was an asshole for what I'd said; no wonder she shut down. She could have said any number of hurtful things back, but she didn't. Wyatt tried to explain why it was so hard for her and that she didn't want to make it about her or have the appearance of it. Why she thought it would appear that way baffles me. No one would think that, if anything, they'd offer her comfort too.

I should've said that.

Two flight attendants elegantly stride towards us, splitting away in the middle, one to serve Wyatt and Julianna, and the other to me.

"Hi there, I'm Elise. Is there anything I can get you? Whiskey? A blanket? Pillow?" She recites in her too-sweet fake voice.

My eyes sweep up her stocking-clad legs, from the black pumps to the matching royal blue pencil skirt and vest over a crisp white blouse. Before meeting Faith, I would've appreciated her beauty, but all I feel is disgust. Her bright red hair reminds me of an overripe tomato, and it matches her bold lipstick, too.

I can't help but compare her fake beauty to Faith's stunning, natural beauty. How the pale pink of her lips doesn't need enhancing colors, or how she has a patch of freckles that spreads over her cute nose, accenting her ever-changing whiskey eyes. Or how she's the perfect height and her head tucks into my chest when I hold her.

I give the attendant a quick shake of my head and lean to the side, looking out the small oval window at the landscape below that's compacting smaller and smaller as we climb a little higher.

* * *

Wispy clouds slice over the wings of the jet, and the pungent aromas of the two flight attendants passing by and checking on us distracts me from zoning out the way I'd like to.

When I shift my focus to the front of the plane, Julianna is sitting before me in the opposite chair, thrumming her fingers over the mini oak table, while the other hand spins her glass of gin, or maybe vodka tonic. Inclining my head to her, I greet, "Julianna."

"Declan." She says matter-of-factly. We stare at each other for a while, studying. I can't tell what she wants, or why she hasn't spoken yet, and I'm two seconds from breaking and demanding what she wants. I lean over the arm of my chair and find that Wyatt's seat is vacant; he must be in the bathroom or he's bugging the pilot.

"Declan, I know we don't know each other very well yet, but I feel like I need to say this to you." Her chest rises, breathing in deeply, and her lips shape an O as she blows it out in a hum. Resting my head in my hand, I jerk my chin for her to continue.

"First, words cannot convey my sorrow for the loss you and your family are experiencing...I need you to know that I'll be there for you as much as Wyatt would be," she offers, but I can tell there's more, so I don't say anything, allowing her to continue. She spins her glass again and takes a long swallow.

"The mate bond can be incredibly intense in the early stages, but it's more intense for alphas—"

"I know," I grumble, slightly annoyed at the topic.

She nods, "I figured...I just...what I mean is, I don't think you and Faith should rush into anything, give her time...but also give yourself some grace," she explains nervously. She downs the rest of her drink and sets the glass down. "And you need to tell her the truth so she can be prepared. *And* don't hold anything against her when she shares hers."

I give her a side-long stare as the words she spewed at me digest. I'd been mulling over telling Faith the truth myself, but hadn't gained the courage to do it. I should be more bothered by the fact that she knows about my issues, but leave it to my big-mouth cousin to dish out my dirty laundry. *Damn it, Wyatt.*

"I-um-Declan, I'm not saying this for your benefit alone, it's for Faith too, give her time to talk to you...ok?" She reiterates, leveling with me with a hard stare. Well, that's cryptic, but I understand her concern.

Julianna twists in her seat, snags her empty glass, and gifts me a wink before ditching me for Wyatt as he rejoins the cabin.

* * *

It's unseasonably cool for summer in Maine, but it suits my mood and the dreariness of the day perfectly. I'd snuck into my family home yesterday evening, and avoided speaking with both my Father and sister, I wasn't capable of forming words yet. Not entirely sure I am now either.

Taking a long sip of whiskey, I survey the black cars dotting the long, sandy-hued, gravel drive. There are too many for me to count or care about. Most of these people loved my Mother, but the rest are only here to garner favor with my Father during his period of grief. Fake ass pricks.

The majority of my pack's self-serving values are one of the main reasons I don't want to take it over. A lot of them are pricks and operate more like the mafia than a pack. I blame the casino. The only reason I would take over is the remainder of the pack that still has morals. They are like my Mother, sweet, caring, and compassionate, but still fierce and loyal.

A sharp snap of bones cracks through the stillness of my rooms, from my neck rolling side to side. Omegas and other servants scurry about bringing in coffee, breakfast treats, and stack after stack of correspondence I have no intention of taking care of.

Bang!

The main entry door slams into the wall behind me. Setting my glass down, I spin to find Estella barging into my room, her reddened face is marred with mascara tracks that crawl down her cheeks.

"Did you plan on hiding out here the whole time and then simply dropping in on the funeral— did you even plan to see me?" She yells, her usually sweet and demure voice cracking with emotion on every word. She storms the rest of the way into the sitting area and the adjoining rooms, hellfire blazing in her aura.

"Stel—"

"Don't Stella me, you've been hiding out here since yesterday. Did you think I didn't see you sneak in, or for that matter, sense your presence?" She narrows her eyes at my glass, "Is that whiskey?" I shrug and take a step towards her. She holds up a hand and shakes her head.

The wrinkling of my nose stings the band of sunburn stretching over the thin skin. I roll my eyes at my sister and cough harshly, chok-

ing on the tightness of my thin black tie as I cinch it up. My head rolls
to each side, popping my neck again.

"Ugh—don't do that," Estella complains, her disgust scrunching up
her face. She sighs and marches over, stopping before me, glaring up
at me. I dip my chin to get a better look at my baby sister.

Her youthful appearance is at odds with her age-appropriate outfit. At twenty-five, Estella is every bit our Mother, but with a sprinkling of our Father in her eyes. The deep navy of her capped-sleeved
shift dress clings to her small curves. The French twist of her pale
blonde hair is so tight it's almost pensive.

My gaze widens, snagging on the strand of gray freshwater pearls
circling her neck. Anguished fingers loom closer to the delicate pearls,
my Mother's favorite piece of jewelry. I had given it to her four, almost
five years ago, for her birthday when our Father had forgotten it because he was too busy with the casino.

While many mate-bonded pairs grow to love each other, my parents were the exception to the rule. At one time, they did love each
other, at least I thought it was evident when I was younger. I never did
figure out what happened, but something did happen shortly after the
twins were born, and they grew apart.

Estella's fingers cover mine as they brush over the opalescent pale
gray pearls. Cold slender fingers cup the side of my face, her thumb
swipes away the hot tears trailing into my beard. Pinching the necklace and turning it over between my fingers, I am taken back to that
day...

*Sweet, summer apple blossoms and sea mist perfumed the corner of the
library. My booted feet crept over the polished wood floors like an assassin.
Sarina McCormick, my Mom, stood regally before the large expanse of windows on the far side, looking out over the garden behind the pack mansion.
Pings and pangs staccato'd against the window pane from the rain pelting the
glass.*

A flash of frustration creased my brow when I honed in on the tears she slyly whisked away, a tiny sniffle following. Her soft hazel eyes reflected in the window, and they swept up to my hulking form in the glass. She spun around, pasting on a practiced smile that didn't quite meet her eyes, no matter how many times she tried.

"Hi, sweetie I've missed you," she whispered, stretching out her hands to me.

"Hi, Ma." My callused hands swallowed her dainty, cold ones. I rubbed the pads of my thumbs over the soft spot near her thumb and leaned in, kissing her cheek. She quickly planted one on mine as I tried and failed to escape her affections.

"Ha, I got you!" She teased, laughing. I searched her features, eager for a break in the facade that would give me any indication of how she was truly feeling. My eyes swept up and bore into her widened, watery eyes, and there, as a single tear pooled and trickled down, she couldn't hide her sadness.

"He forgot again," I said, wishing I was wrong and she was only overjoyed that I was home on leave.

A slight squeeze around my fingers was my answer. She led us to the sitting area near the ostentatious fireplace. We collapsed onto the floral print upholstered sofa, our feet lifting in the air momentarily, and a small giggle escaped our lips. Mom has always repeated the action with me anytime she's able, and at my nearly 30 years of age, she still found it incredibly hilarious.

Before she could hound me about finding my mate and settling down again, I slipped a long, rectangular black box from the side pocket of my fatigues. A toothy grin spread across my face as I presented her with her birthday gift. Her nearly gray, hazel eyes shone in the fading light, gentle wrinkles creased at the sides when she smiled, and finally, one reached her eyes.

"Happy Birthday, Ma," I said and handed her the gift. The oblong box squeaked from the hinges, opening with a snap, but it was her gasp, pure and soft, that had my focus. The simple yet elegant strand of hand-knotted freshwater pearls glinted while she rocked the velvet box to and fro.

"Here, let me," I offered, clutching the box. She relented, and I leapt from the old sofa and darted around it. Clinging to the ends of the pearls, I held it

up and over my Mom's honey blonde head. She pulled the curling ends away from her sleek neck. The pearls nestled gently right below the nape of her neck, a perfect fit. Her fingers slid up, brushing over the iridescent strand.

"It's a lovely gift, Dec, thank you son..." she murmured, with a wistful smile.

"You're welcome, Ma. I knew they'd suit you when I saw them." I bent, placing a kiss on the top of her head, and rejoined her on the sofa.

We'd spent the rest of that evening catching up on the things I'd missed while being away, what I'd been up to, of course, without revealing too much of what I was doing. Mom always worried excessively when I was deployed. One time I divulged too much to my Father, who, no doubt on purpose, decided she needed to know, increasing her worrying threefold..

Blinking away the foggy memory, my hand falls to my side, releasing the pearls.

"I couldn't let Father bury them with her...he's been on the rampage and destroying her things since it happened," Estella admits, sounding more defeated than I've ever heard her. I stare at her in disbelief.

"Destroying her things?" I ask. Shaking my head, I turn away, combing my fingers through my shaggy hair. Perhaps it was a good thing Faith stayed behind, not knowing, but suspecting what she's been through, I wouldn't want to subject her to my Father's bullshit.

"He sounded miserable when he'd called, sobbing," I relay, disbelievingly. His behavior contrasting with what we experienced, but then again, grief has never been a comforting emotion.

"Come on, let's not keep him waiting." Swinging an arm towards her, I grasp her hand in mine, and we stroll to the first floor to get on with the day.

* * *

Traditionally, packs burn their dead, allowing their ashes to return to the earth or, on the wind, to the Moon Goddess. However, ever since my Great Granddad took over the pack, he claimed the Moon Goddess came to him and said covering our dead in the earth would suffice, that she would take their essence as the dead's souls left their bodies. I didn't for one second believe that is what the Moon Goddess wanted, but found my lips sealed shut for a pointless argument over the years.

Both my Great Granddad and Granddad were cantankerous, controlling old men who wanted nothing more than to rifle up the Goddess to get her attention.

The procession of sleek black sedans rounds the cemetery while the skies cloud over, darkening the mourners in a depressing shade of gray.

How Fitting.

Few words are spoken as we say goodbye. The constant sniffling of muffled sobs and the occasional choked-up wail crack like thunder disturbing the peace. Estella and I sit at the front in the creaking, plastic, folding chairs draped in black and stare past the casket to the woods behind. Unblinking, I tip my head back, and a fat, cold droplet splashes on my face.

The last of the white roses is tossed on top of the steadily lowering casket, and a stinging burns the backs of my eyes. I gulp painfully and squeeze Estella's hand resting on her lap. She's dabbing the corners of her eyes again with a light blue hanky, one of Mom's before she returns with a squeeze of her own.

Estella sighs and rises from the creaky folding chair. Dropping my hand, she takes three careful steps to the edge of the expertly carved out hole. She drops the single daisy she's been gripping throughout the entire service, along with the wrinkled hanky. The scrap of fabric flutters to the bottom just as the sky opens up with a crack of thunder and heavy raindrops sprinkle over the three of us remaining.

My father, Emron, stares ahead blankly with puffy, tired eyes and disheveled hair. Estella passes me with a quick side grin and stops before our Father. Cradling his head, she kisses his cheek and then straightens preternaturally quick and dashes through the increasing rain, clutching her purse over her too tightly twisted hair.

I'm not sure at what point my Father and I stand before the open grave, but here we are. Almost two identical men, one with cropped, graying dark hair and the other with longer hair, the ends curling up, and a few strands of silver slicing through.

I lift my chin to the sky, closing my eyes, letting the rain splatter over my face, gluing the ends of my hair to my forehead and cheeks. I swivel back to drop my head and squat before the hole and drop a letter I'd written last night onto her casket.

"Roses aren't even her favorite flower," I grumble, marching away with a deadly glare at my Father. I have nothing more to say to him, and if I can leave without doing so, even better.

Cresting the hill, I turn back and take him in, dropping to his knees with his head in his hands. I don't pity him or empathize with him; the pain he's living with is well deserved.

31

Faith

Faith—" Connor breathes, seemingly relieved. I clutch the handle tight, the pink gone from my knuckles. The initial shock is rapidly replacewith a toppling need to flee.

Why is he here?

A gnawing fear in my mind ripples out a cold sweat over my body. My body that has Declan's scent all over it, mingling. Panic bulges my eyes as they flick behind Connor. Declan's motorcycle is still parked in the driveway, too.

Shit.

Connor's nostrils flare, and his eyes flash to a silvery blue. He lunges, and I swing the heavy door as hard as I can. It doesn't close, just bounces when it slams on his fingers. He lets out a howl and then shoves past the door. My feet move before I have time to think about where I'm going.

Slipping on the carpet runner, I skid to a stop before flying up the stairs, taking two at a time. I slide past my door, losing traction and leaning too far forward, the side of my face kisses the floor, biting the inside of my cheek, copper swims over my tongue.

Harsh, hard hands yank at the base of my scalp, lifting me from the floor, my hair tearing away with each yank as Connor drags me along.

The pain-filled yelp I let out sounds more like a garbled fish breathing out of water as I choke on the blood pooling in my mouth.

"So, you come on our honeymoon, that I paid for, and shack up with another man...after a week?" The accusation doesn't sting as it would have before I'd met Declan, but it still pisses me off. Sharp eyes glare back at him as he continues to drag me back down the stairs, banging my legs against the steps. Connor grabs my throat and crushes it with his other hand when we reach the first floor, and my eyes slip closed for a moment. Not again. He's going to kill me this time.

"You are stronger than you think, Faith," Sienna barks through our link, forcing me to snap my eyes open.

"M-my dad—" I mumble, gasping for air from under Connor's harsh grip around my neck.

"What was that? Something to say? Like, why do you smell like another male?" He hisses, spitting, the warm dollop it splatters on my cheek.

Connor tosses me like I'm a rag doll to the sofa like he always does and laughs. Pain radiates from the base of my neck to the top of my scalp as he yanks another fistful of hair, tugging me up to a sitting position.

"Well?" He sneers.

"My Dad paid for the wedding and honeymoon, you jackass..." I snarl, spitting on him. How does he like it?

He scoffs and shoves my head forward into the arm of the sofa. My face smacks into the cushioned surface and bounces, my body falling off to the side. My nose catches the end of the coffee table with a cracking snap. The motion jars me, and slams my mouth shut, the blood streams down my lip, and drips off my chin, staining the woven gray rug.

Connor's fingers slide up my back, lingering between my shoulder blades, eliciting a disgusted shudder from me. Leaning into me, the shifting of his lips, smiling into my hair, makes me want to puke.

"Hmm...I see I still affect you...you always did like it rough," he murmurs close to my ear. Burning bile races up, coating my tongue, threatening to sputter from my lips. I swallow sharply, craning my neck to scowl at him.

"Hardly...you dis—" His clammy fingers dig into my neck and then wrench into my hair, pulling me back and up to my knees as he stands. Flashes from nights not so long ago, when he'd come home drunk and shoved me to the couch, pulled my hair, punched me, bit my skin, and ripped his claws along my legs pierce and blend into the present. That numb, dark corner appears, and it would be so easy to slide into it and ignore this.

"Don't you dare!" Sienna growls, sending her strength and energy through our connection.

"I don't know if I can do this, Sienna. I'm broken—" I struggle to reply over our link, the pain is shattering through my mind, making it nearly impossible to think.

"No, you're not—"

"You bitch," Connor sneers, and he drags me up the length of his body, skimming his stubbled jaw along my cheek. Inhaling deeply, he groans and jerks me closer, adjusting his hard dick before rubbing it on my thigh. I'm close enough to see the lint fibers stuck on his wrinkled shirt. The weakened citrusy scent of Eliza coats his sweat-slick skin. How had I not noticed it before? My nose wrinkles, and confusion sets in at the lack of alcohol on his breath fanning over my face.

"Mmm...the smell of that male on you, only makes me want to cum all over you, replacing it with mine," he moans creepily, a shiver races from my head to my toes, forcing my eyes closed.

"Declan..." I whisper over our bond, despite knowing he's too far away to hear me, I do it anyway and open my shields.

Connor's sickening wet tongue glides hot over my cheek. Unable to hold the bile back, I choke as vomit shoots out from me, splattering all over his face and chest. Unnaturally quick, he shoves me back by my hair and drops me in a heap to the floor.

With tired limbs, I stretch one arm out to make my escape, but I'm stopped by his biting grip on my arm, yanking me to the sofa again.

"Where do you think you're going? We aren't done!" Connor grunts and jerks me back. The last thing I see is his fist coming at my face, and the world goes black.

* * *

"Wake the hell up! Right now! Faith! Wake up!" Sienna is howling in my mind, pacing back and forth, trying to wrench control from me. My head is pounding to the tune of a drum line. Doesn't she know I need sleep? I was rather enjoying my dream of doing decidedly dirty things with Declan on his bike.

Something cold traces up over my cheek, and something heavy is smothering me. I bolt awake, finding Connor leaning over me. Fear, potent and arctic cold, slithers in my veins. What is he doing here? He sweeps my hair away from my face and leans down. He's straddling my waist; his weight crushing.

"It's about time, darling, glad to see you decided to join me again," Connor says, as the events from earlier slam into me. "I didn't think you'd be out that long, but I did find the pancakes you made, thanks for that, babe." I glare at him, confused as fuck, and shift, trying to wiggle an arm free.

"Nah-ah, you aren't going anywhere. I've had to wait since yesterday afternoon for you to wake up. We have things to discuss." He scolds and smashes his mouth onto mine. I bite his lip, letting go when I taste a pungent iron, and, whipping my head to the right, I bury my face into the cushion of the sofa.

"You bitch!" Connor screams and jumps off me. I scramble to the floor and crawl across the rug. White-hot pain blooms across my back so intense I almost pass out again, as he rakes his partially shifted claws down my back, slicing at the skin of my shoulder blade. He slams into me, his weight crushes into my hips and spine.

His repulsive breath fans the shell of my ear when he whispers, "I know your secret, Faith. Why do you think I kept you so long?" Pure, unfiltered fire rages through me.

"You. Know. Nothing!" I grit out, my jaw locked in a vice. Sienna champs at the bit for control as I hold onto it, cling to it...I will not let her get hurt. *"Dec-lan..."*

Head hanging low and burning from the hair ripped from my scalp and the fresh gouges down my back, I struggle to lift my eyes to Connor.

"Oh, but I do," he taunts, his voice sickeningly smooth.

When my eyes eventually glide up, they snag on shimmering blue and platinum. The pendant, sparkling its sapphire flame in the light, burns a hole into my heart; it's my Grandmother's pendant.

The round, deeply hued sapphire is cradled in a platinum molded northern star. It dangles from a platinum wheat chain. I was told that my ancestors had chosen platinum to show deference to the Moon Goddess and avoid the risk of silver burning their mate's skin. That necklace has been passed down from mother to daughter for centuries. My mother had gifted it to me seven years ago, when my grandmother passed away.

Raw, primal anger rolls through me. Growling, I lunge forward to snatch my pendant from Connor's sickly hand. The pain in my back is slowing my movements to that of a wounded animal.

"Ah-ah-ahh..." he tsks and rips it up and away, swinging his other hand towards me, slapping his palm down hard across my cheek. My head snaps to the right, spraying blood from my nose and mouth. Sharp stinging burns like nettles spiking my skin. Black spots dot my vision, and the creeping darkness beckons again.

"Don't you freaking dare! Faith, get up and fight back!" Sienna growls, her anger palpable through our link. *"If you won't give me control, show*

me you can do this!" At her encouragement, a burst of energy floods my system, and I grit my teeth.

Wrenching myself up with a battle cry, letting loose from my aching throat, I lunge to attack. Again and again, I launch myself at Connor, only to be stopped by the force of his relentless fists smashing into the side of my face and body. My cheek burns, rapidly swelling, and I'm pretty sure I have a loose tooth now, but still, I smirk and crane my head to the side.

Spying the sweat staining his shirt through the slit in my painful, puffy eyelids, I heave in a deep breath, preparing, but that little nagging pinch in my gut stalls my movement. I don't have much left, and everything hurts.

"*Show him you're not weak,*" Sienna demands through our connection. Her white-hot anger races throughout every fiber of my body, disintegrating the doubt in a ball of flame.

Connor is bent over, resting his hands on his knees, "I just need—" he sucks in a deep breath, "—you to imbue your power into this," he rasps. He's more out of shape than he's ever been before. He thrusts the necklace into my face. The sapphire catches the light coming in from the window, strengthening my resolve.

"Fuck. You." I barely manage with my rapidly swelling cheek getting caught between my teeth. Pulling my knee up into my stomach, I scream as my leg shoots straight out, connecting with Connor's shin. An awful crack sounds with Connor's bellow of pain as he falls backwards. My body falls back, smacking into the floor. Heat erupts from my shoulder and shoots up as my head bounces off the carpet.

"*Declan...*"

Suddenly, the front door bursts open, a familiar male's voice shouts, "Faith! Where are you?"

Another male's voice, yet unfamiliar, shouts, "Flik, over here." My swollen lids flutter open and closed as a looming shadow creeps over my face. Flik's dusty blonde locks falling over his tanned face come into view. His baby blues narrow in on me, frowning.

"Shit, Dec is going to be so pissed," he whispers, brushing a strand of hair away from my face. I hiss at the pain; the strand coated in blood is stuck to my skin.

"Sorry—" he winces and then leaps to his feet and is gone before I can register the quiet in the house.

* * *

The burning bite of cold pierces into my skin. "Hey there," it's the unfamiliar voice from earlier. My eyes flutter open to a fair-skinned, blue-eyed male with curly auburn hair that brushes the peaks of his arched eyebrows. Freckles sprinkle over his straight nose and carved cheeks; he's smiling, but the smile doesn't reach his eyes.

"Um..." I croak, scooting back, on the sofa. I'm on the sofa? How? I scan the room and let my sluggish brain catch up. I must have hit my head harder than I thought.

As if on cue, the room starts to spin on an uneven axis and then stops tilting to one side. A sharp, piercing pain stabs into my temple. I cup the side of my head. Cradling it, I lift my eyes to focus on the male before me.

"Hey, hey—take it easy," he says, and waits for me to stop moving. His warm smile comforts and wraps my wary body in a cocoon of safety. "Name's Rhett, a friend of Declan's," he drawls in a sharp southern twang with a hint of Scottish lilt. His accent is thicker than that of Flik's, and he appears to be closer in age to Declan than Flik.

"M-my n-necklace?" I croak, glancing down at the floor. I know I saw Connor had it.

"What necklace, Faith?" Flik asks coming into the living room. I shake my head, letting it go for now. He rounds the sofa and plops down beside me, handing me a couple of pain pills, and Rhett hands over a glass of water. Flik's handsome face crinkles into one of concern as I swallow the medicine and a tiny sip of water.

"Faith, I'm so sorry we weren't here sooner. Declan asked us to protect you, and we failed." He offers, smoothing a hand down the side of my hair. "I know this is, going to be a pointless question, but are you okay otherwise?" He asks, his gaze bouncing up and down my body, stopping on my face. I wince as his thumb brushes the corner of my swollen eye.

"Do you need to see a—" he asks, struggling to finish his question. Based on the look on his face, I know what he's not asking, and thank Goddess *that* didn't happen. I shake my head in answer, and he sighs in relief.

"We stitched your back up, so try not to move too quickly, don't want them to tear out, ok?" He adds, his features softening. "Maybe later you can shift and heal a bit more, yeah?" He suggests and looks to Rhett, having some internal conversation with him.

Taking note of every twinge of pain, I shake my head again. The memory of Connor holding my Grandmother's necklace in my face stabs into my chest, cracking it wide open. I'd lost it the night of my almost wedding to the dickhead and Mom's funeral; at least I thought I'd lost it. He must have been the one to come into my room in the pack house and taken it off of me while I slept. Thoughts race through my mind at lightning speed, zipping from one to the next, trying to sort out how and why and what he wants with it.

"Faith, if you want, we can take you somewhere else for the night," Rhett suggests, breaking my train of theories. Both Flik and Rhett stare at me, waiting, wanting some way to help me. Their guilt rolls off of them in waves, filling the air with the heaviness of it.

A peel of a cell ringing pierces the stark silence. I jump up, ignoring the shooting pain down my back, searching the floor and table. "Hey, take it easy, Faith." Flik cradles my shoulders and guides me back to the sofa.

"Uh, sorry, it's mine," Rhett drawls, answering it. "Hey Dec...yeah, she's here. No, yeah, she's fine, well...mostly. Yes, man, I promise...okay," he speaks softly, never looking away as he hands me the cell. My fingers curl around the device, bringing it up to my ear.

"Faith! Are you there? Omg, Faith," Declan's scared voice crackles through the line, instantly warming my chest.

"Declan—" I answer, voice weak and shaky.

"Thank fuck you're okay," he breathes. His worry is etched in his tone; it scrapes along my heartstrings like a hand running over the strings of a guitar neck. The scratching of his stubble against the receiver, oddly, brings a sense of relief. I can imagine him pacing and raking his large fingers through his dark locks, biceps bulging with each movement.

"Ye-ah..." I supply, not sure what else to say as tears spill over my lids like floodwaters in a hurricane. I want to ask him about his family and how they are holding up, but I find my lips sealed on the topic. Humiliating shame burns the curves of my ears.

"Go to my house and stay there. Flik and Rhett will stay with you until I get back," he orders, attempting to sound authoritative, but it does nothing to hide the worry lining his words. "Please, Faith?"

"Dec-lan, I—" I start, voice faltering, what was I going to say? That I don't want to stay at his house? That I don't need protection, that I don't need...what? I don't know. Do I tell him I'd been about to pack and go to him? Or...

"Faith, please, go for me. I'd feel more comfortable knowing that you are safely tucked away until I can be there." He tries again. I shake my head, relenting, and rub the heels of my palms under my eyes.

"Okay, can we...can...we talk later?" I ask hesitantly, letting out a hard sigh, and close my eyes. My head pounds, seeking relief.

"Sure, sweetheart, listen, there's a fresh pitcher of sweet tea in the fridge, and Connie, Rhett's mate, will be by later with food to stock it up...use whatever you'd like, I'll be home in less than a day...hopefully sooner," Declan rushes out in relief. "We gotta wait for the flight crew to rest up, but I'm so glad you're safe now."

I nod, despite knowing he can't see me, and hand the phone back to Rhett, who takes it and strides off to the back porch—the storm door squeaks and slams following his departure. I get up and take a moment to let my head clear the dizziness away.

Shuffling my feet forward, I stumble over the carpet and catch my fall with my hands on the arm of the sofa. Flik is there instantly, supporting my elbow and side as I right myself and drag my feet towards my room.

Standing before the steps, I grip the handrail and press my other hand to the wall opposite. Counting each step as I climb, there are eleven of them, right? The stairwell narrows and lengthens in my tunnel of vision. The room swells and shrinks back to normal as I heft one foot up the rung.

Wave after wave of memories crash into me as I climb, Connor leaving me at the altar, my Mom dying in my arms, my wolf appearing, Eliza's betrayal, meeting my mate, and Connor at my doorstep, and losing an entire day to Connor's habitual wrath. I don't know how much more I can take before I break. I'm barely holding on with the fraying duct tape holding me together as is.

"You've endured much worse, have faith in yourself," Sienna says softly, brushing herself against our bond, rippling her love and worry into me.

At the top of the stairs, I don't bother wiping the stray tears streaking down my face as Flik and Rhett both join me. Luckily, most of my stuff is easy to repack. I wheel two of the suitcases towards them and then hastily throw the rest of my things in the third suitcase and backpack.

* * *

The guys drop me off at Declan's and help bring in my luggage, which I quickly deposit into one of the spare rooms. Jules and Wyatt have the other primary suite, and I'm not quite ready to share a space with Declan.

I'm unpacking my toiletries when my cell rings, startling me out of a numbing haze. A sharp pain laces through my neck and shoulder as I reach behind and retrieve the phone from my pocket. I groan when I see it's my Dad video calling. Great.

My eyes flick to the mirror, and I grimace as I take in the black and blue marring my skin. I have a split, swollen lip and a cut that slices near the corner of my right eye. Both are pretty swollen and an angry shade of purple; at least the wounds on my back can be hidden.

Swiping answer, I quickly turn off my video and prepare the well-told lie I've been telling for the past seven years.

"Hey, sweet pea, wait, how come I can't see you?" Dad asks, perplexed. His worry is woven into his aging voice as he asks me again. He angles his phone like it's something on his end, making me chuckle a little.

"Hey Dad...no, it's on my end, I turned it off, I'm in the middle of some things-" I reply, sounding more like a dying frog than myself. I'm not lying since I *am* unpacking.

"Faith Rina Bennett, what is going on?" He demands without using his aura, but I know it'll come the minute I don't convince him I'm fine.

"Daddy—" I stutter, swallowing down the burn rising. He turns those glacier eyes on me, and I falter, realizing that I can't lie to him anymore. He will find out eventually. "I'm fine, just tired...I-um...I found my mate...Connor dropped in, and now I'm staying at my mate's house." I tell him, praying he won't judge me too harshly.

"Oh, *okay*- wait-what?" He chokes on his words, and I watch his face contort from concern to shock to anger in the span of a few seconds. "What do you mean-no- just start at the beginning and you'd best turn your video on now, Faith," he commands, and that hint of aura pressing through his tone forces my muscles to flex and teeth to grind.

Baring my neck, I crane it back and stretch my mouth before deciding to obey. "Dad, wait—" I inhale, and try again. "Just give me a minute, okay...I will turn it on, but you need to know I'm okay and that this was unpreventable," I whisper, my finger hovering over the video button, clutching the collar of my shirt. I sigh and tap the screen.

The video comes on immediately, and it's impossible to find the words to describe my Dad's face as he reacts. His beautiful blue eyes cloud over the longer he stares, a pained expression paints his face, and a single tear runs down over his tanned skin. He reaches towards the screen like he wants to caress my face. I break, tears flow freely down my cheeks.

"Who-what, hap-...they're dead," he grates and his jaw bunches as if he's holding back words. His canines lengthen in a snarl, and his eyes flash with the silver of his wolf. I hold up a hand and shake my head, hoping he will allow me to explain.

"It was..." I sniff and hesitate, but only because I know once he learns the truth, he will never forgive me. "Con-...it was Connor," my voice cracks on a sob, filled with debilitating shame.

"What!" The phone vibrates from the sound of Dad's voice, causing it to fall from its propped-up place. A ceramic ring plate clatters as it skips over the counter. I flinch at the sound and, snatching up my phone, I hold it steady as I wait for Dad to calm down.

"You will return home at once. We will send out a party of gammas to retrieve Connor for a tribunal, and he will face m-" he shouts, commanding me, but I stop him with a raised hand.

"Dad, no...stop, I'm fine, I'm protected. No one could've predicted that Connor would come down here...besides, I have two very capable protectors until my mate returns."

"What? What do you mean when he returns? Where is this mate of yours? And who exactly is he?" I shudder as my eyes turn down and away. I knew in my gut Dad would react this way. "Faith..."

The lump in my throat is similar to sludge and is stuck no matter how much I swallow. My eyes shift back to the screen, and I smile a little. My smiles always defuse his anger, but at the same time, I want him to be happy about this.

"Declan McCormick is my mate," I answer, my eyes bobbing back and forth as I watch him. A pride-filled grin begins to spread across his lips. It crinkles the creases at the corners of his eyes.

"Ah, the McCormick's boy, fine young alpha, I know his parents well, they border our pack," he supplies happily, over the lingering anger. He rubs his chin and jaw languidly, then narrows his eyes.

"But his mother just died, is that why he's not there? Why didn't you go with him?" He asks, genuinely curious. "You could've used the jet sweet pea, you know that, right?"

My eyes skirt over the granite counter, I grab my toothbrush and paste, and rearrange them just so, straightening them both to lie horizontally to the sink. My hairbrush and makeup bag follow soon after. I set them down perpendicular to the toothbrush. "I was about to follow when-" I trail off and let the silence rent the air.

"Faith...are you alright?" Flik's sweet voice shatters the numbing disassociation.

"Who is that?" Dad asks, worried.

I give Flik a slight grin and nod, "It's Flik Dad, he is a friend of Declan's," I reply, watching as he leans over in the frame as if he can see him. Rolling my eyes, I angle the phone so Flik is now entirely in frame.

"Flik, this is my Dad, Gerrant Bennett. Dad, this is Flik-" I start realizing I don't know Flik's surname and send him a pleading look, hoping he'll help me out.

"It's nice to meet you, Mr. Bennett, Flik Ryan...your daughter is one amazing alpha, you raised her well," Flik greets, sparing me the awkward moment.

Glimpsing at my phone from the corner of my eye, I watch Dad shift in his seat, scrutinizing Flik and how capable he is of protecting me. I know what is coming next, and before my Dad has the opportunity to interrogate Flik, I jump in.

"Dad, hey- listen...I still have a lot to do, and I appreciate you wanting to protect me, but I have Flik here and Rhett, two of the strongest males besides Declan, and I can assure you Connor was dealt with the best they could...I call you soon...love you," I ramble out all of the excuses I can think of, but he cuts me off.

"We are not done discussing this, and we *will* have this discussion, Faith I—" I don't let him finish and blow him a kiss as I end the call. My shoulders slump as I place the phone on the counter. Why can't anything ever be simple? My phone vibrates again, and I hit decline.

Flik rubs a hand over my shoulder and gestures for me to follow him as he turns away to head downstairs.

injury in meticulous detail. Not only had that piece of shit beat her, but that fucker had sliced her back open. I have no doubt now what those other nicks and slices were from hiding under her tattoos and why Julianna had pleaded with me to give her some grace and time to share. What broke my heart the most was what Rhett told me she was saying in her sleep.

"She was calling out for you, mumbling something about not being strong enough, and that it was nice in the dark," Rhett explained, his voice was pained and rough, like even he couldn't bear repeating everything. She had called out for me, and I didn't answer. I'm not even sure I would've been able to, but no excuse will ever erase the guilt I feel.

Rhett and Flik took the brunt of my anger while she slept. They were supposed to be outside her house well before she returned from walking from mine. I had texted them before we even pulled away from the driveway. Flik was already on his way to my place for something unrelated. He said he would grab Rhett and head over right away. I knew I should've dropped her off myself. If only I had stayed a little longer, if I'd commanded her to come with me, none of this would've happened. Yet, if I'd commanded her, she'd hate me, probably reject me too. It would've been no less than I deserved.

Honestly, I don't blame Flik and Rhett; I blame myself. She's my mate, I should've been there to protect her, but my Mother had been murdered. And she didn't want to accompany me. What was I supposed to do? The desire to rip myself in two has grown exponentially over the last 24 hours. For now, I can breathe a sigh of relief knowing the guys have brought her to my house and are inside keeping watch. Wyatt, Julianna, and I will be home late this evening after the pilot rests and the jet is refueled. Then I can hold her in my arms, kiss away her pains, and finish planning Connor's excruciating death.

3 2

Declan

Pain in the back of my throat scrapes with each inhale as I run to the cemetery. I thought a run would help clear out the shame and guilt piling up in my chest. What a terrific mate I've turned out to be. I've been so afraid of hurting Faith myself that I didn't stop to think of her getting hurt by another. If only I'd listened to that tug, to my suspicions, and asked her about the scars. If only I had waited a little longer, would she have come with me?

Should'a, could'a, would'a, it's all I've got now. I replay the events from yesterday over and over as my feet pound into the ground. I had barely made it to the limo from my Mom's grave when Rhett was finally able to reach me and tell me what happened to Faith. I knew something was wrong, felt it, but couldn't place it.

An unending pit of despair kept swirling in my gut when I was sitting next to Estella during the funeral. Then came the crushing fear, guilt, and sadness that were not my own. The emotions repeatedly crept over my skin, but I was in such a state dealing with everything that I didn't pay much attention to it. Rhett was telling me of how he found her and her ex when the photo he took of her came in.

The sight of her bloodied, bruised, and swollen face caused me to double over, almost retching in the limo. I'd downed a full glass of whiskey from the liquor station. Both Flik and Rhett told me of every injury in meticulous detail. Not only had that piece of shit beat her, but that fucker had sliced her back open. I have no doubt now what those other nicks and slices were from hiding under her tattoos and why Julianna had pleaded with me to give her some grace and time to share. What broke my heart the most was what Rhett told me she was saying in her sleep.

"She was calling out for you, mumbling something about not being strong enough, and that it was nice in the dark," Rhett explained, his voice was pained and rough, like even he couldn't bear repeating everything. She had called out for me, and I didn't answer. I'm not even sure I would've been able to, but no excuse will ever erase the guilt I feel.

Rhett and Flik took the brunt of my anger while she slept. They were supposed to be outside her house well before she returned from walking from mine. I had texted them before we even pulled away from the driveway. Flik was already on his way to my place for something unrelated. He said he would grab Rhett and head over right away. I knew I should've dropped her off myself. If only I had stayed a little longer, if I'd commanded her to come with me, none of this would've happened. Yet, if I'd commanded her, she'd hate me, probably reject me too. It would've been no less than I deserved.

Honestly, I don't blame Flik and Rhett; I blame myself. She's my mate, I should've been there to protect her, but my Mother had been murdered. And she didn't want to accompany me. What was I supposed to do? The desire to rip myself in two has grown exponentially over the last 24 hours. For now, I can breathe a sigh of relief knowing the guys have brought her to my house and are inside keeping watch. Wyatt, Julianna, and I will be home late this evening after the pilot rests and the jet is refueled. Then I can hold her in my arms, kiss away her pains, and finish planning Connor's excruciating death.

32

Declan

Pain in the back of my throat scrapes with each inhale as I run to the cemetery. I thought a run would help clear out the shame and guilt piling up in my chest. What a terrific mate I've turned out to ┝ I've been so afraid of hurting Faith myself that I didn't stop to thii of her getting hurt by another. If only I'd listened to that tug, to my suspicions, and asked her about the scars. If only I had waited a little longer, would she have come with me?

Should'a, could'a, would'a, it's all I've got now. I replay the events from yesterday over and over as my feet pound into the ground. I had barely made it to the limo from my Mom's grave when Rhett was finally able to reach me and tell me what happened to Faith. I knew something was wrong, felt it, but couldn't place it.

An unending pit of despair kept swirling in my gut when I was sitting next to Estella during the funeral. Then came the crushing fear, guilt, and sadness that were not my own. The emotions repeatedly crept over my skin, but I was in such a state dealing with everything that I didn't pay much attention to it. Rhett was telling me of how he found her and her ex when the photo he took of her came in.

The sight of her bloodied, bruised, and swollen face caused me to double over, almost retching in the limo. I'd downed a full glass of whiskey from the liquor station. Both Flik and Rhett told me of every

I come to a walk at the top of the path, and draw several ragged breaths in. Up here in the mountains, a layer of fog lingers over the treetops from the early morning dew. The edge of the dark and dreary forest near the cemetery stokes a cold shiver across my sweating flesh as the pine boughs call for lost souls to return to its depths.

The mesh of my sneakers soaks in the dew from the dark emerald grass spread over the cemetery. My socks are wet, and it's irritating to my toes as I come to a halt next to the freshly upturned dirt from yesterday. There's no grave stone marker; it won't be complete for another couple of weeks. A single wooden stake with my Mother's name inked in permanent marker designates her final resting place.

Thorin's unease and sadness roll through our bond. He loved my Mother too; her wolf was his confidant, his best friend. Pin pricks of stinging pain, like nettles biting into your skin, wrinkle my nose. My eyes squint and I blink away the hot tears gathering in a corner.

A little bluebird sings sweetly in the distance, luring my eyes to where it might be. Not seeing the tiny bird, I collapse to my knees. Mud and wet grass soak into the joggers I'm wearing, darkening the knees from my weight bearing down.

Head bowed, shoulders slouched forward, I lay a small bundle of daisies over the piled dirt. I'd picked them at the bottom of a meadow nearby, remembering how much she loved all the wild flora and fauna, I thought she'd like these today. Mom had treasured every dandelion and clover bud I handed her as a child. When I learned they were weeds, I cringed and only ever gave her daisies and violets from then on. *I miss you so much, Mom.*

A soft chirping draws my attention up from the loose dirt covered in the bright white and yellow flowers. A small blue bird perches on the stake, cocking its tiny head at me. It coasts down to the flowers, hopping around them, chirping and flittering its grayish-cornflower blue wings. The lighter blue and ruddy brown breast feathers identify it as a female. My eyes swivel up searching for its mate.

Off in the distance, a darker, more vibrant version of the tiny bird in front of me perches on a low branch, her counterpart. The little female ruffles her feathers up and keeps chirping, hopping around the flowers. Oddly, my presence has never affected birds. Other animals, and mammals, yeah, but birds, never.

The little blue bird stops and bobs its head down, pointing its beak to the daisy and then back up to me.

"Remember to hang the box about 50 feet up, Declan, it needs the morning sun and afternoon shade..." Mom reminded me as I dashed down the side steps of the house and out to the garden. She was quick on my heels and stood back as I clumsily climbed up the tree we'd selected earlier to hang the nesting box. I had spotted an Eastern Bluebird the day before, flitting and flying about old trees searching for the perfect spot. Afterwards, I'd run to Mom and asked if we could hang a nesting box. I had recently learned about them in school, and I was only a little obsessed with the tiny creatures. They were one of the few birds that weren't terrified of me.

"That's it, right there, that should do it," she called. Dangling from a branch, I hooked the box on a knob jutting out from the trunk, and the bottom rested on a branch almost perfectly.

"I wonder how many babies they will hatch?" I asked her, my smile bright and full of teeth as I dropped to the grass.

"Well, most bluebird pairs will lay 2-7 eggs, so we will have to wait and see. Why don't you run along and help me gather some flowers for the table, hmm?"

The bluebird's chirping and calls filter through my memory, bringing me back to the present. For a moment, while I watch the little feathered friend, I daydream that it's Mom's spirit coming to say hello, but I know that's not possible. Her spirit will remain trapped so long as she's under the earth.

Stretching out my upturned palm, I offer my hand to the little creature, aching for her to hop up into it, even if only for a moment.

The male, who has flown closer, is watching curiously from another gravestone, his slate black eyes analyzing each of my movements for danger.

Their behavior is completely uncharacteristic, but I don't care; these little birds are still one of my favorites. Holding my arm incredibly still, I wait, and wait, and wait. Finally, as my lids slip down, the itty bitty talons of the female dig into the meaty part of my palm. My lids peel open, and a smile turns up the corners of my mouth.

"Well, I haven't seen you smile like that in years. Didn't think I'd ever see you do it here of all places, though." A warm and familiar female voice says, her shadow looming over the upturned dirt stretching out to my knees. A knot tightens in my stomach. I would know that voice anywhere; it haunts my nightmares. Averting my eyes from the visitor, I follow when the tiny bird flies away to her mate for the time and disappears into the woods.

Flicking my gaze up, I swallow the knot that's wedged its way up into my throat. Sophia stands before me, with a bouquet of daisies and foxgloves clutched in her petite hands. She hasn't changed too much, except that her once long, summer-wheat hair is cut to her shoulders now. Her meadow green eyes stare softly down at me, a slight smile curves her lips as she bends and lays her bundle near mine.

Ready to abandon ship and race back down the path to the pack house, I rise and brush the dirt off my pants. I run a hand through my hair and fail to avert my eyes from landing on her neck. A thin white scar runs the length of her neck and dips below the collar of her gray shirt. I haven't seen her since that night. I've tried calling her several times to apologize, but I'd ended up hanging up each time, too swamped with humiliation and shame.

My mind is riddled with the haunting memory of that night, delivering a tremble to my hands, and yet she stands before me, dead still and calm. I hate that I can't turn back time and make it right.

"Declan," Sophia murmurs, and takes a step around the mound of dirt towards me. My chest rises and falls before my lips part to speak, and snap closed, fists clenching and unclenching, I stuff them into my pockets. The heat of her hand seeps into my skin as it comes to rest on my bicep.

"Hey, it's okay, Dec, I'm happy I ran into you," she says, trailing off. Seeking out her eyes, I find a mixture of sadness and relief.

"Hey Soph...I-uh," my words fumble halfway through my thought, and I face her. She's still every bit of summer, but her closeness turns my stomach upside down, and I take a half step back. She's all wrong feeling.

"Declan, I know you're not one for a lot of words, so I'll just say what I need to and then I'll go, okay?" She angles her head to peer into my eyes. I nod and glance towards her, but not at her. I can't bring myself to look her in the eyes.

"I forgive you, Declan. I know you weren't yourself that night, and I've had a lot of time to think about it, and yes, I was scared of you for a time, but I know it was a reaction, not on purpose. I never genuinely feared you," she sighs, and then kneels before my Mother's grave. One of my eyebrows lifts at words. I openly stare, questioning her.

"I spent a lot of time with your Mother after you left. She visited me every day in the hospital, and then we started working with the local VA center in town. It helped me heal and understand where your head was, and by the looks of it, still is," she peeks over her shoulder at me and then fingers a rock within the loose dirt.

"No matter what happened with us, Declan, you are worthy and anyone would be honored to be with you...but you have to learn to cope with it...the ptsd isn't going to go away, but you can learn to cope and maybe one day heal." She finishes and stands brushing the dirt away from her jeans and faces me.

My mind is reeling from everything she said, but like a scratched disc, it's replaying the 'I forgive you.' Never did I think those words would fall from her lips. I swallow down the house-sized brick that's lodged in my throat again and meet her gaze.

"Soph, I-I don't know what to say," I reply, my voice groggy and hoarse.

"You don't have to say anything, Dec, but promise me you'll try for yourself," she replies, so sweet and sincere it pains my heart. Before I know what's happening, she's wrapping her arms around my middle and squeezing. My arms fly out, hanging awkwardly in the air for a minute, and then, slowly relenting, I wrap mine around her in return, trying not to cringe at her nearness. The embrace is all the words we can't say to each other, but also nothing more than I'm sorry and I forgive you.

We release one another, and my hand automatically rubs against my cheek. Wetness greets my fingertips unexpectedly, but as I swipe away the first tear, more follow as the dam opens up. Turning away from Sophia, I suck in a breath and then swipe at my face with the bottom of my shirt.

"You wanna walk back together?" I ask, sniffling and stuffing my hands into my pockets.

"Sure Dec," she replies and bumps into my shoulder, "Besides, I could use your help anyways, before you take off...barn door is stuck again," she laughs and we stride off back towards the center of pack lands.

33

Faith

"Your Dad's right, Faith," Rhett argues, handing his mate and wife Connie a cup of steaming tea. We've been discussing the possibility of me returning home to the protection of my pack for the past few hours, and I'm entirely over it. I know there's no way that I'll be going back there yet, not until I know for sure where Connor is. He has more opportunities to get to me there than here, and I doubt he's stuck around after his beating.

Flik and Rhett gave him quite the walloping after they found him slinking out the back door and down the stairs. Flik drove him to the state line and dropped him off on the side of the road that night.

Meanwhile, Rhett and Connie stitched me up and changed my shirt. They kept watch over me the entire time, never leaving my side until I was awake. I can't remember the last time I had that level of devotion in a friend.

"No, he knows the land there; he doesn't know it here, and while I don't either, I have one thing he doesn't: I have all of you," I say, hoping flattery will end the conversation.

Rhett's lips twist up into a contrite motion and then fall. He shrugs his shoulders and moves behind his wife, wrapping his arms around her growing belly. Connie is seven and a half months pregnant with their first child, and she's stunning. Her soft brown hair falls over her shoulders, accentuating the rosy apples of her cheeks and honey brown eyes. She has been the sweetest for the past two nights, bringing me a home-cooked meal and loads of snacks.

What I need, though, is some peace and quiet or a stiff drink. Declan, Wyatt, and Jules are delayed another day due to the pilot and something with the jet. He'd insisted on finding a commercial flight, but I told him I was okay staying here with the crew.

"Is Flik working tonight?" I ask, praying he's not. A night out would be heavenly, but I also know it won't happen without one of them attending with me. Sienna wants out, too. She nagged me about shifting to heal and stretch the first day. She's been overly quiet the past twenty-four hours but does nudge me every so often to let me know she's still there.

"He is, why?" Rhett answers warily, resting his chin on his wife's shoulder, nuzzling her brown hair.

Good Goddess, they are so cute.

My fingers trace up over my arm and scratch at my elbow before my eyes lift to his, "I need out of this house...I was thinking of getting a drink, maybe shift, have a bit of normalcy?" I admit, shrugging my shoulders and withholding the wince I know they are looking for. It'll be all they need to deny it. They don't want me to get hurt again.

Connie turns in her husband's arms and then steps back. The two of them must be speaking through their link, because when she spins around, she's grinning from ear to ear, and Rhett rolls his eyes.

"I think that's a lovely idea, a local band is playing tonight, and I've got a hankering for French fries and a shake. We can head out in, say, an hour?" She says, beaming. A thrill of excitement shoots through me. I rush towards them and kiss both of their cheeks.

In the short couple of days I've known them, they've been surrounding me in a safety net, but also filled with love. I have instantly grown attached to them both, especially Connie.

Pregnant lady for the win.

I hop up the stairs to get ready. Sienna perks up and paces back and forth, eager for me to let her out even if it's for a moment.

"*If I let you out to heal, will you shift back for a bit? I'll let you out again once we are home,*" I ask, and promise, wanting to have some semblance of balance with her needs and mine.

"*You haven't let me out in weeks,*" she quips back, irritated. I roll my eyes at her.

"*Yeah, well, you didn't show up, let alone want anything to do with me for years, so excuse me for not just relinquishing my control completely,*" I growl, and she growls back, but I don't care.

"*How could I when you were beaten down to nothing more than an omega? I tried, but your shame smothered me, not to mention whatever Connor did—*" Her words bite at me, that shame cloaks me again, and excuses build on the tip of my tongue, but a memory of Declan's lips skimming over my skin burns away that darkness.

When I stand before the mirror staring at my black and blue face, neck, and split lip, Sienna shudders and acquiesces. Shedding my clothes, I turn back away from the mirror standing between it and the bed.

Tingles rush like pins and needles racking over my skin, all at once, my bones snap and shatter as I shift into my wolf. Not fully releasing control, I pad over to the mirror, finally able to see her.

"*So beautiful, Sienna,*" I whisper to her through our link. While Sienna is her own entity, we share the same soul. Taking a step back, I knock into the bed. I hadn't realized how massive she is until now. Her sable-russet brown fur is so stunning, it almost shimmers in the low light. Turning slowly, Sienna takes control and spins us so I can see our reflection in the mirror better.

A knock on the door startles Sienna, and she knocks into the nightstand and mirror. A small lamp falls to the floor, shattering. The door flies open, and Flik strides in and freezes.

"Faith!" he calls, eyes as wide agape as his mouth is. Sienna doesn't lower her head or make a move towards him, instead letting out a subtle wave of our aura, and Flik spins around, as we shift back. I quickly swipe up the blanket on the edge of the bed, wrapping it around myself, and I force the blood rushing to my cheeks to subside.

"Yes?" I ask, swallowing all of my embarrassment. Flik turns, a smile so wide it brings shame to the Grand Canyon.

"You are a beautiful woman, Faith, but your wolf, damn girl, you're–I don't have words." He says unabashedly, raking a hand through his sandy blonde hair, a pink tinge flames his tanned cheeks.

"But-uh don't tell Dec I said that." The same flames lick my cheeks, forcing me to look away.

"*Be proud of our forms, Faith,*" Sienna says, nudging against me.

"I'm sorry I didn't mean to startle you, but I heard you were coming to the bar, and Rhett had to take Connie back to the house to get ready. I just wanted to check on you." He rushes out, seeing my rosy cheeks.

"Oh-I...I'm okay, thanks, Flik. I'll be ready soon, and then we can go. Who's at the bar now?" I ask out of pure curiosity.

"Oh-uh, Lexi is, well, at least until I get back...I'll drive us over when you're ready, and Rhett and Connie will join us there." He says and slowly eases the door closed. I don't know Lexi yet, but I've listened to both Flik and Rhett complain about her lack of work ethic and how much she grates Declan's last nerve, for the past 24 hours. She sounds like a bucket full of fun.

At the click of the latch, I drop the blanket and spin back to the mirror, wincing at my reflection. Four fresh pink scars grace the tanned skin over my shoulder blade. Frowning, I angle my arm to rub my fingers over the raised ridges. At least they're healed, but damn, I was set on not having scars.

"You waited too long to shift...wear those scars with pride...you fought back this time." Sienna offers in explanation. She's right, that doesn't make it any easier to accept.

Turning back, there's no black and blue marring my face or nose. My lip is completely healed, too. My hands comb up the base of my scalp, searching for the spot where a clump had been ripped out. Complete shafts of hair have regrown to almost the same length as before.

Slipping into a pair of ripped and distressed skinny jeans, an old concert tee, and flip flops, I pad into the bathroom and brush on a few swipes of mascara and a pink-tinted lip balm. I slip a couple of hair ties over my wrist and grab my cell and cash before heading downstairs.

Opening the door, I peek my head out and inspect the hallway before stepping out and closing the door softly. A tug in my chest pulls me towards one of the ends of the hall, towards his room.

34

Faith

The door to Declan's room creaks open as I step in and swiftly close it behind me with a click. Sliding my hand along the wall searching for the light switch and turning it on, I lose my breath in a measured exhale as my eyes scan the interior.

His room is a sanctuary of sorts with its dark yet inviting colors and textures. The Prussian blue is almost like velvet against the wall that holds every photograph I've ever sold. My body drifts to his bed as if under a spell, fingers trailing over the bedding, and the delicate friction under my fingertips releases tiny puffs of his spruce and amber scent into the air.

My eyes shutter, head tilting back, I breathe in a deep inhale and melt from the comfort the essence of him brings. Opening my eyes, they skim over to the nightstand, landing on an old leather-bound journal. The thick book is wrapped in several bindings with a black and gold roller ball pen lying next to it. He must have a thing for expensive pens.

Without much thought, I pick up the pen and roll it between my fingers, finding his initials are engraved along the lid. I set it down and swipe up the journal. The leather is old and creased as I turn it over in my hand. It's thick and well-loved; he must write in it daily. Not wanting to push my curiosity, I lay the journal back, placing it exactly how he had it and nudging the pen back beside it.

That tug pulls again. I follow it, and my gaze drifts over the expanse of his bedroom, towards his ensuite bathroom. Flipping the light switch on, my breath hitches. This bathroom is a testament to simplistic craftsmanship. A large clawfoot bath with brass feet is off to the right with a framed, enlarged copy of my photograph of a snowy owl in flight over a field. A single sink dark wood vanity is to the left with a matching wood-framed mirror. My eyes skirt over each of his toiletries, all meticulously laid out, and stop on a line of orange and green pill bottles.

Picking one of the bottles up, my thumb runs over the printed label, and a flutter tickles my stomach as I read the instructions and name of the medication.

Lamotrigine. Take 100 mg twice daily as needed for mood.

Setting the bottle back down, I swipe up another, but the label is partially missing, as if it had been washed or worn away.

Sertraline. Take 200 mg once daily for treatment of—.

Of what, for what? Dammit. It could be for anything. Scanning the other bottles and their labels, I cringe, and a wave of concern washes over me. I hope he's not taking these all together.

Shaking off my unease, I turn from the bathroom as another tug pulls me out. I'm one foot into his closet when—

"You ready?" Flik calls, startling me.

Resisting the urge to bury my face in his clothes, I tear myself away and exit, shutting his door and shuffling down the hallway. Flik stands at the base of the stairwell, jingling his keys with a shit eating grin.

"Get lost, pretty girl?" He asks dryly.

"Of course not," I smirk and join him. He locks up and shows me to his Jeep Rubicon, helps me up, and as he settles in the driver's seat, faces me.

"Hey, are you sure you're, okay? I could always bring you anything from the bar that you want." I don't let him finish with a wave of my hand.

"I'm okay, I need to get out of the house and need to be around people... ok?" I don't have to explain anything to him, but he and Rhett
cared for me while I was injured and have since ensured my safety. But
how will I even begin to explain to them that I need to feel normal?
That after every time Connor inflicted pain, I'd spent hours covering
up each mark and bruise before I forced myself out of the apartment
to escape and then reset. I didn't have a choice.

Flik says nothing in response and drives us to the bar. He hands
me off to Rhett and Connie before getting back to work behind the
counter. The place isn't too packed, but the musicians are already playing a set of southern rock, couples dance while others stand around
the mini stage like groupies. The three of us find the table near the
dart board, giving me a 180-degree span of the bar from the wall.

Rhett leans in and kisses Connie's temple, eliciting a sweet smile
from her. "So, besides an order of French fries, what would you ladies
like to drink?" His southern twang bites in and curls under the hard-
ened numbness, cracking my walls.

"I uh, a cider is good thanks," I say and reach into my back pocket
for the cash I had stashed before leaving Declan's. Handing it over to
Rhett, he frowns and closes his hand over mine, shaking his head. "I
can pay for my own drinks, Rhett," I argue, feeling a little put out, but
he gently pushes my hand away.

"No can do, ma'am. Declan will have my ass if I let you pay for anything, besides, as his mate, you practically own this bar now, too, so
it's on the house." My chest tightens at his explanation, my brain is addled piecing together the implication of what is Declan's, is now mine
as well, it doesn't sit right with me.

Goddess things are moving fast, almost too fast. Connor and I
didn't even share money, let alone a space until much later, but then
again if he was with Eliza the whole time that makes so much more
sense now.

"Um-okay," I supply yielding to the lump in my throat. Rhett takes off to the bar and then behind into the kitchen. Connie leans over and takes my hand in hers, squeezing lightly.

"I know this is all probably overwhelming and all-consuming, but these men really don't have the ability to use breaks once they bond," she says, squeezing my hand again. "I'm not sure how your pack functions, but this rag tag group of males are an all or nothing' type."

I'm not sure what to make of that, but it has been something I've yearned for since I was a young girl. Growing up with devoted parents like I did, had essentially drilled that into my foundation for relationships. In the early years with Connor, it had been similar to this, and then things changed our freshman year of college when we were away from prying eyes.

"So is Declan the alpha then?" I ask changing the subject, a bit unsure if he is here, or if he is supposed to be back in Maine with his family's pack. Seeing as no one else seems to have strong alpha energy, I'd assumed he's the alpha here.

Connie's lips twist into a purse and then release, "well, that's something we've been tryin' and failin' to get him to become, but he's not, he doesn't want a pack, but seeing as he's kept us together for the last four years we respect him and follow his lead as such," she explains, absently staring down at her hands.

It's clear that this group of wolves seemingly without a family pack of their own has forged one and whether Declan wanted it or not, they've defaulted to him; I can see why too.

Rhett returns with a huge basket of French fries, and three different sauces for dipping, a peach milkshake, my cider and a sweet tea for Connie. Her face lights up like a Christmas tree as he slides the milkshake in front of her and then takes a seat, immediately stealing a fry.

"Rhett Pearson! Those are mine!" she snaps with an evil eye trained on him, her lip snarling, but in a blink curls into a smirk. "I am growing your pup and you think you can steal them? Rude," she adds and plucks the fry from his fingers before he pops it in his mouth. He pouts and then kisses her cheek.

"Yes Mrs. Pearson," he drawls, leaning back with his arm over the back of her chair. Connie smiles victoriously and dips a fry into her milkshake, groaning as she bites into it. I can't help but smile at her antics, they are so cute together.

Several songs later, and a couple of ciders, my head is buzzing, but I feel fabulous. Rhett leads Connie to the space opened up for dancing and twirls her rounded belly body into a two-step and cradles her head to his shoulder. Enraptured with watching them, I'm not paying attention. I jump up, startled when a man comes up behind me.

"Hey there, you must be new around here," he ventures and slides a cider in front of me. I settle back in my seat, eyeing him wearily. "I noticed you like the blueberry cider, thought you could use another," he adds and then sits down right next to me.

My vision is a little blurry, but I scrutinize him the best I can from the corner of my eye. Dusty blonde hair falls in straight shafts brushing his darker brows. Pale skin and gunmetal blue eyes, almost to surreal, complement a grecian nose and dark pink lips. Those lips curl up into a dazzling closed-lipped smile, he's quite attractive, practically too charming in a 'my daddy's loaded' kind of way. He nudges the cider to my empty hands resting on the table leaning a bit too close for my comfort. I scoot over the edge of my stool, giving me an inch more of space.

Relenting, to get him to back off, I cage the bottle in my fingers and spin it, collecting condensation on the tips. I remain quiet as I try and scent him. My head's a little foggy from the few ciders I've already had, but I try again anyway.

He smells of fresh snow and ice, must be visiting himself or a transplant, since there is no lingering sea salt odor like I've placed on everyone else who lives here. But the wintery scents are the only two wafting from his body, not even a hint of sweat.

"I'm Keir by the way," he offers as he hones in on me with those immensely captivating eyes. Swallowing hard, my inner warning bells alarm and shock my system in a series of bolts shooting throughout.

"Pleasure to meet you, um-thanks for the drink, but I'm here with someone," I mutter and return to spinning the bottle between my fingers.

His eyes narrow as he scans over my face and then out to the crowd. "Hmm that's fascinating I thought I saw you with another couple. Are you a throuple then?" Flabbergasted at his suggestion, I shake my head and try not to laugh.

"Excuse me? Uh no, he's in the back," I lie and cough on a laugh and go to take a sip, but stop myself. I know better than to drink from an open bottle from a stranger.

"Well thank you for the cider, I'm going to go." I shove back and make my way towards Declan's office, tossing the cider in the trash by the bar on my way. I slip into the darkened room, and slide down the door, sagging to a folded mess and I breathe in Declan's scent thats permeated his space.

After a few minutes I make my way back out to the table and the creepy dude is gone. Reaching over to the sugar packet holder, I grab one, and fidget it with, watching Rhett and Connie sway to a slow song. The tip of my finger traces the crisp edge of the packet and smiling wistfully I recall my first moments with Declan.

Flicking my gaze back to Rhett and Connie, a dull ache pinches my heart. I'm about to get up and head over to the bar when a petite, girl approaches, tray in hand with a cider on it. Her long brown hair is tossed up in a messy bun, strands hanging down frame her round face. The faded white tank top and ripped cut-offs pop against her deeply bronzed skin. Layers of hemp and shell necklaces circle her neck, and several more of the same style wrap around her wrist.

"Hi there! I'm Lexi, I work—" she starts out bubbly and sets the tray down on the table. I quirk an eyebrow at her, so this is the Lexi that grates Declan's last nerve with her piss poor work ethic. "Flik said it'd be okay if I brought this over to you," she says, and offers me the cider. I peer over her shoulder finding Flik. He beams his brilliant smile and gives me a jerk of his chin before tending to another customer.

"Ah, well thanks Lexi, I'm Faith," I offer and take the bottle, and sip. The bubbles rush over my tongue going straight to my head. "I'm so glad he got more of these, they are so good."

"Yep! They sure are. See ya around Faith." Lexi shifts awkwardly and her eyes grow wide, and then she nods, spinning away. I'm taking another drink as Keir slides in next to me again.

"Didn't get too far I see," he conveys, lazily blinking and zeroes in on my mouth, drawing his bottom lip in under his teeth. Darting my gaze back to the dance floor searching for Rhett and Connie, my stomach drops when I don't see them, sneaking a look over my shoulder I find Flik still behind the bar chatting with a customer.

As my head swings back in Keir's direction, my vision blurs and my head spins. Forcing my eyes wide, I try to stand, and I wobble a little. No, this can't be happening, I had my hand on the new cider the whole time, how—Lexi.

"Woah there little lady, I've got you, here let me help," Keir offers and wraps his arm around my middle stabilizing me. My lips open to protest, but quickly shuts when the pressure of something hard and cold presses into my side. His free hand slides up to my throat squeezing, briefly cutting off my air, and caresses down to my collarbone.

"Don't scream or try to flee Faith and no one gets hurt...nod if you understand," he threatens, the heat of his breath curling around my nostrils, making my nose wrinkle. Gasping, I nod emphatically and allow him to lead me to what would appear to anyone watching, the bathrooms, but he turns sharply and slips us out a side door. Leading me through a throng of people he holds me steady as each step I take is harder and heavier than the last.

Keir approaches a dark sedan and opens the back door, shoving me inside before sliding in next to me. "Drive," his barked command is the last thing I can fully hear as the blood pulsing in my head drowns out most of his speech.

I try and fail to keep my eyes open as we speed past street lamps, the lights a streaking blur. Keir's voice is muffled as he speaks to some-one. He drapes his hand over my neck, brushing my hair to the side, and a pinch and sting radiates from my neck. Warm and sleepy, dark-ness floods the corners of my eyes.

35

Declan

Danset, North Carolina

An atrocious sinking fear laces over my senses as Wyatt speeds back to the Outer Banks from the airport. We'd left a few hours earlier when an anxiety-ridden, all-consuming need to get back to Faith as soon as possible had finally eaten away at my logical reasoning. I'd dragged the pilot out of bed and demanded he get us up in the air.

"Almost there. Try and relax, Declan, your anxiety is stinking up the cab," Wyatt says in his way of comfort, but it's not helping ease the sinking pit currently opening up in my stomach.

My cell buzzes in my pocket. As I lean back with a grunt, I pull it out and see Rhett's face light up the screen. A boulder of trepidation lands in my stomach as I answer, putting him on speaker.

"Declan...she's miss—" he states, but I'm already imagining everything that could be happening to her, only hearing part of what he's saying. Wyatt's face falls, and Julianna bursts into tears.

"Flik is searching the houses, and Kiera came in from fishing and is out searching the beaches and surrounding areas," his crippling worry evident in his voice as he finishes.

My heart thuds sluggishly and hard; a paralyzing panic grips my limbs. I refuse to acknowledge that there's a real possibility that she left me of her own free will; that denial is heavier than gravity. "How?" I question, it's all I can manage from the depths of my raw throat.

"I-I don't know, man, she was sitting at the table one minute and gone the next." His shaky answer does absolutely nothing to assuage my fear. I end the call and sit in silence.

"Did you ever get those security cameras put up?" Wyatt asks, and at my non-response, he slams on the pedal, revving the truck past its limits.

After way too long for my liking, we finally come to a screeching halt in my driveway. I bolt from the truck before it's completely stopped moving and race up the stairs, slamming the door open to find Connie, Kiera, Rhett, and Flik inside, all trodden with guilt and misery.

"Anything?" They shake their heads, and then Flik comes to me and nods his head towards the stairs. That atrocious sinking fear boils over again, scalding any hope I have left as we climb the stairs and Flik leads me to my bedroom.

I enter alone and close the door; her scent faintly lingers in the air, layering over my mind in a complementary blend. Had she stayed in here after all? Flik and Rhett both mentioned she'd chosen the other spare bedroom, unless she changed her mind.

Investigating my bedroom, I follow her scent trail to the bathroom, my blood runs cold as I pick up one of my medications I no longer take, but leave out as a reminder. A whisper of white violets and mountain remains on the bottles. Shit.

Spinning out from the bathroom, a fluttering of paper draws my attention to the bed. There on my pillow is a neatly folded piece of cream colored stationary with my name scrolled out in elegant hand-writing.

No, no, no. No! I rush to the side of the bed and swipe up the letter. Ripping it open, my vision blurs as my eyes scan the contents, swallowing a dismal amount of salvia, it scratches my throat on its way down, splashing fiery bile back up.

Declan,

I'm sorry. I can't do this. It's too much too soon.

Please find it in your good heart to reject me and find someone who will love all parts of you.

Faith Bennett

My fingers tremble, shaking the paper as I collapse to the edge of the bed. She left.

Faith left.

She.

Left me.

Muscles contract in my fingers as I fist the note, crumpling it, and throw it across the room in a scream of anguish. Blips of my friend's faces below replay out like an old movie, as I discern their tear-filled, avoidant eyes and their cracked voices. They knew what I was going to find in here.

Determined to prove that they're wrong, that I'm wrong, I seek out the thread of our bond; it's weak, and she's closed off from me, but it's not broken. Did she really leave me? The muscles in my chest shrink and squeeze, a stabbing pain pulses brutally wreaking havoc on my body. White hot ardor rallies, filling my arms and legs with fury.

Wyatt opens the door right as I grab one of the side tables and chuck it across the room. It cracks and breaks apart when it hits the wall. I snatch up the vase on my dresser and pitch it too against the wall, it shatters in a satisfying explosion of ceramic. Adrenaline spent,

I collapse to the floor. He approaches me with caution, hands raised in the air, and comes to sit next to me.

We sit in the stark quiet, side by side for hours. My eyes hurt with an aching dryness from expending an abundance of tears. Icy coldness tingles my digits, arms, and legs, and creeps like phlegm across and around my heart. I failed her. Twice. I'm a pathetic, worthless mate.

"Dec, listen, we have kept looking, I know Connor, he could—" Wyatt tries again for the second time in the last few hours to convince me that she didn't leave of her own free will.

"No! She ran, and as much as it's killing me to respect her wishes, I can't right now, I can't even think," I shout, blood pulsing in my temples, jaw flexing so hard my teeth feel like they're about to crack. I know I shouldn't be so cruel to him, he's only trying to help me, but I can't find it in me to do so. His shoulders slump, and then he gets up, shakes his head at me, and walks out, leaving the door ajar.

* * *

The next morning

"Does anyone care to explain to me why she was out at the bar in the first place?" I ask the next day, sitting at the table with everyone.

Flik and Rhett both share a look, and then Connie shakes her head. Kiera shrinks in her seat and glances to the floor. Swiveling my head like a pendulum towards Wyatt, my brows push together in frustration. He clears his throat roughly running a hand through his hair, and tugs at his shirt collar.

"Give us the room," I demand with a slip of my aura. Kiera, Rhett, Connie, and Flik push back and pat their hands on my shoulder as they pass, heading out the back door to the porch. Julianna scoots closer to Wyatt and stares me down in challenge. "I'm not going anywhere, and don't try to make me either."

After a minute, Wyatt leans his elbows on the table and relents. "Listen, she'll kill me, simply for knowing, but what I'm about to share is something she doesn't think I know about anyway," he starts, and then swallows jaggedly, looking briefly at Julianna. "Back when we were on campus, there would be random week days when she'd call me up and ask for me to take her out. I'd wait for over an hour for her to get ready, and then she'd come downstairs, always painted heavily in makeup and a false smile," he takes a sip of his beer, and a squeak breezes between his lip and teeth before he continues.

"Every single time, she tried hard to cover up the bruises and put on a good effort to keep her bright smile on all night. But I could see the deep purples as they started to fade to green over the week. I never asked her outright why, but my guess was she wanted to be surrounded by people so she didn't feel so alone in whatever she was dealing with at home with Connor," he finishes and chugs the rest of his beer, slamming the empty bottle to the table. He takes in a pained breath and a haunted look passes over his face.

"I'd tried so many times to offer her a way out, any kind of help, but she repeatedly turned it down." He finishes and dips his head down as he sucks in a sniffle. The central air clicks on filling the silence with its steady humming. The three of us, stare at one another, unnaturally quiet. A chair creaks and all eyes shift to Julianna.

"That isn't all," Julianna whispers. Her tanned complexion pales as she flicks her gaze between Wyatt and me. He nods at her to continue, and she locks her gaze on me.

"Since you haven't had the opportunity to talk with her, I don't feel right sharing this, but my gut tells me she's in trouble." She shifts uncomfortably in her chair and sucks down a long drink of her sweet tea.

"Awhile back, I was closing up the coffee shop at the resort, and I overheard Faith's parents talking," she pauses staring off into space. Her eyes gloss over before she blinks it away. "Aunt Alaina was arguing with Uncle Gerrant about Faith needing to be under some kind of additional protection when she came home from college to visit," she says with a worried look at Wyatt. Gauging his facial reaction, he doesn't know what she's about to share either.

"What kind of protection?" I press, eager for her to continue as my foot bounces uncontrollably, knocking my knee into the table. With a sharp nod and a deep inhale, she does.

"Aunt Alaina wanted her to be cloaked by a witch to keep her aura from being tracked by the vampires. She said Isaac had been seen lurking around pack borders several days before," she explains and unexpectedly gets up. She heads into the kitchen, Wyatt and I track her movements. She brings the pitcher of tea over and tops off her glass and then offers us each some. The ticking of the clock in the living room slices away at my resolve as I wait with bated breath for Julianna to finish.

"Where was I?" She ponders and then like a light bulb came back on she nods. "Oh, right. From the crack in the door, Uncle Gerrant's face turned ghost white and then he demanded she explain why on earth their daughter needed to be cloaked when her aura had all but fizzled out years ago."

"I was as confused as he was, because the last time I'd seen Faith's alpha aura was when we were eleven years old, and she'd defended me against another alpha's son from a nearby pack." Julianna laments and sips from her glass, setting it down in a thunk. "Aunt Alaina insisted it was there, stronger than she anticipated, and that she'd taught Faith to mask it when she was a toddler. I never heard the rest of their argument because they had walked off, but it made me question so many things." She adds and bobs her eyes between Wyatt and me.

I too, have so many questions, and no way to get answers right now. Her alpha aura came out as a toddler? How strange. Mine didn't even show until I was ten. What did she say about her Mom being from gifted alphas again?

"*That she had to hide,*" Thorin utters morosely over our connection, he's been in an unbalanced state since we learned of the attack, barely linking with me unless it has something to do with our mate, or to remind me that I'm failing her.

My spine stiffens and then sags against the chair, she wanted normalcy, and needed safety. She wanted to hide in plain sight and I'd forced her aura out, unintentionally, but nonetheless it came out. No wonder she left. She had to have. It's the only thing that makes any sense.

My eyes glaze over into a vacant stare, and I shove back from the table without saying a word. Both of my hands rake through my hair as I walk past Wyatt and Julianna. Their eyes bore into me as I slink past them like the pathetic fool I am and trudge back upstairs.

Nothing and everything makes sense at the same time. I don't want to believe she willingly left, but she literally left me a note saying otherwise, and why wouldn't she? She needs to.

I can't begin to fathom the other reason she's gone, and that thought gets kicked to the far recesses of my mind. My throat closes off as my old friend, shame, grabs a hold of me and cloaks me in a gray cloud fading rapidly to black.

I fucked up.

I lost her.

I broke my promise.

36

Wyatt

2 Days after Faith's disappearance

Declan shuffles past Jules and me, his aura pulsing and fading from his usual blue to black. I reach out and clasp Jules' fingers with my own and squeeze, stopping her from asking him what's wrong. Her concern is rolling off her in waves. I know she wants to help. So do I. We need to.

"I don't believe for one second she willingly left," I whisper to the crook of her neck, when Declan is finally out of earshot. Jules pulls back and stares, unblinking, before nodding in agreement. "We need to start searching while he gets his head back together."

"I agree, but what do we tell my Uncle?" She poses and leans her head on my shoulder. I brush her hair behind her ear and cup her cheek, and guide her face to mine. Our eyes bob back and forth, each of us tuning into one another.

"Nothing yet, I don't want to alert Gerrant until we have to," I say, trepidation clinging to each word. The last thing I want to do is call Gerrant and tell him his daughter is missing, most likely kidnapped. He's a fierce warrior who scares the crap out of me on a good day. I don't want to know what he's like on a bad one.

"I don't know Wyatt, Uncle Gerrant is going to get involved one way or another, but I understand," she tentatively agrees. Her tiny fingers rub patterns on my inner wrist and up my arm.

"Come on, we have to make a plan quickly and get the others involved too."

After making a plan that's more nonsensical than practical, Kiera and Flik head out to start searching the next two towns over. Rhett and Connie head home so that Connie can rest, but Rhett will meet me at the bar in an hour to ask around about that night. Jules will stay behind and keep an eye on Declan and go through Faith's stuff.

That was key for me to know for certain she didn't leave willingly. After moving her Jeep to Declan's, it hit me that she would never leave it behind, let alone her camera. I tried to talk some sense into Declan, but he wouldn't hear it; nothing I said penetrated the shroud of self-induced blame. Declan is spiraling, and my concern for him is growing by the hour. He hasn't spiraled this intensely for a long time. He may not appear that way to others, but I know him; he's keeping it beneath a mask so people will leave him be. What he is, is in denial, afraid to admit that she was taken. His fear of failure is clouding his logic. If it wasn't he would be doing absolutely everything he could to find her. He'd burn down whole cities looking for her.

My feet are heavy walking up the stairs to his room. Standing before Declan's bedroom door, my heart twinges and pulls at the pain he's in, that Jules' is in. I've known Faith for seven years, and she's the sister I never had and always wished for—she's my best friend. We aren't nearly as close as her and Jules are, but she's as equally important to me. I've never told her how much she means to me, and when we get her back I plan to rectify that.

A wretched pain slices down my torso at the thought of something happening to her. She's touched so many lives with her bright smile, and infectious laugh. A small part of me feels responsible for her attack, because I didn't help her escape that douche.

Connor is a worthless piece of shit and deserves whatever is coming to him from Declan, because I know my cousin will shred him limb from limb for every bruise, cut, and scar he left on her. Hell, I want a piece of him too, he's ruined so many lives and I can't wait to see him reduced to scraps.

When Faith and I were in college together, I knew something was up the first time I spotted her out getting coffee, and she was covered up more than she usually was. She'd played it off like it was nothing, that she was fine, but she wasn't and I failed at getting her the help she needed. Failed her in so many ways, I don't deserve to even be called her friend, but Declan? Goddess have mercy on him, because right now he's being an epic idiot, yet I understand where his head is, and what he can and can't help.

Yanking the door open I stomp inside and find Declan crumpled on the floor in front of his bed, staring out the window. Silent tears streak down his cheeks from glossed over eyes. His hands open and close into fists hanging over his knees. I know he senses me but makes no move to acknowledge my presence. Wherever his mind has gone isn't good. I wish I could dive inside his brain, and pluck out the jagged, and dark pieces and burn them. I want my cousin back.

Sliding down beside him, I bump his shoulder, and he glances at me for a moment before returning to his tunnel vision of the window. We are approaching 48 hours gone now, and I know every minute that she's gone is crucial in her remaining alive.

"I told you, I didn't deserve a mate...believe me now?" Declan says hoarsely, as his head falls back to the side of the bed. My lungs collapse and struggle to get air for a beat, while I take him in. He's carrying the weight of the world's problems on his shoulders. He needs to stop blaming himself for what happened to Quinn, and now to Faith, but I know he won't.

"No, actually I don't believe you. You *do* deserve a mate. You deserve her, just as much as she deserves you." I reply and sit with him, until he's sunken further into the depths of his own mind that even I can't pull him out. I retrieve my cell and text both Rhett and Flik. Thankful I got their numbers on the plane from Declan before he slipped into the shadows.

Me: Gonna need you two to help me move him
   Flik: A'right be there in two shakes of a chicken's leg

What the? Okay then, he's so weird.

Rhett: On my way inside now, just got here.
   Me: Perfect.

37

Julianna

I slide a plate of sliced apples and a spoonful of peanut butter onto Declan's nightstand and hold back my tears, taking him in. He's curled up on his side, blindly staring out the window. Wyatt has told me so much about his cousin and what he's battled with for years, but to see it? Well, that is an entirely different type of emotional torture.

Cupping his shoulder, I whisper, "We are going to find her, Declan, I promise." His eyes shoot up to mine and then back to the window before shutting out the world. I sigh and squeeze his arm and tiptoe out, snicking the door closed. He'll come out of it; he just needs to believe it.

Wyatt and Rhett are already out at the bar searching for clues, and Flik has re-joined Kiera. So far, they haven't turned up anything useful. My legs shake when I step forward and down the hall. I didn't think it was right for anyone else to go through my cousin's belongings but me. Yet, I hesitate to turn the doorknob to the room she was staying in. I need her back; she needs to be here when our pup is born. I didn't even get a chance to surprise her with the news yet. I haven't told Wyatt yet either, but I think he suspects. Faith would want me to be strong right now, like she's always been, though she never believes she is. Buttoning up all of my courage, I turn the knob and head into the darkened room.

A lamp is in pieces on the floor, and the mirror has a crack in it running the length of the gigantic glass. Flik said something about scaring Faith when she was shifted in her wolf form, and things broke. I'm a little jealous Flik got to meet her wolf. I got to see her at the wedding and later at the announcement, but didn't get a chance to meet her. Next time, and there will be a next time, if I allow myself to think otherwise I'll end up in a ball like Declan.

Shuttling around the broken ceramic, I heave one suitcase to the queen-sized bed, and unzip it. I don't think I'm going to find anything, since I've already unpacked her clothing a few days ago, but I'd never forgive myself if I missed something crucial.

The soft wildflower scent that is quintessentially Faith whooshes up when I flip the lid back and begin trifling through her clothes. My fingers snag on something solid inside of her short pockets, and I pull out a small pretty shell. I smile, and set it aside, my cousin and her knick-knack habits; always collecting things.

Wiping the back of my arm over my brow, I rub away the sheen of sweat that's accumulated over the past 30 minutes and glower at the chair across the room. I've avoided going through her camera pack, telling myself I'd save it for last. And now, it's the only item left for me to search. Snagging the pack, I set it on the edge of the bed and sit, folding my legs beneath me.

My hands are trembling so hard I can barely get the zipper open. Taking a breath and leaning back on the pillows my hands migrate to my flat belly, and rub tiny circles over it. My thoughts drift to Declan and how he's handling this situation. While I don't truly understand where his headspace is, I do understand how hard it is to get out of it. What I don't understand is why has just given up. I know he doesn't know Faith as well as I do, but to think she would've upped and left without so much as a goodbye is unfathomable. A throbbing in my temples pulls me up. I kneed them with my fingers until the pain abates.

Careful to not break any of her lenses, I grab each one and lay it on the mattress, and then her camera and laptop. Dumping the rest of the contents to the bed, a small blue book thunks out and lands on top of the laptop. Thumbing through it, I pause on a grouping of letters and symbols. I trace my fingers over the writing and stop with a gasp, when I figure out what she's written.

My heart is in my throat and fighting its way out of my mouth by the time I get her laptop turned on and logged in. On the screen is the last thing she was working on and a small box asking for a secure code, the very one she'd penned from our childhood secret language.

Cradling the blue book with my thumb splitting the pages, I type in her code and pray I didn't mess it up. A video clip pops up. "I'm not snooping, I'm investigating, I have to find her," I convince myself and hold my breath while tapping the play button.

Shaky breaths whoosh over my lips, I can't be seeing what I'm seeing. I can't be. I leap from the bed and dash from the room.

"Wyatt!" I shout, bolting down the stairs. My uneven breaths are labored when I finally reach him, in the kitchen. Rhett sets his glass down and raises his brows at me. Wyatt rushes to my side, grips both of my arms and curling his spine meets my eyes.

"What is it? What's wrong?"

Tears streaming down my face, chin trembling, I'm at a loss for words. I stare at him and shake my head. He cradles me to his chest and kisses the top of my head. *I think the vampires have her, or someone working for them,* I relay to him through our bond, the only way I'm capable of right now.

A day and a few hours later, Wyatt and Flik return from Mc-Cormick's, both weary and tired, but with a renewed sense of purpose sketching their features. "We need to pull him out of his head, I think I know where she is." Wyatt says, and pulls me into a hug.

38

Faith

Location Unknown

A tremor vibrating my body shakes me awake. I'm groggy, and there's an ache hammering at the base of my skull. Shifting to sit, I open my heavy lids to a hazy darkness. I try to move my arms, but can't. A burning sting cuts into the skin at my wrist, flicking my blurry vision to where my hands are, cold metal clinks and bites into my flesh...handcuffs. I jerk my hand, and the skin at my wrist sizzles and blisters. *Fucking fantastic... silver.*

"I wouldn't do that if I were you," a velvet-like voice croons in a thick Russian accent that coats every syllable, skating a ghostly sensation down my spine.

"Why's that?" I croak and try to shift up again, cringing when the cuffs dig into my flesh and sear away more skin.

"Well, for starters, you have such luscious skin, and I wouldn't want you to end up amputating your hands from the silver burning and poisoning your flesh," the familiar svelte voice offers, and then the man's hand brushes my hair away from my face.

"Don't fucking touch me, Isaac!" I cut my eyes to the side in time to see the light glint off his nose ring. Flinching, I jerk away, drawing my knees closer to my stomach. Chills race from my head to my toes, and a sour, bitter taste plasters the inside of my mouth. It's quickly replaced with cold eyes and a pounding heart, as blazing heat explodes from anger rising.

"Ah-uh...we can't have any of that now," Isaac tsks, and then a pinch and burn spreads from the meaty part of my upper arm. Icicle fingers skirt up and down my arm and then to my neck. I'm warm all over, as my eyes roll into the back of my head, barely able to hear what he says. "You're so pretty when you sleep."

"Fucker..." I slur as darkness takes over again.

* * *

3 Days later

A pungent, damp, and musty odor forces me to breathe through my mouth as I roll to my side on the thin cot mattress on the stone floor of the dungeon. The only light filters in through a small square opening in the door. Just beyond the door, the evenly spaced sconces along the wall have buzzing bulbs that go in and out from the trickling water above. It's my daily symphony, keeping me awake all hours of the day and night.

I awoke in this shit hole, two days ago. I was free of the silver cuffs, but they'd been replaced with heavy iron ones complete with chains attached to the wall and the excess length drags along the cold floor whenever I move.

Time to start my daily routine. Mustering all of my strength into my exhausted muscles, I rise, dragging the heavy links over the rough stone floor; the metal clinks and thuds against it twinging my ears. Standing before the wall, I lift one leg and press it into the wall while I tug and pull at the ring where the chain is attached, but make no progress. Every day I've done the same thing, desperate for any sort of change, and every day its resulted in the same thing—nothing.

Hours later, maybe minutes in reality, my spine sags and curves forward, my hands fall to my sides, and I back away until the backs of my ankles smack into the soft, cold pad that Isaac calls a mattress. The damp air's icy bite sinks into my bones, rattling out into full body shivers.

Cautiously, I reach out to Sienna, *"Hey, are you okay?"* I hope she'll respond today.

Failure clogs my throat when I'm met with nothing but silence. Not knowing if she's okay chips away at my soul, leaving it in tatters. I fret and pace for hours, the action harkening my mind back to before, when she'd deigned to remain hidden from me, except now, the pain accompanying it is unbearable.

A plaintive whirring and buzzing hums in through the small square window at the top of the heavy iron door. The kiss of frigid air sinks its teeth into my skin, shivering my weakened muscles into a deathly exhaustion. My teeth clatter as the minutes tick by and the cold continues to seep in.

Dropping to the thin, pathetic idea of a bed again, I curl up into a ball, attempting to retain any amount of my body heat. My mind is a blank chalkboard; everything meaningful has been erased and reduced to white dust. After all of these years, Isaac finally has me. No matter how I hid or masked my aura, he found me. I'm positive not too much longer and I'll be before Benedict. I close my thoughts off and listen to my symphony of hell.

* * *

I jerk awake from a thud vibrating the floor. The solid iron door closes behind Isaac and Keir as the pair enters my cell. At some point, my body had given up fighting the shivers and settled into a form of lullaby shaking and rocked myself into a light slumber; it seems to be the routine of my life now.

Keir yanks me up by my elbow, dragging me from the heap that my limp body curled into. He slams my knees into the hard ground and pins my arms behind my back, the chains weighing down over my thighs. I glare up at Isaac, who tilts his head to the side deliberately and quirks an eyebrow. He folds his hands behind his back and curls his spine.

He paces the length of my cell, the clacking soles of his way too expensive shoes against the stone, matching in time with the on and off buzzing of the lights in the hallway. Clack, buzz, clack, buzz, it's a dreary little melody, but beggars can't be choosers. It's annoying and we might as well get this over with.

"What the fuck do you want with me?" I demand raggedly, for the fiftieth time, leaning far away from Keir's hard body. My throat is raw and it feels like I've ingested acid. Isaac glowers, but makes no effort to answer right away. The muscle in my jaw ticks as I grind my teeth, not so patiently waiting for an answer I know he'll give, just not what I want.

"Such a beauty," Isaac tuts, pouting his chiseled lips. His hand shoots out and grabs my face; his fingers clamp down, bruising my cheeks. He thrusts my head to each side as if he's inspecting and ignoring my question. "But such a nasty mouth, you used to have such sweet words for me when you were younger."

Keir strengthens his grip on my arms and yanks me back into his bulging thighs. He bends closer, the soft curve of his grecian nose skims along the nape of my neck, a prickle ripples over my scalp when his tongue tastes my skin up and up and up. Keir's foul mouth closes around the lobe of my ear, he moans out in pleasure, and his hard dick grinds into my back. I'm going to vomit.

"Wanted to get a taste of that pristine skin before we season it with the tang of your blood," he croons and backs away. Isaac's low bark of

laughter freezes my body's shudder of disgust. I lift my chin, faking a bravado I don't think I have much left of, and pin a glare on him.

"What do you want with me?" I inquire again in a grating manner, my teeth hurt as they snap together.

Isaac squats down to my level, his elbows resting on his knees. He balances on the balls of his feet, leaning in and trails his popsicle of a tongue over my temple and forehead, mussing up my hair. Vomit curdles and courses up my throat, I swallow it back down, having learned from yesterday that it's a bad idea to puke on your captors. Isaac leans back onto his heels, and I reel my head back and ram it forward, catching his nose.

A crack rents the air, and my forehead pounds with pain. He falls back, spitting and pawing at his face like a lunatic. He pulls his hand away, his fingers covered in crimson ichor splotches.

"You filthy fucking bitch!" He screams. Fisting my shirt, he forces me to stand. Keir's hands form a vice grip on my biceps. Without warning, Isaac swings his fist and lands a blow to my stomach. A painful grunt slips past my lips and body cows in on itself. He tips his head back in a haunting laugh, and then levels his darkened eyes on me, silencing the eerie sound.

"I don't like having to do this, I'd much rather make your body sing for me in other ways, the way it was always supposed to," he boasts, cracking his knuckles. Inhumanly fast, he pummels my sides and chest in a series of punches. A piercing pain lances my rib cage, following a resounding crack. My body desires to fall forward, and tries, but is restrained by wickedly sharp nails biting into the skin of my arms. Keir's hold doesn't relent and only becomes sturdier with every blow.

My breaths are labored, rattling, and excruciating with each rise and fall of my lungs. Tired lids slide over my gritty eyes, focusing on the memory of Declan's gentle touch, of his lips over my skin, alighting a fire within my flesh.

Skeleton fingers replace the meaty, thick ones biting into my arms, and its twin wraps around my waist. My chapped lips curl in a growl

as Isaac grazes his fangs against the supple skin of my neck. A trickle of blood wells and races down the column, soaking into my dirty t-shirt. Resolved not to show weakness, I channel the familiar unyielding emptiness I'd harness when Connor's fists and drunken anger found my body.

I crack open my cold, dead eyes and leer at Isaac at my side. "Fuck. You." I snap, my throat hot with rage, and each word burns.

"Gladly," he hisses and tightens his hold around my waist, trailing his fingers over my belly. "Say please."

Keir smirks with a hmph and grips a length of the chain connected to my cuffs. "I get her first, but only after she's been taught a lesson," he grumbles, shaking the chains. The heavy links slide over the stone ground, clanking together as he winds up a loop.

Isaac's mouth hovers near my ear, "You shouldn't have rejected Keir at the bar, lil' wolf, he's been eager to taste you—" he whispers, his rancid breath panting along the shell right as Keir lifts the loop and whips it backwards.

The bulky chain, appearing like nothing more than a strand of rope, shoots forward, colliding with my shins. A deafening, obscene snap and crackle penetrates the stone walls. Agonizing, bone-shattering pain shoots up my shins clacking my teeth together and I nearly bite the tip of my tongue off. Another snapping of the chain, and it collides with my ankles.

My head slumps forward in an oomph, copper floods my mouth, drowning my tongue; I've bitten the inside of my bottom lip. A chunk, partially filleted from the smooth flesh, rubs against my tongue.

An evil and malicious chuckle rumbles from behind me. "I told you," Isaac sneers haughtily, making zero sense. He said the same thing yesterday and the day before that. Scorching heat spreads out from the throbbing gash in my leg. The bone is splintered and piercing through the skin. Tears stream down my face in rushing rivulets, joining the snot pouring and bubbling from my nose. Again and again, Keir re-

peats, looping the chain and firing it bashing it into my legs. From my thighs to my feet, bones are broken and shattered.

The words I want to spew at them are lost on a choked sob, my desire to fight dwindling with each successive connection of the heavy chains against bone. Isaac grinds his erection against my hips and back with every cry that escapes my lips. I swallow bits and pieces of vomit with every gyration.

My body collapses to the cold floor, only to be ripped up and forced to stand on broken shins. Isaac's fingers flex and curl into fists, wetting his lips, he inhales deeply, his nostrils and eyes flare wide at the tang of my blood reaching his senses.

He sprints before me, rips my shirt open, and rakes one sharp claw over my exposed breast, slicing the skin. Wincing as dark, hot blood blooms and combines with the salt of my tears falling. A groan vibrates against my breast as Isaac's lips close around the wound. Pure undiluted rage boils in the blood he pulls from my body with each swallow.

"Get off me! You. Repulsive. Leech!" I snarl, shifting my shoulder to shove Isaac away. He releases my skin with a pop and grins wickedly, showing off his blood-coated teeth. "So sweet, yet still so bitter," he retorts, wiping his mouth, then licks his fingers one by one.

He's never marred my face during these beatings, only assaulting it with his mouth and rancid breath. When he slides his hand up my cheek soothingly, my spine braces for impact and falters when he traces his thumb over my bottom lip like a lover would. Blinking rapidly, I gape at him blankly, confused. Isaac trails his hedonistic stare up and down my battered body and smirks before spinning on his heel towards the door.

The room abruptly tilts upside down. My head pounds beating against my skull, and every broken bone screams as Keir drops me like I am nothing more than trash and follows Isaac out.

39

Declan

Danset, North Carolina

4 Days after Faith *disappears*

The sharp rattling of drape rings dragging over the rod wakes me, and the cruel, piercing light that follows momentarily blinds me. The setting sun streaks over the floor and up over my bed, screaming at my retinas with absolutely no remorse. Grumbling, I roll over and pull the blanket over my head.

"Okay, that's it...get the hell up," Wyatt yells, stomping over to the bed, and pulls the comforter from my head, wrinkling his nose, and then steps back, waving his hand in front of his face.

"No," I groan over the never-ending pain in my chest. I'm pleasantly comfortable in the nest of my ever-worsening, bleak outlook on my shit life. Four days of unrelenting, overwhelmingly crippling dejection have weighed down my mind and body. I've had no will whatsoever to move myself from this room, especially when the last of her scent faded after two days. I even cracked open my doxepine to sleep through the pain, which hadn't helped either.

Julianna and Wyatt kept me fed by bringing in plate after plate of food, most of which I'd left untouched for days until my body trembled so hard from hunger that I finally forced myself to eat, only to vomit it all back up promptly. In the days that followed, all I could keep down was broth and crackers. They didn't relent on letting me know that they've been looking for her either.

"No, not no. Get the fuck up, and go find her...stop being a pansy-assed, whiny bitch," Wyatt snarks angrily. He yanks the bedding off, and a shiver of cold slices over the bare skin of my chest.

"Don't care, don't want to, she *left* me, remember?" I mumble, rolling back over to keep ignoring him. He doesn't understand the hollowness that has excavated my chest and weighed it down with a ton of bricks, the second I'd learned she had left. He doesn't understand the constant pang of yearning and pain when I no longer feel her, sense her through our bond.

She hasn't answered any of my calls, nor has she responded to the pounding against her mental shields that I've been sending her way daily. Unfortunately, every unanswered call gave me more confidence to accept that she left.

"No, she didn't, and I have proof," he exhales sharply and crosses his arms over his chest as I roll back, staring at him blankly, furrowing my brows at what he's implying.

"Wh-what?" I rasp over a cracking in my chest spreading the dangerous warmth of hope. The denial has been strong, I couldn't believe in my cousin's insistence that she was taken. If I did, that would mean...I'd failed her, but still that warmth flutters and is quickly drenched. "Proof? Her letter wasn't proof enough?"

"Nope! And I'm not telling you until you get up, shower, get dressed and eat, because Goddess, 1. you stink worse than a dead moose ass, and 2. your face...you look like shit," he orders walking around my bedroom picking up the dirty clothes from last week and shoves them in the hamper and disappears into my closet returning with a pair of jeans, a henley and boots.

"Then and only then will I explain. Come on, up!" He grabs my wrist and, in one swift motion, yanks me to a sitting position. The room spins, and I steady my whirling vision with a hand to my forehead.

After shoving me into the shower with my pajama pants still on, Wyatt finally left me to my own devices. The piping hot water scorches my flesh and warms my stiff muscles and joints.

A redolent aroma of balsam springs to life in the steam as weak fingers scrub at my scalp, once and then again. The shampoo stings at my sore eyes as hellfire water burns away the suds down my head and over my face.

The shower runs cold before I deign to step out and dry off. Wiping a hand over the fogged mirror, my face scrunches in disgust. I do look like shit, gaunt and pallid, I'm essentially death warmed over.

"Tried to tell you that for the past 4 days, but did you listen to me? No...just wallowed away pitifully," Thorin complains, but defeatedly, because he's hurting too.

Dressing in the clothing Wyatt set out before I change my mind, I sit down on the bed, eyes filtering up to the photograph of the stag and jet black wolf; I'd never gotten the chance to tell her. Never got a chance to tell her that the wolf in the picture was me. Dropping my head low, I sigh and then heave myself from the bed and make my way downstairs.

Rich and delectable smoky tendrils waft in the air, my mouth watering in anticipation as my feet hit the first floor. How long has it been since I last ate anything substantial? Sliding into a chair at the round, mahogany table, I twist around to watch as Wyatt plants a kiss on Julianna's cheek. A pang of longing jabs straight into my heart, and wrenches on it hard.

"So, you plan to share your irrational explanation as to why my mate didn't up and leave, effectively rejecting me?" I ask dryly after clearing my throat. I stand, stretch and walk over to interrupt their moment of affection. As happy as I am for Wyatt and Julianna, I'd rather not witness it, not right now.

"Nope! Sit down, and eat," Wyatt demands, twirling his finger upside down in a circular motion. Groaning I tuck tail like a child and do as I'm told.

A plate heaping with brisket, coleslaw, and baked beans is shoved in front of me. Wyatt slides into the chair opposite, resignation written plainly on his face. They were supposed to continue on their trip days ago, but have stuck by my side, refusing to leave while I wasted away in misery. I'm fucking pathetic.

"Well, for starters, I would never leave without looking for my best friend and my mate's cousin. Secondly, I found her note, you know the one you balled up and threw without really looking at it?" He pulls out the crinkled cream paper and flattens it on the table, and then scoots back, dragging the legs of the chair over the floor. His words leave a tightness in my chest that can't be rubbed away.

I gather the coleslaw into a heap with my fork and then push the beans into a pile rather than let them spread out. I stab the brisket slices next and stack them so they're not touching the slaw or beans. I ignore him while I slice into the meat, and then dip it into the sauce seeping out from the beans.

"So, this is not her handwriting. I couldn't be sure at first because it's been some time since I'd seen her signature, and I'm surprised you didn't notice it, Mr. I have every single photograph of hers, but I'm not a stalker," he says fucking with me. I roll my eyes and, lifting my hand in the air, gesture with my fork for him to continue.

That was the conversation of all conversations when he'd found the boxes in my closet a day ago. He read me the riot act and asked me if I'd shown her—hard no. I'd buried my face into my pillows and pretended he wasn't beating me with the other one, while he yelled at me for being a complete idiot.

"Well, like I said her signature is off...like way off." Wyatt finishes and joins me again, plopping a framed picture down on the table. Calm irritation slides down my spine at him moving my stuff...again, before it settles into a blazing, languid pulse. My gaze shoots up and over the framed signed photograph of a fox chasing a butterfly; she'd signed it in the right-hand corner, and...it...it doesn't match. I cower internally as inferiority drapes its shroud over me. How the fuck did I not notice that?

"Okay, maybe she was in a hurry, ya know, to leave me?" I deflect from my inability to catch such an easy sign, reminding Wyatt of the obvious. Moving the beans into a pile again, I swallow back the nausea and shove the coleslaw closer to the edge of the plate.

"Good Goddess, you are a mess, and an idiot—stop separating your food, nothing was touching when I handed it to you," he complains. My head snaps up to him, my lips thinning in anger.

"Sorry, man, please, eat." His apology eases some of the embarrassment rushing to my cheeks, but not all of it, and I continue to move my food, ensuring none of it mixes.

"Anyways, it's the fact that she never signs just her first and last name ever, that clued me in, and it's not simply the irregularities of the penmanship...it's what she says."

But the: 'It's too much too soon' wiggles its way into my mind. She'd told me that, hadn't she? It makes sense. We barely know each other, well, our souls do, but we didn't know anything about one another before.

"Hadn't realized that, guess I was too busy with my soul being ripped out," I supply, jabbing my fork into another slice of juicy and tender brisket, bringing it to my mouth. Julianna sets a tall glass of sweet tea down next to me and briefly touches my right shoulder before disappearing upstairs.

"Right," Wyatt says dryly, "Says the man who has every single copy of National Geographic that her work is in, organized by date and in protective sleeves in boxes in his closet... Uh-huh, totally believable Declan. Do I need to go on?" he taunts again, making me sound like an obsessed freak. I enjoyed her work, and when I found the one with the stag, I had to buy it. No one has ever captured my likeness when in wolf form. He doesn't have to understand it.

"Fine, whatever, she still left," I reply, pointing my fork at him and scowl at him.

He groans, "Fine then, I'm done playing nice with you." He leans back in his chair, tipping the legs up and then slams them back down. "How about this, do you think, Faith, would leave behind her beloved Jeep, or her camera and all of her lenses? For fucks sake Dec, her fucking camera is still in her room," he stresses, the muscles around his eyes twitching.

A wicked, sharp pain stabs in my stomach, doubling me over. Inadequacy slithers under my skin, exposing my worthlessness. Wow, I *am* an idiot. How had I not known that, or thought to search in the room where she stashed her suitcases? "Never mind the fact she was seen with a suspicious dude at the bar." He adds, glaring at me, his aura pulses, and it's plain to see he's withholding his anger at me. Dread pools oily and thick in my gut. I gulp the sweet tea down, needing it to cut through the grossness before it spreads.

"What?!" I screech over panting breaths. A knot forms in my stomach, tightening every second I wait for confirmation.

"Yes."

"Why didn't you tell me sooner?" I stare at him not knowing what to think and tap down my anger.

"You wouldn't listen to me!" He shouts, spit flying from his lips lands on my cheek. Flicking it away, my head falls into my hands and I succumb to the abundance of regret clawing its way inside.

Julianna's steps creak on the last step before she rounds the corner and joins Wyatt's side again. He squints his eyes at me, rolls his lips in on themselves, and sighs.

"She didn't leave you. Jules, can you bring our guest in?" He asks, kissing her cheek, and then turns to me. "You've got to promise me not to do or say anything, all alpha-hole, perhaps I don't know, maybe stay all depressed while he speaks."

Julianna gets up, her footsteps fading as she heads down the hall-way to the front door, opens and closes it, murmuring low, and then two sets of footsteps echo down the hallway. An odorous, earthy campfire and pine needle stench billows down the hallway, temporarily mixing with Julianna's comforting apple and oak moss scent.

Mud-caked boots shuffle and leave clumps of dried mud on the wood floor as a male dressed in thin, ratty clothing follows behind Julianna. The muscle surrounding my eye twitches as I glower at the dirt now flitting over my floors. I can't take any more of this shit today.

"Who in the fuck are you?" I shout and bolt from my chair, knocking it over. The homeless-looking dude jumps backwards, flinging more dirt and mud over my floors. Wyatt races to my side, grabs my arm, and holds me back, snarling at me. A scowl sketches over his face, silently communicating that I need to knock it off. My teeth grate, cracking in my jaw. I draw in a long, ragged breath before I bend and right my chair, the legs clacking on the floor. I plant my ass back in it and pin a menacing glare to the ragamuffin.

"Uh, my name is Dirk Jarrett, and I-uh know what happened to Faith." He replies and takes a hesitant step forward. My brow arches and my head tilts to one side, waiting for him to continue. My body itches with urgency to leave and do what I should've been doing this whole damn time.

"She was shoved into a dark sedan from the bar by some vamp with blonde hair, pretty sure he works for Isaac." My lips pull back, baring my teeth. Exploding from my chair again, I barrel towards him, grabbing him by the collar, dragging him towards the back door, preparing to toss him down the stairs.

"And you're just now telling me this? Why?" I scream in uncontrollable rage, spit splattering on his face. I take one step, throw him to the ground and land on top of him, instantly pummeling his face. Blood and spittle fly onto my hands, arms, and shirt. I vaguely hear Wyatt through the haze of red, and crane my neck to the side, stopping my barrage of flying fists to grip him around the neck. My hands squeezing while Wyatt tries to pull me off of the scrawny Dirk.

"Declan! That's enough! This isn't going to help you find her!" He shouts, the whites of his eyes bloodshot and flickering irises from his leaf green to bright jade.

"Be the alpha, Declan. Get your shit together." He's challenging my instinct to dominate, and then red-hot shame creeps in, filling every frayed nerve ending as I finally connect with leaf green irises, reminding me of the last time I lost control...meadow green eyes filled with the same fear.

A burst of cold rips down my back, dumping over me like a bucket of icy water. I release Dirk's neck and ease off his body. Turning away from him, rubbing my knuckles and regulating my breath, "You decided to tell us this information now...why?" I ask again through my teeth grating against each other, acting like I'm a fraction less irritated, while every bone in my body is on fire.

"Because I'm a rogue...and frankly, you terrify the shit out of me." His unexpected answer makes sense but doesn't clear the blackness edging its way into the corners of my vision again.

"You're absolutely right to be afraid because right now I'm—" I snap, bristling on the edge of losing control. Wyatt grips my shoulder, clamping down, his fingers dig in to the point of pain. Relenting with an exhale, I try again, calmly. "Explain."

"On her way down here, I ran into her, because one of my pack members accosted her at a gas station," he throws a hand up at my growl. Wyatt squeezes my shoulder again holding me back, stopping my lunge, and nods at the kid.

"He didn't harm her, but he became obsessed with her scent and then he disappeared. I didn't want anything to happen to her on account of Eric, so I started tracking him and I spotted Isaac along the way. By the time I made it here, I came up on your bar...and I saw her being shoved inside the car. I'd tracked them to the air strip. And then back tracked here. It took a bit," he rambles everything out, without so much as breathing and shaking the entire time. He pinches his nose as Julianna hands him a wad of paper towels and an ice pack that he doesn't deserve.

Whipping around to my cousin, I lock eyes with him and unclench my teeth. "How soon can we get wheels up and off the ground?" His brows jump up and then settle as he relaxes and purses his lips to the side.

"Fucking finally! I'll get your Dad on the phone," he replies and stalks off, but stops and glances back, I'm sure questioning on whether or not to trust me. "You back now, really back?"

I nod, and swallow the dump truck sized load of shame. When I get her back, if she doesn't forgive me, I'll accept every bit of punishment, and spend the rest of my life making it up to her.

"I'll call Lexi and Elias and Nia to run the bar. And if they're willing, I'll need Kiera, Flik and Rhett, but only if Connie is okay with him leaving so close to giving birth," I mutter, my mind a mush of plans and things I should've been doing days ago.

I right the chair once more, and work my way around to the living room flopping down into my chair and hang my head between my legs. The tremors in my hands won't quit and I don't think I can force them if I was even able to either. An image of my meds on the counter flashes behind my lids.

No! I can do this without that poison.

Mustering some courage and tamping down the elephant-sized shame, I make my calls and stare out the window, up to the dark skies. The new moon hides her silvery essence from everyone tonight, and I briefly wonder if she can see the same stars or if she's being held somewhere with no windows. Knowing Isaac it could be anything, the sadistic bitch.

"So—" Wyatt starts, walking over to me. "First, your Dad is *ecstatic* that you found your mate and is readying a small force for you if you want it, and secondly, wheels can be in the air in 2 hours or less. He never recalled the plane, it's still on the air field here." Wyatt disperses gaining my attention with a snap of his fingers in my line of view.

40

Faith

Location Unknown
6 Days later

The last six days have been a repetitive Deja vu. Keir and Isaac enter my cell. Keir holds me while Isaac beats me until I'm bordering on unconscious, leaving my face alone until the end, where he caresses it and makes me want to vomit. Every day, same time, wash, rinse, repeat.

Expecting the same today when I hear the sliding of the lock clanging, I don't bother to move from the mattress; instead, I pinch my eyes closed, picturing Declan's face, those haunting hazel eyes, and then refocus on the dark, dank stone wall. I've tried and failed to seek out our bond, and what hope I have left is decaying to death. He hasn't come to find me, and I fear he won't be.

My bloodied fingers pick at the loose threads of the thin mattress as I repeat in a whisper only, I can hear, "Shut it down...shut it off...shut it all down..."

As the iron door screeches over the one uneven bit of the floor, I wince, covering my ears and blinking evenly, my heart slows. I let the emptiness inside, let it encompass my already frigid body and wrap its deadened fingers around me.

My cracked, dry lips part as my jaw unhinges in a yawn. I run my tongue over the edges of my teeth, inspecting for any chips or cracks, an easy task as they have stopped clattering for a day or so now. The frosty air is a second skin.

An icy hand curls long, lanky fingers around my wrist and gently lowers it, setting it on my hip, and then just the tips of fingers slide up the bare skin of my arm. My eyes swivel to Isaac, sweeping over his platinum blonde locks perfectly slicked back with pomade, not a hair out of place. His claret red eyes burn through the steel blue contacts he's wearing. I don't know why he bothers to hide, he'll always be a monster.

I drag my exhausted, heavy eyes up over his lanky, but lean body, clothed in a dark gray dress shirt that's tucked into his trim-waisted black slacks. The top two buttons of his shirt are undone, the sleeves rolled up, exposing pale flesh covered in traditional Russian tattoos.

His black oxfords click over the stone floor as he bends to unlock the bulky chain from the wall and then back with the click clack towards me, the iron links clink and clank as they coil to the floor.

Bone-chilled hands scoop under the side of my torso, and outrageously strong, slim arms pull me up into a chest of glacial granite. My cuffed hand flops to one side and smacks into the frame of the door. I groan. Isaac plucks my hand up, draping it back over my chest.

The light that filters into the small opening of the door is now almost blinding as he carries me down the long hallway of blinking, buzzing lights. I skirt my eyes over several more iron doors and strain to hear anything behind them. A steady drip splashes into a puddle ahead, the tang of copper and iron bristles my nostrils and the back of my throat.

Too tired to care, I close my eyes as we ascend what I assume are stairs, judging by the jostling I'm experiencing. So many steps, the incessant clacking of his too-expensive shoes makes me want to rip my ears off and feed them to him if only it will make it stop.

41

Faith

Chanoît, Quebec, Canada
Palais de Sanc

Chamomile and incense surround me, blanketing me in a sickly perfume. I roll into a soft, cushiony pillow and bury my nose, choking when the scent asphyxiates me instead of smothering the smell.

Springing upright, coughing, my entire world wobbles and rights as a low chuckle slices the mud caking my hearing.

"I take it you'd prefer the dank dungeon then?" Isaac mocks dryly and brings a crystal wine glass to his lips, sipping the mahogany-red liquid, which I assume is his dinner.

Shifting to dangle my legs over the edge of the large bed I find myself in, I explore the room quickly, skirting over an antique ivory furniture set consisting of a wardrobe, a chest of drawers, and a large ornate oval floor mirror. Opposite, there is a newer design vanity, its newness makes it stick out like a sore thumb, and it's white, not matching at all, or even contrasting. That little discrepancy is already tiring the muscle on the corner of my eye.

My hands run over my bare legs, and I flick my gaze down at them, confused. I'm healed, clean, and in a new set of clothes. A large brown bear rug with its head attached snatches my attention. It's sprawled out near a fireplace that takes up half of the wall and covers a rich mahogany wood floor.

How old is this place? Where am I?

Deep sapphire drapes hang from the ceiling to the floor, slightly hiding the bubbled mullion windowpanes. The deep blue of the drapes is stark against the creamy ivory walls and bedding of the canopy bed.

Isaac appears, brushing the sheer curtains of the bed to the side, and leans against one of the posts. His usually claret eyes are a haunting jade shade now, and his hair is tidy with an abundance of pomade. There's no way it will move even if a gust of wind blows in from behind.

He extends a hand, confidently swooping a loose strand of hair behind my ear and drags a fingertip down the curve of my jawline. As distressing as his touch is, I don't flinch; I don't think I'm capable of it anymore. Instead, I cut my eyes to the corners and scowl.

Isaac snarls his lip and shoves off from the post and strolls to the tall wardrobe; the doors creak as he opens them. The stagnant silence is broken with the hushed clinking and clanking of hangers sliding and a swishing of material.

He selects something and drapes the ruby red cloth over his arm, bending, he scoops up a pair of black heels, pinching them in his fingers before he closes the wardrobe and returns to the bed. Placing the shoes on the floor, he lingers, leaning in to brush the tip of his straight nose along my ankle. An abhorrent sensation shudders up my skin, and nausea rises to the surface. I swallow it and command my limbs to remain still.

He exhales sharply and clucks his tongue as he unfolds his lanky body and spreads the ruby cloth on the bed beside me. A cold thumb and index finger pinch my chin, forcing my gaze to his deadened irises. Those jade contacts are disquieting and void of empathy as they scan the surface of my features.

"You have only one option, lil' wolf, and that is to do what you're told, when you're told, and this will go so much easier for you," he forewarns, narrowing his eyes at my anesthetized stare. He drops my chin and, shoving his hands in his pockets, storms to a massive wood door with a thick sliding bolt.

Unlatching it, the metal groans and scrapes. He glances back one last time, muttering something under his breath, and leaves. The groaning returns with multiple clicks and clangs as the door locks.

My head tilts listening for the fading footsteps behind the thick door, but there is nothing, not even a hint of muffled noise. A quick burning pain centers low in my abdomen. Goddess, I have to pee.

When was the last time I went?

Leaping from the imposing, but comfortable bed, I hurry to the only other door in the room. Ripping it open, I rush inside and relieve myself. It's not until I'm washing my hands that I fully notice my attire.

At some point, I've been bathed, hair brushed to a shine, and changed into emerald-green silk shorts and a matching camisole. Deep purple, green, and yellow bruises color my skin, some blooming under my tattoos, adding color where there shouldn't be. Tiny cuts and abrasions cover my skin in much the same way an abstract artist creates a masterpiece.

Unable to swallow back the sudden nausea, I sprint back to the toilet in the modernized bathroom and heave the contents of my stomach up, which isn't much.

I shuffle back to the sink and cup my hands under the tap, catching a drink to swish the bile out of my mouth, and then cup them again, slurping over and over, slaking my thirst.

Slinking back to the fluffy bed, I crawl on top of the plush covers, ignoring the blaring red scrap of satin. I scoot back to the headboard and draw my knees up to my chest. My chin rests on my kneecaps, and my eyes circumvent the room again, catching on anything that I can use as a weapon, but come up empty unless you count the paddle hair brush on the bright white vanity currently pestering my mind. Or the shoes in the wardrobe. I can barely sense Sienna, and I'm trying not to think about why.

Declan's rich and husky voice rasps from memory in my ears. A twinge of anguish pinches behind my sternum, my eyes shutter capturing the vision of his arms wrapping around me from behind, murmuring delicious and devious nothings in the shell of my ear.

The stench of chamomile and old incense clouds my ability to recall his amber and spruce with a hint of sea salt aroma—warm wetness trails from my lashes, brushing against the darkened, delicate skin under my eyes.

The click and clanking of gears rolling snaps my head up as the bolt of the door slides and then groans, opening. A repulsive and more potent bubble of chamomile and incense fog the stale air, restrengthening the stench that clings to the furniture as Isaac boldly walks in.

His fake jade eyes slice to my curled up form, his tongue pokes lightly into the hollow of his cheek, as he inhales a tense breath, his teeth make a squeaking kiss noise as the door closes and the bolt slides into place.

"I'm disappointed, Faith, I'd hoped you'd taken my instructions seriously..." he criticizes, the thickness of his Russian accent clipping on the consonants.

"What instructions?" I rasp. The bed dips as his weight settles on the edge. His glacier nearness pebbles my skin in a blanket of goosebumps. I stifle the urge to shiver from his noxious energy.

"I'd rather not punish you, but seeing as you've chosen to be defiant, I find I must bring Keir back; perhaps he will want to assist—" he suggests, but my eyes snap to his pale complexion, shutting him up. My lips curl in disgust as an ache forms at the base of my skull.

"Fuck you," I hiss and scramble further away as his bony fingers glide over the plush comforter towards my legs.

Quicker than I can register, Isaac is on the other side of the bed, and dragging me up from it. He pins my body and arms against his side, and then in one swift motion, he rips the emerald silk pajamas from my body. My nipples harden to buds as they are exposed to the freezing air and his soul-deep cold body.

His menacing laughter ripples over me, causing me to tremble. Isaac's grip tightens, and my toes leave the floor as he lifts me into his side and then drops me back onto the bed.

Wrapping my arms around my breasts and stomach, attempting to shield myself from his disparaging eyes, I will my heart to calm its incessant pounding. Isaac jerks my arms from my sides and forces them up into the air.

"Stay," he commands slowly releasing them, and I obey, deciding it's not worth his wrath even if it means suffering his leering perusal.

Slinky, soft satin cascades down my arms and chest, piling around my waist. He guides my arms back down to my side and then bends, scooping the back of one of my ankles in his palm. The black leather heels slide over my icicles for toes, and he repeats the motion. The heels hug both of my feet perfectly.

He stretches out a hand to me, waiting with a raised brow. My eyes dart up and down and land on his perfectly chiseled lips. Disgust washes over me as they flatten, and his tongue sweeps out.

I follow his hand as it wraps around the back of his neck and then scratches the skin exposed from the collar of his black button shirt. Now that I can see him in the light, the rolled sleeves and barely exposed V of the neck are much more modest than I expected of him. He pinches the bridge of his nose with his other hand and then gestures again for me to give him my hand.

"I can call for..." he threatens with Keir's presence again.

"NO!" I shout and slam my hand into his waiting palm. He yanks my arm towards him, my body flies forward, and I stumble on my heels. Isaac catches my fall and rights me, raking a provocative leer over my body as the satin slips down over my hips and legs, pooling around my feet, hiding the heels.

The deep ruby satin gown is sleeveless save for the thin straps over my shoulders. The deep V cut in the bodice reaches my naval, and the back scoops down into a cowl just above the small of my back.

Isaac lifts my chin and lovingly brushes my hair away and over my shoulders, his hand trails down to my elbow where he grips it and tugs me forward and spins me around. His breath fans across my spine as he dips his mouth to my cheek and then draws back casually. Magically, his hands are at my neck, draping a necklace with a black diamond dangling from the long, dainty chain. The pendant dips down between my breasts. I look like an overdressed wraith, I've lost weight in the time I've been here and nothing can hide his punishments from the dungeon adding to my ghastly appearance.

Without instruction he ushers me to the door, and raps twice on the dense wood.

Did he knock on it before?

The creaking and groaning of the metal as whoever is on the other side unlocks it, resounds inside the room, rattling my nerves. Begging my anxious heart to cease its percussive rhythm I take a steadying breath and keep my head lifted and eyes forward.

Isaac whisks me from the room, his vice grip on my elbow digs deeper and deeper with each footstep away from the cell. Well, chambers, but I'm not kidding myself, it's still a cell, albeit a posh one; it still has locks.

Our path guides over sparkling black marble floors and past steel gray walls devoid of color and decor. The old incense odor is laced with copper and rotting flowers leaving a nauseating burn in my stomach as it swirls up and into my nose. Those too expensive shoes of his along mine click and clack over the marble, echoing off the bare walls and ceiling.

Suddenly, Isaac drags me into a dark room, slamming the door closed, his hand brushes along the wall flipping the light switch on with a click and clunk as the outdated round receptacle comes alive.

My lips part in astonishment, the room is surprisingly beautiful with its elegant dark dining table and chairs over a forest-green area rug in front of a cold hearth. Deep wood panels separate half the walls and are capped with a matching chair rail around. The same forest green is painted above the rail cutting the other half of the room in color. Lively, bright and contrasting abstract paintings hang from the walls in an organized manner that is entirely pleasing to the eye.

The polished table is laden with gold candelabras and three vases of floral arrangements. Before one chair is a set of bone china and dark steel silverware, neatly placed over a cream placemat. In one corner, a phonograph sits undisturbed, its brass fluted sound tube and lacquered base fit into the puzzle of the dining room. The final piece of this charade, is the side board shoved against the wall, littered with crystal glasses and decanters.

Boney fingers dig into my flesh and drag me across the floor, Isaac snakes his free hand out and aggressively pulls a chair back before plopping me down into it and shoving the chair forward crushing my upper body into the edge of the table.

"Sit, we will dine soon."

42

Declan

Rossbury, Maine
Later on the evening of the 4ᵗʰ day

W e'll be landing in about 30 minutes, Dec," Wyatt informs as he plops down in the seat across from me.

"Yep," I utter and continue staring out the window. My anger, bubbling right below the surface, is getting harder and harder to contain and keep in control with each passing minute I've been stuck on this god forsaken plane.

"Listen, I know you're upset about us bringing Dirk, but he can help, and he wants to," he adds, explaining his rationalization of allowing the rogue to join us. Dirk's face is still battered, covered in bruises that mar his features from my tirade earlier.

Flik, Kiera, and Julianna sit across from us and appear to be deep in conversation, yet Flik keeps shooting looks of concern my way and then scratching the back of his neck before turning away. I glare at him, and he quickly hides his face again. Whatever it is he wants to say, he's keeping under lock and key, at least for now.

"Did you hear a damn word I've said to you?" Wyatt barks out of nowhere, jolting my body forward. My gaze darts back to him and hardens at the discontent taking up residence on my cousin's face.

"I heard you, but I don't care, and I won't pretend to care. I know Isaac, and I know Benedict. What information does he have that is going to change what I already know?" I snap back, nostrils flaring, and chest heaving. I muffle the growl begging to be released and lean back in my chair again.

Kicking at my outstretched legs, he asks, "When was the last time you dealt with either of them?" My hands balling into fists, flex and grip the arm of the chair, cracking the wood on the end.

"Actually? Not that long ago, shortly before I left for Danset."

Wyatt hmphs and shifts in his seat. I shouldn't be so hard on him. He's done everything to help me and be by my side when I was wasting away and being a fucking idiot. He also pulled my head out of my ass, and I can never repay him for that. Meanwhile, I allowed Faith to experience Goddess knows what, and that is unforgivable.

"You need to buck up, Declan, and deal with this shit, because so help me, if our mate has been hurt, I'll never forgive you," Thorin links, snarling and snapping at me over our connection. He's been shoving his distress and anger down my throat since the day she was taken. It's already bad enough with my self-induced shame; having his disapproval shoved on me hasn't helped at all.

Wyatt glares at me, waiting for an explanation that won't be coming, and then abruptly gets up and goes back to Julianna. Shaking my head, I lean my chin on my fist, blankly staring out the window again. A worry so wretched, agitates my gut, flipping it over in horrible twists, making me want to heave my meager meal from earlier.

What if I fail her?

What would be the point of my life anymore?

The times I've failed before don't merely weigh me down; they've been suffocating me for years, and I thought I had a good handle on them, until she came and blew that up.

Faith came in like a Molotov cocktail, crashing into my life and bursting everything I had neatly tucked away into flames. But she also brings a calmness I've only dreamed about.

Feelings that I'd long since buried, fight for space and time once more, eating up any energy I have left—thoughts of how I've failed in the past spiral through my mind like a cyclone. When I'd let my team down in Afghanistan and Quinn was killed, I was not handling my issues and I hurt Sophia, and didn't live up to my parents' expectations. I'm so fucking tired. I'd much prefer to shrink away into the most bottomless, darkest hole than figure out a way to feed my soul.

* * *

The SUV pulls up in front of the Blaze Ridge Pack house a couple of hours later, and even though I was here a couple of weeks ago, it's already so different. Dreary in a medieval sort of way, because my Mom's light has been snuffed out, and it can no longer shine without her.

The mansion has always been too gothic for my liking, but it had held a certain homeyness to it when Mom was alive. Now dread, icy and thick, slides through my veins, delaying my body from disembarking with my friends. Wyatt glimpses back over his shoulder, holding Julianna's hand, and nods before he leads everyone else up the stairs.

The door behind the driver's side opens, and Kiera slides in over the seat, closing the door gently. Kiera McCanless has never been one for many words, and most avoid her because of her stand-offish nature, except me. I appreciate her quiet.

She rakes a hand through her pixie cut, teal-dyed hair, and sighs dramatically before turning to face me. "So, what's the real plan here, Dec? Because, I have an inkling you have something else planned entirely," she states matter-of-factly, and she's probably right, but I don't have one yet.

Unbuckling and then pulling my cell out to recheck it, I catch her tapping her fingers on the arm of the door. This girl rarely sits still very long before she starts to get anxious and needs something to do.

It's one of the reasons I got her hired on with a local fisherman, where she can be constantly busy without having to sit too long.

When she's not out on the water, she helps me with the bar in the kitchen. She's an excellent cook, could even give Julianna a run for her money. After all the meals that I have been able to eat since Wyatt arrived, I'll be lucky if I don't gain back every pound I've lost from my self-induced misery.

"I don't have one," I start, and I'm met with her pure incredulity. "Yet... I don't have one yet. I need to speak with my Father about any new updates about the vamps first and then figure out how the fuck we get onto their lands without causing another war," I add. It's the truth, and it's part of the reason I'm still sitting here.

Not knowing the full extent of what's been going on since I've been gone from the pack, let alone knowing why Faith was taken, or why my Mom was supposedly murdered by one, and why Isaac would kill her Mom. Too much has happened for any of it to be coincidental at this point and it would be foolish to rush in. I want to, I want to so badly, but an inkling in my gut tells me she's alive, and they need her to be.

"I didn't want to say this in front of the others, because I know Flik and Rhett are blaming themselves pretty hard, but from what I've gathered from Wyatt and Julianna is that your mate is pretty smart," Kiera says, her voice shaky showing her nervousness which only ramps up my own about whatever she's going to impart next.

"But why on earth would she let herself be taken? Or talk with a stranger, knowing that there were blood suckers after her? She had to be able to tell, right?" she finishes and asks the same questions I've been asking myself, but can't answer.

Drawing a hand down my face, scratching my beard, my head tilts, smacking into the headrest. "Honestly, Kiera, I have no fucking clue. I told her about the vamp that'd been outside her rental, but she also knew he was dead; maybe she thought she was safe from them? Or perhaps she knew she had no other choice? Fuck if I know. Part of me wants to throttle her ass when I find her, the other wants to find every single asshole involved and disembowel them slowly," I reply, trying to bury the rage that's been simmering below the surface since learning the truth; most of my anger is at myself for my stupid denial.

My hands run down my jeans, gripping my knees, and then back up, before I reach for the door handle. "Well, let's get this over with then," I groan and get out of the SUV and head straight up the stairs, Kiera on my tail as we enter the foyer, where my scowling sister greets me.

"How long?" Estella demands incredulously, standing with her arms crossed and thrumming her fingers over her biceps. Brows furrowing, I shove past her, not wanting to have this conversation with her.

"Don't you fucking dare, Declan Reid McCormick! Don't you shut me out, like you did Dad!" she yells, scolding me as effectively as our Mother would, but her words stop me dead in my tracks.

Sluggishly craning my neck back, I'm met with bitter cold eyes consumed with her simmering anger. My shoulders slump as I pivot back to face her, Kiera's lips purse to the side as she takes a couple of backwards steps, spins, and darts down the hallway. As soon as Kiera's footsteps fade away, I move a step closer to my sister, fully prepared to convince her to table this when she holds a hand up, stopping me.

"Did you know she was your mate at the funeral?" She blurts, tears welling in her eyes. Her arms uncross and recross a few times before I find my tongue.

"Yes," I utter and turn on my heel, leaving her there, mouth hanging open, her fury ready to spew.

Out of place, joyous laughter echoes from my Father's study as I round the corner, coming to a stop one foot inside the doorframe.

"She did what now?" My Father, Emron wheezes like he's shooting the shit with his best buddies and not grieving his Luna. Not that I have any room to judge how he mourns, but something about his happiness irks me.

"That's right, sir, she hooked him right in with sugar packets, told him his bar was shit, and the rest is apparent history," Flik chuckles, holding his belly, and then it dies the second his eyes land on me.

The room falls silent, save Emron clearing his throat awkwardly as I walk in and directly to the wet bar. Without much fuss, I grab a glass and a crystal decanter, pouring a couple of fingers of whiskey and throw back the entire contents. Shuffling feet and low murmurs follow as I pour another before turning to find I'm alone with Wyatt and Emron.

The soft leather of his office chairs cushions my back and thighs as I slam down into it and wait for the line of questioning sure to be fired at me point-blank.

Wyatt follows suit and pours himself and my Father a drink before sitting in the chair next to me while my Father takes his seat behind his darkly stained oak desk. The chair creaks as he leans back and then forward again, resting his arms on top of a mess of papers.

"Son, I wish—"

"Let's cut to the chase, Emron, I'm wasting time by sitting here and not out searching for Faith, my mate," I grind out and down the rest of my drink.

"Uhm-okay, Faith? As in Faith Bennett, Gerrant's daughter?" He asks, a little taken aback. Wyatt nods and answers before I can. "Yes, Uncle, she's one of my best friends from college, and my mate's cousin."

Thunderous ticking from the old mantle clock above the fireplace keeps time with the pounding headache I have brewing the longer I sit here. Whatever Wyatt and my Father are discussing is drowned out by the hot irritation burning its way up my legs to my chest.

"Can we dispense with the chit chat? What do I need to know about what's been going on with the vamps?"

Emron takes a languid sip of his whiskey and, as he sets it down, and clears his throat, "Wyatt, would you mind?" he nods in the direction of the door. Without questioning it, Wyatt gets up, lays a hand on my shoulder, his lips drawn in a line, squeezes briefly, and then leaves, shutting the door behind him.

Emron scoops up a stack of papers and roughly shuffles them together, the papers falling in a slap against the wood before he sets them aside and then gets up, striding for the fireplace.

Tick-tock.

Tick-tock.

Tick—any damn day now would be nice.

Scratching a hand from his neck to the base of his skull, Emron glances back at me, grimacing. "What do you remember about the war between our pack and La Luxure de le Mort clan?" He asks, gazing up at the giant oil painting of his Grandfather.

"What does that have to do with anything?"

A heavy sigh comes from him, and he twists, resignation falling over his usually stoic features. "If you'd chosen to take over the pack, you would've learned of this years ago, but I digress," he comments, not quite glaring at me, and shoves his hands in his pockets. "Well, as you know, our pack fought against them in the war they waged against us for decades, and your Great Granddad decided he'd had enough and sought some semblance of peace with Benedict by striking a deal."

I shift my elbows to my knees, quirking an eyebrow for him to continue. I've never heard of my Great Granddad doing anything with Benedict. Many of us assumed they found a new pack to terrorize, and they were ecstatic with the decreased attacks on our people.

"Perhaps, first, I should ask you if you've ever seen a ghoul before?"

43

Faith

Chanoît, Quebec, Canada
Palais de Sanc

Isaac plants his ass down directly across from me, retrieving his cell phone, typing out a message to someone. We sit in pin-drop silence. I glare. He looks up from his phone, briefly connects with my gaze, and then goes back to his phone. My glare hardens as my irritation flares. Finally, he sets the device down and leans back, chair squeaking as I assume the front legs come off the floor and then slam back down, reaching for his glass.

"I do hope you're hungry, I've had the kitchen prepare a feast for you, my pchelka," he mentions conversationally, rubbing a finger over the edge of his crystal wine glass, making it sing eerily into the charged air.

A few seconds later, eight servants burst through the door, bringing platters of food. They each round the table to Isaac, pulling domed lids off in a flare, presenting all of the items to him. He nods, then they move in a sweeping motion as they place the silver-domed platters in a semi-circle in front of me. The last servant to enter jerkily kicks his leg back, slamming the offensive portal closed with his boot.

I wouldn't put it past Isaac to have thralls in his service, and the thought turns my stomach into a pitch. Searching and assessing each of the servants as they come close to deliver all manner of plates and bowls, a small ripple of relief comes as they appear to be well.

A shuffle and thud behind me draws my attention over my shoulder, and I hold in a gasp. A thin, sickly servant hobbles over, a tray in his shaky hands. He pins a ghostly white glower on me, snorts, and unceremoniously shoves the tray before me. The short-statured androgynous human-like being blindly stares with those sightless eyes.

Isaac snaps his fingers in the air, and the servant beside me stumbles forward before bowing and leaving. My nose wrinkles as I fight the urge to recoil; they *have* been enthralled.

"Don't be so shocked, Malishka, they're all here by choice, well, except Yezhov," Isaac offers at my disgusted scrunching facial expression and sips whatever it is he's drinking, probably blood.

Twisting in my seat, I inspect each servant again, and the strap of my dress slips off my shoulder. I catch Isaac arching a brow, and he licks his lips as I dip my chin and fix the strap. When our gazes collide again, he gestures with his glass for me to continue inspecting.

The eight servants, he says, are here by choice, dart across the room like a well-rehearsed ballet. One starts and stokes a fire to life in a matter of seconds. Another places a record on the phonograph and winds it; a sickly violin melody dances over the tension-filled air.

It's all such a production that for a moment I've almost forgotten I'm a prisoner instead of a guest or a patron at the opera. It's been a long time since I've been around any vampires, but most especially being around humans that have been enthralled, it's hard to believe they would choose to be here, but they don't appear to be otherwise.

The last interaction I had with Isaac was almost ten years ago at a council meeting, when several vampires of his clan were accused of murdering a shifter with no justifiable cause. During his tribunal, he'd been arrogant and cocky, as he is now, but less calculating, less bitter at the world, less whatever this facade is. I can't pinpoint it, but there is something off about him, and it's unnerving.

After a few more unbearable minutes, all of the servants scurry out, bowing to us both.

Okay, that is weird.

Right then, a stunningly beautiful woman glides in, the tips of her toes gracefully skimming across the floor. If I didn't know better, I'd guess she's a ballerina, but she's probably his entertainment or lover or worse, dinner. Actually, with that thin dancer-like body, she most definitely is a ballerina.

The flowing white gown with fluttering cap sleeves and scooped neckline she's wearing moves with her skin like a silent whisper. Isaac's eyes don't leave her as she floats over the floor to him, stopping a mere inch from his chair.

"You must eat my pchelka, we wouldn't want you to sour," he commands. When I make no move to obey, his eyes narrow on my fork, then flick up to me and back to the fork before he roughly snatches the woman's wrist and drags her onto his lap.

I draw in a breath with ribs that are too tight for my chest, debating my choices. Not knowing what Isaac wants with me, it's hard to assess his mood, let alone his state of mind. He seems completely off his rocker, but also not; he's entirely too collected. And that is almost worse than being fully aware of what he is capable of doing.

Deciding to obey, because there is no point in not eating, I grab a serving spoon. I need to eat; it's been days since any real nutrients have passed my lips, and I'll need my strength to get the fuck out of here.

With a trembling hand, I scoop what appears to be mashed sweet potatoes up and let them slop to my plate, banging the serving spoon against the elegant china plate to get every last drop, and purely to annoy Isaac.

My eyes dart up and down from my plate quickly, to find Isaac smirking while staring at me from the corner of his eyes, while he sniffs the woman's wrist. I stab a piece of roasted chicken breast next, dropping that too with a smack to my plate.

A groan from Isaac rips my attention back to him, he's shifted the woman to straddle his lap; my heart drops when I discover his gaze pinned on me. A wicked smile curls his lips up, lengthly fangs protrude from his pale gums as he draws the woman's wrist languidly up to parted lips.

A hideous sound squelches in my ears when his fangs pierce her skin, the dancer moans out in ecstasy, not even flinching. Streams of red dribbles down Isaac's chin as he swings his eyes to me, smiling again while his tongue laps at her wrist. Wrenching my face away, I fight the urge to vomit.

"You're a vile... bloodsucking...bottom feeding leech," I sneer, wrath wrapping my tongue and swallow down the pooling salvia in the back of my throat.

His false jade stare darkens as he tears his mouth away with a hauntingly squishy squeak of ripping flesh.

"Barbaric, disgusting, lecherous le—"

"Yes, yes I am all of those things you're about to spout, but you haven't seen barbaric yet," he jeers and yanks the woman's head back exposing her creamy throat. Her jugular pulses with the steady thrumming of her heart, my own ratcheting up.

In a snarl Isaac bares his fangs in a hiss and lunges piercing his sharp fangs into her throat slicing and shredding the tissue. He snaps his head back, spitting the torn flesh to the floor in a splat, blood spraying out everywhere. A fine mist covers the platters of food, dotting the floral centerpieces, and the walls. A drop of hot liquid splatters on my forehead and drips down over the center of my nose.

Do not react. Do not react. Do not— I shout internally to myself, over and over, until I can believe it.

I have to believe it, because otherwise I'm going to lose it. Utterly fucking lose it. I need to be nonchalant, not caring, I've already fucked up by calling him a leech and barbaric, I need to not care how awfully despicable he is.

However, that is going to be difficult with the way he's angled her body. The open vein in her neck pulses and spurts blood in a river of red up into the air like the finest park fountains. Isaac leans over her shoulder, grins, and laps at the stream like a dehydrated dog. Every cell in my body vibrates, zinging together frantically. The hair on my scalp prickles as the pungent copper of the fresh blood rankles my senses.

I do not care.

I do not care.

I. Do. Not. Care!

If I keep telling myself this, maybe I'll believe it right?

Abruptly, Isaac lifts the woman by her torso and tosses her frail body to the table, shocking me out of my thoughts as she lands in a thunk. Her body knocks the candelabras over, flowers crash to the floor as her near corpse slides over the table, leaving a crimson trail that streaks and squeals underneath staining the dark wood.

Her head screeches to a stop centimeters from my plate, blood splatters and gushes out, drowning my food in a gravy of her life force. The poor woman's blood rains down on my face blinding my vision in a haze of red. Hot, sticky blood clings to my hair, the heavy tendrils clinging to my forehead.

My brows pinch together, I fix a sharpened glare on Isaac, scrutinizing his level of insanity again, keen to distract my anxious heart long enough to calm and my body to go numb. For one excruciating minute, my body a statue, a horrible thought crosses my mind, *this has to be my karma, I'm not going to leave here alive.*

Isaac shoves out of his chair the screech of the feet across the marble, screeches like nails on a chalkboard. He stomps over to me, his body rigid as stone beside me, heaving in panting breaths that fan over my shoulder.

He snakes an arm out and punches his fist into the woman's chest, crunching, sloppy noises pound like a heavy bass in my ears matching my thundering pulse. A clawed hand removes her failing heart, strings of tissue snap in half and veins dangle over a gaping hole in her chest. His gaze never leaves mine as he holds the mangled organ. Recoiling, I look away and swallow my dry tongue.

I can't do this.

I can't fucking do this!

"Keep your eyes on me Malishka," he demands and tips his head back lifting the spluttering organ up over his opened mouth. His tongue darts out to catch the hot stream of blood pulsating from the shredded valves.

More thick blood squirts and splashes over me coating my head, and paints my chest and lap. The crimson tide washes his chin and throat in his taunting dinner of death.

Isaac's thinned lips close around one flailing vein sucking on it like a straw, the near empty vessel bubbles and gurgles as he drains the last of the flowing river of red. Disturbingly, he releases the vein and chuckles with a shrug and then he tosses the heart behind him, it lands in the fireplace, the wet slap of meat spits and roasting sounds crackle in the tension filled air.

Gruffly, he hauls me from the chair, bringing our bodies as close together as possible; the frosty bite of his body on mine prickles goose-bumps down my neck. He mutters something in Russian that I don't quite understand and cups the back of my neck drawing us even closer. My chest heaving, pleading for air as every other muscle in my body tenses.

Faster than a viper, his strong, thick tongue strikes my cheek and licks the sticky, cooling blood off my skin. "My pchelka you made my dinner into the finest honey just like I knew you would," Isaac groans and nips at my neck as he cleans his dinner from my skin.

I can't do this.

Unable to hold it back any longer, hot putrid bile rushes up bubbling over my lips and down my neck just as he flattens his tongue over my chin. Isaac jerks backwards, but doesn't let go as he spits the merlot tinged acid to the floor.

"You weak, disgusting worthless wolf!" he barks, as his grip tightens over my neck cutting my air off. My hands flap wildly, slapping at his wrist desperate for him to release me.

"I-I—" I choke, and rasp desperate for him to let go. When I think he's going to loosen his hold, he catches one of my flailing hands, and laces his fingers through it and brings it to his lips, and he bears down on my throat more.

His words echo in my mind, slashing critically, ripping open that bleeding wound I'd thought was stitched back together. But it was only hiding behind every fake smile and barb I slung to the world wishing someone would come fix me. The truth of his words rob me of any remaining strength I have.

Succumbing to defeat, my eyes bulge and the room grows dim before blackness blots his seething ire from my vision.

* * *

An arctic cold presses and seeps into my side, something warm and soft brushes against my cheek. My eyes flash open and cut to the side where the cold is leeching into my body.

"Ah there you are Malishka, I was wondering when my pchelka would wake up," Isaac coos lowly with a devilish grin. The shadow of his hand with a wash cloth, hovering above my head, shades the blaring chandelier above.

As he lowers his hand, my muscles tense and bunch, ready to flee. When the soothing cloth kisses the apple of my cheek, I bolt up and roll off the bed. I get two whole steps away before bone-chilling fingers wrap around my wrist and slams me back into a chest of granite.

He wraps his glacier arms under my silk-clad breasts and presses our bodies together. Glancing down, my lips roll in on themselves as I notice another set of emerald silk pajamas graces my body. I can't focus on that right now, will not.

The rush of his contrasting hot breath against the shell of my ear and his icy skin seeping into mine, causes shivers to run up and down my spine. He whispers something in Russian again, why didn't I take that language in college instead of Mongolian?

"You see my pchelka—" he starts in a voice smooth as velvet but it's mostly broken English.

"What does that mean?" I blurt, he's called me that several times now, and I have no clue what it means. Attempting to shrug from his tight hold proves fruitless, and he clamps down harder, surely leaving behind bruises.

"What?" He asks, feigning ignorance, and I roll my eyes and try again to move out of his death grip.

"Are you serious? What does p-ch-elk ta? Or whatever means?" I stumble over the pronunciation and I know I sound more incredulous than the burning annoyance I was aiming for, but I can't think straight let alone get my heavy tongue to work properly. You would be too if you'd been beaten for days on end, and essentially starving nearly as long.

His unwavering hold on me is more evidence to the weakening state of my body, I can't fight him off at all. As an alpha I should be able to at least contend with him, this is mortifying, no wonder Sienna has tucked tail.

'Weak, disgusting worthless wolf' he'd said earlier. Those words, his tone, they coil red-hot shame, poised to strike and slither up my neck again, and as the scales slide up my back, I cringe knowing he's probably right. I hate this—

"Pchelka, means little bee, Malishka," he answers chuckling and drags me back to the bed where he gently releases me and lays me back on the plush pillows.

I scramble back away from him, feet slipping out from under me, "and what does Malishka mean?" I ask, flinching away from his out-stretched hand reaching for my knee.

Pressing my back against the headboard, and tucking my knees up into my chest to get as far away from him as possible, I plead with my racing heart to turn down a few notches so I can plan or try to. I need answers and a way to try and escape from here as soon as possible. I may be weak and pathetic, but I can at least try right? I can't hope that anyone finds me important enough to even bothering to come for me.

"That means, baby girl...now are you hungry?" He finishes, curling his fingers back and resting them near my bare toes, his pinky barely brushing against the tips zaps them with a frigid bite.

"I am starving but—" Sliding my feet back under me, but stop when he's at the door faster than I can blink.

"Wait!" I shout reaching out a hand and fall forward into a pile of blankets. I try and fail to untangle myself from the bedding, appearing like a damned fool.

He flies to the bed and helps by ripping the blankets up and away, essentially spinning and flopping my body to bounce on the bed. My hair snags and pulls when he yanks on my ankles aggressively sliding me down the silk sheets. The pajamas roll up and exposing my belly. The bed dips and creaks as he straddles my calves.

His deceivingly heavy body leans over mine as he crawls up, pinning my wrists above my head in one swift movement too fast for my eyes to track. He collapses and crushes his rock hard body into mine. No joke his muscles are like granite, he's hard everywhere...and oh...my...Goddess...he is NOT. Oh for fuck sake he is.

His steel hard and shockingly well-endowed dick presses into my belly as he slides one thigh between mine. I don't know what's more disturbing, the fact that he's turned on, or that it's not grossing me out. What the hell is wrong with me? I'm in shock; that is the only log-ical explanation.

Shaking my head to shove those thoughts away, I find his heated stare boring into me. Gone are the jade contacts, and the claret of his blood red eyes subtly glows.

He's kind of, sorta beautiful...

What? No!

Closing my eyes for a moment to gather myself, I make a mental note to ask Sienna about this situation later if she'll even answer me. Eyes flashing open, my teeth grinding, I wiggle and give him my most menacing glare possible.

"I wouldn't do that if I were you Malishka," he groans and leans in closer, his breath a whisper against my skin.

"What do you want with me? Why did you take me?" I demand, this time sounding as angry as I should be and struggle against his hold.

Isaac scrutinizes me as if I'm something precious to him and it's wholly unnerving. The blood rushing to my cheeks burns my flesh and all I want more than anything, is to shove him off of me and run down the hallway to freedom, yet I'm rooted to the spot.

"Why don't I get you something to eat first my pchelka hmm? And then we can talk like civilized people...sound good to you?" He rasps, wincing as if he's in pain.

He lowers his lips to the side of my face, "well Malishka?" A blush spreads from my chest up my neck to my face burning hotter than before. Isaac takes my silence as an answer and as he pulls away the tip of his straight nose skims against my cheek to my nose and then in a flash he's gone.

The sheer drapes that surround the bed dance back and forth the only indication he's breezed past them and the sliding click-clocking of the lock gears of the door sounding of his departure.

44

Declan

Rossbury, Maine

So have you ever seen a ghoul before, son?" Emron asks again, my mouth slackens as I kneed my brow, refusing to believe that he asked me about a creature not seen or spoken of in centuries.

"What does that have to do with anything at all?" My voice squeaks like a pubescent teen forcing me to swallow down the dryness.

A knock at the door stalls whatever response he was going to give, and Wyatt pops his head in. "Hey, we are heading out, going to loop Alpha Bennett in on the situation, and Julianna wants to check on Hollie," he says quickly, and then, with a wave from both Emron and me, he ducks back out, and the clicking of the door as it latches reverberates up my spine.

"Sit down, son, we have a lot to discuss," Emron says, almost too solemnly. It riles up my instincts and has me on edge more than I already am.

"Whether or not you believe me, ghouls still exist, and all of them live within the vampire clans all over the world," he explains, as if what he's saying is common knowledge, and takes the chair across from me, sipping his whiskey. I remain silent, because frankly, what the fuck am I going to say at this point?

"They're created by using a vampire's vitae sourced from one of the Four Princes; their vitae is fed to a recently deceased human, or preferably a supernatural being or creature—"

"Wait, what the fuck is vitae, and who the hell are the Four Princes?" I interject and get up to bring the decanter of whiskey over to the desk. After pouring us each a few swallows and handing one over, he continues.

"Vitae is an essence of life-force found with a vampire's blood, but it's most potent in the primordial vampires, the Four Princes, as it were. I don't know that history well, but I do know that despite being our mortal enemies, they are distantly related to us through their matron."

What in the actual fuck?

Leaning back in the worn and aging leather chair, I take a generous swig of the amber liquid, letting its smoothness burn down my throat.

"Okay...don't care too much about the princes' part for right now, get to the part where ghouls matter to me," I mutter with little patience left. The fingers of my left hand drum over the arm of the chair, faster and faster the longer I wait.

He sighs and gulps his drink, staring at me with a worried expression as he pours another drink. The clinking of crystal on crystal is loud enough that it could be a cracking of thunder.

"Ghouls are the reason our pack remains alive and intact, after the deal your Grandfathers made with Benedict years ago, one right after the other. They are the sole reason we haven't been wiped out," he admits, and slumps forward in his chair, resting his elbows on his knees. He sounds almost bereft, like there's something else he has yet to say. Perhaps I shouldn't have drunk so much whiskey on the plane, or now, my mind could be clearer for this shit.

"*Not making great life choices again, I see,*" Thorin links with disdain. I roll my eyes, shrugging him away internally.

"*Shut up.*"

"What aren't you saying?" I ask hesitantly, leery to find out honestly. Emron lifts his head a bit and then, with a huge sigh, drops it again.

"We bury our dead so the vampires can claim whomever they wish. In doing so, they can make new ghouls when they see fit," he releases with a long sigh. We do what now? I fucking knew that whole 'we're doing it to appease the Moon Goddess' line was a bunch of bullshit.

"What the actual fuck? Why?" I shout, my nostrils flaring as I jump from my chair. The muscles in my arms are twitching with a need to strike out, to smash something or someone. My throat aches, as if the flesh itself is being torn from within, it's too tight.

"Calm down, son," he reprimands me like I'm a pup. Calm down? Fuck that.

"This is asinine, shifters submitting to leeches? How long have you been lying to me?" I bark, throwing my glass across the room, it smashes into the wall, explodes and shatters in a clinking, whiskey running down the panels.

"We give them bodies, so they leave us alone! We don't have to like it, but let's face it, unless you plan on taking over as is your birthright, then set your judgment aside Declan," he snaps as he slumps back down in his chair, running a hand over his exhausted face. He looks so defeated.

Chest heaving, I run over what he's explained and admitted to; but there's one thing I need an answer to, well, two.

"Do these ghouls need a soul?" I rasp, my throat hoarse from being drawn tight. My Father shakes his head no, but way too quickly for my liking.

"Is my Mother a ghoul now?" His head pops up, eyes wide and stretching across his face, brows lifting to the ceiling.

"Well, you said vampires killed her, how do I even know if that's my Mother's body in the casket? I never saw it, neither did Estella, for that matter, and with how much you stopped caring years ago, I wouldn't be surprised if you didn't know for sure either," I point out , anger seething, and narrowing my frustrated eyes on him.

"Get. The. Fuck. Out!" He screams, leaping from his chair. His hands smash into my chest, knocking me back a few steps. Thorin rushes forward, wanting to take over and demanding respect. I almost let him too, but, interestingly, my Father is reacting this way when for years his indifference towards my Mom was his status quo.

"Go! Get the fuck out, Declan! Just fucking leave!" He bellows, his voice rough and coarse, whiskey-laced spit flying from his lips. His eyes, full of red-hot rage, and his cheeks flushing hot. His eyes swivel back and forth, his wolf skirting the surface now, too.

A ravaging ache assaults my heart as I recall snippets of Emron's past actions, and nothing lines up with how he's behaving right now. For nearly 20 years, he's remained at a distance. Never showing much emotion on account of my Mom, the two of them lived like strangers who occasionally offered the barest of affection to each other. They argued over everything, even the trivial stuff, but he never blew up at her, never her, just cold indifference. They only ever agreed on one thing: me finding my mate.

My vision blurs with a building heat behind my eyes; he's hiding something. I blink, and the next thing I know, hot liquid copper explodes in my mouth, an electrocuting pain jolts out and sinks into my jaw and face. My hand reflexively blocks the next fist thrown my way, and I stare down at my Father, no, Emron, he can't even be called Father, as Thorin lends me some of his strength.

Distinct crunching and a yelp permeate the space. I squeeze my fingers around his fist until one last snap sounds, and I drop it like it's a hot coal. He falls to his knees, cradling his broken hand, head hanging in shame as I walk out and slam the door behind me, rattling the pictures littering the walls.

"Piece of fucking rotting shit."

Rhett and Flik find me in the hallway, take one look at my face, and immediately find the floor interesting. Rhett calls out as I brush past, "Hey, I need to head back, man, I'm sorry...Con—"

"Pup time?" I interrupt him morosely. He nods quickly, "early too," he says with a mixture of pure joy and horror coloring his face.

"Go, take the plane, I don't mind, and my *Father* sure as fuck won't either...congratulations, man," I say, mustering happiness for him the best I can and clap him on the shoulder. Out of nowhere, he wraps his arms around me in a tight hug, and cold shock worms its way through me.

"Thanks, man, you know this means you'll be Uncle Dec from now on?" He smirks and then steps back and starts to jog down the hallway, grabs his bag from by the door, and waves as he runs out.

"He's utterly terrified he's going to screw it up...like drop his pup on its cute head or something," Flik comments as we both keep staring at the door.

Digging down inside, I search and rip through the tangled mess of emotions, trying to dredge up a sliver more of happiness for Rhett and Connie, but I can't. I want to, desperately so, but it's buried so far under that I don't think it will surface anytime soon.

I smudge a hand over the swollen side of my face and wipe off the blood dripping from my mouth. If Flik wanted to say something, he decides against it and claps his hand on my shoulder a couple of times and walks off. He's been around my broody asshole-ness long enough now to know not to pry until I'm ready.

Making my way up to my rooms to change and leave, I try tapping into my link with Faith for the hundredth time. I stumble back a step, my hand flies out to the wall to steady myself, when I'm met with static, almost like a radio tuning in. Can she—my heart stops and starts again, a little flare of hope flickers, maybe she can hear me?

"*If you'd marked her like a proper mate, you'd be able to track her and link with no problem,*" Thorin barks at me through our bond, and resumes his nonstop pacing since we left the runway in North Carolina. He growls and grumbles low before sitting.

I plan to get geared up, and head towards Benedict's territory, and wing it—

"I'm not dismissing the trauma you both have faced, but neither of you has truly dealt with it, only compartmentalizing it. Doing that, though, will only hold what you were meant to be back...both of you." He adds a bit more somberly and out of nowhere.

As his words sink in, pins and needles spread down my limbs, making them useless, as scorching shame blooms in my chest. My knees buckle, falling to a rung on the stairs, I slump back and slam against the wall near the landing.

Thorin's right. I'd convinced myself I only bonded with her out of an instinct to keep her safe. Told myself that keeping her at arm's length was what was best for her, to keep her from coming to harm at my hands. I suspected she'd suffered enough at Connor's; she didn't need mine too, and I had planned to reject her, but then my stupid mouth went and accepted.

Sophia's words trickle in through the thick fog crowding my mind, "...the ptsd isn't going to go away, but you can learn to cope and maybe one day heal..." she's right, too, but I-I'm too damn—

BANG!

The front doors bursts open, flying off the hinges and split down the middle as they crash into the walls. A giant gray wolf looms in the settling dust and debris, one foot hovering over the threshold, panting heavily.

Unwavering, glowing onyx eyes expertly scan in an arcing sweep; it raises its nose in the air, sniffing. Outside, curses and heavy breathing announce Wyatt and Julianna as they skid to a stop over the porch and leap inside next to the wolf, leaving no doubt as to who broke my doors down, Gerrant Bennett.

"He was on his way here when we ran into him," Wyatt spits out in between heaving breaths, bending over to his knees and then flings himself upright.

Wyatt dashes past him and into the first closet ripping out jeans and a t-shirt. He's covered in sweat, beads of it are dripping off him, leaving a splattering trail over the floor.

Julianna meets my gaze and rests a hand between Gerrant's shoulder blades and whispers something to her Uncle. Onyx eyes find my glittering hazel-gold ones as I scurry my way back down the stairs.

Wyatt tosses the clothes to Gerrant imposing paws and guides Julianna away by her elbow, with a wary glance over his shoulder to me before shuffling out of sight. I should be worried, but for some reason I'm not. If I die today, its been a long time coming.

Before my feet hit the first floor, Gerrant is pulling the t-shirt over his head and stalking towards me. I don't want to deal with more parental bullshit, but he's Faith's Father and if Goddess forbid something happened to my daughter I'd be fuming like he is right now too.

"Don't worry, you'll have a few daughters I'm sure, so you best get used to the protective Dad role," Thorin says dryly through our bond and his chuckle echoes through my body leaves me bewildered at his sudden good mood. And, I'm not touching that comment right now, first Gerrant.

"Where. The. Fuck. Is. My. Daughter?" Gerrant asks pointedly, each word slicing clean through my resolve.

I swallow haggardly, forcing myself not to choke on my tongue, I open and close my mouth a few times before I finally spit out, "Isaac has her." It's all I can say, because I don't know anything else.

I shouldn't even be here right now. I should be racing across our pack lands and giving no fucks as I cross into vamp territory, ripping the leeches to shreds to get to her. But, I hardly have a plan in mind, and that will not serve anyone well so, I remind myself that Faith is strong, stronger than she gives herself credit for and I know she'll fight until I can get there. But, it doesn't mean the swell of absolute dread and guilt isn't eating away at me every second I'm delayed in leaving.

Gerrant's hard glare softens the tiniest bit as he searches my face before returning to angry, Papa-wolf-mode. He mutters something in French and then strides right past me into my Father's study.

My hands slide into my pockets as I pivot on my heels and follow silently behind. Gerrant's bellowing borage of French and English is being slung at Emron in rapid succession, bouncing off the hallway floor; now I know where Faith gets it from.

Stepping into the study, I come to a blunt halt. Both brows bunch together, my tongue probes my cheek in amusement. Gerrant has Emron on his knees in a chokehold. Both of their faces are beet red, and eyes bloodshot and watering from their spat. Looks like Gerrant got a good couple swings in; purple blooms across Emron's chin.

At my footfalls, Gerrant releases my Father, he falls to his hands, spitting blood and oh—a tooth to the floor.

"Karma?" I think ironically and toe the molar back across the wood floor. It tumbles and rolls stopping at Emron's knees.

Gerrant stops his pacing to the window, and quirks an eyebrow at me. *Oh! Shit.* Guess I said that last bit out loud, oh well, he deserves nothing less. Gerrant pours himself a healthy measure of whiskey and leans against the edge of the desk, chest heaving, he takes a shaky sip.

"Now, who wants to explain to me how my daughter, the last First Daughter of the Moon Goddess was fucking kidnapped and has yet to be retrieved by her mate, the last Second Son of the Lycans?"

My stomach flip flops upside down and my heart full on crashes at his words.

The what and the what?

45

Faith

Chanoît, Quebec, Canada
Palais de Sanc

Now that Isaac's gone, I can breathe fully without feeling like my ribs are going to explode from being too tight. I know Isaac is cracked in the head, but that? That was next-level insane behavior. What's worse is how I wasn't entirely repulsed by him being so close to me, and that doesn't make a lick of sense. Did he do something to me while I slept? Or to Sienna?

She's been too quiet, and I fear she's retreated from me again. It would be no less than what I deserve, though. I've acted like a total bitch to her, well, to everyone.

Sliding from the bed, I catch my pink cheeks in the floor mirror and swallow down a bucket of chummed-up shame. As I stare back at frustrated amber-brown eyes criticizing every flaw of mine, I can't brush away the sharp pain that stabs in the center of my breastbone.

I've asked myself a hundred times, what happened to me? When did I become so reactively angry or so blindingly numb? When did I lose my sassy, smiling self and start painting on the fake ones I managed to make and appear genuine? When did I submit to the pain and comply with demands so easily? I'd only started to feel like myself again around Declan.

Besides, I've asked those and many others similar to it a hundred times and never found an answer, but it's not because I don't know. I—no, I shake my head, desperate to shut it down, I can't deal with this. My hands find my temples, the pads of my fingers massaging to relieve the pressure building there.

"*You need to deal with this, Faith,*" Sienna says softly. Following with a wave of warmth, her calm whooshes into me, comforting me. Relief, sweet and soothing, floods my senses at hearing her voice. This is how it should've always been between us for years: trusting and supportive. It's been so long since I've been truly taken care of that a pang pulls at my heart for the lost time in my bond with her.

Another pang tugs the other side of my heart as blips of the mere days Declan and I had together surf through, leaving an emptiness behind.

He'd comforted me on the beach, not knowing me at all, showed up to protect me, and accepted a bond he didn't want because of his demons. Hell, in a way, he'd unknowingly been there for me when I showed up to his bar to drown my sorrows and told him what a dump his bar was. I never told him I went home and unleashed some of that pent-up grief.

He took care of me and helped me through my heat. Memories of those tender kisses and strong hands holding me in place as he laid claim to my body wash over me again; as he possessed me in a way that should have terrified me, but didn't.

And what did I do? I was too consumed in my grief, and pushed him away. I went and let my fears make choices for me, while I hid where I wouldn't get hurt anymore, and no one could see the scars.

I've been pushing everyone away so I won't have to face their rejections or watch them leave when their blinders come off, and see how worthless a creature I've become.

This battle I've waged against myself? It's an ever-expanding black hole, ripping through my soul, tearing it to shreds one day, leaving me to waste away with the buzzards the next. It can last for weeks, and these are my personal favorites of self-imbued torture. There are rare times when the black hole shrinks, almost winking out. Its invisibility lets me put on my khaki shorts and pick up my camera. It's those days when I don't have to bear the crushing weight of its looming shadow.

Thinking about it, the frayed edges of its soul sucking energy loom and curl in my peripheral, stretching over me. The longer it drapes over my shoulders, the worse I miss him. I shouldn't, I don't deserve him.

"*That's enough! Do you have any idea how hard it's been to watch you choose to live in denial to live in fear? My dear sweet Faith, you flee from anything that appears too big, too real. You've pushed our mate away because you are afraid.*"

"*Stop! Please stop! Please...*" I beseech, sobbing my plea to Sienna, sensing her pain as I know she's sensed mine. A stunning, shinning silver box appears.

"*Don't do it, don't shut down now,*" she whines through our link, shoving all of her energy at my wall, keeping the box away.

"*I know you're trying to help, but right now of all times? I can't, Sienna, I just can't... And speaking of mates,*" I interrupt her, preparing to argue with me about how I shouldn't currently be stuffing those pesky bubbles of love, boulders of issues, and books of unpacked trauma back into their metal box.

Sienna scoffs, letting out a groan, already annoyed with my choices again, but I swear I'm doing it for the right reasons right now.

"*Well, what about them? Now that you've finally decided Declan is worth all the sweet tea in the south, you've got questions about mates? And only after being rolled on by a decrypted leech?*"

Goddess, I forgot how much of a bitch she can be. Guess we're a matching set. "*I didn't do that on fucking purpose!*"

Folding my arms across my chest, my tongue presses against the back of my teeth, and I take a deep breath before I answer and head back over to the imposing canopy bed.

I smooth a hand over the silk sheets; they're soft, a bit too soft. A lingering warmth dissipates as my fingers splay and spread out, inching their way toward the edge of the blanket. Dragging up the down comforter, I curl my legs up and under, covering back up.

"*Why—*" I start to link, as the door flies open and Isaac appears carrying a large tray in both hands. He smiles so bright like he's the luckiest man in the world and kicks the door closed and glides across the floor placing the tray down on the bed.

There's a platter of cheeses, rolled meats, a smattering of fruit, and a small domed lid covering whatever hot food he had made. Steam puffs from the neck of a quaint little teapot; two cups and saucers complete the set with honeybees and flowers painted along the creamy porcelain.

Pchelka-little bee-he's been calling me. The painted, fuzzy, little bees have dashed lines behind them in swirling loops, and it almost makes me choke on a laugh. The psychopathic vampire has a cute tea set? This is too comical and surreal.

Isaac, grinning like the fool he is, leans in, with one thigh up on the mattress, hesitantly brushing a loose strand of hair away from my cheek, curling it behind my ear. My entire body and Sienna's shared soul shudder at his touch, in both disgust and what is that? Yearning? *Gross.*

"*He feels and smells like our mate,*" Sienna says almost sleepily, like she's drunk, maybe a little love sick? I don't know, but this whole thing is weird. Something has to be going on; she wouldn't allow this to happen.

"*Do it, you'll see,*" she yawns and stretches out lazily. What is wrong with her? Do what? It takes me a second to piece together what she's asking me to do...and no!

Fuck no. I refuse to believe that could even be possible.

It's not possible, right?

Fuck I don't know. I'd rather eat a moldy shoe than be attracted to Isaac Larionovich. My eyes bug out when he clears his throat. I'm sure I'm giving off dying clown who needs to puke vibes. Yep.

"Did you miss me, Malishka?" the leech croons, smirking with a hint of fang peeping. Fuzzy warmth curls around me, and my brain gets a little crossed-wired.

Oh, hi there, sharp and pointy...okay, okay. I might admit, if I were into fangs, and that's a big if, and I'm obviously—no. I'm not so there's nothing to worry about. But, if I were, I'd say that little move there was kind of hot. *The hell?*

"*Smell him, take an itty bitty whiff. He smells like our mate, and you are into fangs- or did you forget you all but combusted when Declan scraped your neck?*" Sienna adds nonchalantly and then fades into the recesses of my subconscious like a fading memory. Some help she's gonna be.

"Malishka? Did you hear me?" Isaac asks, voice dipping low and way too inviting, my head tilts to the side, like compulsion, inviting? Did he use compulsion on me and I not notice?

I find his gaze, eyes bobbing back and forth over his, searching for the slightest hint of him trying to compel me, because that is the only thing that would make any sense as to how I'm reacting. No, that can't be, alpha's can't be compelled.

As I study him, his eyes, a deep red, glisten like a freshly poured merlot; his pupils are disturbingly steady and of equal size—his otherwise ice cold resolve cuts over every sharp edge.

At my silence, he begins again, "Ah, clearly not, well then, I was saying that you, my pchelka, are the Last First Daughter, descended from a Goddess, and—" he pauses, puts a finger in the air, and climbs up onto the bed.

His long leg arches up and over my blanketed legs, his knees snug against my outer thighs. Hovering in a straddle over me, his hands fall on either side of my head in a soft thunk. He's damn close again, and suddenly I can't think, as his nostrils flare tersely.

Hooded, merlot eyes dip to my emerald-green wrapped cleavage and then back up as he tips to the side and flops back then scoots closer to reach over and grab a bowl of strawberries from the polished, pewter, filigreed tray. It really is a pretty tray, with ergonomic handles and not too busy with the rose pattern engraved in the base or the thorny vines around the edges.

Roses and Bees...where has my mind gone off to?

"You really need to eat Malishka, here...please," he pleads and my fogged up-addled brain gets hung up on the way his Russian rolls off 'Malishka.'

Patiently waiting for me to respond, he offers up the delicate white bowl full of plump, freshly washed strawberries with the greens cut off. Tentatively, my hand lifts, palm up for him, nerve endings are firing off all sorts of red flags.

Did I ignore those with Connor? Or was I blind to them too?

Isaac's frigid fingertips graze along the backs of my knuckles as he places the bowl gently in my palm. I suck in a breath. Choosing to ignore this abnormal behavior from him, like I should have been doing this whole time, I stuff a juicy berry past my lips and dart my eyes back and forth to Isaac and the end of the bed honing in on the little carved bird at the point.

He's glued to the movement of my mouth and throat, sharp awkwardness penetrating each time I catch him. A sourness swirls in my belly and I quirk my brows, praying he'll continue explaining. He's right about one thing, although I'd never tell him, he doesn't need the ego boost, I do need to eat. Especially, if I'm going to figure out a way to escape soon.

"Erm—oh right, so here's the thing, you're the one I need to get rid of my Father once and for all," he explains simply. He starts rambling about there being some prophecy that he thought was bullshit, until he'd seen a truth he couldn't unsee or deny. That he wants me to be by his side. I'm only half listening to his never ending rambling, holding on to bits that seem important as I scan the room and nod to him occasionally and stuffing bits of food into my mouth.

Landing on the door, I skim it twice to be sure I don't have a case of wishful thinking. I do it one more time and I have to hold in a squeal of excitement, the gears are all rolled back; he didn't lock it. If I can—

"Faith! Are you even listening to me?" Isaac suddenly snaps, a blip in his recently changed demeanor, peels back to a layer of his usual self in the sneer of his voice and a cruelty only he can muster in the creases of his eyes.

Now that I'm back on what appears to be solid ground with him, a rush of relief sails through me. I leap from the bed and slip my feet into the fleece lined moccasin slippers placed neatly beside the nightstand and begin pacing.

At some point he'd left the bed, while I zoned out, and paced the area rug, leaving tracks behind with each pass. His usually perfectly combed back hair, save that one blade of bangs that hangs over his eyes, is mussed and sticking out at odd angles. I'm all of three steps from him as he slips a hand into his pants pocket and reaches for my cheek with the other as he looms closer. Instinctively, I take a step back and he curls his fingers in, dropping the rejected appendage.

"I don't know what some forgotten prophecy has to do with me? Yes, I know, I'm descended from the Moon Goddess, I've known my whole life. And not to mention, we are two totally different species Isaac what you're suggesting, I don't think would work," I make my point and accentuate his name as my brain turns over what I may have missed.

"Yes and no, but you wouldn't believe me anyways even if I told you. I'm surprised your Mother didn't teach you anything about what has been passed down to every Last First Daughter, over several millennia," he mutters, defeated and a little annoyed.

Something snaps inside me, at his mentioning of my Mom. Red slides over my vision, and fire licks at an old pain for revenge, reigniting it, fresh and new, a wild fire in my veins. I sense my mouth moving before my brain has caught up.

"Don't speak about my Mom! You don't get to speak about her!" I yell and reach out to shove him, but miss, fingers grasping thin air.

A cold hand palms the crown of my head, icy fingers digging into my scalp, hold me at arms length; while I swing at him like an angry baboon, red nose and all. He lets go and I almost topple over when he breezes back and sits on the edge of the bed all regal and unaffected.

It's fine...it's totally fine, I didn't just swing at him like a hangry toddler and he didn't gracefully deflect me like Bruce Lee.

What the fuck is wrong with me? Thinking I could go at him in my state.

As my temper tantrum cools, it dawns on me that I can and should ask him why. He was the one who did it. He's the one who stole her from me.

That stupid silver nose ring glistening from the light above, is screaming at me to rip it out, *just do it.* I feel freaking crazy right now, completely off my own rocker.

No, not worth it, it'd be funny though.

My fists clench, fingernails dig into my palms, leaving little half moons indents as I try and bring my head back to clear. I haven't felt this way in a long time. Drugged up and raring to go at the same time.

An invigorating heat buzzes to life deep in the darkest parts of my chest and pushes outward as a thought comes to life, the proverbial light bulb moment so to speak. I can do this, I tell myself, even if it sounds weak and pathetic, and completely unbelievable.

Isaac walks around me, and an invisible ripple pulses around me.

Yep I'm doing sooo...good dealing. Look at me dealing. I kind of want to throw my head back in laughter...I'm fucking losing it, but hey, I'm dealing. Something clearly isn't right with me. I shake my head and then shudder shake, wiggling rest of my psycho off.

I stop from rolling my eyes at my crazy showing and cross my arms covering my flushing chest from Isaac's leering perusal. The slinky, while cute, silk pajamas, do nothing to keep my breasts from spilling out with every movement.

Isaac comes closer again, and I step away. That pulse radiates again.

All it would take is one slip of the strap or a good jostling and boom! Titties would be popping right on out. Honestly, it could be a potential part of a plan, seeing as he's clearly distracted by them. Mom would be rolling on the floor right now if she could hear my thoughts.

Thick, syrupy hot grief slathers my heart and I can't breathe. Oh-oh nope! Back down you go, nobody asked you join the insanity train. Obviously, my tickets have been upgraded to: needs a padded room. Especially, with how much I'm internally talking to myself. I squeeze my arms tighter over the reckless D cups and toss the plan.

I can't do this, but I want to, no I need to know why. It's only five little words...

"Why did you do it?" I rasp so softly I'm surprised I even said anything out loud. My body so tense, I'm bedrock. A set of rolling waves breaks the bank of my stuffed down emotions, and like the unwavering tides they've been since my wedding day, relentlessly assaulting, they roll up and crash over me, drenching me in memories of her.

"Faith...breathe...take a breath, I know it hurts, it's going to for a long time, but you can do this, I know you can," Sienna whispers through our link, sounding groggy, but she's more present than she was a little bit ago. Whatever is affecting me, is affecting her too. Steeling myself once more, I summon my inner bitch, and let the brat fly free. It seems to be the only thing keeping my mind clear.

"Well? Did you loose your tongue? Perhaps you swallowed it...ya know while you were being too thirsty for my help?"

I blink and he's before me, leering down at me, that tuft of blonde hair tickles the tip of my nose. It's so...white, I want to—what the actual? Huh? What do I want to do? Flick it? Maybe my finger will accidentally stab him in the eye, it'd serve him right with all staring his been doing. *Bitch mode remember!*

He does smell good though, and familiar like a safe—*oh my Goddess!* My hand flies to cover my mouth and nose, stifling an embarrassingly loud gasp. He smells exactly like Declan, the realization is a cruel slap across the face, complete with stinging cheeks and eye watering clarity.

Schooling my face from the bouncing ball of humiliation at everything that has crossed my mind in past few hours, I narrow my eyes and step back from his bubble of whatever it is he's trying to pull. Jazz hands wave in front of me while my head shakes emphatically no, no, no.

"You know what? I don't want to know. You probably did it, because you're as cracked and scrambled as an egg in my breakfast," I reply dryly angling away, ready to turn when his popsicles for fingers wrap around my arm and slide down to my elbow stopping me.

"I didn't mean to kill her," he blurts and immediately swallows, his eyes soften drawing me all the way back in. "Connor was—no, is working for Benedict, and I thought if I took him or you out, that it would either reveal my Father's plan or maybe weaken him enough so I could kill him, except your Mom moved so fast, faster than she should have, destroying my hope in a second," he says, without a hint of remorse in his tone.

A sharp pain jolts down my throat to my chest like an electrical shock-induced pain, similar to damaged nerves firing, hot and quick. That buzzing sensation ratchets all the way up this time, spinning out and filling me up. The tips of my fingers burn and my whole body vibrates with rage. I want to incinerate him, to peel the flesh from his bones and serve it to dear old Daddy Benedict on a silver platter. He'd probably consider it fine dining.

'Destroying my hope in a second.' His words slice through the last stitch holding all of my broken, unworthy pieces together. The suture snapping and falling to floor along with all of my give a damns.

"You think my Mom, my sweet, loving, do anything for anyone Mom, ruined your hope...your hope?" I shriek, laughing manically, I'm shaking all over. Tears slip from the corners of my eyes, with each cackle of crazed laughter.

Throwing my hands forward, to lash out, I once again grab thin air, as he slides to the left dodging my reach easily. I can't focus on technique or skill, I'm nothing, but flailing arms and anger. I don't really have a clue what I'm doing either, merely acting on instinct alone.

"What about you, huh? Destroyer of dreams, what about my hopes, my dreams, for a normal fucking life?!" I yell and swing my fist again, this time making contact with his cheek. A loud crack disrupts my tirade, wincing as my hand smacks into rock and flies backwards.

I suck in a wheezy breath and shake my fingers out. "Fucking hell," I yelp, and cradle my throbbing disco ball of a hand to my chest. My, definitely need to get my vision checked, glowing blue, disco ball of a hand. I stare in dubious horror at the pulsing blue light that's tingling each of my fingertips and wrapping around my arms to my neck.

At a hacking-gagging noise, I twist around and I'm met with cringey satisfaction at witnessing Isaac hacking up and spitting out a bloody tooth to the floor.

I did that.

A grin splits my lips and I ball my fist up again, about to lunge towards him, but he's quicker. Viper fast he snatches both of my hands and spinning me, bends one hand behind my back, and brings the other up above my head. Releasing the hand behind my back and quickly snaking it around my middle, he yanks backwards, hard, pinning me to his ice rink of a chest.

In the next blink, a pinching crunch and then fire, explodes under my skin. Liquid flames lash at my glowing skin covered by Isaac's mouth. Lava explodes where his fangs have pierced and intensifies with each long draw of my blood. The sky blue glow fades from my skin and sputters out with each undulation of his throat.

Heat envelopes me, spreading up and around from my lower back, and crawls up my neck. My chest pushes up, pajama top slipping down, nipples playing peak-a-boo under the silk. My spine curves, the force tipping my head and shoulders back into a pleasantly muscled chest.

Too heavy limbs slump, and strong, warming arms hold my weight with ease. A growl rumbles low at the base of my neck, hooded eyes flutter close and jolt back open as one last burst of buzzing rises and dies pulsing along my arms, hands and each finger. Bright painful light implodes from my chest and palms, blinding me and all I can smell is Declan.

Faintly, as oblivion darkens everything, I swear I hear him calling my name.

46

Faith

Chanoit, Quebec, Canada
Palais de Sanc

The room is bobbing, or maybe that's my head? My neck flops like a wet noodle, and everything hurts. Aching muscles protest under too-tight, too-warm skin, overstretching and pulling at every jostle. I already know opening my eyes is going to hurt like hell, but it's now or never. Cracking one eye open, burning brightness streaks over my retinas, forcing them to snap closed. Tiredly, I try again. The chandelier windmills like it's about to drop and crush my face. Nope, it's too much. I squeeze my eyes closed against the pain and vertigo.

I pray this has all been a nightmare, and I'll wake back up in my rental, or hell, even the dungeon at this point would be better. Nothing makes sense, and the biggest one? Isaac. His about-face behavior has me whirling harder than I ever did with Connor's narcissistic tantrums.

Connor may have been an asshole whom I couldn't quit because I was blind to all his glaring red flags, but at least he was a predictable asshole for the most part. Maybe I'll unpack all of that guilt later, when I wake up from this freakish nightmare.

My wishes are busted as this weakened body I call my own, sinks and snuggles into something soft and cozy, my eyelids flutter, bits of blurry light shine in and then out as they close again...to bright.

Someone is saying my name, but whatever is hugging my body is too good, and I want to wrap myself up in it, like an overwhelming force of peace.

Brisk, cold wetness slides over my forehead, and a trickle of fluid rolls into a corner of my eye. Heavy lids flash open to be greeted by a pair of pale lavender eyes scanning the length of my body. It takes my sluggish brain one second too long to remember and catch up with what happened earlier.

Isaac, me fighting no better than a toddler, glowing hands, prophecy nonsense, and he...I glance down at my wrist. Where two angry red punctures should be are faint white marks marring the otherwise smooth skin. He bit me! He bit me and I'm already healed because...oh-oh. Fuck.

"Believe me now?" Isaac asks incredulously and sweeps his soft fingers over my brow. Unable to pull my eyes from his, I run through everything one more time. He's acting like Mr. Please Love Me, and it's wigging me out. Did I hit my head or something? There are missing pieces to this 3000-piece jigsaw puzzle, and the room reeks of deceit.

I need to figure out what to do next, but I can't focus with that amber, spruce laced with a hint of driftwood fogging up my thoughts.

My brain is too hung up on why he smells very much like Declan. It's so surreal, like he's standing right next to me, lighting me on fire with those golden hazel eyes. Maybe I am hallucinating, or Isaac is deliberately fucking with me. I choose the latter.

Two can play whatever game Isaac is trying to play with me. This 180 of tenderness and seduction can't be real. It's been a minute since I've flirted on purpose, like I'm about to, and never in my life with a freaking vampire! Certainly not to get information and get someone's guard down.

A stitch of heaviness in my stomach stalls my decision as doubt creeps in. Can I do this? What if he takes it for real and...no, I cannot think about that. But what if something does happen and Declan finds out? Would he hate me? Probably, I'm sure, since I've been a brat to him and begged him to reject me. I need to make things right as soon as I can; what that will look like right now, I don't know yet.

But I digress. If flirting back gets me answers from Isaac and a way out of here and back to Declan, then I'll suffer his lips, too. On second thought, I can be sweet and endearing, no flirting.

Finally, I nod in answer to him, and lift a hand to his cheek, a subtle coy smile curves my lips. "I do, believe you that is, I'm sorry, I-just-it's too much," I go with a partial truth and drop my eyes before slowly dragging them back up to him, praying that my shyness and embarrassment shows. He assess me, probably thinking the blast knocked me silly, but I need him to think otherwise.

Come on, come on, lean in, you know you want to, I only need one good whiff to make sure.

Color me surprised when he does, like I'd summoned him, and he cups my cheek. "No, no, I'm sorry. I didn't think and we apparently bring the worst out in each other, but—" he murmurs and stutters to a stop, like he'd didn't mean to say any of that.

His ash blonde brows pinch together so hard that the motion wrinkles the skin on his forehead. His head bobbles like those dolls you get at ball games. He's so lost in thought he hasn't stopped tracing his thumb over the apple of my cheek, the friction beginning to be painfully warm.

"Mistakes can be fixed," he says again and sighs. "Thank you for releasing my lycan from the eternal cage he was damned into 1,299 years ago," he whispers and slowly turns, lavender eyes seeking and longing for something from me.

I return his wistful smile and relax. For a moment, everything that is usually glazed over him in ice, melts. Then it's gone in a flash, giving way to whatever he's thinking. His smile falls and he closes his eyes.

"It's strange, not actually being alone in my head, but I've always had voices in here," he rambles and with his other hand he taps a finger to his temple. He catches my gaze again, absently rubbing his thumb over and over.

I have to have stepped into some kind of twilight zone, or something, because he's being so weird, and it's freaking me out. Strangely, though, I don't have the urge to kill him at the moment or the desire to flee, which is really bad. *I need to get out of here.*

I lift a hand again, cupping it over his lightly, and relax my cheeks, softening my eyes, reeling him in. He leans closer, our foreheads almost touching, and I tell myself to pretend it's Declan, over and over.

I hold in a wince as his lips brush over my forehead in a wisp of a kiss. The moment his lips press fully against my skin, he bolts backwards away from me. The sheer curtains billow from his vanishing act, along with the intense draw towards him. The door slamming closed.

Oh, thank fucking Goddess.

Waiting for a count of twenty before I move and to give myself time to find some bravery as my head clears. I jump from the bed and dash to the door and tug, it doesn't budge. I try it again anyways, and again nothing not even a wiggle. Pressing my cheek against the cold wood to listen, my heart leaps up into my throat, nothing save the whooshing of my blood in my ears. Shoving away from the door of Fort Knox, I cross my arms over my chest as I walk in a zigzag back to the bed, thinking.

"There has to be a way out of here—" I mutter and "—oomph!" My toe snags against something and skids over the floor, tipping my balance too far forward. My hands smash into the floor taking the brunt of my fall.

"*Been walking long?*" Sienna links and rumbling an equivalent to a laugh.

"*Oh shut it!*"

I'm a bit stunned for a moment, then glance back at my legs twisted around a blanket. "What the?" Dusting myself off after getting up, I see the window, and my brain clicks through the channels of memories. I don't recall there being a window. Or I was so out of it I've forgotten? Confident that prick did something to me now, that my memory is shot to hell.

Frantically, I run to it and push against the trim where it should open. Nothing but starry night sky stares back at me. I bang my fist against the cold dark pane, not even a shudder of sound. Swallowing the rising panic I check every nook and cranny in the room and then race to the bathroom.

I'd forgotten the small square of sky shining through when I was in here last. I climb into the tub, and pop up on my tip toes to pound my fist against the glass. A stabbing of pain shoots up my toe. My foot gives out and I bend over, rubbing my sore toe—a thought hits me and I jump out of the tub sore toe be damned and bolt to the wardrobe again and fling it open.

Shoes.

I grab a pair of stiletto heels, which are cute as hell. Better to break things with than my neck walking in them.

Running over to the window, and stand off to the side by the fire-place, I arch my arm behind me and let the shoe fly. The spiked heel smacks into the glass and bounces right off. I grab it and take to bashing it into the glass. Nothing happens, well to the glass at least, the heels are destroyed and my hand is an unhappy red. I'm well and truly caged in.

My shaky hands drop the heels, and cover my choked sob of panic. Backing away slowly, I try to not let the ache of defeat cave in and overwhelm me. I will not cry. I won't give up, not now, not when I don't want to for the first time in a long time.

The backs of my thighs smack into the bed, and absentmindedly my ass sinks into it and scoots back. Sliding my legs under the blankets, my knees curl up, and my chin rests on them. The soft feathery down crinkles as the blanket bunches in my fingers under my chin. How could I have been so stupid to think I could outwit Isaac, the calculative psychopathic vampire? A single hot tear rolls down my pink cheek.

47

Faith

Chanoît, Quebec, Canada
Palais de Sanc

The bed dips, flinching me awake, and my hand gets sandwiched between my thigh and his. "Feeling better, Malishka?" Isaac asks with those strange lavender eyes, fixated on me.

"What are you?" I wonder out loud, sitting up and pushing my back into the headboard. A knowing smile stretches his full lips, his eyes never leaving mine, and he reaches to the nightstand for a glass of water, silently offering it.

Taking the glass, I sip and inspect all of the changes in Isaac. Besides his eyes being a beautiful shade of lilac, he's a little bulkier all over, and the crude, harsh edges of his features have rounded but remain chiseled. He catches me skirting up the curve of his tattooed neck to his lips, and he lifts one corner of his top lip, revealing the same protruding snowy white fangs as before; he darts his tongue out, sliding it over the tip. A tiny pool of burgundy bubbles to the surface as he releases it and smoothes the pink flesh over his top lip, and bites his bottom simultaneously.

He has to be fucking with me...because in no universe should I want to rub my thighs together from his display of fang erotica. Blinking rapidly like it will cure whatever the hell is wrong with me, I find the chipped nail polish on my toes exciting.

"I'm a hybrid," he chuckles and retreats to lean against the post at the foot of the bed and props his long legs alongside mine. "A true one now anyway. I was born a lycan, kidnapped after my parents were murdered, and then a witch bound my lycan from surfacing when he should have. By the time that happened, I'd already met who I believed to be my Father for years, and my brother, and then my Father, Benedict turned me," he says matter-of-factly and adjusts his shoulders against the wooden post.

"Have you thought any more about my proposal?" He adds, eyes loosely closed.

"You're what now?" I ask, a bit dumbfounded, but I honestly have no clue what he's talking about. How long was I out? I vaguely recall checking the door and windows, feeling stupid, and then waking up to him staring at me as if...as if he can't live without me. He hasn't stopped staring either, every time his eyes are open they are glued to me.

So, unless he told me of this proposal when I'd been tuning him out earlier, I don't remember. Because let's be real, all I could breathe in, hell...taste, was the essence of Declan, it was like taking a hit of Molly.

Wait!

Maybe he's been drugging me this whole time, and I'm hallucinating Declan? But it doesn't explain the heady and familiar bubble of safety I want to crawl into and then pop so I can bathe in his scent.

Which, upon remembering, I lean in and blatantly sniff him, that cloyingly gross incense and rotting chamomile has been replaced with a pleasant cedar and a slight hint of iron, no deliciousness present now...interesting and relieving. I'm musing over the possibility of him drugging me, when his voice startles me.

"I'd offered your region of wolves and lycans protection from the vampires, so long as you agree to help me take my Father out and become my Queen when I take his throne," he repeats, exasperated. He pops one eye open from where his head rests on the post. Then he closes it again when he's satisfied that I've heard him.

My mind rewinds to his first answer. A lycan? And vampire? What the fuck...Am I going to do? Tease him into a coma with my piss poor skills at seducing? He'd probably be willing to get a lobotomy after witnessing it...I can see it now, and the award for the most cringy worthy seducing goes to Ms. Faith Bennett!

Enough deflecting, seriously, what will I even be able to do now? Lycans are notoriously strong, and there are so few of them left, well, at least to my knowledge. There are so few reported that they are practically legendary, but a hybrid? Goddess, no, I'd be dead in an instant.

An uneasiness creeps in and scuttles over my skin thinking about what I may have to do, but I can't shake loose the fact that he's smelled like my mate for two days, effectively driving me into crazy fits.

A dull ache forms in my temples from trying to sort out facts from possible hallucinations. The ache sharpens, stabbing my sides with an ice pick, forcing my fingers to them and kneading small circles until the pain lessens. I need answers, and the only way to do that is to ask questions myself, knowing he will most likely lie to me.

"Perhaps, I'll agree, if you answer one question for me," I say, and pray I sound convincing because there is no way in hell I'll become his Queen, no fucking way, not happening.

He cracks that eye open again and then, nodding, waits for it. I slip from the bed and walk over to the window, press a hand to the cold pane, the slight shock doing wonders for my system, and face him when I sense him approach.

"Why do-did you smell like Declan?" I rush out, casting my gaze down to my curling hands pressing in at my sides. I focus on the anger bubbling under the surface. I can do this, and then maybe I can do something to distract him long enough to get the upper hand.

"A-and why could I sense a pull towards you? Like I do him?" I finish, that is what I want to know, because that is the only thing that is bothering me. My head dips to my shoulder and crooking up a little to see him better, did he get taller too?

"I-I—" he coughs, "I-fuck," he chokes, and pounding a fist into his chest, he clears his throat again.

"Don't die on my account," I smirk, hands going to my hips, remembering that my anger and bitchiness kept my head clear last time. "Wouldn't want to deal with that mess, I imagine it would be the equivalent of watching a overcompensating owner of a red pick up crashing...worthless bits everywhere," I snort, twirling a finger in the air and spin on my toes, the sensation is lighter than I have felt in ages despite how stupid that was.

"Wait—is it even possible for you to die again?" Isaac's pale skin is tinting purple as he tries and fails repeatedly to speak. "What? Lycan got your tongue?"

His eyes bulge, and then he gasps, "Ask me something, anything that you know I can't lie about...like my name," he pleads, reaching his hands out to me again. I step back, scrunching up my nose, what is he doing?

"Ok-ay...what is your name?"

He clears his throat and replies with: Isaac, confidently, his coloring and voice returning to normal.

"Now ask me something I could lie about," he insists.

I don't hesitate.

"Why are you being so nice to me?" The words tumble right out of my mouth before I can think. He shifts forward and then runs a hand through his hair. He angles back, and his cheeks are red. Is he blushing? He stretches his neck up, like he's got something stuck in his throat, and groans before resigning to whatever it is he's struggling with.

"Because, when I'm around you, I get a taste of peace, a blissful quiet, a reprieve from the," he says, tapping the side of his head, reminding me of his craziness. "It's intoxicating, the past week being around you constantly has brought a calm to me that I haven't had before." That same reaction of bafflement colors his face as he spouts words he didn't intend to.

You've got to be kidding me.

Do you count the torturous beatings you inflicted for the majority of the week as me bringing you peace?

His chin tilts to the side a little, and then he turns away, not answering. Not sure why I expected an answer. Of course he does, and then it dawns on me. The tremendous shock of his admission, or rather his lack of one, slakes off me in a flash...Oh! My! Goddess!

I'm sure my face is equivalent to a fish out of water, staring wide-eyed, mouth gaping open and closed. He can't lie! He pretty much set me up to figure it out; it's embarrassing how slow my thinking has been.

My feet move on their own, stopping when our toes touch. "Answer my first question, and because I know how much you love yourself... don't die trying to lie," I quip, jabbing my finger into his clay soft chest, no longer the granite that could break my fingers.

Sienna stirs and ripples her energy throughout my body, joining with the warm buzz growing again, already preparing for whatever it is he has to say.

"Well, as you know, shifters and vampires are incredibly drawn to their mates, and after years of watching you both for my Father, I had a witch confirm my suspicions," he answers and swallows, staring at me.

"It's a tactic we've used for years to capture and subdue enemies' mates to control them," he shakes his head with a pause before taking a long breath. "So an opportunity came, and I stole some of his pheromones and scent when I'd knocked him out from behind during our spat a few years back. I'd honestly forgotten I had it, and after the second or third time in the dungeon, I-I'd hoped using it... would calm you enough to—" he answers, but sounds like he'd rather rip his tongue out than admit what he had planned.

"Why, am I not surprised at all? You fuckers will do anything, won't you? What was your spat over?" I snap as a rush of heat pulses the shells of my ears and spreads down my neck. It builds and grows to an inferno.

He doesn't stall this time, the pensiveness on his face falls, his head following as he mutters, "he came to avenge his baby sister, the twin I'd killed, he lunged and I struck," his voice trails off, and without warning, that same blinding blue light erupts from me again.

"You did what?!" I scream, veins pulsing from my neck. Eyes blaring wide and spit flies from my lips, landing on my chest and the floor. A pain not unlike my own for my Mother, slices at me, and I know it's the bond making me feel what Declan did for his sister.

Isaac's forearms cross, covering his eyes. And on instinct, driven by some forgotten memory, I burst forward, knocking him back with a blast of power shooting from my open palm.

Landing atop him, I straddle his waist, claws shifting with a flick of my wrist, ready to unleash the fury whipping inside of me. Swipe after swipe, I attack his face and pummel him to the ground. Bits of fabric and platinum blonde hair fly, the sounds of threads tearing and skin shredding in squelches, rent the air.

Right as I'm about to pummel his stupid, pretty face, I freeze. He's not moving, just lying there, but he's still breathing, heart beating like a hummingbird's. He's not fighting back.

Why isn't he fighting back?

"Don't look a gift horse in the mouth. Get up. Let's get the hell out of here now!" Sienna growls, ready to run. I don't second-guess her this time. I

scramble off him and bolt for the door. I tell her I'll give her full rein once we don't need opposable thumbs.

I'm so amped up, when I creak the door open, it yanks back and slams into the wall. "Well, shit, there goes that tactic," I mutter to myself and take off down the hall, the skin of my feet squeaking on the black marble floors.

My heart is hammering in my chest as I careen around a corner. I didn't think this all the way through. What if my power drains like last time, and I can't fight off anyone else? The tiniest flare of doubt sparks, and at the click clack of footsteps, my head swings back, scanning the way I'd come from. Empty, not even a candle flickers from the outdated sconces. I must be hearing things.

Calmly as possible, my fingers curl around the smooth, polished edge of the corner. I peer around it, smother a hand over my yip, and jump back when I think I see someone.

When no other sounds echo, I roll my eyes. Oh, fucks sake, I'm a wolf, and I take a good whiff. Sensing no one, I push off the wall and bolt straight down the long corridor, hair snapping back with my speed. Shoving my hands against the large wood and wrought iron medieval doors, as soon as I have enough space, I fly down a set of stone steps.

The cooler northern air bites at my skin. I really should've grabbed a robe or something; whatever, I don't have time for this. Isaac will be on my ass soon, laughing as he tracks me down and throws me right back in the dungeon, since I'm sure he's done playing with me after I've exploded and attacked him.

Arms pumping, I race to a looming brick arch in the distance. As I approach, a vast, old metal gate comes into view, blocking my path. I skid to a stop, tearing open the soles of my bare feet. At the foot of the gate, I yank on the chain that's dangling to the side.

Chains rattle and clank, dropping the weight that makes this whole ancient get-up work, and the gate slides up. I don't wait for it to finish and dip under it and then scramble up to slip and fall face-first in the mud, eating a mouthful of gritty clay.

My fist pummels the ground in frustration, and my cheeks heat. I will not cry, I will not cry, I chant, and pull myself up and take off again. Dashing past brambles and thorn-covered sticker bushes, my legs, stomach, and arms sting from the cuts peppering them.

* * *

My lungs are burning, and the dread that keeps coiling and striking, forcing me to peek over my shoulder every few seconds, grows and grows. It keeps growing as the trees become thick and the rushing of water pierces through my fear as a river cuts through the forest. I don't stop, I don't assess, I leap, ice cold splashes up, numbing my toes and legs in an instant. I can do this, I can do this, I repeat through chattering teeth as I climb my way across the riverbed to the other side and up the bank.

A blanket of exhaustion spreads out over me when I reach the top. I can do this! This time, I shout it, using the rage and momentum building from it, and push myself up to my feet again.

I don't know how long I have been running, but my feet are numb, and I think I have more holes and cuts than I have piercings and tattoos; the dead weight of expired energy folds me over in a heap.

My hands rest on my knees as I take in ragged breaths, willing my body to calm. Once the burn in my lungs and throat recedes a bit, I keep on, walking while I gather strength.

"*You can take over anytime now,*" I link to Sienna and take another shaky step, lungs on fire, begging for relief.

"*Nah...you're doing great! Keep going, I'm proud of you,*" She says back a little condescendingly.

Freaking wolves.

48

Declan

Rossbury, Maine

A Lycan? There's no way he's implying that *I'm* a-a Lycan, Thorin would've told me, I would've felt it, and wouldn't that make my Father one too? I have so many questions and not enough time to get answers.

"You're the last second son of the Lycan Declan, and I'm sure none of this makes any sense, but it's the truth—"

"No wait," I snap, and let the truth settle once more. "How can I be the second son, if I'm the only son?" I ask, a sickening cloud of betrayal rolls over me, no, it can't be.

My stomach clenches again, harder this time, as Gerrant's words roll over in my head a few more times, the last First Daughter of the Moon Goddess and the last Second Son of the Lycan. I seek out my Father, and I'm not at all surprised to see him, not shocked, but resigned. He has many secrets I don't know of, and he has no plans to share them when I need them most. None of that matters, though. I have somewhere to be, and I've been stalled long enough.

"You are, but I suspect that is a question your Father will need to answer." Gerrant tries to explain, but his emotions are not in check, as he stares at me and then at Emron. His aura is glowing and radiating out from him.

"I don't have fucking time for whatever you're about to explain, save it for later, I need to get out of here," I growl, turning to leave and find her, vampire rules or not. Gerrant grunts something and then is at my side before I take another step.

"Wait, son, there is something you need to understand about my daughter," he sighs and claps a hand to my shoulder, detaining me further, and ramping up my irritation. Every fiber in my body wants to shift and run to her, too many hours have passed since landing, and thinking of everything she's already most likely experienced coils the burning nausea in my stomach ever tighter.

Gerrant takes my silence as an invitation to explain whatever it is he needs to. "From the moment she was born, we knew what she would be forced to do when the time came one day, and her choice could potentially change our world the way we know it, but without your bond, you may never unlock the true spirit within you now," he starts and drops his hand at my bafflement.

"What choice?" I ask hoarsely, as dread, thick and icy, spreads like the first frost through my body. Gerrant heaves in a breath. I seek and connect with his eyes again, and a sad resignation swims in the cool blues.

"You have not marked her, correct?" He inquires even though it's none of his business and a personal invasion, but at my nod, he continues. "Then I'm afraid to say this may not end as you hope. I know my daughter and I fear she will choose a path to keep the peace—" he doesn't get to finish as an annoyingly loud chiming from my phone alerts me of an incoming text.

I hold up a hand silencing him, and retrieve my phone. Several more messages are being sent in succession.

Unknown number: Image received.
Unknown number: Image received.
Unknown number: Image received.

I open the first image, and a desperate sinking pain hollows out my insides as it loads, and sharp pangs snap in my jaw as my teeth clack down so hard one cracks. In the image, there is a shackled, bloodied, and beaten Faith with an unmarred face that hangs over her chest, as Isaac holds her up, licking the side of her face.

My feet are moving as a red haze slides over funneling my vision. My phone dings again as I sprint from the mansion and down the steps. I whip past Wyatt, Flik, and a group of men who've agreed to help in the fight to rescue Faith. Wyatt calls out to me, but upon noting the ire coloring my face, steps back, hands held up in the air.

Unknown number: Image received.
Unknown number: Image received.
Unknown number: "Come and get your lil' wolf...cousin."

What the fuck? Cousin? I'll deal with whatever the fuck that is later, right now, getting to Faith is paramount to everything else. Shifting in one fluid movement, I relinquish all control to Thorin as he dashes through the woods, splashing through streams and bounding over rocky terrain with a finesse I could only wish for in my human form.

We don't communicate at all. We don't need to. We are experiencing the same thing. What we should have been doing the minute the jet landed. I'm more angry at myself for allowing anything to get in my way of finding her, especially knowing what Isaac is capable of. I'm angry with myself for so much, and how I've handled things, but like I've done with everything else lately, I compartmentalize it to deal with later.

I lend Thorin all of my strength and energy, so together we can push ourselves to reach Benedict's lands and prepare for the carnage sure to be waiting for me.

* * *

We run for hours, and by the time we've crossed deep into vampire territory, it's dark. There should be a river not too far from here that cuts through their lands and into ours, and from there it's not too far to Benedict's relic of a stronghold.

Thorin slows, and I catch it at the same time he does. It's faint, but it's there, wafting on the wind, bristling the limbs of the white pines; wildflowers in the mountain air, Faith's scent. With a renewed sense of energy and strength, we surge forward, dodging around the thick trunks and roots easily.

A bit later, Thorin stops again to check the direction of her scent, and we pick up on another's. It's odd, it smells like iron-cedar and a dash of a shifter, and a drop of that decaying floral that almost all bloodsuckers have. I don't get much of a chance to decipher it further when a shadow shudders from between the trees.

Isaac strides out from around a tree, clapping slowly and smiling, a little unhinged. "Ah, cousin, I see you got my messages...right on time," Isaac says dryly, cocking his head to the side and then tossing a pair of jeans at a snarling Thorin.

"Oh come now, we have so much to discuss, shift," he taunts, and I don't want to shift, I'll have no way to take him down otherwise, but something urges me, and I shift without thought.

Snagging the jeans and slipping them on, I keep my focus on Isaac as he stalks closer, dressed in a shredded dress shirt and slacks. Red claw marks mar his tattooed skin; they appear fresh, but are healing. Dried blood covers him and his clothes, and as he gets closer, Faith's scent becomes stronger and stronger.

"Where is she?" I demand, the muscles in my jaw feathering, teeth cracking under the pressure, and cross my arms over my chest to keep myself from killing him too soon. I will not get any closer to this psychopath either. My nose twitches, and I inhale again; that odd scent is coming from him.

"*He's what he was always born to be, Declan, dread carefully,*" Thorin links and then slinks away.

What the fuck?

"What are you?" I question as he stops a few feet away from me and then starts to pace around me, so I follow in the opposite direction. We size each other up, beating a circle into the sparse grass in the small opening of thick trees.

"That seems to be the question of the day, well, night," he says pointing to the sky and narrows his eyes on me. The thumbnail of moonlight filters down, and a soft lavender glows from his eyes. Isaac cackles, throwing his ice blonde strands back; they sway stiffly from his head, and then he stops, like someone hit pause on a video, and crooks his head towards me.

"A hybrid, half vampire, half lycan," he says matter-of-factly, and then he starts his dance with me again. A hybrid, well fuck that, that's awfully inconvenient right now, but surely he can still die. My thoughts get interrupted again when Isaac starts to say something, but I've tuned him out while I think of a way to take him down, until I hear Faith's name cross his lips.

"You know, that sweet-tasting beauty agreed to be my Queen?" He licks his lips and smirks. "I must say, though, she's quite the little seductress. She's got a fang kink, did you know that? Probably not, seeing as her neck was free of a mark," he rambles on, every word igniting a fury deep within me. I don't respond, I can't, I need him to keep talking, so I watch and wait, feeding my rage like a masochistic psycho.

"Does she bring the calmness inside you, too, cousin? She's like a lullaby, singing and quieting away the voices—" That's my mate he's talking about. My mate.

Nope! Never fucking mind, I can't do this, he needs to fucking die. I lunge, half shifting with the motion. My claws rake across the flesh of his chest, tearing and slashing up to his collarbone, and dark crimson sprays my bare chest and face.

Isaac returns my attack and slices into my side as I try to maneuver away, hot searing slashes against my ribcage as my skin is torn open. He lunges again as my hand goes to clamp over the gash. More burning pain erupts from my leg as I jump back, his claws slicing down my thigh to my shin.

"You need to let go, Declan, don't fear what you can do," Thorin links, and it's then that I notice the image of him has changed slightly, he appears larger, and more menacing, an aura of silver glints off the darkest midnight fur. He's always seemed bigger than normal shifter wolves, but now he's a giant compared to what he was.

Undiluted power ripples from him, into me, and my side stitches itself up inch by inch; my leg following shortly. Removing my bloodied hand from the wound, I find Isaac doing the same with his chest. We share a look, and he grins knowingly.

I let the power build under my skin and snap my wrists out again; my claws are more elongated, sharper than before and black. My muscles rush with a warmth and swell as we both sprint towards each other, colliding in a clashing boom of bodies.

Isaac matches me blow for blow, both of us heaving and claws slashing against one another's flesh, tearing it open. He jumps away, hissing, holding his abdomen, and pulls his hand away slowly to lick each of his fingers.

Right as I'm about to launch forward, a blood-curdling scream rents the air, and I freeze. That was Faith. She can't be far, her scent is all around me now, and I can't tell which direction I need to go. Too distracted to notice Isaac and whatever it is he's doing, I lift my nose in the air and inhaling I take a step towards where her scent is strongest.

"Oh cousin, didn't anyone ever tell you not to turn your back on your enemy?" Isaac jeers, his arm snaking around my front, as agonizing white hot pain rips through my stomach and up my chest. I stagger back and collapse to my knees, my hands instinctively going to my middle. Wet, hot, squishy tissue slops into my hands. Dazed, my head dips down and I find myself gutted, my insides gaping open and organs spilling out.

No! This can't be happening. Not now.

Isaac's shadow looms over me in the moonlight, as I fall to back, landing on my side, barely protecting my intestines from spilling out further.

"You see, I've learned that lesson a time or two, just as you have now, to never turn your back on someone who's more powerful than you are," he laughs, and rips what remains of his shirt off. Pale silver and white slashes cover the expanse of his entire upper half. He catches me staring and laughs hysterically, he's fucking losing it.

"You like my Father's gifts? Or shall I say my great-great uncle's?" He squats down, and grabs me by my hair and jerks upwards. Excruciating pain tears down my spine and middle, darkness wavers in and out dotting my vision.

"See the thing is cousin, oh and yes we are by the way, very distant and all that, but nonetheless cousins, I don't want to have to kill someone of my only remaining family, but I have to," he says manically, his voice all over the place and cracking with every word.

"I have to so my Malishka will stay, and keep my head good," he adds, his voice deadly serious as he points to his head and smirks as my head lands in a thud in the crushed grass.

I blink in a daze, his feet disappearing over the mound is the last thing I see.

49

Faith

Chanoît, Quebec, Canada
Weeping Forest

The moon is high and bright in the sky, I've slowed to a walk and round another set of trees before coming to a meadow. It's eerily similar to the one on the hill above my pack house, even down to the wildflowers swaying under the gentle light of the moon.

Exhaustion and hunger pound at my ragged body. I don't think I have enough energy to go any further, but I have to. Why did I believe escaping without planning was a good idea? My arms fly out to my sides to keep my tired body balanced as I spin around slowly, trying to get my bearings. I have no idea where I am now. I thought once I'd crossed the river that I only had a little further to go before I slipped into shifter territory, but it seems I've turned myself around somehow.

My gaze skirts over the meadow again, and a tingling of memories wrinkles my nose.

Mom.

"Goddess, I miss her so much," I whisper, and bite my trembling lip. Questions bombard my mind and drag the little self-confidence I had back down.

Why didn't she tell me about being the Last First Daughter?

Why didn't she tell me more about my powers?

Why did she lie to me?

Am I that much of a fuck up? She didn't think I deserved to know?

Is that why she had me learn to mask my scent, how to hide my alpha aura? Is that why they wanted me to find my mate so badly? I'm so confused and frustrated, I don't know what to think. Everything I've ever known has been a lie.

Thoughts spiral out of control, whirlpooling my mind into madness, everything from the last few weeks combines, and it's too much, too heavy. That pin-prickling, bubbling sensation balloons again, and I fall to my knees, letting out a scream as the pain I've held in for too long boils over.

Pain from losing my Mom, pain from possibly losing Declan before I've had the chance to fix it, pain from Isaac's torture, shame of my stupidity and naivety, and the betrayal from learning the truth. My arms cross over my middle as I rock back and forth, sobbing. I try to reign it in, try to remember I'm strong, but the crushing weight of everything I've lost is too much to bear, and I let go.

As my sobs finally subside to hiccups of tears and snot bubbles from my nose, I take a raw, shuddering breath in and stare up at the sliver of moon. I want to shove my ire at the Goddess who rules over it. I want her to know my pain, my wrath, as the grief morphs into anger. Why does it have to be me?

"Your Mother did what she thought was best to keep you safe," Sienna links, as I pull myself up from the cold ground.

"I'm sure that's what you want to think," I reply and swipe at my legs, flicking bits of grass and mud away.

"*It's what I know, Faith. I've watched every one of your ancestors over the centuries try to protect their firstborn daughters from bearing this curse. You are more like Princess Azlena than any other daughter, which is why she sent me to you; she knew the burden of having a power that comes too soon to someone so young,*" she says, and comes forward in my mind, her warmth wrapping around me again.

"*And what is this curse? I was always led to believe it was a secret gift?*" I counter and hope I don't come off as snippy, as it sounds.

"*That I cannot answer, for now at least. But I can tell you that, Azlena knew of the pain you would come to suffer and wanted you to be the last to carry this burden that her Mother unknowingly placed over her.*" She offers and sits, ears twitching as the squeaks of bats and the hoot of an owl silently flying by fill the night air. I have so many more questions. I have no idea what the future holds or what this curse means. Not entirely sure I want to.

"*Faith, I am so proud of you. Do you see everything you've overcome so far? Don't give up now, you are stronger than you think, than you believe,*" Sienna says softly, nudging me with her essence through our bond. It fills me with a blooming of hope, and while I may not believe I can do whatever it is she thinks, I allow her essence to wash over me. I can use this energy to get home, and then, I can unpack all these confusing and conflicting emotions.

A twig snaps behind me, and I flinch, the hairs on the back of my neck standing on end. Whipping around, I scan the dark forest behind me. Finding nothing, I turn around and suddenly a cloth comes over my mouth and nose. I breathe in a rancid smell, gagging, and I fight to pull at whoever's hand is clamped down over my face. A shiver races down my spine as an all too familiar voice vibrates against my ear. How did he creep up on me without me sensing or smelling him?

"Hello darling, miss me?" Connor croons and jerks my head back into his chest and drags me backwards. A second of frigid-laced fear drapes over me, freezing me to the spot and smothering my muffled arguments.

Another second passes, and my mind stalls and goes into auto mode, shutting down the desire to fight back. Then a burst of that bubbling, pinpricking energy and power surges through me.

"Fight back!" Sienna shouts through our bond, growling and snarling. She wants to kill him.

"I've missed you, babe," he says, forcing it out between ragged breaths. "I've been looking for you for weeks. Imagine my surprise when I learned you were right where I needed you to be. I should thank Isaac," he laughs and continues dragging me back to the forest. He's moving faster than he should be able to, like a vampire, my eyes flare as realization floods my veins with a glacial dread.

At the mention of Isaac, something inside me bursts open, and it pours gasoline all over the inferno I had earlier to get away from him. I will not let Connor take me. My feet kick up and out against the ground, flailing and falling in a thud, my heels trench a path through the dirt.

I let the pulse of power in my chest out and use it to wrench myself free of his hold. Shoving him back away from me, I answer his dark, reddened eyes and cringe with a snarl of my own. He smirks and bares his teeth at me, revealing two fangs. I stumble away and weave, trying to get my balance back. Whatever he had on that rag has messed with my equilibrium.

"Let me help you," Sienna growls, and I nod. Connor cocks his head to the side, watching me.

"Just let me get one good one in, yeah?" I ask and shake my head until the topsy turvy movement stops.

"Give him hell."

50

Benedict

Chanoît, Quebec, Canada
Weeping Forest

The rough bark of this damn tree keeps digging into my shoulder as I lean up against it, but it'll have to do as I settle in to watch everything I've waited over three millennia for to unfold. Faith's heart is beating like a little hummingbird, and her anger pulses out in a bright blue with every strike she throws at that bottom-feeder's face. It's a glorious sight, and I have to say I'm pretty proud of my little beauty and how far she's come.

She's destroying the man who tried to destroy her. Of course, it was at my behest, but that's a trivial matter...can't have a weakling now, can I? She circles him as her little claws fling out, screams, and charges him. I debate helping her and then smirk as she tackles him to the ground, screaming every debauched and evil thing Connor's ever done to or said to her. The squelching sounds of ripping flesh and cracking of bones are music to my ears.

It's pretty sexy to watch her unleash all of her power on him. All that unfettered, pent-up, raw power and resentment she's kept inside for all those years.

My vicious little Faith...oh my little darling feed your darkness, it looks beautiful on you.

Tipping my head back, I pick up the faint sounds of Isaac toying with his food again, that boy, just as crazy as his Father, and his Father's Father. Azlena will never admit that I did our family a favor by ending that entire line with Isaac. That boy is not quite right in the head, but perhaps he'll do something right for once and take out that pathetic lycan for me, giving Faith no other choice but to choose me.

Then again, I may take him out, let myself be on her bad side. I quite like it when she's mad; it turns me on. She's hellishly vindictive when she wants to be, well, at least she had been over the years, according to my spies, until Connor.

With a twitch of my fingers, I cloak Isaac's and Declan's scents as the wind changes direction, so lil' miss vindictive here can't pick up on them and dash off to ruin my plans. I slip my hands into my pockets and stifle a groan as Faith shifts into her wolf.

Oh hellooo Sienna, long time little wolf...

She turns that sable head towards me, copper eyes swirling and then back, as she prowls to a trembling Connor. He crab crawls backwards away from her, but it's too late for him. Sienna leaps and lands, biting into his neck, shaking his body back and forth, ripping half of his throat out.

Faith shifts back and stalks around him and drops to her knees. Straddling his filleted open stomach, she plunges her fist into his chest and tears out his heart. Pride rumbles in my chest as I behold her gripping the bloodied organ in her hand and starts laughing, or is she crying? Isaac did a number on her for sure. I could give him an Etta boy for that. She's become a bit unhinged, and I fucking love it.

My gaze rakes over the curves of her naked body, and my cock twitches at the thought of tasting every line of ink and every dip and rise of her skin. Soon, I've waited this long, what's a little longer?

Steam rolls off her heaving naked body, her lovely head of brunette falls back as she lifts her face to the moon. My fang pierces my bottom lip as I imagine sinking them into the curve of her neck exposed in the silver light.

All of those thoughts go to the wayside when Isaac appears behind me. Without removing my hands from my pockets, I take control of his neck and squeeze his throat closed.

"*Tsk, tsk, tsk, son...*" I chastise him in his mind. He's considerably stronger now and tries to fight back this time, his face turning a calming shade of violet. I dive further into his mind, and oh, would you look at that, he's figured it out...well, we can't have him coming in and fucking up my plans now.

My fingers slide from my pocket and flick behind me, "*I do believe it's nap time, son,*" I order into his mind, and a loud crack snaps. He was always a fussy baby, never going down easily for naps.

Isaac drops to a heap on the forest floor, his neck bent at an odd angle, arms and legs twisting awkwardly. He's not dead, but at least for now, he's out of my way.

Craning my neck a little, I listen for his toy and hear the faint beating of Declan's heart and the sloppy sounds of a wound gushing. "Hmm..." It appears my son only played with him and didn't rip another spine out. This will be interesting indeed.

Deliberately stepping on a twig, I move towards Faith, expecting her to flinch, and a sliver of disappointment slithers over me when she remains frozen chiefly, but slyly peers over her shoulder.

I remove my suit jacket and offer it up to her, "Hello, my little darling," I greet and smile with pride at her triumph over that waste of cells cracked open and bleeding on the grass. Her plump lips and face are freckled in blood splatter, and her hair is coated in bits of Connor's skin and organs.

Her eyes swirl with Sienna's copper shimmer, and her body is radiant with its illuminating blue glow. Her deranged and a little bit psychotic appearance only serves to make her more stunningly beautiful. I can't get enough of her. I'm dying to sink my fangs into her and thrust my cock between her thighs until she can't walk.

Faith's gaze slides to my hand with the proffered jacket and then back to me, before she spins and picks up the scraps of silk Isaac had dressed her in. I still need to punish him for touching what is mine, but later.

"I'm not your little darling," she scoffs and sniffs, refusing my jacket. "I'm not your little anything."

I shrug, *fine by me, more to enjoy...*

"Oh?" I query and take another step towards her. "I beg to differ," I disagree gruffly and offer the jacket once more, as goosebumps scatter all over her skin. Faith turns around, holding the scraps of silk to her chest, and sighs.

Eyes rolling, she drops the scraps and rips the jacket from my fingers and slips it on, wrenching the lapels over her full breasts and hourglass waist. The hem skims her shapely, inked thighs, those thighs that I've dreamed of curling over my shoulders one too many times.

She marches the three steps towards me and stares daggers up at me, "So brave little one," I whisper, leaning in to her ear, and my eyes roll back in my head getting a whiff of her. She smells divine. "Do you know who I am?"

"No, nor do I care... what do you want?" She snaps, snarling her tiny canine snagging on the bottom lip.

So cute.

Such a little liar, I can hear her heart rate skip over a beat and then pound harder. Those haughty eyes scan the length of my body up and then down and back up, reuniting the windows of our souls.

"Ohh...I think you do, but we can pretend for now if that makes this easier for you," I croon and snake my hand out, tucking a wave of wild chocolate strands behind her ear, and drag my finger down the apple of her cheek to her lips, collecting the blood splatter. She tracks my movements as I suck the blood off my fingertip like a straw and release it with a pop. "His vintage is a bit bitter, don't you think?"

She snorts, one brow arching, clearly deciding on how to deal with me. I'd love nothing more than to dive into her mind, but out of the billions in the world, she's the only mind I can't penetrate. However, what does remain true is that I don't have to use my arcane magic on her, as our connection is strong enough to hold her captive for the moment.

"What do you want?" Faith rasps as she takes a step back.

Smart girl.

"Never mind, I don't want to know, leave me alone, I've had enough of asshole leeches to last me a lifetime," she spits, her anger like a bonfire roaring to life.

Oh yes, please do get angry.

Hesitantly, she takes another step away from me, but I match her and step right up to her, our chests a breath away from touching, and dip my head, getting lost in the depths of her soul. A breeze of cool night air ghosts across my skin, sliding a shiver up and down my spine.

The skin on my finger scalds from the touch of her skin as I lift her chin to me. Those whiskey eyes bobbing back and forth over me leave behind invisible burning scars, searing heat right to my cock. In three thousand years, I've never been this hard for anyone, and I'm so close to bursting.

I dart my eyes to her throbbing pulse at the base of her neck and then back to her face before answering.

"You," I whisper, fighting the desire to lean in and— "just you, darling, I want you to be my bride, my queen." A little gasp parts her lips, and her nose scrunches in disgust, but I'm not bothered at all. She will be mine whether she likes it or not.

"That's rich, taking a page from your son? I'd rather stab myself in the eye with a thousand lemon-soaked toothpicks than be anything to you," she says sardonically and takes another step away, ripping her chin from my pinched fingers. A few more steps, and she'll be pinned up against the tree a few feet behind her.

"Where do you think Isaac got the idea from, sweetling? But, I will give you the same offer; however, mine comes with an expiration date," I reply, lowering my voice an octave and stepping into her again.

She takes two steps back and murmurs something about nurture versus nature being evident, and then adds, "You can go crawl back into the depths of whatever hell you were born in; I'd rather die than be your wife."

Oh, she's so cute when she's bound in fury..

I move in, and her back smacks into the trunk of a white pine. She yelps and puts a hand up. Those lovely fingers press into my bare chest. Shock ripples across her features at my warmth, and confuses her beautiful face. This moment is worth every second of withstanding this torturous need to devour her while she deduces why...she won't be able to, but I'll let her try.

"That can be arranged, but I daresay we'd be going to the same place if that happened, so you'd still be stuck with me," I whisper and cup one side of her cheek, and slide it down to the back of her neck. "Here's the terms, my dear little one, you will have until the next two full moons to decide the fate of all of shifters and Lycans in this hemisphere," I offer and retrieve her incentive from my pocket.

Dangling her grandmother's, well, Azlena's necklace, up, it sparkles and shimmers in the moonlight, the tiny droplet of her ancestor's blood flares to life between us, and Faith's eyes go wide.

"Ah-uh..." I scold and slip the necklace back into my pocket. "If you choose to come to me willingly and accept my terms, I will spare them and you may have this amulet back...if you do not...well, let's hope you're smarter than that," I offer and brush the tip of my nose along her cheek to her ear, she shudders and it goes straight to my cock. Her skin is like velvet, driving me mad, one touch at a time.

Overcome with need, I latch my mouth to her, stealing a kiss I've waited lifetimes for. She freezes, her body ramrod still, but she doesn't back away. I slip my tongue over her lips, and dip inside, only a moment, but enough and pull back. Scowling she swipes the back of her hand over her lips.

"I'll see you soon, my lil' darling...mate," I whisper on a fiery breath, and as I pull away, my fingers twitch behind me, releasing the cloaking spell over Declan, and catch her gaze. Let the games begin.

Her button nose scrunches up in disbelief, her eyes clamp closed, and a hand flies to her chest. The thrumming of her heart ramps up to a dreadful torrent and then thuds to a slow rhythmic beat as her eyes fly open again. Pure horror wreaks havoc over her face as Sienna, languidly confirms the truth, my lips curl up, and I zip away.

"How? How is this possible?" She falls to her knees, rasping it over and over.

I swoop over to where I left my worthless son and throw him over my shoulder.

Soon my lil one, I'll be seeing you very soon.

Before you go!

I'd love to hear your honest review!
Thank you!

Declan's and Faith's story continues in The Blood Prince, Book 2 of
The Blood Cursed Series.

Acknowledgements

Thank you so much to: JJ, T & K, My Gurls (you know who you are) Asshat, Sissy, Shawners, & all of my Lil' Peanuts. For my family.

Thank you for putting up with my never-ending texts, countless photos, emails with drafts and FaceTiming to hear me read aloud. You are all my rocks, my team and my family.

Without your unending support and love, I wouldn't have had the courage to write this. Y'all are my strength to get up every morning, battle my demons, and keep smiling.

XOXO

About The Author

L.N. Wandrei was born in the Pacific Northwest, but New England is her true home in her heart and soul. A military veteran, she has traveled the world and continues to explore the nation with her active duty husband. She can be found traversing forested trails, scouring sandy beaches, and climbing rocky terrain with her menagerie of four-legged fur babies, capturing magnificent photos, and transposing them into delicate and beautiful paint-ings. When not pursuing outdoor adventures, she immerses herself in the worlds of romance, fantasy, comedy, historical fiction, manga, and anime. She enjoys spending time adventuring in the world of Dungeons and Dragons with her two sons and husband.

Some of her favorite Indie Authors are: L.J. Andrews, K.M. Moronova, Briar Boleyn, C.J. Sweet, Lacey Lehotzky, R.B. Sturn & J.D. Linton.

The Blood Prince

Please enjoy a sneak peek of the Prologue of
Book 2 in The Blood Cursed Series

Nyelia

2,489 Years Ago

It's a splendid night to meet my demise. I wonder if my death will be brutal, bloody, or peaceful. Midsummer's Eve night is the warmest it's been in ages, and the slight breeze drifting between the stone columns is sweet with the aroma of wild mountain flowers. This high up on the mountain, it should be cooler, but Canos whipped a heat wave for the beginning of his season.

The stone floor is warm beneath my bare feet as I make my way to the front of the temple. I squint at the intricate patterns carved into the flutes of the columns, barely deciphering the ancient symbols of the Gods and Goddesses that reside within this monstrosity of a temple. It's one more confirmation that my time as Queen is coming to an end. Not that it matters that it will be tonight, and by sons' hands, no less. If it weren't to be them, it would be Paine, my husband, and King.

Paine seems content with his secret lover, Ilena, who isn't as much of a secret as he thinks. Never understood the draw to the Goddess of Water and Seas, but I am not one to judge. I have had my fair share of lovers, too. So long as he doesn't find out about Lupin and Seth, all will be well.

The scuffling of sandals over stone draws my attention down the 100 stairs of the temple to the lone woman ascending. She's late, of course, and without her brother, but I find myself not caring all that much. Rhazien and Azlena are my favorite children and will become my successors once I'm gone from this plane.

Azlena ascends the steps gracefully and with purpose; the purple of her peplos is dark, even in the moonlight. It billows behind her, along with her waist-length brown hair. The moonlight casts an ethereal glow about my only daughter, highlighting her beauty.

"Mother," Azlena says, crossing her arms over her chest and bowing. "You summoned me."

I reach out and run a finger up under her chin to her cheek, and say a silent prayer that one day she will forgive me.

"Yes, daughter, come."

We walk through the columns to the right and slip into the second door. Azlena's eyes widen when she sees Otaris, the Goddess of Fortune and Fate, and Enas, the God of Destiny and Chance, reclining on the chaises covered in goat hides. She quickly crosses her arms and bows.

"Remove your necklace, Lena," I say, and I continue to stand beside Otaris.

Rising slowly, Azlena hesitantly removes the large sapphire stone from around her neck. The deep navy stone dangles from her outstretched hand, sparkling in the candlelight.

"Mother, what is going on?" Azlena says.

"Nothing that can be undone," Enas answers, speaking directly into all of our minds. If my daughter is shocked, she doesn't show it; she merely stands as unmoving as possible. The other gods and goddesses make both twins incredibly nervous, particularly Azlena, who has only visited the Halls of Gods and Goddesses Temple a handful of times.

"Hold out your palm, dear," Otaris speaks, breaking the tenenous energy in the air. Azlena does so without opposition. The Goddess of Fortune and Fate glides to her, and quicker than most could detect, she slices her silver blade over my daughter's palm, and takes the sapphire in her hand. She holds it, angling to coat the gemstone in Azlena's blood.

Otaris heals my daughter's hand and shuffles her way to Enas. The two disappear to the open patio with hushed whispers as a white glow emits from their hands.

"Mother?"

"There's no need to fret, my cherished daughter, a precaution is all." I offer in place of what I want to tell her.

Otaris and Enas return, nodding towards me, confirming they could do what I asked. Enas gently loops the necklace back around Azlena's neck. The sapphire, now nestled in a pendant resembling the Northern Star, sparkles and shines, its secret hidden within.

The moon is at its highest when my sons arrive, and I decide to meet them at the door. Perhaps I should offer them some wine? No. They are most undeserving this eve.

What I must do, is begin the ritual. My bloodline is tainted; their petty squabbles and feelings of inadequacy rule their decision-making. They've brought this upon themselves.

Sabien and Benedict enter, bloodlust dripping from their eyes, and daggers raised. Benedict at least has the decency to have shaky hands. He could've been so much more than he will become.

I stop their procession, with a raised hand, turning away from them, before dropping to my knees under the midnight sky. With a flick of my fingers, the moonlight dims to its dark side, and the shadows of my domain rise.

"It will do you no good, Mother," Sabien sneers.

"You have made a mockery of your sons; we will not stand by while you play favorites with those bastards," Benedict condemns.

My incantation, not more than a whisper over my lips, begins to unfurl with my magic and seeks out each of my children. My sons' footsteps are muffled as the magic takes hold in my body, ready for my blood to spill.

Carefully, I drag the long braid of my black hair over to one shoulder, exposing my neck for them. A tear slips down my cheek when I speak the last words loud enough for them to hear.

"You will become the monsters your soul feeds, you will remain in the shadows beneath that of the moon, never to feel the sun, and be consumed with the blood lust you seek," I sigh and wave them both over.

"What nonsense are you babbling about now, Mother? Your prayers won't save you." Sabien taunts, flipping his dagger end over end.

"To be free of your chains, you will heed the truest call of your hearts," I finish and bow my head.

As the cool steel of my sons' blades slices along both sides of my neck, I seek out the threads of my curse, and my breath hitches. No! No, no, no. It wasn't supposed to go to them.

"Find your mates, your one true love—" my whisper gurgles as my severed head falls to the stone floor, and my magic is released with the spilling of my blood.

"What the fuck did she just do?" Benedict hisses.

www.ingramcontent.com/pod-product-compliance
Lightning Source LLC
Chambersburg PA
CBHW020007120726
47903CB00004B/1182